DIANA, HERSELF

Expecting Adam:
A True Story of Birth, Rebirth, and Everyday Magic

Leaving the Saints:
How I Lost the Mormons and Found My Faith

Breaking Point:
Why Women Fall Apart and How They Can Re-Create Their Lives

Finding Your Own North Star:
Claiming the Life You Were Meant to Live

The Joy Diet:
10 Daily Practices for a Happier Life

Steering by Starlight:
The Science and Magic of Finding Your Destiny

The Four-Day Win:
End Your Diet War and Achieve Thinner Peace

Finding Your Way in a Wild New World:
Reclaim Your True Nature to Create the Life You Want

The Martha Beck Collection:
Essays for Creating Your Right Life

DIANA,

An Allegory of Awakening

HERSELF

MARTHA BECK

CYNOSURE
PUBLISHING

Published by Cynosure Publishing, Arroyo Grande, California
Copyright © 2016 Martha Beck
All rights reserved.

ISBN: 978-1-944264-03-1

Library of Congress Control Number: 2016934549

Jacket, cover and book design: Laura Shaw Design, www.lshawdesign.com
Front cover painting © Martha Beck
Back cover art © Elizabeth Beck
Front cover art photo: Allyson Magda, www.allysonmagda.com
Author photo: Phyllis Lane, www.phyllislane.com

Across The Universe
Words and Music by John Lennon and Paul McCartney
Copyright © 1968, 1970 Sony/ATV Music Publishing LLC
Copyright Renewed
All Rights Administered by Sony/ATV Music Publishing LLC,
424 Church Street, Suite 1200, Nashville, TN 37219
International Copyright Secured All Rights Reserved
Reprinted by Permission of Hal Leonard Corporation

ACKNOWLEDGMENTS

I had more fun writing this book than I've ever had writing anything, mainly because I strong-armed so many people into helping me. Gratitude is a feeble word to describe what I feel for these people, and for all the others who've given me inspiration and encouragement to be as strange as I really am.

First, my brilliant and generous collaborator, Kat Forster. You may think there's some nepotism involved in our working relationship, since she happens to be my daughter, but you would be wrong. I've simply never met such a gifted story surgeon. Kat can cut through anything that doesn't work with a delicate but unflinching scalpel, then stitch together what's left and breathe life into it. All the bad ideas in this book are mine; most of the good ones are hers. Thanks, too, to her husband, Scott, whose quiet intelligence and gentle precision buffed off so many rough edges.

And while we're at it, thanks to the far-seeing imagination and impeccable artistry of Elizabeth Beck—Lizzy, Elly, Liz, however you know her—who finds unfamiliar worlds in everyone and everything. Then there's the pure magic of Adam Beck, who sees the forest animals with his "deep eyes" and reminds me that the foxes love to hunt. That these three people survived the childhood I gave them to become such fabulous adults is the greatest miracle of my life.

A major part of that miracle was performed by Karen Gerdes, my better half, whose constant nurturing presence has healed the wildness in so many people—but I got to keep her! (As one of my dear friends puts it, "Get your own damn Karen!") Her presence in my life astounds me every day. It's enough to make me a believer in the benevolence of the universe.

My ranch family, who are wild enough to live with me as a kind of gutsy sociological experiment, are all heroes in my eyes. Koelle Simpson, Travis Stock, and Katja Elk have supported and encouraged me every day since I ran away to the woods. Through good times and T-Rex emergencies, you've become as much a part of me as my own heart. This book wouldn't exist without all of you, and I probably wouldn't be here either.

Of course, many members of my ranch family live off-property. Matthew Dowd, a soul-brother who is much more magical than he lets on, steered me toward the place my heart wanted to live, and ultimately catalyzed the writing of this book. Bridgette Boudreau, comrade and co-adventurer, read every draft of every chapter, reshaped my schedule so that I had time to write, and would have taken up a life in avocado farming to get me where I needed to go. For years she's kept my company and my life running more and more joyfully, and her wise, wry, loving presence in my life is a gift beyond reckoning. The same may be said for the whole fellowship of coaches at MBI, especially Abigail Steidley, Jessica Steward, Jennifer Voss, Sandra Trca-Black, Kris McGuffie, Deb Droz, Jen Falci, and my former assistant Jessica Reisenbeck.

Maria and Timothy Shriver have both spent long hours talking with me about the possibility of healing individual souls, humans in general, and the Earth. I love them like siblings, and am so grateful for the huge and beautiful scope of their will to do good in the world.

I owe my career as a writer to the generosity, kindness, and endless energy of Betsy Rapoport, my first editor and adored friend. Her keen intelligence, hilarious wit, and magical mama-bear valor truly make her my Besty, and her editing has made this a much, much better book.

Susan Casey, the astonishingly multitalented former editor in chief at *O, The Oprah Magazine*, has supported my writing for many years, in more ways than I can list here. She's been a champion, an advisor, a visionary, a cheerleader, and a brilliant example of a word-smith who can churn out superb writing in the midst of every distraction imaginable. (I know I'm using the word "brilliant" a lot. But these people all happen to be brilliant, so we'll just have to live with it.) I have endless gratitude and admiration for Susan. The same to Rennio Maifredi, who read an execrable early version of the book and cheered me on with boundless love and enthusiasm nevertheless.

My African family—Dave, Shan, Bronwyn and Boyd Varty, Richard Laburn, Kate, Mo and Maya Groch—made me hope that the planet Earth (and the human race) were salvageable at a time when I'd pretty much given up. Their love, their incredible devotion to healing people and places, their humor, their magic, and their general brilliance—yes, I said it again—are an inextricable part of me and this book. They gave me the invitation to seek solace in nature, something I thought I'd left behind with childhood. As long as people like them are on Earth, there's hope for us all.

They say there are friends of time and friends of like mind, and a very few who are both. Annette Rogers and Lydia Nibley are friends of time and like mind who offered their extraordinary intellectual and literary gifts, reading drafts of this book and giving me cogent feedback. So much love and thanks to them.

For much of my life, two great souls, Stephen Mitchell and Byron Katie, have been near the center of my thought and spiritual practice. They have loved and nourished me through countless difficulties with their inspired writing and with the extraordinary example they set as they simply live their lives. I am dumbstruck with gratitude that I can call them my role models, teachers, and friends. Other readers who know their work will see their influence everywhere in this book, and though I'll never rise to their level, I hope some of their wisdom will filter through my work to other readers.

My shamanic friends—you know who you are—can feel my gratitude in the Everywhen. But just in case you feel like doing things the Western way, here it is in black and white: Thank you for everything. If you think you see bits of yourself in the magic I "made up" for this book, you are correct.

Speaking of magical people, the brilliant (Yes! Brilliant!) novelist Rowan Mangan was gracious enough to read a manuscript that was making my eyeballs go numb, and offered inspired corrections.

Thanks to the coaches who have been through my training program. You are my favorite. I wish I could send each of you a magic pig.

Many, many thanks to Janica Smith, who oversaw the physical production of this book with a rare combination of patience and enthusiasm. Laura Shaw's talents as a designer, and Lisa Canfield's as a proofreader, contributed a great deal to the final product and to the process of creating it.

And finally, thanks to anyone who has ever received coaching from me, come to an event where I've taught, or read anything I've written down. You have given your time and precious attention to my words. My love and gratitude are all I can give back, and you have them in spades.

FURIES

Five minutes ago, Diana Archer's life was running along quite smoothly. Now it's in shambles. You know how that goes, beloved. The same sort of thing has happened to you, probably more than once. Maybe your world wasn't perfect, but it was okay—and then suddenly it wasn't. A drunken teenage driver T-boned your car. A smirking stranger in a cheap suit served you divorce papers. Or, like Diana, you lost the dead-end job you desperately needed to survive.

Of course, in retrospect, it wasn't the end of the world. You survived, after all. You prevailed. You probably even told yourself you had come out the other side a wiser and deeper being. But oh, beloved, in the minutes and hours after the blow fell, weren't you just *demolished*? No, wait, don't try to remember. It was bad enough when it happened, and there's no need to relive it now. Instead, let's focus on Diana as she endures her own catastrophe.

At its best, Diana's life has never been easy, so she knows trouble when she feels it coming. The moment the loudspeaker at the Super Big Mart ordered her to report to the back office, she felt a sick twist in her gut. Now, as she knocks on the door of Gussman's office, she feels like a rabbit watching a hawk drop out of the sky, talons outstretched.

"Enter!" booms a voice from inside. Buck Gussman, Diana's boss, prefers this to the less elegant phrase "Come in." At twenty-five, Gussman is a decade younger than Diana and earns nearly twice as much as she does. No one at Super Big Mart has ever seen him display a shred of wit, allure, or managerial skill.

Gussman looks up from his desk as Diana closes the door behind her.

"You wanted to see me?"

"Yeah, yeah." Gussman takes a slurp from the MondoGlug soda cup on his desk, wipes his wispy blond mustache, and stands up. His eyes barely flick to Diana's face before proceeding to her breasts, where they always tend to linger.

Since Gussman isn't looking at her eyes, Diana takes the opportunity to roll them. Being the object of lechery has always baffled her. Comparing herself to the Photoshopped models on the magazines and packages she stocks every day, Diana believes herself to be far below average attractiveness. But she is wrong.

In point of fact, Diana's body is exactly average. Precisely, mathematically so. In fact, beloved, if you measured every physical aspect of every female human presently alive, then added it all up and divided by head count, Diana would be the result. Her height and weight are smack-dab on the global mean. Ditto for her bra and shoe sizes. Also the curvature of her cheekbones, the tilt of her eyes, and the width of her lips. Her skin tone falls exactly halfway between the shade of the darkest Jarawa in the Andaman Islands and the palest Icelander in Reykjavik.

Diana, of course, has no idea how extraordinarily average she is. Nor does she realize that this actually makes her very attractive. She's quite oblivious to the fact that when she walks past, her caramel skin, honey-gold eyes, and espresso hair make most men—and a fair percentage of women—daydream happily about sex or Starbucks, frequently both at once. Diana never thinks of herself as delicious, because her self-esteem is also exactly average for a woman of her time. Which is to say: low.

"Should I sit down?" asks Diana.

Gussman shakes his head. "No need. Let's just get this over with." He takes a deep breath. "Management's cutting back staff, big D. I'm letting you go."

Diana's gut tightens like a hangman's noose as the trapdoor flops open. "What?"

"Retail's not a fairyland any more, Diana." Gussman chews at his mustache. "Online shopping is killing us. It's eating our frigging lunch."

Diana squints at him, trying to imagine how the echoing cavern of Super Big Mart, with its pervasive polymer odors and sputtering fluorescent lights, could ever, by anyone, be mistaken for a fairyland.

"But . . . my car's not paid off." Her face feels like wood. "My rent—"

"Read the newspapers, *chica*," says Gussman. Diana would bet her last dime he's never read a newspaper in his life. "It's the economy, you know? The government won't do nothing for nobody, except maybe the illegals."

Diana flinches. She was born on American soil—probably—but people have always tended to assume that like many dark-haired, brown-skinned people in Los Angeles, she's an invader from California's neighbor to the south. Not that it matters anymore. The awareness of her newly unemployed status is spreading like poison through Diana's body.

Gussman picks up a slip of paper from his desk. "Well, we don't cut people off without a parachute," he says. "Management's giving you fifty bucks. They don't have to do that, you know. You should be grateful." When Diana reaches out to take the check, Gussman grasps her precisely average hand in his large damp one. If the gesture is meant to feel comforting, it fails. "Don't worry, D-dog," he says, squeezing her hand but still gazing at her breasts. "You'll find something else."

Well, B-dog, thinks Diana, *at least I'll never have to see you again.*

She keeps her face blank as she leaves Gussman's office. Watching her, you'd have no idea she's scrabbling desperately through her mind for any trace of hope, optimism, or courage. She comes up empty. It's time for the Furies to rise up and fill Diana's mind with their chorus of horror.

You know how the Furies work, beloved—you have your own. Every human does. They're all-purpose demons, vicious little bugs in the software of everyone's mind. They all shriek variations of the same tunes: *You're useless, you're stupid, you're ugly, you're failing, you're so, so screwed. You'll never be loved, never be good enough, never accomplish enough, never be rich enough, never be safe. What the actual hell are you doing with your life, you squishy, repulsive, aging bag of pus?*

Or words to that effect.

As she takes her purse out of her locker, leaving her plastic nametag in its place, Diana's Furies reach hurricane intensity. The fear they generate feels as if it will physically kill her. What can she do now? How will she pay her rent? What if she gets sick? Thank God, Devin will be all right; he has a full scholarship, an on-campus job, student health insurance. But Diana herself can't think of anything to tide her over to her next lousy minimum-wage job—assuming she can even get one. *You're going to die of nothingness,* scream her Furies. *You'll end up on the street, no teeth, no hair, no home, no love, no purpose.*

That's what it all comes down to, Diana realizes, shambling past her former coworkers. She has no purpose. Her life has felt long and painful in progress, brief and meaningless in hindsight, and there's no reason for it all, no meaning. *I have no purpose,* she thinks, walking across the parking lot. *I have no purpose!* She reaches her secondhand Hyundai. *I have no purpose!* Fumbling in her purse for her keys—*I have no purpose!*—she accidentally hits the orange "Panic" button on the remote control, and the Hyundai blares at her like an angry walrus. *I HAVE NO PURPOSE! I HAVE NO PURPOSE! I HAVE NO PURPOSE!*

Trapped in the unbearable cacophony from within and without, Diana tries to recall which button on her electronic key turns off the car alarm. But her mind has been swept entirely into panic. Diana's heart is pounding, her face sweating, her knees failing.

And then, right in the middle of her torso, Diana feels something else. A faint prickling sensation that frightens her more than all the rest of it put together.

She's kept that feeling at bay for years, ever since Devin was born. She's fended it off, dodged it, forced it back into hiding. Until this very moment, she thought she'd wiped it out for good. But now Devin is off at college, and she has no job, and there's nothing to hang on to, nothing to stop it, no reason to stop it.

With a long, shuddering breath, Diana gives up, and gives in.

•

When she comes back to herself, it's almost dark. Diana looks around quickly, trying to assess what's happening and whether she might be in danger. She's standing in a parking lot behind a row of deserted industrial buildings. The last streak of sun on the western horizon has turned the smoggy Los Angeles skyline a muddy shade of orange, and in the dim light she can see that the tall buildings are far away. She's traveled several miles from the Super Big Mart. To her vast relief, Diana sees that there are no people around her, just the hiss and rumble of traffic on a nearby freeway.

In the next moment she notices that she's holding something soft and warm in the crook of her left elbow. Her right hand has been stroking it absentmindedly since she came to. Looking down, Diana sees that the object is a large, very relaxed rat. It returns her gaze, its black, shining little eyes half-closed in bliss.

To you, beloved, this kind of thing might come as a shock. To Diana, it causes only mild surprise. She spent large segments of her childhood and adolescence in a cycle of losing and then regaining consciousness, often in the presence of some mangy animal, and she's never been afraid of rats. She and Devin, whenever they heard pattering little feet in the ceiling of their tiny apartment, referred to them as "night squirrels." So she doesn't scream or hurl the little beast into the twilight. She just sets it gently on the asphalt, giving its small head a final pat. The rat gazes at her for a moment, then scampers away.

Diana straightens up and looks around her in the smoggy gloaming, hoping to find her car. It's nowhere to be seen. That, combined with the weariness of her legs and the extensive scuffing on her shoes, tells Diana she's probably spent the whole day traveling on foot. She checks herself for wounds, and is relieved to find nothing more than a couple of broken fingernails. She's voraciously hungry. Typical. She's always been hungry after a span of lost time. It amazes her how vividly the memories return, even after so many years of remission. As if the last fugue state before this one had happened last week, not eighteen years ago.

Diana looks around for something to eat—a discarded pizza crust, a half-eaten apple—then stops abruptly, shocked. How could she backslide so quickly from her hard-won normalcy to the animal barbarity of a runaway child? The thing to do, Diana tells herself, is not to forage like a cockroach, but to purchase food like a civilized person. This is when she notices, with a sinking chill in her heart, that she isn't carrying her purse. She pats her pockets anxiously. No cash, but at least she's got her car keys. This presents a new concern—did she drive somewhere during her time away? She's never had a fugue state and a driver's license at the same time, and the complexities this situation presents are legion.

You might as well give up and die! scream the Furies, and with that the morning's disastrous events surge back into her mind like a flood of sludge. Out of work. Virtually no savings. No purpose, no purpose, etcetera, etcetera, ad nauseam.

Diana rubs her forehead with the heel of one hand, trying to push away the dark chorus. Her childhood practice, when emerging from a fugue state, was to return to the last place she'd slept. This time, she decides to head back to Super Big Mart and hope to find her car in the parking lot. If it's not there, she'll walk back to her rat-infested apartment—which, the Furies are quick to remind her, is a gilded heaven compared to the places she'll end up if she doesn't land another job, and soon.

As she turns the corner of a dilapidated warehouse, Diana stops like someone running into a glass door. There it is, right in front of her. The Dumpster. The place where her useless, meaningless, purposeless life began. Diana draws a long, quavering breath. Should she climb back into the Dumpster, find a shard of broken glass, slide into death in the place where she'd slid into life? Maybe that was her whole reason for coming here, but as attractive as suicide undoubtedly appears (*Die! Die! Die!* scream the Furies), Diana can't do that to Devin.

By now, beloved, it should be clear to you that Diana's history is as unusual as her body is average. You may be thinking that you have very little in common with her, apart from bilateral symmetry, the memory of suffering, and a full working set of Furies. If so, you are in error. It takes Diana some time to walk from the Dumpster back to the Super Big Mart, time we will use to recount part of her strange history. In many ways, no doubt, that history is very different from your own. But in others, you'll find that Diana's story and yours are more alike than you would ever suspect.

INSANITY

The Furies rise to fever pitch as Diana plods past the Dumpster. *Garbage!* they shriek. *Trash baby! Even your own mother could see you were nothing but a waste of space!* They clamor on as she numbly sets her course toward the fading horizon. As near as she can tell, she's somewhere in Burbank, or maybe North Hollywood. The Super Big Mart is in Van Nuys. Could be eight miles away. Could be ten. Diana's feet hurt. Her legs hurt. Everything hurts. *Junk!* scream the Furies. *You're a walking chunk of junk!*

Shaking her head and setting her jaw, Diana forces herself to remember the happy side of her birth story. Not everyone had treated her like toxic waste, she reminds herself. Quite the opposite. As soon as local news teams ran the story of a tiny baby discovered by sanitation workers on a routine pickup, hundreds of people donated blankets, teddy bears, and diapers to the hospital where Diana was taken. Dozens more volunteered to foster her. *That's because they didn't know what you really are,* shriek the Furies. *They didn't know you were a worthless, purposeless junk-chunk.* Her attempt to focus on the bright side fails miserably as the Dumpster fades into the smog behind her.

Your beginning, beloved, was probably quite different from Diana's. Odds are your newborn self was welcomed into the world, not left in a Dumpster to die. And yet, when you've hit the lowest ebbs in your own life, you too have felt like an abandoned child: lost, alone, friendless. Your vulnerable core hurt the same way Diana's hurt when she was tiny, the way it hurts now. At life's worst moments, everyone—male or female, old or young—wants to cry like a little girl.

Diana clamps her teeth and manages not to burst into tears as she heads into the seedy neighborhood near the warehouse. She follows a sidewalk of broken concrete past rows of small rectangular buildings that compensate for their utter lack of architectural charm with a profusion of iron bars. Bars on the windows, bars on the doors, bars on the air-conditioning vents. Liquor stores share strip-mall space with pawnshops and tattoo parlors, most with even more sliding panels of bars crisscrossing their glass fronts. Above Diana's head, hundreds of power lines compete for airspace with billboards advertising seedy clubs, tobacco products, and auto repair services.

She's walking fast, both to keep warm in the damp evening air, and to send a message. This is clearly no place for anyone to be walking alone at night, and walking alone *slowly* would be tantamount to suicide, which she's already ruled out once today. But she's less frightened and disoriented than you might be in her circumstances, beloved, because one thing Diana gained from her unusual childhood is the ability to navigate the City of Angels like a flesh-and-blood GPS. She wasn't raised in this neighborhood, exactly. It's more like she was raised in all of them.

Her first foster parents, Bob and Nancy Archer, lived several miles and a few economic worlds away from here, in the posh Pacific Palisades, not far off the water. Both Nancy and Bob were software engineers in their late thirties who'd proven wildly successful at making money, less so at making babies. They'd resigned themselves to infertility until the very day they brought the little Dumpster girl home, named her Diana (Nancy had been a huge fan of the late princess), and promptly relaxed enough to conceive twins.

Diana barely remembers the Archers, with their marble floors and immaculate yard. She's more used to sandpaper-rough neighborhoods like this one. Ahead she sees several broken streetlights, which she knows have been shot out for two reasons: target practice, and the improvement of hunting grounds. In the pool of darkness gathered under the broken lights, dark figures are moving. Diana crosses the street. A man in a hooded jacket moves out of the darkness and drops in behind her. From the corner of her eye she can see a second man walking parallel to him on the other side of the road.

Diana's heart rate doubles, but she keeps her pace steady until she reaches the electric-peach light of a working streetlamp, at which point she whirls around and puts her hands on her hips. "Really?" she says in a hard, bored voice. "Seriously?"

The man behind her skids to a stop. "Shit!" he yelps. "You!"

"That's right, me." Diana's brain is shouting at her to *run, run, run,* but her voice stays cold and calm. Street instincts never fade.

The man backs up, holding his hands out in front of him. "Listen, lady, you said we were good. You said—we're good, right? Sure, sure, we're good."

"Are we?" Diana says, cocking her head as she takes a step toward him. "You want to find out?"

"No, no, I—" The man turns and runs, shouting to his companion across the street, "Get out of here, man! It's that bitch from before! She's crazy!"

Diana watches them disappear between two storefronts. Then she lets out a long, shaky breath, pushes her trembling hands into the pockets of her khakis, turns, and walks on. She's grateful for the man's reaction, but not as surprised as you might think.

There are precedents.

Once, when Diana was fifteen and living on the streets, she popped out of a fugue state to find herself standing in front of a closet in an unfamiliar house. A large man she'd never seen was cowering in there, begging her not to hurt him. She never did figure out why. Another time she suddenly found herself in the living room of a bungalow in Beverly Hills, next to a coffee table covered with drug paraphernalia. A naked, badly bruised woman crouched behind her. In front of her, several obviously stoned young men stared at her in gape-jawed horror, as if they'd just found out she had Ebola.

In such situations, Diana had never thought it prudent to stop and ask for descriptions of her own behavior during the preceding hours. Instead, she had simply assumed a homicidal stare and stalked away from whatever strange situation appeared around her, leaving the other players to their own devices. Afterward she would move on to a different part of the immense Los Angeles metropolitan area, where no one yet knew she was crazy as a bedbug. So Diana has no idea what went down between herself and the hooded man earlier today, but whatever it was, she's glad. She smiles thinly. The best thing that's happened to her all day is just more evidence of insanity.

Psycho, psycho, psycho from the get-go! the Furies shout as she trudges on, passing into a residential neighborhood where small houses hide behind tall fences. *Looney Tunes! Certifiable! Unfit for human companionship! Just plain nuts!*

And when it comes to this subject, the screaming creatures can back up their accusations with scientific data.

Diana's abnormalities began appearing just months after the Archers adopted her. It was no surprise that the baby from the Dumpster should have Psychological Issues, but Diana's were particularly unnerving. From infancy, she would often fade into nonresponsive blankness that lasted several minutes. Her amber eyes would focus on the middle distance as if mesmerized by some scene playing out in the air. Then she'd snap out of it, often with a violent jolt or a scream, and thrash around desperately, trying to escape her parents. The more mobile she became, the more frequently she succeeded.

As a toddler, Diana often shimmied out of her crib and disappeared through doors or windows that seemed impossible for such a small child to open. After Bob and Nancy padlocked every entrance to the house, Diana broke windows to get out, routinely cutting herself in the process. Her parents found themselves following trails of her blood all over their lovely neighborhood. Even after they finally located Diana, watching ants under a hedge or following a mouse through a dry irrigation ditch, the Archers would be emotionally drained for days.

By the age of three, Diana had added delayed speech to her repertoire of disconcerting attributes. She clearly understood language, but rarely spoke except to repeat the word "Why?" until adults around her nearly lost their minds. Diana's silence wasn't the sort that fades into the background, either; it was profound, unnerving, almost creepy. She would move up behind people, silent as mist, contemplating them with unblinking eyes until they turned and emitted little shrieks of surprise. Generally this sent Diana into one of her own panics, and she'd be out the door, wedging herself into a culvert or under the crawl space of a nearby house, before anyone knew what was happening.

Having spent so much childhood time in hidden places, Diana still has excellent night vision. Now, as she walks past a small house pocked with bullet holes, her eyes catch another shape moving in the shadows, and her adrenaline spikes again. But the shape turns out be a skinny stray dog. Diana stops and whistles, and the dog comes up to her, sniffing tentatively. It whines and licks her outstretched fingers. She scratches it behind the ears.

"Hey there, fella. Want to walk with me for a while?"

The dog wags its tail. When Diana sets off again, it trots along beside her. It's a motley thing, but good-sized, with Rottweiler stockiness and German Shepherd ears, and Diana feels much safer.

She remembers the time she came out of a fugue state with her knee on the swastika-tattooed, bald head of a man she didn't recognize. The scene was a little patch of bare-dirt yard inside a chain-link fence. Surrounding them circled at least a dozen pit bulls, all barking and snarling like something from a horror movie. One of the dogs was peeing on the man as Diana held him down. When she had walked away that time, all the dogs had followed her, then scattered into the night. She wonders, even now, why she was never afraid of them.

Diana was about four when she started to display an obsession with animals. She began smuggling creatures into the house: starving cats, wounded squirrels, reluctant toads, confused lizards. Around the same time, she began carrying weapons. These included a butter knife she'd sharpened on a rock, slingshots she made out of sticks and rubber bands, and a closed umbrella she carried like a javelin. The Archers began to fear for their twins, who were blond and chatty—the diametric opposite of their wide-eyed, silent sister. The specialists they consulted diagnosed Diana with dozens of conditions: attachment disorder, attention deficit disorder, hyperactivity, severe dyslexia, even schizophrenia. No one ever said "future serial killer" right out loud, but on the day Nancy found Diana with a roadkill chipmunk in one hand and a meat cleaver in the other, the Archers finally admitted they were out of their depth.

So began Diana's adventures in the wide and varied world of foster care.

Between the ages of four and thirteen, Diana lived in ten different homes. All her foster parents tried to normalize her—some with sweetness, others with tough love, still others with thinly veiled rage. She was put on pills, exercise regimens, cleanses for the liver, colon, and blood. Nothing helped. Experts kept adding to her list of possible diagnoses: Asperger's syndrome, post-traumatic stress syndrome, borderline personality disorder. Her classmates and foster siblings used shorter labels: stupid, psycho, crazy, freaky, weird, retarded.

Diana had believed them all.

She still believes them.

Was your childhood completely unlike Diana's, beloved? If so, you probably learned very early to shape your actions, words, even thoughts into the forms considered "normal" by those around you—and you've never stopped, right to this very day. Think about it: Do you turn and flee when you encounter an odd stranger in an elevator? Do you run from every room that feels suffocating? Shout at the slow stranger ahead of you in the grocery store line? Fall asleep in meetings that bore and annoy you? Of course not. You may not even realize you want to do such things. You may have no idea *what* you want. The price of normalcy is the loss of connection to the simple truth of your own feelings and desires—which could actually be a little crazy in itself, though few people ever notice this.

At any rate, Diana's many diagnoses ended when, at fourteen, she grew breasts of exactly average size for an adult woman. This led to the discovery that there were people who didn't want her to talk, didn't need her to attach, and didn't care if she occasionally bolted through a window. They were all men, most of them twice Diana's age or older, and she soon stopped asking them "Why?" because the only reason they ever wanted her to do anything was always the same. Shortly after she ran off with her first boyfriend—if a thirty-year-old crack dealer could be called a "boy"—Diana's overworked social workers finally gave up and lost track of the now-teenaged garbage child.

Diana has arrived at a street that underpasses the Hollywood Freeway. She knows this area from the few months she spent here shacking up with various males of questionable character, sharing their drugs and booze until a fugue state interrupted the pattern and she moved on. Though she's grateful to see familiar landmarks, she knows this is still not the best area for a nighttime stroll.

The Rottweiler-Shepherd walks beside her for the hour it takes to reach the Super Big Mart parking lot. Diana almost weeps with relief when she sees her car sitting in the middle of the lot, apparently unmolested. She limps up to it—her legs are trashed—and clicks the door locks open. Then she does start to cry, because praise the Lord, there's her purse, with her wallet inside it, tucked beneath the front seat. Apparently—at least today—her fugue-stated self isn't completely without strategic awareness.

She offers the dog a chance to hop in the backseat, but it veers away and begins searching the area around the Super Big Mart loading bays for discarded food. Diana is sure it will find something tasty there. She always did, back in her runaway days.

She starts the Hyundai, glances in the mirror, and frowns. Someone has written a line of symbols with a finger in the dusty glass. She turns to stare at it directly, but it still makes no sense: vὸτυᴅƺᴏ ɹθῶvγ. Diana feels a prickle of gooseflesh on her arms. It's nothing, of course, probably just some kid playing around, but she feels a deadfall drop in her gut. She puts the car in gear and drives out of the parking lot, thanking her stars that the weirdness of today is finally over. Now, job or no job, she can go back to normal.

But the Furies know better, and their barely muted voices are pushing into Diana's awareness as she drives. Beloved, if you have lived long enough, you, too, may be smiling ruefully now, or shaking your head just a little. You know perfectly well that most of the times you've had that thought—"Now everything can go back to normal!"—the weirdness was just beginning.

CHANGE

Diana is almost too tired to drive. Even her little Hyundai seems to be struggling to put one wheel in front of the other. The clock on the dashboard tells her it's almost eleven. Devin might have called while she was tromping around the city, and Diana is worried by the thought of him worrying. But her cell phone, joining in the general exhaustion, sputters out when she tries to call him. Her brain feels as if it's been pounded with a meat tenderizer. The thoughts that terrified her earlier in the day are still churning away, but weariness has dulled the Furies' shrieking to a listless repetition of ugly truths: She's out of a job. Her fugue states are back. She's falling apart.

The only thing Diana wants more than sleep is food—she must have walked at least twenty miles today, with nothing in her stomach but morning coffee. In a way, she's grateful for the sharp hunger. It's the only thing keeping her alert. She's so tired that if a cop pulls her over right now, she'll have a hard time proving she isn't drunk or stoned. She can feel that her reaction times are slow. The lighted billboards and neon signs on each side of Van Nuys Boulevard flash past before she can read them. She pinches herself on the leg, trying to stay focused, worried that she'll plow into another car without even noticing.

The radio might help. Diana turns it on and hears the distinctive crooning of the Beatles. It's one of their more acid-fueled songs, all about broken light, wind-tumbled thoughts, a million eyes calling across the universe. Diana can't really follow the lyrics, but she sings along as well as she can, and when the Fab Four get to their chorus, she's glad she did. *"Nothing's gonna change my world,"* sing the Beatles. *"Nothing's gonna change my world."* The thought is comforting, and Diana reaches to turn up the volume as she repeats the phrase.

Nothing's gonna change my world.

Nothing's gonna change my world.

Have you ever taken refuge in that thought, beloved? It's a lie, of course; your world has never stopped changing, and it never will. As you read this, everything you know and everything you are is dropping away, and away, and away, into the irretrievable past. Sometimes it's fairly easy to ignore that, of course. You create a career, a relationship, a child, and you tell yourself things are as they should be, forever. It's a lovely fantasy while it lasts, and it can be hard to let go when the illusion of stability inevitably ends.

As it's ending for Diana right now.

She makes it to her neighborhood and cruises the streets until she finds a parking spot a block and a half away from her apartment complex. The complex itself has no parking lot—one reason the rent is low enough for Diana to afford. Unlike most of the structures nearby, her building is not boxy, unattractive, and small. It's boxy, unattractive, and large—big enough for fifty tenants, give or take the few visitors who are always recovering from meth binges in this unit or that. Diana gets out of her car and presses the fob to lock the doors. The night is cold, blurred with slight fog. From the vast city around her, Diana can hear distant sirens and honking horns. Occasional shouts— laughter, anger, fear—issue from the crowded houses on both sides of the street. The only person in sight is an old woman, shuffling past a streetlight fifty yards away. She's leading two cats on leashes. Trying to, anyway. The cats have twined around the woman's legs and she's wrapped up, Diana thinks, like a lumpy little Maypole.

"Oh, gosh darn it to heck, you guys," the woman fusses under her breath. Her weak, quavering voice carries eerily well in the foggy stillness. "No, Steve, I said clockwise! *Clockwise!* Michelle, you just hold still."

Diana feels a sudden stab of empathy for the old lady, stuck out here in the damp, hopelessly entangled in cat leashes and dementia. She feels an urge to help, which she instantly suppresses. The last thing to do on any night, on any city street, is connect with a stranger. Instead Diana just watches the cat lady from the corner of her eye and sets off toward the gate of the apartment complex.

Yes, take a good look, hiss the Furies. *That's your future, right there. That's where you're headed. You've already got a mother lode of crazy. Just need a couple of starter cats.*

A low, calm, conversational voice cuts through the night, interrupting the Furies. "Oh, I'm not crazy, Diana."

Diana can't help herself: She stops, turns, and stares. The old woman's eyes lock onto hers, glittering in the streetlight, sending twin needles of ice into Diana's chest.

"I'm not crazy," the woman repeats in that rich voice. "I'm wild. You of all people should know the difference."

Diana's heart hammers. Did this senile old bat just call her by *name*? No, that couldn't be. It must have been Diana's imagination. A delusion. A hallucination. Just behind the old woman, a juniper tree shifts in the slight breeze, and for a moment Diana sees faces moving in it—green, shifting faces. She forces herself to turn and walk steadily forward. A few steps later she hears the woman muttering "Oh, my heck!" and "Gosh darn it!" Her voice is old again, thin and reedy.

The warm, prickling sensation—the one that signals a fugue state beginning—wells up in Diana's chest. Some alien *other* is rising from a depth as distant as the bottom of the ocean, intent on occupying her bones and limbs.

"No, no, no!" she whispers frantically. With a burst of will, she pushes the *other* back down into the depths. A moment ago her legs could barely walk, but now insanity is after her—she can feel its breath on the back of her neck—and she almost sprints down the street, through the gate of the apartment complex, and up the stairs to her apartment. She fumbles with her keys, bursts through the door, slams it behind her, and leans against it, panting.

In the glow of the one lamp she always leaves on, the room looks quite normal. Cheap but clean IKEA furniture, old but clean carpet, pictures of Diana and Devin on the walls. As her heart rate slows, Diana feels her usual sense of empty surprise that her son no longer lives here. He's been gone more than a month, but it still shocks her to see the foldaway bed where he slept for most of his life tucked back into its rickety couch. There are no video games scattered on the coffee table, no schoolbooks or sneakers on the floor. The place is heartbreakingly tidy. Diana feels another jab of worry about next month's rent. But at least for now, this is home.

She heads for the tiny kitchen, plugs in her cell phone, makes a peanut butter sandwich, and practically inhales it with a glass of milk. Then she eats another, and another. By the time she feels satisfied, her phone has also absorbed enough energy to function. It chirps perkily as several texts come in. They're all from Devin.

The first message, sent at 6:12 P.M., says, "Hola! Que pasa?"

At 7:22 P.M.: "You there?"

At 9:15 P.M.: "Buzz me when you get this."

At 10:30 P.M.: "Should I be worried?"

Diana smiles despite herself. She keeps bracing herself for Devin to disappear into college life and start thinking of her as a nuisance—that seems right and natural for an eighteen-year-old. And it's true, he rarely calls. But it seems that the texts they exchange every couple of days may be as important to Devin as they are to Diana.

If you are lucky, beloved, you have a Devin in your life—someone or something so bright that in its presence every form of darkness recedes. Diana doesn't know if any child would have affected her this way, or if Devin is truly as extraordinary as he seems. In any case, since the moment he was born (nine months after Diana's one-night stand with an itinerant sitar player who'd gone back to India without ever telling her his last name), Devin has been Diana's anchor to normalcy. The social workers who helped her get off the streets before his birth actually placed bets on how long it would take the hapless Dumpster baby, now seventeen, to toss her own infant into the nearest landfill. But Diana had surprised everyone—most of all herself—by proving to be an excellent mother.

The white-hot love she'd felt the moment little Devin had been placed in her arms ultimately gave her the resolve to abandon almost all her bad habits. For Devin's sake, Diana stopped drinking, drugging, and dating unwholesome strangers. For his sake, she obtained her GED, a job, and her first tiny apartment. And for him—most important of all—she somehow managed to stop her fugue states, cold turkey.

Until now.

She takes a last swig of milk, pulls herself together, and taps the FaceTime app next to Devin's number. He answers on the second ring.

"Yo, maternal unit!" The phone screen brightens, showing Devin's merry dark eyes, then pulling back to reveal his whole smiling face. "Where've you been?"

"Right here, just sitting around," Diana lies cheerfully. "Sorry I didn't get your texts earlier. My phone went dead and I didn't even check it until just now."

"That's okay, I understand." Devin smiles. "I figured you'd gotten carried away by—I dunno—romantic fantasies or whatever."

"Yeah, because that would be so me." Diana arches an eyebrow at her phone.

"Go ahead, admit it." Devin's smile grows to a grin. "You've been daydreaming about you and Buck Gussman together at last, sharing sangria on a Caribbean beach, riding horses, wearing matching peasant blouses—"

"Wait, who's wearing the peasant blouses?" Diana interrupts. "Us, or the horses?"

"All four of you," says Devin solemnly. "Everyone in this scenario gets a peasant blouse. I'll wear one myself when I come to visit—it's not really my thing, but I know how much it'll mean to Buck, and since he'll be my new daddy . . ."

Diana dissolves in giggles "Gah! Ew! Buck Gussman!" Just saying the name brings back all the worry of the day, and she stops laughing.

"Wow, Mom, you're looking kind of wiped out," says Devin. "Seriously, are you okay? Do you have a cold?"

For just a moment, she considers telling him the truth—at least about being fired. She'd rather die than tell him about the fugue state; it would worry him to death. In the end, she decides it's easier to come up with a wholesale lie than a partial truth. "Oh, I decided to go for a run after work," she says. "I got lost. Ended up doing a lot more mileage than I expected." She shrugs and smiles dismissively, then changes the subject. "So how's Stanford treating you today? How's that advanced thing going?"

"The string theory seminar? It's—well, it's pretty hard. If I can learn this stuff, Mom, I'm telling you—I can learn anything. Almost everyone else in the class is, like, thirty. They're all grad students. But they're nice. They treat me kind of like a mascot."

"A hairy mascot," Diana says, peering at her phone. "Maybe a yeti, or something? Have you stopped shaving?"

Devin grins sheepishly, rubbing one scruffy cheek. "Well, I haven't had time to get my hair cut, and I was starting to look like a girl. So . . ."

"I like it," says Diana. He's right; his thick black eyelashes and storm of curly hair would make him too pretty without the hair on his face (she can't really call it a beard). "It makes you look like someone in an ad for—I don't know—Jeeps, or beer, or barbecued meat with fur still on it. Something manly."

She doesn't really hear Devin's response, just lets his voice soothe her like music while she watches him, the way she used to watch him when he was little. She never tired of looking at him: his newborn tininess, his bright intelligence as a toddler, the drive to succeed that grew along with him. Devin was as high-achieving a child as Diana had been odd. He was the valedictorian of his (admittedly subpar) public high school, winner of two national science exams, admitted to Stanford at seventeen on a full-ride scholarship, living stipend included. Diana decides that she won't tell Devin about Super Big Mart until she's in another job. A better job. Much, much better. Then she'll surprise him, make him proud. Though she can't imagine anyone ever being as proud of her as she is of him.

" . . . so now I have this extra paper to write. Unless I find a way to get out of it. I've been thinking of stowing away on a Merchant Marine vessel. That would work. I could foment mutiny, take over the ship. It'd be fun."

"Oh, right." Diana laughs again. "Just run away, after all the work I went to making you out of simple tools I found around the house. You may have a fancy scholarship, your dudeness, but you still rely on me for . . . I don't know, mom things. Homemade cookies. Perpetual nagging guilt."

"Well," Devin pouts, "you never send as much nagging guilt as the other guys' moms."

"I'll work harder," Diana promises solemnly.

"Cool. I'll start doing street drugs as a logical and natural consequence."

"I guess we've both got our work cut out for us."

"Yep." Devin yawns. "Well, *mama mia,* I'd better go hit the books now. Or the crack pipe or whatever."

"Okay. Bye, sweetheart. I love you."

"Love you, too. Devin out." The screen of Diana's phone goes blank.

She sits at the kitchen table for a moment, basking in ordinariness. Her stomach is full, her apartment in order, the Furies dispersed by Devin's effervescent presence. She's still bone-tired, but for the first time since morning, Diana isn't dogged by the sense of everything falling apart.

She feels a draft from the door of the bedroom and realizes she's left a window open. As she trudges wearily over to close it, she hears a thin, wandering voice from the sidewalk below. It takes Diana a second to recognize the voice—the old woman with the cats. She's singing, and it's that same Beatles song, but cat lady is getting the lyrics all wrong. *"Something's gonna change your world,"* she warbles. *"Something's gonna change your world. Something's gonna change your world. Something's gonna change your world . . ."*

Diana slams the window, but it's too late. She knows the song is meant for her, and it's taken root in her mind. Just like that, *bang,* her heart is racing again, her mind whirling. Diana sits down hard on her bed, clenches her fists, and presses them to her eyes. Just a panic attack, she tells herself. Not insanity, not annihilation. Nothing to fear but fear itself. She just has to pull herself together, be normal.

Oh, right! shriek the Furies, their laughter like nails on a chalkboard. *Good luck with that, you crazy bitch!*

Doing her best to breathe slowly, Diana turns on a lamp and finds the remote for the TV. She presses the power button with shaking fingers, desperate to see bright lights, to hear chatty voices. She's trembling so hard she drops the remote and has to scramble for it on the floor. Then she begins surfing channels, looking for a cheerful, comforting, familiar program. She finds one.

And just like that, wouldn't you know it, something changes her world.

ROY

Ordinarily, Diana has little interest in *The Nightly Show*, though of course, like almost everyone else in the world, she's familiar with it. Tonight the program's familiar set and smiling, handsome host take the edge off her panic, so she kicks her shoes onto the rug, climbs into bed, and settles down to watch. On the screen next to the host sits a tall, laughing man with sandy hair, a deep tan, and striking gray eyes. Looking at him, Diana experiences a sudden, almost audible *click*.

It's her first sign that from this point on, everything in her life will be different.

For a moment she worries she's going into another fugue state; she feels the warm pins and needles of the *other* in her chest. But instead, the energy in her torso rises up and turns inward on itself like a tornado, a whirl of feelings so powerful and complicated that

Diana can't follow them. Then her attention gathers and focuses, as if the tornado is being forced into a kitchen funnel and projected, with unbelievable power, toward the gray-eyed man.

It's the most intense thing she's felt since Devin was born. By contrast, everything else inside her has gone blessedly, blessedly quiet. No Furies. No panic. No regret. No pain. In the silence, Diana hears her own voice whisper something she has never said before. *"I have a purpose."*

At that very moment, the gray-eyed man pauses, turns, and looks straight into the camera, his brows gathering slightly as if he's heard a strange noise in dim light. Against all reason, Diana knows that somehow he can see her—*feel* her—watching him. She doesn't even know the man's name, but the vortex of attention turning her toward him is also turning him toward her. She's certain of it. She also knows that it's no coincidence she's watching this program now, after a day that's shaken her to the core. Some inscrutable power is working on her. Through her.

It may be, beloved, that you've gone through something similar to this: a surge of destiny so strong it made you believe in miracles. Such bolts from the blue seem to hit when weariness or ill fortune have plowed through the ground of reason, breaking it up so that magic can take root. What follows is so perfect that to call it accidental defies reason. You're rejected by your first-choice college, only to find the perfect mentor at the one you didn't want. After missing a plane, you meet another stranded passenger who becomes your best friend. An unwelcome job transfer takes you to the city that turns out to be your favorite place on earth. This is often how destiny finds us: as a storm of desolation leading to a bright discovery.

Now, as she watches the *The Nightly Show,* Diana feels an unfamiliar sensation steal through her: calm. It soaks into her body like a healing drug as the man on the screen leans back, pulling his left ankle up to rest on his right knee, utterly relaxed.

"I've always wanted to ask you something," says *The Nightly Show*'s charismatic host, who seems downright drab compared to his guest. "How do you get the cojones to call yourself a 'life coach'?"

The audience ripples with laughter.

"I mean," the host continues, "it's not like there's a Life Olympics where you can win six gold medals and then say, 'Well, I think now I'll go into coaching,' right? I mean, what gives a person the sheer, raging chutzpah to tell people, 'Yes! Come to me, and I will coach your entire life!'?"

The man laughs along with the audience, the slight crow's-feet at the edges of his silver eyes making them look sweet, rather than steely. He pushes back a lock of his thick, longish hair, then stretches out one muscular arm to pick up a book from the host's desk. He flips the cover open and reads from the flap.

"Roy Richards—that's me"—he gives the audience a self-deprecating grin, and gets a cheer in return—"is the star of the popular television series *Conquest*. He has earned degrees from Yale and Oxford, summited Everest, rafted down the Amazon, and crossed the Sahara on camelback while living with a Bedouin tribe. He has lived with Greenlandic Inuits and the Karapuna people of Papua New Guinea, and passed traditional tests of bravery and strength in seventeen different tribes of North and South American Indians. His personal empowerment seminars attract hundreds of thousands of people annually. He made over half a billion dollars in a single day when his company, Conquest, Inc., went public."

The audience cheers along, growing louder with each item Roy Richards reads, until they drown out his voice. He stops reading to beam at them, raising both arms like someone opening a window, goading the crowd into turning up the volume.

The Nightly Show's host throws up his own hands in surrender. "Okay, okay," he says with a laugh when the crowd noise finally dies down. "I'm in! I'll be at your next seminar. With bells on. I'll bring my bells—you just bring your massive, massive balls. God, you make me feel like such a failure!" The audience laughs.

When *The Nightly Show* goes to commercial, Diana types "Roy Richards" into the computer tablet she bought on sale at Super Big Mart. Her hands still tremble slightly with fatigue and excitement. Wikipedia alone teaches her more about the gray-eyed man than she knows about most of the people who raised her. It begins, "Roy Richards (born Leroy Duncan Richards) is an American television star, life coach, and author consistently listed among the most influential celebrities in the world." The entry goes on to enumerate Richards's many achievements, the landmarks in his career, his luxurious homes (one on a private island), his long string of dalliances with movie stars and supermodels.

After *The Nightly Show* ends, Diana turns off the television and keeps researching. She watches several YouTube outtakes from *Conquest,* Richards's hit TV reality show. Each episode shows Richards forging his way through some horrifically inhospitable natural environment, teaching viewers how to conquer any obstacle life may throw at them.

"You can't let yourself lose confidence out here—or anywhere," Richards proclaims from a desolate glacier, where he's just made a fire by using a plastic bag of his own urine as a magnifying glass that concentrates sunlight.

"Confidence is the root of conquest!" he shouts as he rows a hand-built raft away from a desert island.

"If you don't feel confident, fake it 'til you make it," he advises from a steaming Amazon jungle, and punctuates the sentiment by eating a large cockroach and a small snake, both of them alive.

Diana feels her weary heart blazing with new energy. If Roy Richards can do all that, she tells herself, she can get a job—a good job. At first she's not confident of this, but she fakes it, and sure enough, as she watches video after video of Roy Richards, her fears and Furies fall silent again. She clicks and watches, clicks and watches, until her eyes refuse to focus. When she finally falls into exhausted sleep, her hand still resting on the tablet screen, all her dreams have gray eyes.

•

It's already bright daylight when she wakes up. Diana feels a jolt of worry about missing work before she remembers: There is no work. Then a different worry begins to arise, but before it can take hold, Diana grabs her tablet and brings up another Roy Richards video. Instantly, she feels his confidence lifting her like a rising tide. She can breathe again.

Beloved, you may have fastened onto something similar at difficult times in your life. A book, a preacher, a friend, a philosophy—something that pulled you beyond the limits of your courage and gave you a new place to stand. Diana relies on this effect completely for the next three days. Staying in her pajamas, slowly eating her way through all the food in her kitchen, she watches every "quest" Richards has ever filmed, clicks through every page on his official website, reads everything she can find about him on fan sites. The more she rivets her attention on him, the better she feels. Whenever she thinks about her logical next step—looking for a new job—panic, the Furies, and the tingling rise of the *other* frighten her into near paralysis, and she returns to Roy Richards for another dose of courage.

For a while she worries that she won't be able to keep Devin from sensing that something's wrong, that she's lost her job and has no idea what to do next. But the deception turns out to be easy. She chats with Devin about her days as if she's still working at Super Big Mart, knowing she'll soon have better news to tell him. Her new life philosophy— Roy Richards's teachings—flows into every empty, fearful place in Diana's psyche, filling her with hope. No, more than hope. Destiny.

Have you ever felt your destiny unfolding, beloved? Have you experienced the intensity of the hunt, the fixation of attention that only fate can explain? Have you ever told yourself your feelings were excessive, but known that something huge and pivotally important was carrying you along like a riptide? You can fight that current all you want; you know it will still have its way with you. Or you can try swimming along with it, and grow amazed by your own power— until you pause and realize that you aren't moving but being moved. You're not in control, not at all, and that's what makes the feeling so exquisitely exciting.

●

A week after being fired, Diana is running out of cash and food, but has a huge supply of information about Leroy Duncan Richards. She knows his parents' names, his favorite foods, his earliest memory. She's also figured out (by triangulating one of Richards's photo

Tweets with landmarks on Google Earth) where the production team for *Conquest* films its promotional videos. The location is nearby, in the foothills around Los Angeles.

An idea begins to form in Diana's mind.

Madness, whisper the Furies. Diana just watches another video of Roy Richards and tells them, *No. Destiny.*

Thus, one sunny morning, Diana showers, dresses, heads to a factory-outlet mall, and accrues an incautious amount of credit-card debt. She buys several outfits far sexier and more expensive than anything she's ever worn before, basing the look on photos of various women Richards has dated over the years. True, he favors tall Nordic models, and Diana is so . . . well . . . average—but with high heels, pushed-up breasts, and makeup applied by the saleswoman at the cosmetics counter, she's almost as confident as Richards tells her she should be. With his advice ringing in her mind, she's ready to pull off a wild, ambitious quest of her own.

It's an hour's drive to the location where *Conquest*'s crew is filming a promotional video. Diana's Hyundai gamely grinds over the final few miles of bumpy dirt road until she sees a huge RV trailer squatting on a grassy field. A few other cars and trucks and a scattering of camera equipment stand nearby. She parks a few yards away, gets out of her car, and wobbles toward the site in her strappy high-heeled sandals.

A group of ten or twelve people, mostly men, all dressed in grungy jeans or cargo pants, are sitting on the bumpers of their cars munching pizza and sandwiches. Most of the men stop eating—some in mid-chew—as Diana walks up to them. She can feel herself, or perhaps her *other,* pulling their attention like a magnet, making them unable to look away. Usually the stares of men in packs unnerve Diana, but suffused with the strange power that's been working in her from the moment she first saw Roy Richards, she feels no doubt or fear at all.

"Hey," says one of the men uncertainly. "Who are you?"

Diana just looks at him, aware of the way her breasts and hips shape her faux-snakeskin silk dress. She knows (without knowing how she knows) that all these people are, at this very moment, becoming enchanted. Before she can speak, a short man in rimless glasses steps through the open door of the RV trailer.

"You've got to wear the safety harness," he says. "The insurance company—"

"Oh, screw the insurance company," says another voice. Diana's heart almost stops. In the next instant, there he is, even taller and handsomer than he looks on television.

"I'm not wearing some nancy-boy harness," says Roy Richards. "The viewers aren't paying to see me go to a damn spa. If we're saying I'm in danger, then I'd better be in danger."

The first man doesn't respond. He's seen Diana, and is eyeing her uneasily. From her Internet research, Diana recognizes him as Kyle Whittingham, the producer of *Conquest*. He looks her up and down. He can't help it. Diana knows he can't.

"Who are you?" he says.

"I'm here to apply for a job." Diana keeps her voice low and normal.

Kyle Whittingham rolls his eyes. So do several men in the crew. For an awful moment, Diana loses her nerve. *What the blue shit are you doing?* scream the Furies.

Then Diana sees that Roy Richards isn't dismissing her like the others. He's watching her intently, his head cocked a bit to one side. Diana feels his eyes on her, the heat of them, the hurricane power of the connection between them, and her confidence soars again.

"You don't know it yet, but you need me," she says calmly, addressing the whole group but looking at Roy. "I'll do whatever no one else wants to do—run errands, get props, sweep floors. Anything."

Whittingham moves toward Diana, shaking his head. But Richards takes two long steps, blocking the producer's path, and gets to her first. She looks up at him, barely breathing. Richards smiles at her, the muscles in his face accentuating the bold anvil of his jaw.

"You don't even have to pay me minimum wage," says Diana. "I'll work for less."

Richards nods slowly. Then his smile broadens into a boyish grin.

"So . . . this forty-year-old virgin walks into a brothel," he says, loudly enough for the whole crew to hear even as his eyes—those storm-gray eyes!—stay locked on Diana's. "It's his birthday, and he's there to get laid, come hell or high water, right?"

Diana smiles back at him, feeling the warmth spread through her whole body.

"This smokin'-hot prostitute walks up, sits down right next to him," Richards goes on. "She says, 'Hey, mister, I'll do anything you want for two hundred dollars—as long as you can ask for it in three words.' The guy says, 'Seriously? Anything I want?' The hooker says, 'As long as you can ask for it in three words.' So the guy thinks for a minute, and then he gets so excited he can hardly stand it. He leans over like this, so she'll be sure to hear." Richards bends slightly, until his lips are just a few inches from Diana's ear. "And the guy says to the hooker, 'Paint . . . my . . . house.'"

After a moment of silence, Diana bursts out laughing. She's worried she sounds manic, but everyone else is laughing just as hard. It's not just the joke. It's the energy, the torrent of charisma that fills the whole space around Richards. "My point," he says, "is that it's crazy to turn down a pretty lady who offers to work hard for bargain prices." He extends his right hand to Diana, the muscles in his arms rippling. "Hi, I'm Roy. And you are . . . ?"

"Diana."

She takes his hand, and the feel of it—both rough and soft, gentle and strong—is shockingly familiar.

"*Enchanté, mademoiselle,*" he says, and she knows (maybe he knows, too) that he means it literally. She also knows he'll insist on hiring her, over the protestations of his producer. She knows she'll end up working closely with him—very closely. Neither she nor Roy really has any choice in the matter. Diana senses, in fact, that they've already made their choices, in some time and dimension beyond their ability to imagine.

And if you've ever been enchanted, beloved, you know she's right.

CONQUEST

Working in television is intoxicating. Her whole life, Diana has lived in the world's greatest media mecca, without ever becoming part of The Business. During her hapless teenage years, she often reflected that Los Angeles probably had the best-looking homeless population in the world. The prettiest cheerleaders and handsomest student thespians from every small town in America fed a constant trickle of beautiful people into the LA area. Every cab driver or convenience-store clerk wanted to act—or, at the very least, was working on a screenplay. Diana watched so many dreams die she long ago lost count, so she's always viewed the TV and movie industries with a jaundiced and skeptical eye.

But that was the old Diana.

The new Diana—the one who rose into existence at her first sight of Roy Richards—loves everything about creating a TV reality series.

Even without Richards's electrifying presence, the high-speed demands and sheer adrenaline rush of the work make Diana's blood seem to fizz in her veins. And, it turns out, she's very, very good at it.

It helps that she's obsessed with Roy Richards as a person and with *Conquest* as his best-known showcase. After watching, rewatching, and re-rewatching every episode, Diana has an instinctive feel for the way the show fits together. Her first job, other than running general errands, is creating what the director calls "supplemental locations." When Roy Richards returns from some remote environment, the video he brings with him occasionally lacks bits of explanation or demonstration. To fill in these gaps, the *Conquest* crew simulates the original locations, building sets to match the terrain, foliage, light, and weather conditions. From her first day on the lot, Diana displays an unusual aptitude for the task. "I don't know why," she tells Devin happily, three weeks into her new life. "I just seem to know how to visualize any place he's been. Swamps, ice fields, big ol' mountains—I've never been to places like those, but somehow I can just close my eyes and know how everything would look. And I can put together a set that looks pretty close to the real deal. It's so strange—I think I'm actually good at something."

"News flash, Mom." Devin beams at her from her phone screen. "You're good at everything that interests you. You're just not *interested* in everything."

In the old days, this compliment would have flown right over her head, but recently, Diana is beginning to entertain the thought that she may not be a complete loser.

"You may be right," she tells Devin. "Anyway, I feel like I'm finally working up to my potential." Unexpectedly, the phrase brings a sting of tears to her eyes. Beloved, if you've ever been told that you're "not working up to your potential," you know how that sentence cuts, like a dull knife to the heart. It's a monster that's haunted and shamed Diana from birth.

Well, actually, since one particular day.

Diana was five years old, being tested by a new set of foster parents to see what sort of school might have some chance at educating her. Various child psychologists had labeled her "differently abled" (a phrase that could mean virtually anything but good news) but hadn't

nailed down exactly how different she was. Diana's IQ had been esti-
mated at 70 or 80—educable, but as she overheard one psychologist
remark to a colleague, "definitely a few rings short of a circus."

The latest in the string of experts to evaluate her was a jittery
young man named Marvin Piper, whose ginger hair and pink, beard-
less skin made him look as vulnerable as a cooked prawn. When Diana
accidentally kicked her chair leg, he flinched as if she'd stabbed him.
Watching this reaction, a new idea occurred to Diana: Other people,
besides her, might also be "differently abled."

She regarded Marvin Piper with intense curiosity. His every
move betrayed his differences: the way he caught her glance and
then immediately looked away; the slight tremor of his hands as he
opened an official-looking booklet and smoothed it flat on his desk;
the uncertainty in his voice when he explained that he'd be asking
Diana a series of questions that would grow progressively harder,
and that she should answer them as best she could until she no longer understood them. The poor man grew more miserably self-con-
scious with every word, until he was sweating right through his tie.

Diana looked upon him, and took pity.

She had no idea why Marvin Piper so desperately wanted her to
give him the answers to the questions in the booklet. Why didn't he
just read them himself? They were written right there, under the
questions. Diana suspected it was impossible to watch as much *Ses-
ame Street* as she had without learning to read. She'd been doing so,
fluently, from the age of fifteen months. She often scanned books and
magazines held by the adults around her, and as a result, she could
read peripherally, at any angle, including upside down. She never
told anyone she could do this, because no one ever asked.

But Marvin Piper seemed so desperate for the answers to the
questions in his booklet that Diana decided to read them to him,
even those that were incorrect. For example, the answer to the question, "Why is an octopus like the month of October?" was not, as
the booklet said, "Because an octopus has eight legs and October is
the eighth month." For starters, Diana thought, October is the tenth
month. And even forgiving that, the eighth month since *what*? Since
humans decided a year began? The year could begin any time from
the perspective of an octopus; it would probably think the eighth

month started seven months after it was born. Honestly, she thought, months were a human invention that would make no sense at all to an octopus. It couldn't count time—not the way it could count its legs.

As she contemplated this multifaceted issue, Diana's eyes glassed over, headed for a fugue state. But then the ginger-haired man's Adam's apple began bobbing as if he'd swallowed a live hamster, and Diana remembered to soothe him by reading the answer from the booklet. Worked like a charm.

As they got toward the middle of the booklet, and then the end, Marvin Piper seemed surprised, then increasingly pleased, then weirdly joyful. After she'd answered the last question, he stood up and bolted out of his office into the waiting room. Diana heard him stammering excitedly to the social worker who'd brought her. The word "genius" was used. Also "savant," an unfamiliar term that nevertheless was clearly a compliment.

Climbing out Marvin Piper's second-story window—she went outside as a matter of course whenever any adult left her unsupervised—Diana registered the fascinating discovery that if she simply told adults things they already believed to be true, it made them happy. She herself preferred to learn things she *didn't* know, but perhaps that was because she was differently abled. Diana was still pondering this when Piper found her in an empty lot half a mile away, sharing half of a discarded cheeseburger with a one-eared mongrel dog.

Ever since that day, people had been telling Diana she wasn't working up to her potential. The foster parents who took her to see Marvin Piper had returned to their house and spent a week trying to teach her to count cards at blackjack, aiming at a life of leisure in Las Vegas. But the game had seemed pointless to Diana, and she couldn't focus on it.

The same could be said for virtually everything she was taught in school. Though she remained a voracious reader, and her IQ scores continued to sail off the charts whether or not she could read the answers off a booklet, Diana could never harness her own mind, never put it in the service of a standard education. The punishment and scolding she received for that failing were far worse than being considered a simpleton. Frustrated educators added "oppositional defiant disorder" to Diana's list of diagnoses and treated her with poorly restrained contempt.

Now, working on the set of *Conquest,* Diana finds her whole intelligence finally cooperating with her intentions, quickly and expertly calculating exactly what's needed to improve the show. She initially gets paid for two hours' work each day, but willingly puts in ten, often more. Before long she's not just making coffee and creating supplemental locations; she's holding microphones and light-reflecting panels in perfect position. Sometimes even the cameras. She learns quickly, enjoys even the most mundane tasks, and never forgets. Her salary rises accordingly, and the fear of losing her apartment blessedly fades.

At the heart of all this enthusiasm, of course, is her obsession (she's honest enough to call it that) with Roy Richards. That entranced feeling, the sense of connection between them, increases every day. But Diana is too wise to throw herself at Richards. Somehow she knows that she's hunting, and that the single most important virtue for a hunter is patience. She finds any way she can to be near Roy Richards, but rarely even glances in his direction. She can feel how this intrigues him. The sense of his eyes on her back is a physical pressure that fills her with heat and desire. Diana isn't sure he feels it, too, but she has her suspicions.

One reason she is reserved in her pursuit is Roy's "camera assistant," a fretfully beautiful blond actress named Summer Fields, who has accompanied him on his last several quests. Diana tactfully learns what she can about the relationship from her best friend on the crew, a makeup artist named Melanie who shaves her head, wears an army jacket, and sports at least twenty visible piercings.

"Roy's always had an arm trophy," Melanie tells Diana one day at lunch. "I'd call them the flavor of the month, except it's always the same flavor. Thin, blond, stacked, drop-dead gorgeous. I can't even tell them apart. He takes them on his quests as 'location assistants.'" Melanie makes air quotes with her fingers. "But he doesn't mind everyone knowing he's boinking them off camera. It's part of his image—you know, 'A real man doesn't just keep himself alive, he protects his woman, too, blah blah.' All very macho."

From Melanie, Diana learns that Summer Fields was born a brunette—several years earlier than she admits—and named Sarah Feldman. "Her middle name—get this—is Rain." Melanie sniggers. "I guess she thought 'Summer Rain Fields' would look awesome on movie marquees. As if." The makeup artist's smile makes her lip rings clink against her teeth.

"Well, maybe she'll get a big break. A movie or something." Diana tries not to sound hopeful.

"Are you high? She's pushing forty! She's never getting another acting job."

Diana nods. Both she and Melanie are used to watching Hollywood fantasies die on the vine. And yet, Diana reflects, both of them still want to believe in their own. Melanie is sure that after her work on *Conquest* (mainly poufing Summer Fields' hair and artfully smearing dirt onto Roy Richards's cheekbones) she'll move on to big money in high-budget films. She's even shown Diana a tiny "vision board," a collage of images glued onto a five-by-seven card, hidden inside her makeup kit.

"This totally works," she tells Diana. "It's called the Law of Attraction—everything you think about, you create. You manifest it with your mind."

"Really?" Diana barely manages not to laugh. If she created everything she thought about, she and Roy Richards would be making love at this very moment.

"Absolutely." Melanie gives the serene smile of a true believer. She points to her vision board. "See this Mercedes convertible? I put that photo there a week ago, and I've seen, like, ten of them since then. Also, this picture of a dog? My neighbor just got that exact kind of dog. I mean, seriously!"

"Wow," says Diana, thinking that despite her carefully cultivated façade of toughness, Melanie is just another gullible girl huffing the opiate of the New Age masses. And still . . .

Have you ever half-believed something too ridiculous to be true, beloved? Have you privately said a special prayer, consulted a psychic, checked your horoscope and let it encourage you? That's how Diana feels. At home she has her own vision board, this one glued onto a large piece of poster board. She'll never show it to Melanie—or anyone else—because even she thinks it's ridiculous, possibly patho-logical. Almost every image on the board is a photo of Roy Richards. Roy in swamp gear, Roy covered in a parka, Roy holding a spider the size of his hand, Roy eating that very spider alive.

Anyway, Diana figures, at worst her vision board won't harm any-one. And at best . . . well, sometimes she can swear she feels it work-ing. The vortex of power between her and Roy Richards seems to swell as she prints, cuts, and glues ever more images to her vision board. The evening after her conversation with Melanie about Sum-mer Fields, Diana stops by a 7-Eleven, buys a copy of *Soap Opera Digest,* takes it home, and glues pictures of Summer to the cover.

A few days later, Kyle Whittingham sends Diana back from a sup-plemental set to the RV for an extra camera battery. As Diana locates the battery in a cupboard, she hears Roy Richards's voice from the other side of the closed bedroom door. He sounds troubled.

"But this is a major quest, Summer. You can't just cancel at the last minute!"

"*Your* major quest, not mine!" Summer Fields is more than trou-bled. She's almost always angry; now she sounds enraged. "This is the break of my *career,* Roy. You are *not* going to hold me to my con-tract, or I swear, I'll go public with all those videos we made. How would that affect your political future?"

"I could sue you," says Roy, his voice low but intense.

"Go ahead!" shouts Summer. "Do you know how long I've been going to auditions? It's regular work, and it's *acting,* Roy, *acting*! My *craft*! You really think I'm going to give up an opportunity like this to follow your ass around some godforsaken swamp?"

"It's not a swamp, it's a forest," says Roy reasonably. "And where am I going to find another camera assistant on such short notice? Have you thought about that?"

"*That is so like you!*" Summer yells. "Me, me, me! Can't you be happy for someone else, Roy? For once in your narcissistic life, could you *please* be happy for *me*?"

"But—"

"Oh, for God's sake, Roy! You can start a fire with your own piss. I'm sure you can find another woman to bang on your precious little quest."

"Okay." Richards's voice is calm and level. "We're done here." The next instant, the bedroom door bursts open and there he stands, looking straight at Diana.

"Oh!" she says, jumping violently. "Oh, I'm so sorry. I didn't mean to—"

"No, no, don't apologize. It's fine." Richards takes a deep breath and lets it out slowly. Behind him, Diana can see Summer Rain Fields sitting on the rumpled bed, pulling on a pair of khakis. Diana knows for a fact that Summer hates khakis.

"I just came for this," says Diana, holding the battery up and keeping her eyes down. She heads for the door of the RV.

"Stop!" Richards's voice is like a wizard's spell; Diana freezes in her tracks. "You're not in the way," he says kindly. She can feel the blaze of his eyes on her. "In fact, Diana, could I talk to you for a minute? In private?"

"What? Sure—yes—of course—yes, yes," she stammers.

Summer Rain Fields pushes past Richards, her hair tousled, her lips pursed as tightly as their injected silicone will allow. She stops, looks from Diana to Richards to Diana again, and rolls her eyes. "Oh, for God's sake," she says. Then she bares her teeth in a feral imitation of a smile. "He's all yours, bitch. Good freaking luck."

She walks to the door, stops, takes one look back at Roy, and hisses, "Sayonara, douchebag." The door slams behind her.

And Diana, as she's always known she would be, is alone with Roy.

OSCURA

From above, Sierras Oscuras National Forest looks like a gigantic field of broccoli. Diana alternates peering out the side window of the Fire Service helicopter with sneaking glances at Roy, who's belted into his seat facing hers. She's never been in a plane, let alone a chopper, and the wonder of the bird's-eye view—coupled with the fact that she's about to spend a month alone with the man she worships—is almost more than she can absorb. She closes her eyes for a moment, determined to tolerate the joy. When she opens them, Roy is smiling at her.

"How you doing?" he shouts. She can't hear him—her noise-cancelling headphones, plus the almighty *thub-thub-thub* of the chopper, drown out any auditory communication—but she can read his lips.

Those perfect, delicious lips.

Roy and Diana have been lovers since the very hour that Summer Rain Fields stormed out of the *Conquest* trailer. Something far more powerful than feeble human will propelled their bodies into a passionate embrace—that day, and every day since. It's been just under a week, and already Diana knows Roy's body better than she knows her own. She loves everything about him: the tiny mole below his left shoulder blade, the ticklish spots on his ribs, even the fact that he hates feet. Diana has been with many men who didn't bother to take off their socks during sex, but Roy is the first one to request that she leave hers on as well. From a man who regularly dines on live insects, Diana finds this odd, quirky little aversion adorable.

"I don't know what it is about you," he says as they lie, naked but for their socks, on the RV's king-sized bed. He reaches out for a curl of her long chestnut hair. "Don't take this the wrong way, Brownie Girl, but I don't usually go for your type."

"Thanks a lot." Diana laughs.

"No, really, I'm just trying to understand this. I can't stop thinking about you. I can't stop wanting you. I'm almost starting to feel as if I'm not really in control here." He sounds puzzled, even slightly nervous.

Diana kisses his hand. "Well, I know why I can't stop thinking about you. You're perfect."

Roy laughs, his beautiful white teeth and those silver eyes flashing in the dimness.

Diana, too, feels deliciously out of control. The bond she has with Roy astonishes her. Everything about him draws her like a magnet: not just his perfect sculpture of a body, but the loftiness and scope of his vision. She's never known anyone who thinks in such grand terms, who expects the absolute best of everything and everyone, who will accept nothing less than perfection.

Watching him from across the helicopter's small cabin, Diana marvels again that such a man has chosen her for his bed—and for a month-long expedition. It's Roy she loves, not his wealth, fame, or power, but she can't help feeling dazzled by all of it. For Diana, to love Roy is to love everything about him, from his smallest concerns to his most legendary triumphs.

Roy winks at her, then turns his attention back to the shot list for the episode of *Conquest* he and Diana are about to shoot. She takes a long, trembling, joyful breath and looks out at the view.

They've been in the air nearly three hours. From Los Angeles they flew north up the Pacific coast to the first redwood forests. Then they turned inland, cruising over the fields and vineyards of California's fertile central valleys, then beyond them into the sparsely inhabited oak savannah, and finally the deep old-growth forest. Now they're above the very center of the Sierras Oscuras, a virgin ecosystem virtually untouched by human activity. From horizon to horizon, Diana sees nothing but endless hills peaking and dipping like petrified sea swells, carpeted with that deep green, cruciferous foliage.

The machine finally stops over a golden patch of dry-grass meadow, hovering deafeningly. Roy unclamps his seat belt. Diana removes hers as well. Her heart is thrumming like a snare drum. She's practiced this descent mentally and physically over the past couple of days, but being lowered from a Fire Service training platform in Los Angeles is nothing like the trip from an actual helicopter into an actual patch of wilderness.

The copilot unbuckles and joins them in the main cabin. He and Roy help Diana into the rescue basket, which is already partially loaded with camera equipment and survival gear. Roy clamps Diana's safety harness to the basket, double-checks the carabiner, and gives her a kiss. Then he and the copilot push the basket out into thin air.

Diana expects to be afraid, but all she feels is wild exhilaration. As the basket descends into the small windstorm created by the chopper blades, she gapes down through the whipping strands of her own ponytail at the treetops thrashing below. What looked like a vegetable garden from thousands of feet up now looms toward her as the canopy of an ancient forest, massive oaks as tall as skyscrapers.

Diana has a flash of memory: the green juniper bush behind the old cat lady in her neighborhood, the green faces appearing and disappearing as foliage moved in the breeze. The oaks below Diana don't have faces; they have arms—thousands of arms apiece, millions of fingers reaching, grabbing, beckoning. They remind her of a mosh pit, a crowd dancing wildly, begging Diana to throw herself onto them and let them carry her over their heads. For a second she has the disorienting certainty that if the chopper weren't so loud, she'd hear the forest roaring her name.

The prickling warmth of the *other* appears in her chest. She looks up at Roy, who's gazing intently down, guiding the basket. Diana fastens her whole mind on his face, and the vertiginous *other*ness disappears.

The trip to the forest floor is longer than Diana expected, the trees around her taller than she would ever have imagined. When the basket finally bumps to the ground, she unbuckles her harness and quickly unloads the equipment. Once everything is piled in packs and crates on the dry grass, Diana yanks the cable sharply three times. The basket lurches upward. She watches it diminish until the helicopter sucks it in.

Diana finds her backpack, takes out a small video camera, focuses it on the hovering chopper, and presses "Record." Through the viewfinder she sees Roy emerge from the chopper. No basket for him—not even a safety harness. According to the *Conquest* shot list, Roy is using a descent technique called "fast-roping," perfected by British Special Forces in the Falkland Islands. Wrapping his legs around the cable, he rappels down to the forest floor as easily as a child slipping down a slide. He beams into the camera as he nears the ground, then steps away from the rope and holds up his hands, showing blisters on both palms: friction burns. "You do *not* want to try this at home!" he shouts into the camera, pulling a piece of torn skin off his hand. Diana tries not to ruin the shot by wincing.

The rope rises and disappears. The chopper waggles in the air, waving good-bye, then flies away. Diana and Roy look at the empty spot in the sky until the mechanical thunder becomes a grumble, then a whisper, then nothing. Diana turns off the camera. Even then, they don't move. The quiet is softly stunning. Have you ever heard the silence of a forest, beloved? No motors, no hum of industry, not even a human voice? Just the gentle sussuration of wind in the oak canopy, the buzz of occasional insects, and a soft, hypnotic symphony of birdsong. This is the first time Diana has heard a wilderness. Her skin tingles with it.

"Nice, huh?" Roy smiles at her.

Diana can only nod, her eyes filling with tears of gratitude. Even if she wanted to speak, she couldn't find words. She stretches and takes a deep breath, waiting for her eyes to dry. The last thing she wants is for Roy to think he's stuck in the woods with a weepy hormone case. Diana is well aware that she's probably the least attractive girlfriend Roy has ever had. She's determined to compensate by being the most accommodating. She goes to Roy and hugs him, not too tightly. She has never been this happy.

Roy kisses the top of Diana's head and then says, "All right, let's get this show on the road. Actually, two shows." He goes to the pile of equipment and begins sorting through it.

Diana wonders, as she has since boarding the helicopter, why they need so much kit. The *Conquest* script calls for them to simulate the predicament of a couple stranded by a small-plane crash, with just a few items of survival gear. She's always assumed that there was television equipment behind the scenes of *Conquest,* but Roy is famous for creating truly taxing conditions, and for his scorn toward other survival celebrities who pretend to be in dire straits when they're actually spending off-camera time at a Holiday Inn.

Now Roy is crouching near their gear, sorting it into two piles, one much smaller than the other. Her own backpack, filled mainly with layers of clothing fit for a wide range of temperatures, is in the little pile (clothing is something plane-crash victims might legitimately be assumed to carry in their luggage). Along with it are several packets of peanuts, a few small liquor bottles, and a first-aid kit. No cell phones, of course, though there is a radiophone they'll keep at the drop-off point and use only when Roy's quest is over. The second pile is made up of canvas and nylon cases. She sees two sleeping bags, which, according to the script, they aren't supposed to have. Diana is intensely curious about the second pile, but the last thing the foster-child garbage girl plans to do is pester her wealthy, gorgeous, famous, brilliant boyfriend with stupid questions.

Instead she turns in a slow circle, amazed by wildness. All around them, huge, mist-gray trunks spiral upward like pillars. The light filters through their leaves, which turn it soft and green and shifting. The forest floor's golden dry grass is punctuated by cream-colored boulders and wildflowers in every kind of jewel tone. The whole place feels sacred to Diana, and also, somehow, deeply *normal*. The familiar spreading warmth tingles in her chest, and she immediately turns her focus back to Roy. He's opening a large nylon case that looks as if it might contain a violin. But inside, each couched in its own specially shaped foam aperture, nestle the components of a huge gun.

Roy sees Diana's jaw drop. He chuckles. "Never seen an M16?"

Diana shakes her head, trying to look nonchalant. "Um . . . only in the movies."

"Well, feast your eyes." Roy grins. "Check these out, too." He opens another case and shows her two blocky-looking handguns. "Glock nine-millimeters." He picks up one of the guns, pops the empty cartridge, and pushes it back into place with a heavy, satisfying click.

Diana's mind is bursting with questions she forces herself not to ask. The *Conquest* script specifies that she and Roy will be armed only with a Swiss Army knife, plus a wooden bow and a few homemade arrows they'll fashion on location. But Roy is strapping a holster across his shoulder, another one to his ankle. He slides a Glock into each one.

"So, Brownie Girl," he says as he begins taking parts of the M16 out of their case and assembling them. "Aren't you going to ask me why I've got all this?"

She smiles. "I figure you'll tell me when you're ready."

"Good answer," says Roy. "But I'll bet you'd like to know."

"Sure." Diana gives him a shrug and a giggle, remembering advice she once got from a foster mother: *Always let men take charge. They like that. Don't be a nosy posy or a know-it-all.*

Roy nods slowly, his expression unreadable. Then he asks her the very last question she would ever have expected.

"Brownie Girl, do you believe in magic?"

Diana feels a chill ripple through her whole body. The night she first saw Roy on the television comes back to her in a rush: the lost time, the strange symbols on her windshield, the old woman, the almost physical force that had compelled her to focus on Roy's image. *Something's gonna change your world.* How improbable is it, she thinks, that just a few weeks later she's here with him?

"Sure," she says. "My mind is open."

"That's what I thought you'd say." Roy grins. "I didn't trust Summer, but once you came on board . . ." He clicks the barrel of the M16 into the stock. "I've been waiting to do this for a long time, Brownie Girl. With you along, I decided I could add it to the quest." He chuckles. "There's shooting," he says, glancing at Diana's video recorder, "and then there's *shooting*." He hoists the assembled rifle with one muscular arm.

Diana tries mightily to wait for his lead, but she can't repress a question. "What are we shooting?" she asks. "I mean, what are we, you know, *shooting* shooting?"

"Don't worry, Brownie, you're just on camera duty." Roy laughs. "And we're not even starting that for a while. Have you noticed that we could finish the whole shot list for the episode in about five days? Three, if the weather cooperates."

Diana says nothing. Of course she noticed. Five weeks seemed like a very long time to get the necessary video. She'd assumed they were staying in the forest more than a month to honor Roy's well-known insistence on real survival, genuine hardship. Not that five weeks alone with Roy sounds like hardship to Diana. She's already told Devin not to expect to hear from her until he's home on Thanksgiving break.

"You see, there's this . . . project I started once, years ago," Roy goes on. "I was living with the Chuchunk people—nomads in Siberia. A culture fifteen thousand years old. Spend a few nights with them, Brownie, and you'll have more than an open mind about magic. I've seen things that would turn your brain inside out." His eyes take on a distant look, and he's silent for a moment before shaking himself back into alertness. "Not just in Siberia, of course. Not with just the Chuchunk. All the ancient traditions are wiser than anyone realizes."

Diana watches him put the M16 into a nylon holster attached to his backpack. She stays silent.

"Anthropologists study these people and think they understand— pah!" Roy snorts in derision. "They know about as much about the ancient rituals as a butcher knows about bull fighting. Hack everything apart with the mind, and you kill it." He fastens a Velcro strip across the gun barrel to hold it secure. "Me, I've actually *participated* in the ceremonies. A lot of them are just horseshit, but some of them, Brownie—" He stops and looks straight at her, his eyes like silver daggers. "Some of them are more real than anything we call real."

Again, Diana feels the shiver—what is it? Excitement? Fear?—run through her blood. Her whole body is cloaked in gooseflesh.

"So, aside from a little television, that's what we're doing out here," says Roy. "I need to finish what I started in Siberia, and I think you're the person to help me. Sorry I didn't tell you before, but the ceremony has to happen in secrecy. I hope you're okay with that."

He stands up, giving her his best boyish smile, and the chill leaves Diana's body. She smiles back at him. "I'm in."

"That's my girl." He kisses her, a long, slow kiss that sets her whole body on fire.

"Hey," she says, slipping her hand inside the waistband of his jeans. "Do you have another gun in there, or are you just happy to see me?"

"Mmm," he murmurs. "You know, Brownie, I'm thinking we should test those sleeping bags before we do anything else. See if they can take a little rough handling."

"Absolutely," says Diana. "Have to check the equipment. That's just a smart survival strategy."

Roy nuzzles her neck. "Leave your socks on," he says.

It turns out the sleeping bags work just fine.

QUEST

It takes Roy about half an hour to sort all their gear, then wrap the equipment for the *Conquest* shoot, along with his gun cases, in a waterproof nylon bag. He attaches the bag to a nylon rope, tosses it over an oak bough, then hoists the bag of gear fifteen feet into the air and ties the end of the rope to a branch near the ground. "There!" he says, giving the knot a final tug, his arm muscles rippling. "That'll keep the bears and raccoons out of the peanuts."

Diana looks up at the bag as it twists in the gentle breeze. "Our peanuts are in there? All of them?"

Roy laughs. "Don't worry, Brownie Girl. We'll have plenty of food. That's what the guns are for, mostly." He pats the M16, which sits snug in its nylon holster.

"But the script says we only hunt with a bow and arrow."

Roy nods. "Well, sure, we'll do that for the show. But that will only take one week, and we're here for five. My quest is separate." He cocks his head thoughtfully. "But now that we're talking about it, why don't you get your camera out right now? You can film me while I make the bow. That's something I'd do right away if we'd been in a plane crash."

For the next couple of hours, Diana records Roy's preternatural skill at fabricating primitive weaponry. He chooses a long branch of Pacific yew, stiff but flexible, and whittles notches into each end to hold a bowstring. A disaggregated strand of nylon rope—something that might be found in a small-plane crash—provides the string itself. Then Roy sharpens the tips of several more sticks for arrows. All the time, he's chatting with the audience on the other side of the camera: charming them, impressing them, making them feel as if they're the ones with the encyclopedic mind, the endless range of useful skills, and the sharply cut triceps.

"All right," Roy says when the operation is completed and Diana's camera stowed. "Let's get going."

"Going?"

"Yes, we're headed deeper into the forest."

"Why?" Diana mentally kicks herself for asking two questions in a row.

Roy regards her for a long moment. "I can trust you to keep this to yourself?"

"Of course."

"Diana, I need to find a certain animal and . . . master it. Kill it, to be blunt. A real conquest, not some ridiculous television show. I need to engage my spirit animal. I need a wolf."

Diana blinks several times. "Wow. I . . . uh . . . I didn't know there were wolves in California."

"They were hunted out about a hundred years ago. But biologists are reintroducing them to the Sierras Oscuras. That's why I decided to come here."

"But if they've been reintroduced, why are you allowed to kill them?"

Roy laughs, a long, tickled chuckle. "I'm not *allowed* to kill them, Brownie Girl. But there are maybe five forest rangers for thousands of square miles out here, and not even many hikers. I'll just do what ranchers do when they see a protected predator—shoot, shovel, and shut up. I mean, after I've done the other things that are necessary for the ritual. I've got to put the 'quest' in *Conquest,* kiddo."

"Oh." It takes all of Diana's willpower to hold back a hundred more questions. In the end she says nothing but "Wow."

"The wolves were planted about ten miles north of this point." Roy waves an arm vaguely northward. "They have a huge range—fifty square miles, sometimes even more. We're close enough to hike into their territory. But I told Kyle we're going on a long hike south. No one's going to catch us, Brownie, 'cause no one knows where we are. We'll finish the ritual, hike back here, and then shoot the episode. By then we'll look like hard-core survivors. Grubby, hairy, and lean. Camera-ready!"

A twinge of uncertainty—is it worry?—pulls at Diana's gut. She ignores it. She refuses, absolutely refuses, to ask more questions. Instead, she stands up tall, swings her knapsack onto her back, and asks, "When do we start?"

Roy chucks her under the chin. "Brownie Girl, I love that can-do attitude. No bitching and moaning, just action. Where have you been all my life?"

They set off under the noonday sun, a breeze and the shadow of the oaks keeping the brightest light out of their eyes. The weather is still warm, but the first showers of autumn have fallen in the past few days, and everywhere new greenery is pushing through the golden remnants of dried-out summer grass. They follow game trails under the murmuring canopy, surprising gentle deer and, once, a bobcat, which hunkers down into the stubble of a dead sagebrush, glaring at them. Above them, in the clear blue spaces between the leaves, hawks and vultures circle idly.

Roy points out edible plants as they go: wood rose, salmon berries, wild parsnips, and a variety of edible mushrooms. When they come to a shrub covered with fruit Roy identifies as huckleberries, they stop to forage, stowing berries in a bag made from one of Roy's T-shirts. Diana eats as much fruit as she saves. They've been walking for hours, and she's famished.

"Wait here," Roy tells her, and slips off into the forest as Diana goes on foraging for berries. Ten minutes later she hears the snap of a gunshot, then another and another. Roy comes back to the black-berry patch with the carcass of a rabbit.

"Your dinner, *mademoiselle*," he says, bowing. "But first, your camera."

Diana wipes blackberry juice off her purple fingers and gets out her camera. Roy props the dead rabbit under a bush, hiding its wounds with leaves. Then he has Diana film him pretending to see the rabbit. He nocks an arrow into his homemade bow, creeps close to the animal, shoots. When the arrow hits home, Roy jumps straight up into the air, punching his fist at the sky in victory—something he does often during his motivational speeches on YouTube. The whole process might have shocked Diana before she joined the crew of *Conquest,* but by now she's familiar with the bits of stage-craft that go into making television—and, after all, it's not as if Roy couldn't take down the rabbit with a bow and arrow. The show's policy is never to pretend the impossible, but staging the probable is a daily occurrence.

Roy chats amiably with the camera as he guts, skins, and prepares the rabbit's corpse for cooking. He eats the heart and the liver raw, making sure Diana gets a close-up of his bloody hands popping the dark wet meat into his mouth. She almost gags, filming this, but she knows viewers will love it. Diana tries to convince herself Roy is just eating more juicy huckleberries. She's quietly proud of herself for getting through the shoot with professional aplomb.

As the sun sets and the air turns chilly, Diana helps Roy build a stone fire circle and roast the rabbit on a spit. Roy takes a small salt-shaker from his backpack, cuts off a hind leg, salts it, and offers it to Diana. It's the most delicious thing she's ever tasted. By the time they finish eating, the sky is dotted with the night's first bright stars, and the forest rings with the love songs of crickets and frogs. In the fire-light, Roy looks like every hero in history: a Viking sailor, a Roman general, a movie star.

"So, Roy," Diana says. "I bet you know some good campfire stories."

He gives that low chuckle again. "Oh, Brownie Girl, you have no idea. I know stories people would die to hear. Stories people *have* died to hear."

Diana feels a sudden, delicious chill. She leans closer to the fire. "What do you mean?"

"I can't tell you."

"Oh, come on!" She laughs and throws a dead oak leaf at him. It lands in the fire and bursts into flame. "You can tell me anything!"

"No, I can't," he says seriously. "Some things are meant to be secret. Like the Chuchunk ritual. I know a lot of secrets, Brownie. Keeping them is one of my specialties."

"Well, you have to tell me *something*," Diana teases. "Isn't that one of the sacred rules in some tribe or another? Like maybe the Boy Scouts?"

He stares into the fire for a long moment, considering, then breaks into a grin. "Okay, I'll tell you one story—a story about not telling stories."

Diana gives a little squeal of delight and puts her chin on her knees. Roy pokes the fire with a stick as he speaks.

"You see, when I go to live with the old ones—tribal people, wherever they are—I'm after ancient knowledge. The real magic. Not every tribe still has that, you know. Most of it's been lost. The few tribes who held on to the real power did it by keeping their secrets, no matter what."

He glances up at Diana, and she nods soberly.

"I'd heard that this tribe in Papua New Guinea—the Karapuna— were the real deal. Neolithic culture. Unbroken connection to the jungle. Rumor was that they were still cannibals, that they still hunted people from other tribes for food."

Diana's eyes widen. "Is that true?"

Roy sighs. "I kind of hoped it would be, you know? I wanted to go to the limit. But no, they stopped that a hundred years ago. Didn't do it all that often before that, actually. People like to sensationalize."

He stirs the fire thoughtfully for a while, then goes on. "Anyway, I went out for a quest with them. Met a Karapuna warrior who'd come out of the jungle to live in modern society. Gave him a gun, a few hundred dollars. Made friends with him, you know. He agreed to guide me back to his tribe. We hiked for two weeks, no paths, no roads. A lot of climbing cliffs and fording rivers. I'd keep my eyes on his feet, always on his feet. He didn't wear shoes, and his toes were like fingers. They'd grab branches or rocks the way you'd pick up a baseball." Roy makes a face. "The whole time I was there, the feet were the only thing that really disgusted me."

Diana laughs. "So, did you find the tribe?" She knows the answer, having read Roy's book about that particular quest, but she also knows that some questions are an integral part of every campfire story.

"Oh, yes, we did," says Roy. "We did, indeed. At first the warriors came out—big bones stuck sideways through their noses, red and yellow plumes in their headdresses. They spent about an hour arguing with my guide. Wanted to kill me right away." Roy laughs heartily. "He convinced them I'd be more use to them alive than dead. Showed them the gun I gave him. After that, they treated me like a king."

"How long did you stay with them?" Diana says, though she already knows.

"About four months. I gave them gifts, went hunting with the men. Learned their language well enough to have a basic conversation. Then one day we were crossing a river—big river, fast, cold—and one of their guys lost his footing. Everyone else just stood there, but I went after him. I was bigger than any of them, and a better swimmer. I got to him just before he went over a waterfall."

Diana nods silently. She's read about the incident, but hearing it told aloud, by the crackling light of a fire, makes it thrillingly vivid.

"So after that, I was the big man on campus. The shaman took a shine to me, let me ask questions. One day he was explaining a ritual and he started cracking up, laughing. He told me that when he was a boy, a white man came to study his tribe. British dude, from the sound of it. Probably an anthropologist. Wore a pith helmet, the whole deal. He started asking the Karapuna about their rituals and beliefs."

Diana cocks her head. This information isn't in the book.

Roy is laughing. "Well, of course no one was going tell this moron anything. But he was so persistent some of the villagers started making up stuff, just to get him off their backs. They said they used special hair braids to ward off demons. He freaking loved that, so they told him toads made their wishes come true. Said they took orders from a certain kind of moss. Said they knew the future by staring at each other's belly buttons. All complete bullshit. He ate it up. Ate. It. Up."

Now Diana's chuckling, too. "Did he ever publish all that?"

"Oh, no. Hell no. He fell out of a tree and broke his neck." Roy bursts out laughing again. "Or, who knows, maybe someone pushed him. Would've served him right. What an idiot!"

Diana shivers. "Weren't you afraid something like that would happen to you?"

"Well, if it did, it would've been because I screwed up. Because I failed in some way. And that means I'd deserve killing, at least in my book."

He looks up at her, the firelight bright orange in his pupils, hot lava in the pit of a volcano. "I don't know if you can understand this, Diana, but there's something in me . . ." His voice fades away. Then he gathers himself again, as if he's made some inner decision. "Diana, my destiny is to go as far as anyone can go, you understand?"

"I do," she says immediately.

"I have to conquer everything there is to conquer. Achieve every goal there is to achieve. Know every secret there is to know. The Karapuna shaman could see that. After a few weeks he officially adopted me. He taught me . . . a lot more things I can't tell you."

"Real magic," whispers Diana.

"Yes." Roy falls silent. Story time is over.

They zip their sleeping bags together, make love again, and fall asleep as the fire burns down to embers. Diana dreams of men with feathers in their hair, of wickedly powerful rivers, of a strange, black, tusked creature following her through an endless forest. She wakes up with a strangled gasp and moves even closer to Roy's comforting warmth. It's a long time before she can sleep again.

•

They head out at dawn the next morning, Roy holding the M16 in one hand as if it's no heavier than a plastic toy. He constantly scrutinizes the landscape, assessing whether the terrain is right for wolves. They've been walking for two hours when he stops, stares at the dust, moves on a few paces, squints along the ground like a golfer setting up a putt, and then clenches a fist in quiet jubilation.

"Check it out, Brownie Girl!" He points to the ground with the tip of the M16. Diana crouches down, stares. At first she sees nothing, but then it pops into focus: a paw print the size of her outstretched hand, each of its four toe-pads an inch across.

"Is that a wolf track?" she whispers.

Roy's eyes shine like new dimes. "The quest goes forward," he says, and then breaks into the huge smile that always softens Diana's very bones.

A few yards away he finds another footprint, then another. All day they trail the wolf, progressing at uneven speed depending on how clearly the track shows in different substrates. At noon they eat leftover rabbit as they walk. When he's on a quest, Roy tells her, he doesn't stop to eat.

The sun is lowering toward the western horizon and Diana's energy is flagging when Roy suddenly stops short, his eyes fixed on the ridge of a steep hill fifty yards away. Heart hammering, Diana searches the brush for a glimpse of a long, gray body, a plumed tail, piercing yellow eyes. She sees nothing.

Slowly, smoothly, Roy raises his rifle. He glides forward, feeling the ground gently with each foot before putting his weight on it. Diana tiptoes behind him, awash in gooseflesh. Then, suddenly, she sees what he's hunting.

She knits her brow, confused. It isn't a wolf. Not as long as a wolf, but bulkier, with charcoal gray hair that gleams reddish-brown in the sunlight. A bear? But it doesn't move like a bear. It's too compact, not furry enough. It bounces a bit with each step, slipping between bushes as fluidly as a fish swimming through seaweed.

Finally, the thing steps out of the bushes into a slant of full light, and Diana can see it clearly. She's dumbstruck with surprise. The creature in front of her is the monster from her dream last night. The black, coarse hair. The small, burning eyes. The sharp tusks.

It looks like a pig, and absolutely not like a pig. It's three feet tall at its massive shoulder, which tapers down a muscular neck into a blocky head with a long, agile snout. The coat of blackish bristles, limned auburn in the golden light, thickens almost to a mane on its neck and head. The creature's eyes are strangely beautiful, small and glistening and heavily lashed.

Somehow Diana knows that those eyes aren't just seeing her, but *watching* her. Deliberately. Intelligently. She can't look away from them. Her nightmare thunders in her mind. She can't quite catch her breath.

"You ever cooked a wild boar, Brownie Girl?" Roy breathes, his body absolutely still as he closes one eye and begins to curl his fingers around the trigger. "Because that's what you're going to do today."

And that, of course, is when the fugue state hits.

DISASTER

A millisecond before Roy squeezes the trigger, time slows almost to a stop. Diana—but not Diana, the *other*—surveys the scene calmly, at perfect leisure. Around her the oaks smile and wink, their great green faces slowly appearing and disappearing in the shifting air.

As the moment of no-time stretches on, Diana's *other* mulls over the situation, makes a decision. With a sideways step, she gracefully collapses against Roy's body. She watches an orderly sequence of bullets emerge from the M16. If she wanted, she could reach out and pluck them from the air. They spray like bright water drops into the canopy of a nearby oak, startling a flock of mourning doves, who rise from the tree as languidly as a handful of helium balloons.

Then, as quickly as it came, the fugue state is over. Time accelerates into a moment of complete chaos. Diana slides helplessly down Roy's side as he fights to remain upright. The slope of the hill and his heavy pack compromise his balance so that he slips, flails, and tumbles. One windmilling arm hits the back of Diana's head, pitching her forward into Roy's fall line. Together they skid and bounce down the steep escarpment, dislodging rocks and saplings. Then Diana's foot jams into a gopher hole just as her torso smashes against a tree trunk. She feels her foot turned almost backward, the tendons and ligaments pinging like overstretched piano wire. There's a moment of silence, dust, and pain as everything settles back to earth.

"Jesus Christ!" Roy scrambles to his feet, covered with dust and small scratches, but somehow still holding the rifle. "What the *fuck* was that?"

Diana curls up like an armadillo against the base of the tree, gritting her teeth against the pain in her twisted ankle. She manages to ease it out of the gopher hole—barely—but almost blacks out from the agony of movement.

"Never, never, *never* fucking *touch* a hunter when he's shooting!" Roy shakes the M16 at her, his face bright red. "Do you hear me?"

Diana can't reply. The urge to vomit overwhelms her, not because of the pain in her ankle, but because of the horror of what she's just done to her relationship with Roy. "I'm sorry," she gasps. "I'm so, so sorry."

"We would have had meat for days, Diana! Days!" Roy slashes at a tall weed with the gun. "And still have had plenty left over to bait the wolves!"

"I know. I'm sorry."

"Oh, *I'm sorry, I'm sorry!*" Roy whines. "Stop groveling, Diana. It's disgusting." He turns away abruptly and takes three deep breaths, a simple self-mastery technique he teaches in his seminars. When he turns back, his voice is softer, slower, and colder. Much colder. "Do you know what any reasonable tribe would do with you right now? They'd eat you. Not out of anger, just to stay alive. When you ruin a hunt, Diana, the people have no meat. When the people have no meat, they use yours. It's a logical consequence. Not rocket science. Natural law."

"I'll gather more food," Diana whispers. "I'll make it up to you." *How?* scream the Furies in her head. *You can't even walk, you clumsy idiot!*

"That is not the *point*!" Roy's jaw works as he brings himself under control. ("A real man conquers his environment by conquering himself," he always tells his audiences. "Controlling your world begins with controlling your emotions.")

He looks away for so long that Diana's attention turns to her ankle, which has become a hammering throb of heat. She swallows a surge of panic, steeling herself for what will surely be an excruciating hike out of the Oscuras. Once Roy calms down, she'll leave, go home, tell him to quest on. She'll get back to Los Angeles by herself. Anything, anything, anything to keep his love.

Roy holds out his hand, but his face is like granite. "Get up."

Diana takes his hand, struggles to her feet, gives a smothered gasp, and goes down again. "I'm so sorry, Roy," she says when the stars stop swimming in front of her eyes. "I can't . . . my ankle . . ."

Still expressionless, Roy takes off his pack and crouches beside her. He pulls her sock down and examines her ankle, which has swollen to the size of a softball. When Roy palpates it with his fingers, Diana goes light-headed again from the pain, but she manages not to flinch or gasp.

"It's not broken," says Roy. "Sprained. You may have torn a ligament."

"I'll be fine." Diana sounds pathetically unconvincing, even to herself. The ankle is still swelling, trapped blood blooming purple against the tightening skin. None of that bothers Diana nearly as much as Roy's blank face. His quest is irreparably compromised. He'll never forgive her. She'll never forgive herself.

Roy opens his backpack, takes out a tin canister of matches and a Swiss Army knife, and sets them on the ground next to Diana. He pours water from his thermos into hers, filling it to the brim. Then he breaks several dead limbs off a fallen oak and stacks them next to her. Diana watches him through tear-blurred eyes, looking desperately for a smile, a nod, a kind glance. Nothing.

"I won't leave a gun with you," says Roy tonelessly. "The Glocks don't have a safety mechanism. You'd be more likely to shoot yourself than anything else. Take these." He sets the wooden bow and quiver of arrows by the firewood.

Leave, thinks Diana. He used the word *leave.*

Roy stands up, a tower of muscle, mind, and will that fills Diana's universe. "I want you to know," he says in that frozen voice, "that I blame myself for this. I never should have brought a woman. Wait here."

And he walks away.

Beloved, have you ever watched the person you love most leave in anger? Have you felt the wind hit the ragged shards of heart that remain in your chest? Then you know what the universe will be like when the last stars die, and what Diana is feeling now. Her world loses all its color, becomes various pointless tones of gray. For hours she doesn't move, just stares numbly at the place where Roy vanished into the forest.

Wait here, he said.

So Diana waits.

As night falls, her mind begins, slowly slowly, to work again. She tries to calculate how long it will take Roy to return to their drop-off site, contact the *Conquest* staff by radiophone, and guide a helicopter here to rescue her. She remembers all the videos and books in which Roy has given advice for a situation just like this one. If she focuses hard enough, she can almost believe she *is* Roy, full of confidence and resiliency. She imagines joking with the rescue team the way he would—"Hi, guys, what brings you here?"—when they finally arrive.

Which won't happen tonight.

Beloved, you may have heard stories about being lost in the forest, but if you've never experienced it, you have no idea how frightened Diana is. As the night begins, she can sense the dark-dwelling creatures roaming around her, prowling, hunting, being hunted. Strange shrieks, caws, and growls echo through the box canyons, sending bolts of panic through her body. Every rustle might be the footfall of a wolf, a bear, a mountain lion. They're looking for prey that's weak or crippled. Diana is both.

She remembers Roy saying that for a lost hiker, a campfire is the difference between psychological disintegration and healthy optimism. Practically every episode of *Conquest* shows him building a small blaze and telling the audience how good it makes him feel, even when he's tired and hungry. The night isn't cold, just nippy, and her fleece jacket, waterproof hiking pants, and top-of-the-line sleeping bag are all Diana needs for warmth. But she's definitely short of good cheer. For that reason, she clears a space in the leaf litter, stacks twigs, and drags a few dead limbs into a pile to feed a campfire. She ruins half a dozen matches with her numb fingers before she finally gets the wood to burn.

Roy is right (of course). The fire immediately eases Diana's terror. Something about the little circle of orange light seems almost magically protective. She unrolls her sleeping bag next to it and lies down, pillowing her head on one arm and watching the flames, almost comfortable despite her throbbing ankle. Roy and the rescue team will find her in the morning. All she has to do is survive the next few lonely hours.

She hears a hushed crackle on the other side of the fire, raises her head slightly, and sees two green spots moving in the dark like glowing lamps. Eyeshine. An animal is watching her. Diana's heart pounds. She sits up, grabs a burning stick, and waves it, shouting, "Go away!" The green reflections wink out.

The firelight no longer feels like a reliable barrier. As minutes and then hours crawl by, Diana imagines footsteps in the brush behind her, to her left, to her right. Soft, ruffling crashes overhead make her flinch and stare upward, sure that any moment a mountain lion will leap from the trees. She sees fanged shapes in the smoke, strange patterns in the grass, more glowing green eyes. By the time her firewood runs out and the sky bleaches to the charcoal gray of pre-dawn, Diana is so exhausted she's almost hallucinating. The plants and stones around her seem as much alive as the birds and insects. Everything seems to chuckle and whisper in a language she once knew, but no longer remembers.

She dozes off just after sunrise, dizzy with relief that the night is over. But her dreams bring back the darkness. She has nightmares, unbelievably vivid, of a hundred deaths at the jaws of a hundred predators. Jaguars, crocodiles, saber-toothed tigers seize her in their foul-smelling mouths. A clan of hyenas runs behind her, snapping at her guts as she struggles to escape, half-eaten. An eagle's talons hit her with the force of a sledgehammer, closing like razor-tipped vise-grips around her neck. A school of piranha strikes from every side at once, and she watches the water go frothy pink with her blood and small chunks of her flesh. By the time she finally fights her way back to consciousness, Diana is more tired and terrified than when she fell asleep.

She's also famished. As the day warms up, she emerges from her sleeping bag and searches forlornly through her belongings for anything edible. She finds a few smashed huckleberries and eats them with a long drink of water, trying to fill her stomach. She pokes at her ankle, which looks like a small eggplant, purple and plump. It hurts, but not as much as it did last night. She settles in to wait for the rescue party.

Which never comes.

Diana spends the hours mentally reviewing Roy's books, videos, TV episodes. She knows them so well she can almost rewatch some of them in her mind. They comfort her, but also remind her of the horrible reality: She has scuttled her relationship with Roy. That moment with the wild boar plays over and over in her mind, a nightmare form of the funny looping videos Devin likes to send her over email. Why, why, why, did she do what she did? What disobedient, fractious, perverse part of her seems determined to ruin everything that might make her life worth living? The Furies are having a heyday. *Headline, headline, read all about it: Crazy trash baby once more snatches defeat from the jaws of victory, misery from her chance at happiness.*

By afternoon, Diana's stomach is a dull ache and her limbs feel like wet cement. She falls asleep again, and now the nightmares are even worse. Over and over, she becomes a dying creature, helpless against the teeth and fangs of the hunters. A rapid slideshow of horror runs through her, clickclickclickclickclick. Each moment, she hears her various bodies screaming in different voices—no words, only the incoherent shrieks of creatures at the furthest extreme of horror.

She's awakened by a heavy thump and shuffle. A turkey vulture has landed on the ground next to her. It smells like death. She grabs Roy's bow and waves it frantically, giving a strangled yell right out of her nightmares. The thing flaps awkwardly away, but remains in the sky above her, circling. By sunset, it has been joined by several others.

That night, Diana builds another fire and sleeps a few hours from sheer exhaustion. Her dreams are oddly peaceful. In them, she is still a series of hunted beings, but instead of fearing death, she is resigned to it. Her screams for help fall silent. Her body—infinite bodies—slackens in the jaws of the leopard, the osprey, the shark. The world dims as her eyes go fixed and sightless, over and over and over and over.

By morning, she's finally able to face the truth: No one is coming for her. Maybe the search party can't find her—but no, Diana can't believe Roy wouldn't be able to lead them here. That means he must have decided against even attempting a rescue. He's seen the truth Diana has always known in her heart: She's not worth saving. Her heart goes as limp as the dying creatures in her dreams.

As the day progresses, she realizes she's made a drastic mistake by drinking her water so quickly, and by using all her matches to light those first fires. She's delirious with hunger, but that won't kill her for days. Exposure and dehydration are much more clear and present dangers. She's begun to cry listlessly, off and on, and she wonders if losing water through tears will hasten her death. She has no real desire to live, now that she's lost Roy. But there's Devin to think about. No, no, she doesn't want to leave Devin. If she survives the night, she'll have to look for water.

When darkness comes, and with it a half-conscious sleep, Diana doesn't dream of dying beings. Now she is Death itself. She rides from creature to creature like the vultures ride thermal air currents, barely moving, magnificent, carrying lives away from bodies. She feels no fear. No love. Nothing. When an oak leaf falls onto her cheek, waking her up in the faint starlight, Diana doesn't startle. If it were a wolf or a bear, she would welcome it. She's past caring.

At sunrise she crawls from her sleeping bag and prods at her sprained ankle. It's still purple and swollen, but it hurts even less, and the edges of the bruising are turning a bilious shade of yellow. She rolls up the sleeping bag, packs her things in her knapsack, slings the quiver of arrows over her shoulder, and drags herself upright, standing on her good leg, using Roy's unstrung bow, which is so stiff she can barely bend it, as an awkward cane. The gray world turns black again, and she sways precariously until the blood finally reaches her brain. Then she takes a hesitant step. A stab of agony runs up her leg, but she doesn't fall.

Her plan is to head downhill, saving energy and moving into the most likely terrain to find a spring or stream. As Roy always tells his viewers, slopes lead to brooks lead to rivers lead to civilization.

Limping and hopping, she proceeds very slowly toward a drainage line. The brush around her is thick with shrubs and new autumn grass. There's plenty of cover for predators, should anything decide to hunt her. She remembers her horrible dreams. They don't frighten her any more. She's sick, she's tired, and above all, she's lost Roy. Death has very little to take from her.

That day she travels maybe five miles over rough, overgrown terrain. Her pack feels impossibly heavy. Her ankle throbs and stabs. Her vision blurs. She allows herself to rest and take a tiny sip of water every hour or so. By afternoon her thermos is empty.

She comes to a small, dry ravine where winter streams have carved a deep cleft in the sandstone. It would be easy for Diana to cross it on a normal day; she could either build a small bridge with sapling trunks or climb down one side of the stream bank and up the other. But right now, it might as well be the Grand Canyon. Diana looks around for any evidence of a spring, but the stone and soil are dry. They mutter to her, inviting her to join them. Dust to dust.

Diana drops to her hands and knees, crawls back uphill, and finds a spot under a huge oak tree where the ground is relatively flat. She spreads out her sleeping bag but doesn't build a fire. She has no intention of surviving the night. With total dehydration still a few days away, hypothermia is her quickest option. She settles her weary bones onto the sleeping bag, takes the Swiss Army knife from her pack, opens the knife blade, and holds it next to her left wrist.

She knows better than to slice sideways, as she used to do during her teens, when the ache of not belonging could be kept at bay by the sharp sting of a blade. She needs to open an artery, preferably from wrist to elbow. Diana presses the point of the knife into her skin and watches the blood slowly pool around it. Then she sighs and pulls it back. If someone finds her body before it's eaten or rotted away, she doesn't want Devin to see that she abandoned him. She never wants anyone to hurt the way she hurts over Roy. So instead of cutting deeper, she smoothes out one leg of her pants and writes on it in blood, dipping the knife in her wound the way an artist wets a brush.

"Devin, you are perfect. I love you forever. Mom."

It takes a long time to finish the message, and by then Diana's energy is utterly spent. She lies back on the sleeping bag and welcomes the end of her sad little life. Which, it just so happens, has lasted thirty-five years, ten months, two days, nine hours, and fifty-two minutes.

The precise average age of every female human living on Earth at this moment.

Diana closes her eyes—the lids are like sandpaper—and lets all the breath run from her body. The grayness closes in, and in, and in, and in. The hours pass.

•

"Diana."

The voice seems to come from very far away. Roy? No, it isn't Roy's voice. A woman's. A low, mellifluous alto.

"Diana, dear. It's time."

Diana moans. "Time?" she whispers.

"Yes."

"To die?"

A low chuckle. "You could say that."

"Okay," Diana mumbles. "I'll die."

"No, love. Not like that."

Diana feels a warm pressure on her arm, on the back of her neck. Something trying to lift her head.

"Come now, Diana. You don't want to get all the way here and then stop it."

Diana frowns, her eyes still closed. "Stop . . . wha'?"

"Waking up, sweetheart. It's time for you to wake up."

In the gray universe, a tiny flame of curiosity flickers. With an unspeakable effort, Diana opens her eyes.

Standing above her, its huge head blotting out the sun, stands the wild boar.

BEWILDERED

A Taser bolt of adrenaline shoots through Diana's body. She tries to roll sideways but only manages to flop like a landed fish. "Shoo!" she croaks, thrashing a hand in front of her face. "Go! Get away!"

The boar regards her silently, blinking its tiny, long-lashed eyes.

Diana scrabbles for Roy's bow and holds one end in trembling hands, pointing it at the boar's face. The creature's physical bulk is shocking, incomprehensible. The massive body, thick bristles, and long, limber snout belong in some ancient cave painting, not Diana's reality.

"Go away!" she yells again, jabbing with the bow. "Go away right now, or I'll . . . I'll . . . "

"What?" the boar says in that rich alto. "Poke me with a stick?" She opens her rosy mouth, revealing short, sharp tusks on her lower jaw. From that savage-looking orifice issues a jolly, grunting laugh:

"Hoink, hoink, hoink."

"Gah!" Diana blurts, almost fainting as her mind tries to reconcile the sound of a woman's laughter with the boar's twitching snout. "No—nuh! Buh . . . wha . . . y—y—you can talk?"

"Better than you can, it appears," says the boar. *"Hoink hoink hoink!"*

Diana squints hard, trying to focus. "Am I hallucinating?" she whispers. "Or . . . dead?"

"Mmm." The boar's head tilts left, then right. "Yes and yes. You've been hallucinating practically from birth, like every other human. And you've been dead—well, mostly dead—for years and years." She sits down on her haunches and yawns, her tusks sharp, her tongue bright pink. "But in the pedestrian sense, Diana, you're still alive. And I aim to keep you that way."

The creature leans over and noses Diana's thermos, which is standing upright on the ground. "I filled this for you while you were sleeping. Which, I must say, was not the easiest process in my current form. Good thing you left the cap off. Drink."

Diana sees that her thermos is slightly dented in several places where the boar's teeth have gripped it. A terrible thirst seizes her, overwhelming even her amazement. Cautiously, she sets down the bow, lifts the cool metal canister, and takes a long swallow. The water runs down her throat and blossoms like a flower in her stomach. She gulps.

"Not too fast, dear," says the boar, "or you'll throw it all up. I'm not going through bulimia with you twice."

The water clears Diana's mind astonishingly fast. She expects the boar to vanish, but instead it becomes more solid, its edges crisper.

"How do you . . . what . . . why can you talk?" Diana wipes her chin with the back of her hand. "And how do you know my name?"

"Seriously? The one useful thing Roy ever taught you, and that penny still hasn't dropped? Oh, goodness." The boar clucks her tongue. "I hoped we'd be further along than this."

"Roy?" Diana is instantly alert. "What do you know about Roy? Where did he go? Is he coming back?"

"Oh, Roy's fine." The boar gives a small snort. "He's completely lost, but that's been true since he was about twelve. *Hoink hoink!* But enough about him. Let's talk about you."

"Roy's lost?" Diana's mind races. How could Roy be lost? He's world famous for finding his way in the wilderness. And yet . . . she feels a slight warming in her frozen heart. Maybe he didn't abandon her. Maybe this hallucinated pig—a fragment of her unconsciousness, a projection, intuition, or whatever else it might be—is telling the truth. Roy went for help, and somehow he got lost, and there's a chance that he'll get over his anger. That he still cares for her.

"Look here, I brought you some acorns," says the boar. She nods toward a small mound of plump nuts piled near the base of Diana's oak. "They've been soaking in spring water, so some of the bitterness has leached out. Though I myself prefer them right off the tree, and I suspect you do, too. For reasons you may later recall."

Diana picks up an acorn. It's larger and heavier than she expects. The meat has swollen so much the shell is cracked. She takes an experimental bite. To her ravenous body it tastes delicious, not unlike an almond, despite its bitterness. Diana peels off the shell, swallows the meat almost whole, and starts on another. Her newly hydrated mind is clearing, which allows her to reach the only possible rational conclusion about her situation.

"I'm dreaming," she says.

"Well, that's for sure." The boar nods. "You're dreaming me, I'm dreaming you, that tree over there is dreaming us both. There's nothing but a dream to be found anywhere, and noticing that is just another dream."

Diana frowns. "What?"

"*Hoink hoink!*" The boar stands up and trots in a small circle. "Three dimensions! Don't you love it? So quaint! So primitive! So *fun!*" Abruptly, she plops sideways like a Volkswagen blown over by a high wind. She keeps rolling all the way onto her back, then begins to shimmy in the scratchy leaf litter. Her belly is smooth and whitish, not as armored by bristles as the rest of her body. All four short legs stick straight up, wiggling in the air.

"Oooh, loo loo loo!" the boar croons, eyes half-closed with pleasure. Then she stops writhing and looks up at Diana, her upper lip flopping open to show the full ferocity of her tusks. "Look," she says solemnly. "It's almost like I'm upside down." With gravity's pressure on her snout, the sentence comes out "Id'z albozd lige I'b ubzide dowd."

"Almost?" says Diana. "You *are* upside down."

The boar bellows with laughter, rolling back onto her side. "Oh, that's funny, Diana! As if anything could be upside down!"

"You're crazy," Diana says, half to herself, half to the animal she's conjured up. Even as dreams go, she thinks, this one is bizarre.

"Whoops!" says the boar, clambering to her feet. "We're going to have to work on your lying, darling. Lying . . . lying is a problem."

Those bright little eyes fix on hers, and Diana finds that she can't look away. She feels suddenly nervous, edgy. "I hate this dream," she says out loud. "I want to wake up now. It's time to wake up."

"Which, if you'll recall, is exactly what I told you when we met," says the boar, shaking leaves and twigs out of her bristles. "Remember that, Diana? The good times we had back then?" She sighs happily.

"Back then?" Diana frowns. "You mean, like, five minutes ago?"

"Oh, wait, that's right," says the boar. "That's not a lot of time for you, is it?" She doesn't wait for Diana's answer. "I said 'time'!" she squeals joyfully. "I said 'back then'! *Hoinkhoinkhoinkhoinkhoink!*"

Diana slaps herself across the face, hard. It fails to awaken her. She does it again.

"Now, Diana!" The boar's voice is suddenly low and penetrating. Diana freezes. "You see that right there, sweetie?" says the boar. "That whackity-whackity-whacky thing? You don't get to keep that."

Diana covers her eyes with her shaking hands. "Aagh!" she moans. "What's going on? Why is this happening to me? Why won't you go disappear, or explode or something? Just go away!"

"*Hoink!*" the boar giggles. "You said 'go away.' As if *that* were possible."

"You're not making any sense!" shouts Diana, closing her eyes tightly. "Nothing about this makes sense!"

"I certainly hope not. If it did, I wouldn't be doing my job."

Diana opens one eye, peering between her fingers. "You have a job?"

"Oh, yes, indeed. I'm here to bewilder you."

"What? Why?"

"Waking up is the goal, bewilderment is the method."

Diana contemplates this. Then she sighs and drops her hands into her lap. "Well, congratulations, pig. I'm bewildered."

"I'm not a pig."

"Of course not. You're a dream."

"*Hoink!* The dream that is here to wake you up. But not the way you think."

"What do you mean? What the hell are you?"

The boar beams. It isn't a physical smile, just a slight lift of the head, but a bubble of pure pleasure pulses outward from her hairy barrel of a body. Joy briefly suffuses Diana, like the smell of cookies baking.

"I am Myself!" says the boar.

"Uh . . . that's pretty obvious."

"Not as obvious as you'd think." The creature drops her head, sniffs the pile of acorns, selects one, and chews it, smacking loudly. "True fact," she says. "In some parts of the British Isles, it was once considered bad luck to mention a pig to a fisherman."

Diana stares at the boar's long, strange face. "What?"

"I know. Bizarre. *Hoink hoink!* But humans are very bizarre creatures." The boar shrugs, the bristles on her shoulders bunching and releasing. "Anyway, these fish-mongering folks were so superstitious they stopped using words like 'pig,' or 'boar,' or 'sow' altogether—after all, one never knows who's a fisherman and who isn't, does one?"

"I guess one doesn't." Diana picks out another acorn herself. Her fear is easing, and she can feel her hunger again.

"So when these humans wished to speak of even-toed ungulates such as yours truly, they called us 'Themselves.'"

"Even-toed what?"

"The things you call pigs, and other animals that have the good fortune to be piggish. Please note that I myself am not a pig. Not any more, that is. I'm a boar. A *wild* boar."

"Okay." Diana takes another drink from her thermos. "You're a boar. Got it."

"Now, since human language possesses a certain amount of magic—not much, but a little—when those humans called us 'Themselves,' they gave us a power known to members of no other species, least of all their own. Since then, each of us has known itself to *be* Itself. Ergo, I am Myself. Of course, technically, I'm also Yourself. *Hoink hoink!*"

Diana frowns. "You're yourself and also myself?"

"Exactly!" says the boar. "But that's simple for you, because either way you can call me 'Myself.' Except when speaking about me in the third person. Then it's probably best to use 'Herself.' Otherwise, things could get confusing."

Diana chews slowly, swallows, picks up another acorn. "I think that ship has pretty much sailed."

"*Hoink hoink!*" The boar wiggles like a monstrous, happy puppy. "Don't worry, it will all make sense when you see that no such thing as a self ever existed in the first place. That's always so clarifying."

Diana closes her eyes. This illusion, whatever is causing it, makes her head hurt. "I just want Roy to come back," she says plaintively.

"Ah, yes, sweetheart," says the boar. "I understand. Unfortunately, Roy can't find his way to you just now. As I said, he's quite, quite lost."

Tears fill Diana's eyes. "Is he in danger?"

"No, no, heavens, no! Of course not. Nothing is ever in danger! What a strange thought!" The boar pauses. "Though, come to think of it, you might not see things that way. Hmm. Yes, indeed, from a human perspective, he's in an enormous amount of danger. More danger than most beings will ever face."

"Oh, my God!" The familiar fist of anguish closes around Diana's heart. She has feared for her own life in the past few awful days, but it's nothing compared to the thought of something bad happening to Roy. She begins to cry. "Is he suffering?"

"Oh, yes," says the boar, chewing another acorn. "Terribly."

Diana gasps. "What's happened to him?"

"*Hoink!* Diana, that's a looooong story. Much too long to tell right now."

Diana can't stop crying. "I have to help him!" she sobs. "How can I help him? Please, pig—I mean boar—"

"Myself."

"Okay, whatever, Myself—can you help Roy? Please. If you're real, *please* go help him."

"I'm here for *you*, dear. I can't help him. He can only help himself. Though you can show him how. In your hearts, you and Roy both know that. That's why you became lovers. It's why you're here."

Diana is so surprised she stops crying. "What?"

The boar smiles again, sending that lilt of warmth into Diana's body. "You'll help Roy if you follow your destiny, dear, because your destiny is to help *everyone*. I believe you humans call it 'saving the world.'"

"I don't understand anything you're saying."

"You have to save the world," says the boar. "Remember?"

"That's ridiculous!" Diana exclaims. "I don't want to save the world, pi—I mean, Myself. I only want to save Roy."

"Can't save Roy without saving everyone, can't save everyone without saving Roy." The boar swallows and smacks her lips. "But of course you're always free to choose. What do you say, dear? What will it be? Will you accept your destiny, or reject it?"

Diana feels a tingle of warmth in her core—the *other* rising up. She pushes it back down—*don't go crazy, don't go crazy, don't go crazy*—as if chatting with a talking animal isn't evidence that she's already completely insane. Diana decides that the "dream" explanation is more comforting than the "insanity" option. If this strange creature is a dream symbol, it might have a message from her unconscious mind.

"Well . . . what would I have to do?" Diana says. "To, um, accept my destiny? To save Roy?"

"You'd have to go home."

Diana blinks. "That's all?"

"*Hoinkhoinkhoinkhoinkhoink!* 'That's all,' she says." The boar chortles. "Oh, Diana, my little piglet, you are *hilarious!*"

"Can you help me go home, then?"

"Are you asking me to?"

A spike of anxiety flashes through Diana's heart. In her life, asking for help has rarely proven to be a useful strategy, or even a safe one. *But what the hell*, she thinks, *it's my dream*. So she says, "Yes. I'm asking you to help me go home."

"Aha!" squeals the boar, dancing another small circle. "In that case, I not only can, I must!"

Diana feels a wash of relief. The thought of her tiny apartment in Van Nuys, with its barred windows and IKEA furniture, is like a vision of paradise. "How long will it take?"

The boar stops circling. "To get you all the way home?"

"Yes, please."

"Mmm, let me think. About a month, give or take."

"A *month*?"

"Wait. Is that a long time?" The boar cocks her head quizzically.

"Yes, it's a long damn time!"

"So . . . longer than five minutes?"

"What is *wrong* with you?" Diana yells.

"Sorry, I have a little trouble keeping it straight. Time is the most difficult part of this whole illusion for me to imagine. I mean, you have to admit it's weird. Minutes, months—don't you find it all surreal?"

"Really?" Diana shouts. "Seriously? That's what you find surreal about this situation—that months are longer than minutes?"

"More that months *seem* longer than minutes. I can't quite track it. I get a little—"

"Bewildered?" Diana snaps. "Welcome to my freaking world."

The boar's little eyes open wide. "Why, piglet, you are correct! I *am* bewildered!" Another bellow of laughter. "You're bewildered, and I'm bewildered! You know what that means, don't you?"

"No!" Diana yells. "I do not know what that means!"

"It means, piglet, that the process has already begun. There's no way of stopping it now. Wooohoooo!" Herself points her snout skyward and shouts, "DESTINY!" Then she goes into another gale of laughter, the effervescent *hoinkhoinkhoink* echoing and bouncing off the silent hills.

TASKS

Diana has eaten more than twenty acorns, and strength is flowing back into her body like a blessed tide. The boar stands patiently nearby, humming a strange little tune full of soft grunts. Of course, Diana doesn't believe the creature is real—she's not that far gone—but in a way she's proud that her mind, lumpy, defective instrument that it is, has conjured up such an elaborate illusion in some last-ditch effort to survive.

She's heard about similar things—maybe you have, too, beloved. An accident victim trapped in a flooded car, liberated just in time by a stranger no one else can see. Soldiers witnessing guardian angels in their hour of greatest fear. A near-dead mountain climber counseled by a disembodied voice to get up and climb one more slope, to the place where a helicopter finally sees him. Diana knows such things happen, but she's not sure how to deal with her own situation. Roy never covered the issue of hallucinated talking animals in any of his books or speeches. For now, she decides to keep addressing the boar as if it's real.

"I'm not hungry anymore," she says, swallowing one last acorn. "So I guess I'm ready to go."

"Go?" says the boar. "You mean physically? Leave this apparent place?"

"Well, yes," says Diana. "You just said it's going to take a month to walk back to Los Angeles. I don't want to waste any more time."

The boar laughs until she hiccups, which makes her laugh even harder. "Oh, piglet!" she says between hics. "Who said anything about Los Angeles?"

Diana frowns. "You're taking me home, right? You just said you would."

"*Hoink hoink!* Of course, piglet. But I meant your *real* home."

"Which, last I checked," says Diana acidly, "is in Los Angeles, California, United States of America, solar system, planet Earth."

"Hmm," says the boar, hiccupping dreamily. "That's what you think, darling. Tell me, can you say you've felt really at home at that address? Haven't you been homesick your whole life?"

Diana is startled to feel her eyes filling with tears. There's something about the boar's manner that evokes a strange helplessness. The creature's shining eyes give Diana nothing to push against, no hard surface of disdain, judgment, or annoyance, only a strange depth that makes them seem huge, rather than tiny. The warm tingle of the *other* fills Diana's chest. She looks away from the boar and wipes her eyes roughly with the back of her hand.

"If you're not taking me back to Los Angeles, where are we going?"

"Why, into the Tasks, of course," says the boar. "They're the only way for any human to get back home. Do you mean to tell me you've forgotten even that?"

"I don't know what you're talking about." Diana means to make her voice sound angry, but it doesn't come out that way. The Tasks. The Tasks. Something about that phrase makes her torso thrum like a bell. The *other* stirs in her chest the way Devin used to move in her belly before he was born. The hair prickles on her neck, and a flush of warmth runs through her arms and legs. Instead of frightened or annoyed, she feels overwhelmed by an incongruous curiosity, a pull almost like sexual desire. The Tasks . . .

"That's *enough!*" she barks, forcing the feelings away. "I'm getting back to LA where I belong, whether you come or not, you crazy pig."

"Hmm." The boar sings her words to the sweet, strange melody she's been humming. "I don't think so, my love. I think you want to stay here. I think you want to wake up. I think you want to fulfill your destiny. I think you can't help it."

"Shut up," says Diana, but it ends up sounding more like a question than a command. She looks at the boar with a mixture of fear and yearning, seduced by the melody, feeling herself pulled by something as sure and insistent as gravity. "What's happening?" she says. "Are you casting a spell on me?"

"You're just stirring in your sleep, piglet," says the boar softly. "Reality is calling you. The reality where what you call 'magic' is simply the way of it. Remember reality, Diana? Remember?"

The force pulling her toward the boar is so strong it makes Diana's head whirl. She feels her heart speeding up. Because she *does* remember. She does. She remembers . . . what? When she tries to grasp it with her mind, the memory slips away, back to the shadows just beyond her conscious thoughts. Her curiosity has become a maddening itch Diana can't quite scratch. You may have felt this incongruous pull yourself, beloved, turning you in some new direction at a crossroad in your life.

Diana fights the strange pull as she gets to her knees and begins putting her few possessions—the thermos, the Swiss Army knife—into her backpack. She tries to keep her mind on the only objective that makes sense to it—a return to Los Angeles and the resumption of her ordinary life. But her soul has already reached the crossroad, already turned, and in her heart she's aware that she's already headed into the unknown.

The boar gives a little yip of joy, and Diana jumps as if she's had an electric shock.

"Good!" crows the boar. "Everything is aligned. Let it begin!"

Diana's body thrills with an excitement that makes no sense whatsoever. Her heart is pounding now, but she tries to keep moving methodically, purposefully, ignoring the dream-boar, staying sane.

She pulls her blue nylon sleeping bag toward her and smoothes it flat—or tries to. The bag is oddly heavy and lumpy. As Diana begins rolling it up, a shape bulges in the center, moving slowly from side to side. With a sharp yelp, she drops the bag. The shape inside keeps shifting, rippling upward. Then, from the soft inner pouch, a blunt triangular head emerges. Behind the head, pouring and pouring from the bag, comes a limbless body as thick as Diana's arm.

"Oh, shit!" Diana screams, scuttling backward like a crab. *"Snake!"* she gasps when she can form the word. *"Snake! Snake!"*

The mud-brown body is still sliding from the sleeping bag, not slithering now, but *extruding* itself straight forward in a way that makes Diana's flesh crawl. The snake is as long as she is tall, and when the tip of its tail finally pulls free from the bag, Diana sees a many-segmented rattle. The snake's head whirls around to fix its lidless eyes on Diana. A shiny black tongue flickers rapidly in and out.

"Run!" Diana screams, forgetting to disbelieve in the boar. *"We have to run!"* She turns, takes a step on her bad ankle, and collapses onto the ground with another little shriek. The snake accelerates, whipping the bulk of its body into a coil and raising a third of its length into the air, a thick, writhing hangman's rope. A harsh buzz fills Diana's ears as the snake's rattle disappears in a blur of speed. Everything about that sound tells her to flee, fight, jump off a cliff if necessary—anything to *get away*. She scuttles backward into the trunk of the huge oak tree, bumping the back of her head, and lets out an involuntary whimper.

The boar watches all this placidly, hiccupping from time to time. "Diana, dear," she says, "I'd like to introduce your First Task. Beautiful, isn't she?"

The snake's demonic head bobs, tongue flickering. It feints slightly toward Diana, and she screams again.

"Go ahead, darling," says the boar sweetly. "Proceed with the Task."

"What?" Diana shoots a wild-eyed glance at Herself, then gasps as the rattlesnake opens its hideous mouth. It actually seems to be flexing its fangs, like a fencer warming up.

"Calm her down, sweetheart," says the boar. "That's always the First Task. I can't believe you don't recall this. *Hoink hoink!* I mean, of course that was the plan all along—for you to forget everything, I mean—but this Task is so *obvious*, you know, that one would think—"

"Stop talking!" Diana shouts. "I'm in *danger*, here!"

"Hoinkhoinkhoinkhoinkhoink! Of course you're in danger, dear heart! And this sweet little one is just trying to help you learn that." Herself turns toward the snake. "Idn't dat so, my widdow snakey wakey?"

The rattlesnake hisses. The buzz of its tail grows louder.

"All humans are snakes at heart," the boar goes on, "or, I should say, at brain. *Hoink hoink hoink!* You have a serpent in you, Diana. All humans do. That's the very thing that's making you so jumpy-wumpy right now."

Diana slowly pulls herself to standing, leaning heavily on the trunk of the old oak, breathing in trembling gasps, keeping her eyes fixed on the rattlesnake ten feet away from her.

The boar chuckles. "Oh, come now, sweetie. If you pant like that, you'll never get her to relax. Loooong, slooooow breaths."

This advice reminds Diana of Roy's self-mastery techniques, so she decides to follow it. She inhales deeply, then lets her breath go in an extended exhale, just as Roy always does in his demonstrations. (If you tend toward nervousness, beloved, you should use this strategy; it never hurts, and it often helps.)

Herself squeals with pleasure as Diana slows her breath. "Perfect!" she says. "Now you're calming the snake in your brain, and see how our little friend appreciates it?"

It's true; the rattlesnake seems less tense, its head lowering, the buzz from its tail growing softer. Diana's head clears enough to form a plan. Slowly, she reaches behind her, finds a small branch growing out of the oak, and breaks it off.

"She's just a mirror of your fear, you see?" the boar says as the rattlesnake pulls itself into a snug coil with its head at the center. "Oh, you humans! Always popping your reptile brains into fight-or-flight, imagining a universe full of evil. It's been that way ever since Eve. Your Bible story is quite mangled in translation, but it gets that right. It's the fear of the serpent—and the fear *in* the serpent—that you humans use to cast yourselves out of Paradise. Believe me, I was there with Eve the first time it happened."

The snake has grown much quieter, so Diana risks another glance at Herself. "Wait. Are you saying Eve was a real person?"

"Oh, yes, indeed. We saw it on the news once, dear, don't you remember? Every human on earth is descended from the same ancient mother." The boar sighs happily. "Oh, what a gorgeous thing Eve was! Big brown eyes, silky black hair running all the way down her back. Not much on her head, of course, but you can't have everything. *Hoink hoink!*"

Diana feels slightly better with the branch in her hand. She keeps breathing slowly, deeply. It definitely helps. She's able to think again. Even with her sprained ankle, Diana figures she can dodge in plenty of time to avoid a strike. Her hands are still shaking, but not as violently as they were a minute ago. She white-knuckles the branch more tightly for reassurance.

"Very good, piglet!" says the boar. "See how the serpent outside reflects the serpent inside?"

The rattlesnake is definitely relaxing. The wicked-looking head is now resting on its coiled body. The rattling has stopped.

Diana's plan is based on a famous encounter between Roy and a cobra he stumbled across somewhere in Asia. Roy wrote that he prodded the serpent with a long stick until it tried to slither away. Then he grabbed it by the tail, jerked it backward, and stomped on its head with the heel of his hiking boot.

"You might want to get out of the way, pig," Diana says, sounding braver than she feels. "I'm going to kill that thing."

"*Hoinkhoinkhoinkhoink!* Oh, you are such a cutup! Sweetheart, even if you did manage to kill this innocent creature—who's done nothing more to you than spend a night in your sleeping bag, soaking up body heat you weren't using—another snake would take her place. And then another, and another. As many as it takes, my love, for you to learn. The dream is endlessly generous that way."

"What the—soaking up my *body heat*?" Diana grips the branch so tightly the bark almost breaks the skin of her palm. "And there are *more* of them?"

The boar scratches one cheek with her back trotter. "I repeat: as many as it takes."

Diana isn't listening. It's time to act. She holds the stick out stiffly, as far away from her body as she can get it, then limps toward the snake, imagining how she'll heel-stomp its head. That head rears upward again as the snake rattles furiously. Diana jumps backward. Her hurt ankle gives way, and she crashes to the ground. This time, she can see the snake slithering rapidly toward her.

"Help!" she screams. *"Help! Help! Help!"*

"Ooh, a request! How *lovely*!" says the boar. She trots into the shrinking space between Diana and the rattlesnake. The snake hisses, lashing toward her.

Diana screams again. *"It's going to kill you!"* She scrambles away, back to her position under the oak tree, panting and trembling, terrified to know what's happening behind her. But when she turns to look, the snake seems to have frozen in place, the slits of its pupils fixed on the boar.

"Hoink hoink hoink hoink hoink! It can't kill me, darling. I'm not alive."

"What?"

"I'm not dead either, of course," the boar goes on. She's swaying gently where she stands, and the snake's body begins to move in rhythm. The boar begins singing the same little tune she was humming earlier. "This apparent body lives, Diana, but I am not alive, because I am Life. Birth and death travel through form like the back-and-forth of the snake as she travels through this dream. Birth, death, birth, death, on and on and on. But Life, you see, has no opposite."

The words, and the strange, sweet tune, help Diana begin to breathe again. She pulls herself to a sitting position and hugs her knees to her chest. Long inhale, long exhale.

"There you go, dear heart!" sings Herself, still rocking gently. "Well done, well done!"

The snake is no longer rattling. Diana can see its head on the other side of the boar's huge back. It's looking from Diana to Herself, swaying to the tune the boar is humming. For the first time, it occurs to Diana that the snake has as much cause to fear her as she does to fear it. More, actually.

"Now wish it well," the boar sings softly. "You know how this goes."

"Uh, no I don't," says Diana. "What do you mean, wish it well?"

"Oh, heavens, piglet! Just say something loving." She hums for a second and adds, "And make sure you mean it."

Diana scowls. The snake's head has dropped behind the boar, below Diana's line of sight. "I don't have anything loving to say to a poisonous snake."

"Then say it to yourself. It's the same thing." The boar rolls her eyes. "As if *that's* not obvious."

"Huh." Diana feels a good deal calmer now, but not enough to know what she should do. Then she remembers how the boar reacted when she screamed for help. *"Ooh, a request. How lovely."* She clears her throat. "Um, Myself, I'm not sure how to . . . What I mean is, could you, um, help me? Please?"

"Ooh, loo loo loo!" the boar squeals. "Piglet, I'm so proud of you! You're already mastering the Task!"

"I am?"

"Yes, indeed. You've got the first two steps: When you feel afraid, breathe deeply, then ask for help from me. Which is to say . . . ?"

"Ask for help?" Diana repeats.

"Yes, love. Help from whom?"

Diana thinks furiously, trying to anticipate the creature's thinking. "From Myself?" she guesses.

"Yes, yes, yes, piglet! From the Self that was never born and will never die, that is Life without form or limit. Now I can help you with step three. Because you asked. If you don't ask, I can't help. See? *Hoink hoink!* That's the way everything works."

Diana stares at her. "Um, okay."

"Watch your fear—the serpent within, the serpent outside, it doesn't matter which—and repeat after me. 'Be well, my dear one.'"

"Seriously?" Diana winces.

"Be well, my dear one," repeats the boar.

Diana heaves a petulant sigh. "Okay, whatever. Be well, my dear one."

"Be safe, my love."

"Be safe, my love," Diana repeats doggedly. But her hands stop trembling.

"Live in joy and peace, sweet friend."

"Live in joy and peace, sweet friend." As Diana says this, something in her softens. It's stupid, she tells herself. It's corny. It's trite. Again she feels tears stinging her eyes.

"And repeat," says the boar, still moving gently, side to side, side to side. She goes back to her humming. Diana murmurs the words again: *Be well, my dear one, be safe, my love, live in joy and peace, sweet friend.* Then again. And again. Slowly, the fear drains from her body, leaving her absolutely spent. Her head droops forward onto her knees.

"Now, look!" says the boar softly. She walks forward. Diana raises her head and sees that the rattlesnake has become very still, settled into its own coils.

"What's it doing, Myself?"

"She's sleeping," says the boar. "Isn't she beautiful when she's asleep?"

To her astonishment, Diana realizes that the answer is yes. She stares at the snake, its elegantly mottled diamond back, its fierce eyebrow ridges. "She looks kind of like that kid who was in foster care with me at the Eichenwalds," says Diana. "Cloyd. Remember Cloyd?"

"Of course," says Herself, coming to sit by Diana. Her coat is rough and scratchy, but the warmth from her body is overwhelmingly comforting.

"Poor old Cloyd," says Diana. "He acted so tough, but only because he was afraid of everything. I mean, I was afraid of a lot of things, too, but Cloyd was afraid of, like, socks. Dirt. Oatmeal. Stuff like that."

"He hadn't mastered the Tasks," says Herself. "Not even the First. But very few humans do, love. Every tantrum, every war, every argument, is just the human reptile brain fearing for its own well-being, attacking others. So few can see that the danger comes from inside, and only there can it be healed."

Diana frowns at the snake. "You may see it that way. For me, that thing is definitely outside me, and it's still definitely dangerous."

"Yes, love," says the boar, hiccupping. "To see danger as real is the essence of the dream."

"Dream? You're still trying to tell me danger is a dream?" Diana's voice rises a little. The snake stirs slightly in its coils. "Are the people who die of snakebite every year dreaming? What about shark attacks? Or murder? Or war, or tidal waves, or malaria or—"

"*Hoink hoink!*" the boar chuckles. "Just experiment with the Task, Diana. Breathe. Ask. Love. If you can't love your enemy, love yourself. Soon you'll see there is no difference. You are that snake, and she is you. And if you can calm her, you can learn to master this realm of being."

"Whatever you say," says Diana wearily. "Talking pig trumps normal world. I am frigging Cloyd, and frigging Cloyd is me." She reaches down to scratch her sprained ankle, then blinks in surprise. The bruises are gone. The ankle only itches, the way cuts itch when they're almost healed.

"Hey, Myself?"

"Yes, darling?"

"Look. My leg. It's different." Diana pokes her ankle with a finger, then lifts her foot and taps it on the ground. No pain. "A few minutes ago it was killing me, and now it's completely better. It's like a miracle or something."

"*Hoink hoink!* Yes, of course," says the boar. She hiccups. "Because that's how life works once you are awake. Because while apparent danger is the essence of the dream, my darling, apparent miracles are the essence of awakening."

As Diana flexes her ankle, the tingling warmth rises in her chest, stronger than ever before. It seems to ride on the boar's song, the words of kindness that calmed the serpent. She hears Roy's voice saying, *"Brownie Girl, do you believe in magic?"* And she realizes that three decisions have occurred within her. She didn't make these choices voluntarily; her *other* committed to them before she even had the chance. First, Diana has decided to believe that the strange talking boar is real. Second, she isn't going back to Los Angeles. Not now. Maybe not soon. Third, she will find out what the Tasks are, and she will master them.

Not one of these choices makes any rational sense, but as she accepts them, a fierce, unfamiliar joy fills Diana's whole body. She has left normal, leaped into the unknown. And though she thinks she should be afraid, the snake tucks its head more deeply into its coils and grows very still.

POISON

Diana has fallen into an exhausted doze, tucked up against the big oak with her head on her knees and the boar's comforting bulk between her and the silent rattlesnake. Exhausted as she is, her sleep is shallow and troubled. She keeps remembering what the boar said about Roy being in terrible danger, and her urge to find and help him won't let her rest deeply. Also, despite her meal of acorns, she's very hungry again.

For a while, the first topic seems by far the more important. But as time passes, the second issue slowly pulls even, until it's leading by several lengths. She's nodding off again when her Furies begin to scream. *You're going to starve out here!* they shriek. *You'll shrivel up and die, and never see anyone you love, ever again! Idiot! Moron! Loser!*

Diana's hunger is so great that the Furies' words spark a flicker of panic. Immediately she hears the snake rustling and hissing on the other side of the wild boar. She lets her mind go silent, attentive, and the snake-sounds disappear.

Diana wonders what Roy would do in this situation. It's painful to think of him, given her fears about his safety and everything she's done to their relationship, but he's still her best role model for surviving. If he were here, under this tree, he'd take stock of everything he could possibly use to his advantage. He'd find something, anything, he could eat. Diana lifts her weary head and sets her jaw. She can do this. She can forage just like Roy has done in so many episodes of *Conquest*. She takes a deep breath and stands up.

"Oh, *goodie*! Is it playtime?" The wild boar hasn't moved a bristle for three-quarters of an hour, but her voice sounds wide awake. She raises her huge head. Dry leaves stick to the short, stiff mane on her neck.

Diana lets out a frustrated sigh. "No, it is not playtime. I'm hungry. I'm going to find food. To try, anyway."

"Oh, hu*zzah*!" squeals the boar. "It *is* playtime!" She clambers up to her small, forked feet, careful not to disturb Cloyd.

"No! I told you, I need food," says Diana grumpily. "It's serious."

"Well, certainly, piglet! The more serious the problem, the more playful the solution." The boar bats her long eyelashes. "So, what's your plan?"

"I need more food," says Diana shortly.

"How wonderful!" The boar skips a few steps.

"I liked those acorns you brought me," says Diana. "There must be more around here somewhere."

"You're welcome!" crows the boar.

"Yeah, yeah, thank you for the acorns," says Diana.

"Yes? And?" The creature turns her head, looking at Diana with one eye, then the other.

"And I want more."

The boar doesn't move for a moment. Then she says, "That's it? That's the entire plan?"

Diana begins walking in a slow circle, kicking up dead leaves and sticks, looking for acorns. "Do you have a better idea?"

"*Hoinkhoinkhoink!* Of course I have a better idea! Which means that you do, too, if you'd bother noticing."

"I don't have any plans," says Diana wearily. "I'm just hungry. I need to figure out what I can eat."

"Aha! *There* it is!" the boar almost shouts. "That's the ticket! I knew you'd get to it, my darling. Well done! Continue!"

Diana looks at her through narrowed eyes. "Hunger is not a plan."

"Wanna bet? *Hoink hoink hoink!* It's the only plan most animals ever have. Yet you humans manage to almost entirely squelch it out of one another!" The boar clucks her tongue, her head shaking slightly. "Good lord, how *tame* you are." As she says the word "tame," her skin shudders.

"Here's an idea," says Diana. "I'd love some pork chops right now. Maybe some bacon. You look crunchy. How's that for a plan?"

The boar bounces in place, as if she's on a pogo stick. "Wonderful, piglet! Maybe your instincts aren't past repair!"

Diana scowls. It seems impossible to offend this animal, with her weird, smiling snout. Watching the boar's nose wiggle, Diana has a thought. "Hey, maybe you could get me some truffles. Aren't pigs supposed to sniff out truffles?"

"Are you asking for my help, darling? Do I hear an actual request?"

Diana pauses. "Maybe." Then she decides there's no point in being cautious. "Yes," she says. "Please help me find food."

"To whom are you speaking, please?" says the boar coyly.

Diana rolls her eyes. "To you."

"To . . . ?"

"To you, Myself," says Diana wearily. Then she grumbles under her breath, "Geez, what a stupid name."

The boar seems as untroubled by this criticism as by anything else Diana can say. "Wonderful!" she beams. "Now I can help, and that's my favorite game of all! Come, piggly-wiggly!"

She bounces out of the little grove and onto a game trail. Diana follows, glancing at the torpid Cloyd, eager to be away from the snake but also uneasy about letting it out of her sight.

The boar stops after a few hundred yards, standing in a spot of sunlight where low-lying plants abound. "Now," she says, "the proper process for finding nourishment—and I'm not just talking about food here—is not to bother looking *around* until you've first looked *within.*"

"Within," Diana repeats.

"To the hunger you feel there." The boar nods. "Ah, hunger. Such a useful and loving teacher. But you tame humans have all but robbed it of its purpose—and in the process, your own. Most of you have no idea what you want, whatever the circumstance."

"Hunger is a teacher?" says Diana.

"Oh, yes, dear. One of the most constant and truthful teachers you'll ever have. Here, darling, feel this."

Suddenly, the pangs in Diana's stomach go from muted to intense. The desire to find food cuts like a sharp blade through her mind and body.

"Now that you're focused, look around, piglet." The boar's voice has changed, from joyful to gentle. "Not just with your eyes, not with your mind. With *all* your senses. With your whole body. With your gut. What is your hunger saying? *What do you want?*"

Ravenous, Diana begins taking long breaths through her nose. The air is suddenly full of subtle perfumes: the clean scent of wood, the fragrance of crushed grass, the rich aroma of earth, a hint of fresh water on the breeze. One particular smell, like a blend of sweet parsley and wheat sprouts, makes Diana's mouth water. She looks down at a patch of herbs a few feet away.

"That's it, piglet," the boar encourages her. "Trust yourself."

The plant that has Diana's attention seems to have become unusually vivid. She feels drawn toward it, pulled by the tiniest echo of the feeling that drew her to Roy Richards. She squats down, plucks a soft leaf, and sniffs. The scent brings back memories of the green smoothies Roy's personal chef makes every day for breakfast. Diana's stomach rumbles.

Tentatively, she puts the leaf into her mouth. The Furies go into red alert. *What are you doing, you fool? You can't just eat stuff off the ground! Wait until someone tells you it's not poison! Death! Death! Death!*

"You're doing very well, love," says the boar. "Just notice."

The taste of the leaf fragment on her tongue, mild and sweet and somehow deeply *green*, makes Diana close her eyes and sigh with pleasure. Her whole starved body wants to swallow it. Even more strangely (*You're freaking NUTS!* shout the Furies), Diana could swear she feels the plant wanting to become part of her. It's only a tiny bit, after all. Why not experiment? (*Poison, that's why not!*)

Diana chews and swallows. A tingle of pleasure runs through her gut into her arms and legs.

"Well done, my pretty piglet!" the boar squeals. "Oh, well done, indeed! This lovely little plant is called miner's lettuce. One of the best wild foods in this forest. So nutritious it kept thousands of starving forty-niners from dying of scurvy. Feel what it's doing for you already."

Diana's whole body is responding with a sort of comfortable rejoicing as the nutrients from the plant flow into it. The taste and smell are indescribably delicious. "Why didn't you just *tell* me about it?" she grouses. "Why did you let me take that risk?"

"You still want to do things the *tame* way?" Herself shudders. "And rob you of your chance to master the Second Task? Oh, Miss Scawlett, Ah would *nevah! Hoinkhoinkhoink!*"

Diana feels that thrill again, the jolt of curiosity. "Wait," she says. "So this is the Second Task? Learning to be a hunter-gatherer?" She picks another leaf, inspects it from all angles, puts it into her mouth, and chews. Delicious.

"*Hoinkhoinkhoink!*" The boar hops over and nuzzles Diana's leg. "Darling, you've always been a hunter-gatherer. It's just that you've never hunted and gathered—well, except during what you call your 'fugue states.' Other than that you've been tame, terribly tame, like a bird in a cage so small it can't even open its wings."

"So what's the Second Task, exactly?" Diana munches another leaf of the miner's lettuce.

"Learning to choose what nourishes you, not what poisons you."

Diana nods, too busy eating to speak. The feeling of health flowing into her cells gets stronger with each leaf she swallows.

And then, suddenly: *Don't.*

"What?" Diana stops chewing.

"I didn't say anything." The boar blinks innocently.

Diana realizes she's right. She didn't hear a verbal command from the boar, or even from the Furies. It was a twist in her gut that made her stop eating. She brings all her attention to the taste on her tongue. There's a faint, unpleasant tinge to the mouthful of leaves she's chewing. The taste makes her stomach grip again. She turns her head and spits green mulch onto the ground.

"And that would be blue nightshade," says Herself. "Just a teensy sprig, sweetheart. Worked its way in there, don't you know—not enough to kill you, but if you'd eaten it, you would've had a nasty little bout of vomiting, delirium, paralysis, that sort of thing."

"Geez!" Diana spits again, then rinses her mouth with water from her thermos. "Nice of you to mention it!"

"*Hoink hoink!* I didn't need to mention it, my love. Your body did. I must say, you're mastering this Task even faster than you caught on to the first one. Though, of course, we always knew you'd be a quick study. Go on, try it again! Choose another plant!"

And so, for the next hour or two, Diana practices the Second Task. She touches, smells, and tastes her way through the forest, her whole body learning in a way that is both strange and familiar. Sometimes the boar tells her the name of a flower or tree, but labels are unimportant compared to what Diana's body senses about each plant's character. She recalls the times her old boyfriends shared drugs with her, blasting her nerves with stupefying or hyper-stimulating chemistry. Now various plants travel her body along the same channels, but far more subtly and beautifully, each species whispering to her brain and bloodstream the nature of its own particular magic.

"Are you making me good at this?" she asks, nibbling on the berries of a tree the boar calls a Madrone. She's definitely better at sniffing out food when the boar is close to her.

"You were born good at it, darling. Though I am bewildering you a little. Just enough to help you forget what you came to believe, so that you can remember what you've always known."

"Huh," says Diana, swallowing more berries. "You know, I've heard pigs have a better sense of smell than bloodhounds."

"That's quite true, angel. And wild boars even better than pigs. I know that firsthand. I was a farm pig myself once, you see."

Diana's jaw drops. "Shut up!"

"Yes, indeed." The boar nods. "When I first took this particular body, as a wee piglet, I was almost tame. Pink and soft as bubble gum. But I escaped, you see. And when pigs live in nature, we revert to our wild form. Within a few weeks of reaching this forest I found friends—wild boars from Russia that were brought here to be hunted by men, many years ago. Soon I noticed that my skin was darkening to the same color I saw in my wild friends. I could feel my bristles and tusks growing in. Now I am as you see me."

"I've never heard of an animal changing that much," says Diana, wishing she could Google the phenomenon to see whether the boar is telling the truth.

"Feel it," says Herself. "Smell it. Taste it."

"What—this?" Diana holds up a berry.

"No. What I just told you. You were wondering whether I was lying to you. Taste it and find out."

Diana lowers one eyebrow. "*Taste* it?"

"Your body knows what's nourishing and what's poisonous, piglet. And lies are poisonous. Literally. Telling the truth makes you physically stronger, and lying makes you physically weaker. Try it. Go on. Lie a little. The way you usually do."

"The way I— What? I don't lie! Ow!" Diana's gut twists as she speaks.

"Oh, sweetheart! *Hoink hoink hoink!* You've been lying all your life. Not just with words, but with actions."

"What are you talking about? That is *not* true! Ow, ow, ow!" She puts one hand on her stomach.

"Any time you do something that opposes your true nature, darling, you're lying," says the boar. "Remember how much your gut hurt when you were working at Super Big Mart?"

"Well, that was because I had irritable bowel syndrome," says Diana. "The doctor said so, remember?"

"Yes, piglet. Irritable bowel syndrome is one label for your 'tell.' Ever played poker? Your tell is what gives you away. Every human has a tell by which they can recognize their own lies. Your kind have all sorts of names for your various tells—panic attacks, addiction, depression, tension headaches. But the universal cause is tameness. Rejection of your true nature. What you did when you took that job at Super Big Mart, and stayed with it no matter how much you hated it."

"It was the only way I could pay my rent," says Diana. "OW!" She doubles over again, grabbing her belly. "Myself, please make this stop!"

The boar gives a sympathetic murmur. "I can't, sweetheart. Only you can."

"How?" says Diana, straightening up cautiously.

"By mastering the Second Task, dear. By promising to taste whatever you eat, drink, say, do, or think, and refusing to swallow any more poison. To choose nourishment with every action and every word."

"Well, I've never lied much with my words— *Oowwwww!* Damn it! I'm *not* a liar, Myself! I'm not I'm not I'm— *OW!*" Diana's gut kinks so hard her eyes water.

"Hmm," says the boar dreamily. "Darling, your mind is chock-full of lies."

"Is NOT! *OW!* GEEZ! STOP THIS!"

"Ooh, I have an idea!" says the boar. "Why don't we review some of the names you've called yourself this very day?" She takes a deep breath. "Stupid crazy ugly idiot hideous loser dumb disgusting lunatic psycho moron imbecile fool whackjob mouth-breather—"

"All right, all right! *Shut up!*" Diana's gut is so knotted up she thinks she may vomit.

The boar regards her, blinking her thick-lashed eyes. "Not exactly motivational speaking, is it? Nothing but a river of falsehood. And I've been listening to it for *years*. As have you, my sweet liar."

To her shame, Diana begins to cry. "I was doing my best," she says, and notices that there is no new stab to her gut.

"Yes, dear, and your best has been . . . well, I'm sorry to say this, but it's been downright civilized. Ugggh!" The boar shivers.

"But isn't that good? To be civilized?"

"Well, civilized people killed over a hundred million of their own species in the last century or so, and have come near to destroying their home on this planet. Civilization hurts things. You tell me if that's poisonous or not."

"But I've never hurt anything— *Ow, ow, ow, ow, ow!*" The pain in Diana's gut brings tears again.

"*Hoink!*" the boar's laugh is curt. "Just like any civilized person, you've spent practically your whole life torturing an innocent wild creature. Starved it, then force-fed it, cut it, cursed it, driven it to exhaustion. Imprisoned it with other creatures who tormented it."

"What?" Diana shakes her head in miserable confusion. "I don't even kill spiders! I never wanted to hurt anything."

"The innocent wild creature to which I refer, my darling, is you."

Diana opens her mouth to answer, then closes it again. Several seconds later she says, "Oh." She wipes her eyes with the sleeve of her T-shirt. "Well, what am I supposed to do about it?"

"As I said, you can decide not to swallow poison again—not with your body, not with your mind, not with your life. Now I must warn you, dear, that taking this vow will increase the sensitivity of your tell. Basically, you'll live in either complete integrity or horrible pain. It's always been true, but the difference will be more noticeable than ever."

"So that's the Second Task?" asks Diana, just to be sure.

"Yes, darling."

"Okay, but..." Diana feels her pulse speed up. "I'm scared, Myself."

"Yes, sweetheart, that would be your reptile fear of the unknown. You know how to handle it—use the First Task. This is why the Tasks are learned in order—each one is necessary to support those that come after it. So, then. You know this. Deep breath, and then...?"

Diana closes her eyes, breathes slowly, and mouths the words of the First Task. "Be well, my dear one," she whispers. She feels like an idiot, but her gut begins to relax immediately. "Be safe, my love. Live in joy and peace, sweet friend." Blessedly, the pain in her gut is gone. Diana basks in its absence.

"There," says the boar softly. "Do you feel how the kindness nourishes?"

Diana nods.

"Are you ready to make the vow?"

"Yes. I'll never take poison again. I promise."

The boar beams. "Then it is done." And all at once, the smells of the forest become a hundred times more vivid.

If you've ever used a pair of binoculars, beloved, and seen a fuzzy image leap into clear, crisp focus, you have some idea how acutely Diana can suddenly smell and taste. She picks up dozens of layered scents, fantastic in their beauty and complexity. The soil smells of dying leaves and sea sand and grass roots and dozens of other ingredients she can't name. The boar's wet-penny smell divides into separate scents: sun-baked skin, damp hair, a vaguely appetizing porky aroma.

In fact, Diana notices that among the million new scents are many delicious smells. Suddenly she knows that she is literally surrounded by food. Berries hidden under bramble leaves. Tubers rich with starch. Herbs tangy with vitamins.

"Myself, what's happening to me?"

"Feeling a bit bewildered, are we, piglet? *Hoink hoink!*"

"Everything's so clear."

"Delicious, isn't it?" says the boar. "This, my love, is how you know the truth. Your whole body is tasting, always. And when you cleanse yourself of lies, nothing blocks your talent for knowing food from poison."

"It *is* delicious." Diana nods. Then she laughs. "Myself, a minute ago, I thought I might starve out here. And now I feel like this whole place is trying to feed me. Like it's been trying to feed me all along."

"And do you feel how that thought nourishes, just like the plants?"

"I do. I really *do*," Diana giggles again, like a kid set loose in a candy store.

"Welcome to the banquet of this world, Diana. Welcome to the feast of life."

"Thank you," says Diana. And she follows her hunger deeper into the forest, knowing clearly, for the first time, what she wants and doesn't want.

ARCHERY

In the days after she learns to forage, Diana begins to feel healthier and better fed than ever in her life. But her mind is less cooperative than the forest. She can keep troublesome thoughts at bay when she's foraging—the woods are like a fascinating puzzle she's solving with her senses, and it requires her full attention—but when she's lying in her sleeping bag at night, the Furies rise up again. *You're nuts!* they shout. *You're a brain-dead moron roaming around the butt-crack of nowhere with a pretend pig, squandering what little is left of your so-called prime!*

Diana might go along with this hatefest, as is her usual custom, but now, every time she heads in that mental direction, a hot knife slashes into her gut, twisting and cutting until she manages to shake the Furious thoughts from her head. Then what she calls "the stabbies" blessedly abate.

Her most tenacious stabbies come from thoughts about Roy. When she focuses on him—which in those first days is every few minutes— her stomach goes into wrenching, complicated knots that match the confusion in her mind. She can't tell whether she's torqued up with regret over driving Roy away, or the fear that he no longer loves her, or the thought that she'll never see him again.

Eventually, just to get some sleep, she learns to imagine her Roy-thoughts as helium balloons that keep stubbornly appearing and appearing and appearing again in her fists. She forces her mind open the way she'd pry Devin's baby fingers from a dangerous object, until Roy's adored image floats away and peace gradually returns to her vital organs.

Devin himself is another object of worry. Is it missing him that makes her gut ache, or is it her fear that he might not be all right? Every now and then she feels a desperate urge to find her way back to civilization and check on him, but this thought always brings on an attack of the stabbies so incapacitating that to act on it would be well nigh impossible. Since Devin isn't expecting her back for weeks, she's usually able to calm her worry about him.

Occasionally, the screeching of the Furies grows so loud it drives Diana into a panic. This always activates Cloyd, who rears up and begins rattling and striking aimlessly, a display of reptilian self-defense that delights the boar and makes Diana's skin crawl. It takes her more than a week to master the art of calming the snake quickly, but Diana practices the First Task often and gains skill by the hour. She is highly motivated.

She loses count of the days as autumn weather cools the forest. New plants, dormant in the savannah's dry summer, emerge and bloom all around her. The constant monologue of her thoughts begins to fall silent, replaced by sensory vividness: the *rowr* of a bobcat calling its mate, the metallic fuchsia flash of a hummingbird's feathers, the dazzling sweetness of a tiny wild grape bursting on her tongue. Diana doesn't realize that she's beginning to move differently, more like an animal, silently following ribbons of scent through the forest, lifting her head to sniff the breeze. One day she discovers a plant that, when crushed, produces a fragrant, cleansing lather. Diana uses it to wash her hair, then forgets to put her springy curls back into a ponytail. Everything about her is growing wilder.

"You're doing so well, piglet," says Herself one morning as Diana uses a stick to calmly move a drowsy Cloyd away from her sleeping bag. "I'd say you're ready for the Third Task."

"Really?" Diana feels absurdly pleased by the boar's approval. The warm tingling rises in her chest.

"Yes, piglet. I expect it to present itself to you very soon."

Diana feels a burst of energy. She shimmies out of her sleeping bag. The morning cold feels refreshing, rather than chilling; her body seems to be adapting to the temperatures the way animals do. She pulls on shorts, socks, and hiking boots before retiring modestly behind a bush to pee. Then she follows the boar into the woods, her curiosity and anticipation pulling her along. She imagines how she would have felt if, on the day she was fired from Super Big Mart, she'd been given a glimpse of this moment in her own near future. She laughs and shakes her head. The boar's favorite word, "bewildered," hardly begins to cover it.

After half an hour's march through thick brush, they reach the base of a fragile-looking sandstone cliff, where Diana sees that a narrow game trail climbs rapidly upward in a series of switchbacks. Diana is slightly nervous until they're twenty feet up. After that, she's extremely nervous. She hushes her Furies before they can begin screaming that she'll most certainly fall to her death, which would bring on an attack of the stabbies and create exactly what she fears.

When they eventually reach the top, she's breathless and trembling, but the view is worth it. Wave after endless wave of golden-green hills undulate into the distance, punctuated by stands of ancient oak. Diana finds herself thanking the terrain for being so rumpled and inhospitable that humans rarely even travel through it, let alone settle down here. She follows the boar along a razorback ridge, then down another game trail into a patch of forest. From inside, the grove is a cathedral, its stained-glass leaves shifting as the sun shines through them. Tiny goldfinches flit through the oaks, their butter-yellow feathers perfectly matching the brightness of sunlight through illuminated foliage.

It's then that the hair on Diana's arms begins to prickle. It takes her a moment to realize why. The forest around them is unusually silent. Too silent. Diana frowns, looking around her, sniffing the air. Then she follows Herself around a stand of scrub oak and stops as if she's been punched in the face. Before them lies the carcass of a deer, its throat torn out, great gouges of flesh missing from its side. Its eyes, wide open and vacant, reflect the green and blue world above. Blood still seeps from the body into the earth.

Diana's first reaction is a surge of horror, then sorrow that the poor creature is dead (this produces a jab in her guts that she doesn't understand). Right behind this reaction, consuming it like a flame, comes fear. Diana breathes slowly, but her heart is still racing.

"Myself?"

"Yes, piglet?"

"Whatever was eating this is . . . still eating it."

"Astutely noted, darling."

"It's somewhere around here."

"No doubt."

"Why didn't I smell this?"

"It's downwind, sweetie."

Diana exhales again, mentally repeating *may you be well, may you be safe, may you live in joy and peace* until she feels a bit calmer. Still, her senses are all on high alert. She circles the dead deer until she catches a strong scent: iron and salt and water, the inland sea that is a mammal's blood. She lifts her head, sniffing and looking for the predator, thinking she should run now. Fast. But this brings a quick stab to her stomach. To her shock, Diana realizes she's ravenous, and the deer smells delicious.

"You need protein, darling," says the boar. "You need it badly."

"What? Are you saying—oh, Myself! Ugh! I could never eat a dead animal! It has eyes and everything, and OW!" Diana's stomach clenches harder.

"And yet you are so very fond of hamburgers."

"But that's . . ." Diana's voice trails off. She feels drawn to the carcass the same way she's drawn to edible plants, the way she'd sniff out bread baking in an oven. Appalled, Diana realizes the most appetizing smell comes from a wine-dark slab of meat just above the rosy coils of intestine. Her mind tells her she should be ready to vomit, but instead, she's salivating like one of Pavlov's dogs.

She looks anxiously at the boar. "What' s wrong with me, Myself?"

"Diana, my darling, you're low on iron and several vitamins, as well as protein. That liver would do you a great deal of good right now, and your body knows it."

Diana looks down at the gore before her, the warm prickle rising in her chest. Suddenly a bewildering array of images flashes through her mind. She's running across hard-packed snow toward a man in a fur parka who holds out a piece of raw seal liver like Santa Claus offering candy. She's crouching on a hot plain, chasing away hyenas so that two spotted lion cubs can get to the liver of a gazelle. She's offering a piece of liver to an eagle who sits heavily on her wrist, triumphant to have brought back a rabbit. Then she's just Diana again, kneeling beside the dead deer, anticipating the return of an unseen predator, her stomach rumbling.

"It's *scrumptious*," says Herself encouragingly.

Diana feels herself capitulate, exactly the way she used to give in and eat ice cream three days into a weight-loss regimen. She takes the Swiss Army knife from her pocket. "I'm so sorry," she tells the deer. And then, "Thank you very much." With deftness that shocks her all over again, she cuts the liver free from the carcass. It's warm and slippery and bloody. Diana should be revolted. And isn't.

A flock of scrub jays begins squawking loudly a hundred yards ahead of them. Diana looks up sharply, everything in her body shouting *predator!*

"Cover me!" she yells to the boar, and sprints back along the path they just traveled, wondering what that even means. They always say it in the movies. She can hear trotters galloping behind her, and the low *hoinkhoinkhoink* that means Herself is having a fabulous time.

They run all the way back along the crest of the ridge, rocket down the switchback trail on the cliff face, and finally arrive at camp, wheezing and gulping for air. All the way, Diana cradles the fragile trophy of the deer's liver against her body. When she finally reaches her sleeping bag, she bursts into hysterical laughter.

"Holy crap!" she gasps. "Myself, I could've been killed!"

"Yes, indeed!" says the boar. "How wonderful that would have been! You could have fed a mountain lion or a pack of coyotes!"

"What? Myself, that's an *awful* thing to say!" Diana feels a gut-stab. "Okay, maybe it isn't," she says. "After all, if I were already dead, getting eaten wouldn't be so bad."

Cloyd is poised for combat under a large rock, her rattle buzzing like an electric saw. Diana spends a moment calming the snake back into a relaxed coil. Then she examines the deer liver, which is a pure, deep, soft crimson. Diana's hands and wrists are covered with blood, yet still she feels no disgust. The liver looks . . . beautiful.

"I should cook it, shouldn't I?"

"Well, you have no fire," says the boar. "And no matches. So good luck with that."

Diana has read about people lost at sea, how as they slowly starved, the eyes and internal organs of fish began smelling and tasting appetizing to them. She's also seen her share of vampire movies. She's wondering which applies right now. Either way, there's no denying it: The liver is making her mouth water. She cuts off a small piece and puts it into her mouth. Her body rejoices. She swallows. Delicious.

"I must really be losing it," Diana mutters, and gets a stab in the gut for her trouble. "When I get back to LA, I'm going vegan," she adds. No stabbies.

She eats the liver in small bites, her body soaking in the rich nutrients like a plant being watered after drought. By the time it's gone, she feels more vibrant and energetic than she remembers feeling since . . . ever. She's also ready to confront the obvious problem posed by her discovery of the dead deer. Something her size was just killed, very close to her, and she didn't even know it. She needs a weapon for self-defense in case she gets jumped by a mountain lion, or a bear, or a wolf.

She opens and inspects every tool on her Swiss Army knife. All of them are pathetic as defense against large predators. She wanders around the nearby forest until she finds a long, reasonably straight stick to sharpen into a spear. As she whittles at it, the boar trots over to Diana's pile of possessions and noses the bow and arrows Roy made on that first day in the forest.

"What about these?"

"What about them?" Diana looks up briefly. "Those are Roy's. I don't even know how to use them. *OW!*" She drops her knife and curls up in pain. "Sweet mother of God," she gasps through gritted teeth. "What is the *problem*?"

The boar says nothing but *"Hoinkhoinkhoinkhoink!"* She laughs so hard she collapses onto her side, where she wriggles around joyfully, scratching her back on the sand.

Diana glowers at her. "I'm so glad you find my agony hilarious." But her eyes glance off the boar and land, with an almost audible *thock,* on the bow and arrows, as if she's never seen them before. The warm prickle rises just below the center of her breastbone, as primordially delicious as the liver.

Perhaps, beloved, you remember a moment when something you would come to love first registered in your consciousness. Maybe you saw a phrase written in a language so beautiful you simply had to learn it, or heard a particular instrument being played and felt the sound entrance you. Maybe you knew, right then and there, that hours and hours of your life would flow into this strangely alluring thing. That the thing was part of your destiny, a tool of your personal magic.

Slowly, Diana stands up and walks toward the bow. She bends down to pick it up by the handgrip for the very first time. As soon as she touches it, a shock runs from her arm to her solar plexus, then explodes through her body like a bomb. Another vivid dazzle of images flashes in her mind, each one too quick to register: a hundred thousand bows, a million arrows, a blur of settings flickering from jungle to desert to tundra to swamp to mountain to sea. Diana jumps back as if she's been electrocuted.

"Jeez! What the . . . ? Myself!" She looks over at the boar, who has fallen asleep on her back, twitching her tail and snoring softly.

Diana backs away from the bow the way she once backed away from Cloyd the rattlesnake. For the rest of that day—and the next, and the next—she barely dares glance at it. The simple staff of carved yew with its nylon string, which at the moment hangs slackly from one tip, terrifies Diana. Not because it feels unfamiliar, but because it's as familiar as breathing.

At night (and all night, for several more nights) she has endless dreams of bows and arrows. She stands in the courtyard of an elegant palace holding a long bow above her head while instructors dressed in black robes watch her appraisingly. She perches in the limbs of a huge, mossy tree as a tiny bearded man with blue tattoos hands her an arrow.

She rises up in the stirrups of a galloping horse, her head steady and still, and shoots at a straw target swaying in the prairie wind.

Each morning Diana specifically avoids looking at the bow, keeping her head turned away from it as she goes off into the forest to seek more vegetarian meals. So it's several days before she notices something teasing at the back of her mind: The bow and arrows seem to be moving. Every day they're in a slightly different place. The thought gives her a blast of gooseflesh, but no stab in the gut, which only makes the whole thing creepier. That night she forces herself to look straight at the bow and arrows, memorizing their exact position at the base of a young oak. The next morning she looks again, and what she sees makes her heart jerk so hard that Cloyd almost gives herself whiplash.

The bow is right next to Diana's sleeping bag.

She jumps to her feet, trembling. "Myself! Where are you?"

"I'm at the spring, love!" calls the boar.

"Did you move my— Did you move Roy's bow?"

"Not I, piggly-wiggly." Diana hears a faint *hoink hoink,* which turns to a gurgle as Herself begins blowing bubbles.

"Dammit, Myself! Stop messing with my head—it's not cute, and it's not funny!"

No apology comes from the direction of the spring, just happy humming and splashing. Cloyd is rattling furiously, so Diana takes a moment to calm her, and this, in turn makes Diana calm. She stares at the bow, lying next to her on the ground like a dog waiting to hunt. She's sick of feeling the thing—fearing it, and also wanting it. The familiar prickling glow blooms in her solar plexus. Slowly, slowly, Diana reaches down and rests her left palm on the handgrip. This time there's no slideshow of images. No shock. Just ease and comfort, as if she's sliding into a conversation with an old friend after a long separation.

She picks up the bow and twirls it. The string, attached at one end, looped loosely around the other, makes a whistling sound in the air.

"Well, well, well!" Diana looks up to see Herself trot into the clearing, her bristles glittering with water drops. "Look at you, piglet! You're all over this Task! Tremendous!"

Diana stops twirling the bow. "The Third Task is shooting a bow?"

"Mm, well, not exactly," says the boar. "But close enough. Here's an idea—why don't you string it?"

Diana tries to bend the bow by putting the handgrip against one knee and pulling back on the ends with both hands. It bends—a little— but there's no way for her to put the loose loop of string into its notch. "Here's another idea," she says. "Why don't you show me how?"

The boar extends a foretrotter. "Darling, do you see an opposable thumb here?"

"Well, for crying out loud, then, how am I supposed to figure it out? I can't even bend this thing!"

"Indeed you can't, love. Not your meat-self, anyway. That's the whole point."

"My meat-self?"

"Your body, without your meta-self. The meta-self can do things the meat-self could never manage in a thousand years. That's why so many people have used archery for the Third Task."

"Wait, wait, wait," says Diana. "Go back. What's a mecca-self?"

"*Meta*-self, darling. *Meta* meaning *beyond*. Something *other* than the body you think is you. Your meat-self—your physical body—is as helpless without its meta-self as that deer who so kindly fed you the other day. Call the meta-self your soul, your angel, the Force, the intelligence of Nature, the ghost in the machine. Call it whatever you want, but learn to use it."

Meta. Something *other*. Diana feels a chill run over her skin, while deep in her solar plexus, the warm prickling energy grows hotter. The *other* is the one who takes over when . . . She shakes her head, hard. She's been fighting the *other* her whole sorry life.

"Myself, I don't think this is a good— Owowowowowow!" The stabbies hit so hard Diana has to stand still and breathe, eyes closed tight, for a full minute. Then she looks beseechingly at the boar. "Are you saying this *is* a good idea?"

"I'm not saying anything, angel."

It's like her attraction to Roy, like the feel of her hair curling wild around her shoulders, like the taste of the raw liver. Diana feels something fracture in the very center of her body as she gives in to it. Gives in to the *other*.

Smoothly, her body places the strung end of the bow on the

ground, braced by her foot. Her right arm pulls the bow down as her left slides the string up into its notch.

"Holy crap!" Diana whispers. She has no sensation of moving deliberately; movement simply happens. Her whole focus is on the energy of the *other,* pulsing from her center, radiating through her limbs, using the body to do things—no, to not-do them. This isn't doing, Diana thinks, but an absolute lack of doing. She almost stops breathing at the strangeness of it. Then she remembers to exhale. Her mind repeats the calming words of the First Task. Her gut rests in the comfortable familiarity of these alien actions.

Herself's tiny eyes twinkle. *"Hoinhoinkhoinkhoinkhoink!* You are *so* clever, my darling! It took many a samurai years to let his body string his bow. And here you are doing it the way young Mozart played the piano!"

"I . . . it's . . . what . . ." Diana is so confused—so bewildered—that she can't put words to the experience. She watches her body lean down, pick up an arrow, nock it. Then she takes over, awkwardly holding the bow up to her face and pulling back on the string. Nothing happens, except for mild pain in her fingers. The bow is much too stiff for her to bend.

"See, now you're *doing* it," says the boar, "and doing—well, it has its uses. Most humans get along all right using nothing else. But not-doing is so, so, *so* much stronger. How about not-shooting, dear?"

So Diana tries not-shooting, though it makes no sense at all. She stands under the trees, holding the bow and feeling stupider by the minute, for most of the morning. Once or twice, when her attention wanders in a certain way and Cloyd looks particularly limp, a surge of fire rises from her solar plexus and the weapon suddenly feels pliable. The bow is pulled (Diana is definitely *not* pulling it) but immediately snaps back as she notices what's happening and tries to make the action continue.

This goes on, with short breaks for eating and sleeping, for three more days. Diana becomes obsessed with the Third Task, so much so that Herself has to do much of their foraging. Every few hours the boar arrives at the clearing, dragging Diana's backpack full of roots and nuts, to offer a little coaching.

"No, sweetheart, you're exerting effort. No muscle needed. Relax, relax, relax," she says. Or, "That was very good. You weren't trying at all. Just hold the intention and wait." Or, "Do you realize your brain is actually developing an area devoted to the bow and arrow? As if they were parts of your body. Which, from your meta-self's perspective, they are."

By the fourth day, Diana is so exhausted, frustrated, and disillusioned that she finally puts down the bow. She joins Herself at the spring, washing her hair with the lathering plant the boar calls "soaproot." Diana throws a glob of lather at Herself, who chases her around the spring until they're both covered with bubbles. They splash each other clean, laughing. For a moment Diana tells herself she's getting too comfortable in her strange banishment from civilization. But this makes her gut stab so unpleasantly, and relaxing into the moment feels so nourishing, that the thought dies away almost before she has time to think it.

That night, instead of lying down in her usual spot between Diana's sleeping bag and the ever-cuddly Cloyd, Herself disappears into the forest and comes back moments later with a tiny daisy held delicately in her chops.

"Time for target practice," she crows, and trots off again.

"Myself? Where are you going?" Diana begins to follow.

"No, love, you stay right there," Herself calls, and comes back. "There! I put the flower on the fallen tree—you know, the big one with the lightning strike scar down the side. You're going to shoot it."

"Oh, ha ha. Let's go to bed," says Diana.

"Don't you feel like just giving it a try?" says the boar.

"No—ow—oh, all right." The strange compulsion to shoot the bow pops back into her body, and Diana grins wearily. She retrieves the weapon, along with her favorite arrow. Funny, her body has actually come to feel incomplete without them. The boar must be right, Diana thinks. Her brain has added these tools to its sense of self.

"I'm not sure what to do here, Myself!" Diana calls into the gathering darkness. Her gut sends up a warning flare.

"Yes, you are, Diana!" the boar's voice calls back. And, of course, she's right. Some inscrutable part of Diana knows exactly what to do.

She relaxes, dropping her head, feeling the deep calm silence of the forest pervade her. The *other* arises, first a warm tingle, then a buzz, then a blaze of energy in her solar plexus. Diana is too tired to try. She lets the *other* feel the bow, the string, the arrow. And then the boar, the pool of joy around her, the sweetness of playing, the safety of being loved.

"I don't want to hit you by mistake!" she calls.

"Diana, my love," Herself calls back, "no offense, but you have literally never hit anything! *Hoink hoink hoink!*"

Diana can't help smiling. The boar's jolliness, her continuous and causeless enthusiasm, is impossibly infectious. As her own laughter bubbles up, Diana's body raises the bow high over its head. Her left arm, by itself, comes down straight and true. Her right elbow bends, pulling the bow nearly double, the nock of the arrow beside her ear. The *other* sends out its blazing energy, feeling within itself: human, boar, dead tree, tiny daisy.

Diana doesn't even notice when the arrow is loosed. She only knows that the flower and the arrow's tip have come together. It all happens so simply, just as all your own skills were finally mastered, beloved—in the quiet, without ceremony or effort. Like old friends hugging. Like long-time lovers, with absolute trust, reaching out to touch each other in the dark.

"Bull's-eye," says Herself mildly, sounding far away. "But you knew that."

BAREFOOT

That first perfect shot proves almost impossible to replicate. Diana spends most of the next three days standing in the rain draped in an ultra-light Mylar poncho, bow and arrow in her hands, and eyes fixed on a pinecone she's chosen as a target, waiting for her meta-self to shoot. Her mind is so focused—not thinking, but feeling for the state of not-thinking—that she barely notices the chill or the water dripping from her curls. She's not concentrating, exactly; it's more that she's opening, letting her mind drop away so that her body will be free to shoot.

On the fourth day the rain finally ends, leaving the forest clean and bright and electric green. Tender young grasses and flowering plants spring up everywhere, mosses flourish on the rocks, and the ancient trees put out thick sprays of pale newborn leaves. Late that afternoon, after hours of standing and waiting, Diana's thoughts vanish into all that green, and once more she feels her body raise the bow, draw back the string, and touch the arrow's tip to the target, fifty yards away. She looks around, checking whether Herself saw the shot, but the boar is off in the forest, foraging.

The next shot comes only a few hours later, the next only a few minutes after that. By the time Herself arrives home, hauling a backpack full of acorns, Diana has learned to drop into not-shooting almost as fast as she can calm Cloyd.

"Watch this, Myself!"

"Watch what, love?"

Diana raises the bow, tries to pull the string, hurts her fingers. "Darn it! No, wait, wait, wait a second." She composes herself, relaxes. The body—not even Diana's body now, just *the* body—inhales deeply and raises the bow. *Thock!* The arrow goes straight through the pinecone, pinning it to the log.

"Hah!" Diana punches the air with her fist. "That's what I'm *talkin'* about!"

Herself lets out a loud *HOINK* of praise, and the two of them spend several minutes doing a jig around the clearing. Then they sit down, breathless, Diana fanning her face with her hand. She takes off her hiking boots and wiggles her toes happily.

"You know what it is, Myself? I figured it out. It's a feeling in my *head*. You'd think it would be my body, but there's this place in the very center of my head that sort of warms up when I let go enough for . . . for my, uh, meta-self . . . to shoot. And everything sort of appears and disappears at the same time—I don't know how to describe it."

"Well, dear, the inside of your head is more like Play-Doh than most humans are used to assuming. Quite malleable, really. And you're re-sculpting yours—the Tasks do that, you see. *Hoink hoink!*" The boar tilts her head to one side, twitching her ears. "I think you might be ready to take on the Fourth."

"Really? The Fourth Task?"

"Mm-hm."

"Well, what is it?" Diana feels the familiar tingle of anticipation.

"Would you like to start learning it?"

"Yes! Of course!"

"Right now?"

"Sure!"

"All right, then," says Herself. She comes a few steps closer, opens her tusky mouth as far as it will go, and closes it on the uppers of both Diana's hiking boots. Then she raises her head, the boots protruding from her snout, and gallops off into the forest.

Diana leaps to her feet. "What the . . . ? Get back here with my boots! Are you crazy?"

But the boar is already gone. Diana can hear her galloping off through the soft grass, her laughter muffled by the cargo in her mouth: *"Hng hng hng hng hng hng hng hng hng hng hng hng hng hng hng hng hng . . ."*

Inside Diana's head, a proliferation of catastrophes bursts forth. How many times has she heard Roy say that in the wilderness, barefoot equals dead? The Furies, rousing and revving their engines, crank out a few new tunes. *You let a freaking hallucination steal your shoes! You'll pick up a thorn! You'll go septic! You'll get gangrene! Out here in the middle of nowhere that means dead. Barefoot equals DEAD, DEAD, DEAD!*

Beloved, you, too, may have had moments when fear rose up so powerfully that nothing else seemed real. The trigger may have been a number on a bank statement, a boss's sideward glance, an angry comment from a lover—anything that pinged your Furies into action. By the time you were conscious enough to form thought at all, terror was already in the driver's seat. And, in that moment the spike of fear overwhelmed you entirely, as it's overwhelming Diana now. As she panics, Cloyd wakes up, hissing madly and rattling like an industrial-strength maraca. Finding nothing to attack, the snake bites savagely at an exposed tree root. Diana's gut spasms so hard she can't breathe.

She forces her mind back to what she's learned. Step one, step two. Calm the snake. Release the poisonous thoughts.

Peace.

For the next two hours Diana waits, munching acorns, watching Cloyd free her left fang from the tree root, and fuming as much as the stabbies will let her. Which isn't much. Finally her fascination with archery pulls her body back to its bare feet, which wiggle tentatively against the cool ground. Once again, Diana marvels at how her body has adapted to the cooling temperature; she half expects her feet to go numb with cold, but instead they feel refreshed, freed from their tight leather bindings. The body walks carefully to the fallen tree, puts the pinecone back in its place, walks carefully back, and keeps practicing.

Thock!

Thock!

Thock!

Every shot is dead-on now, so Diana chooses another target, smaller and farther away. She tenses up a little, tries too hard, loses her form. Step one, step two. Calm. Release poison. Find the warmth in her solar plexus, spreading upward to that place in the center of her head.

Thock!

By nightfall, Diana has found that while her meat-self still can't even draw Roy's bow, her meta-self can hit a single leaf bobbing in the breeze at the tip of a branch a hundred paces away. She's so deep in not-thought that she feels only a wisp of worry that Herself still hasn't returned.

"Better bring my damn boots back," she grumbles as she crawls into her sleeping bag. "You big psycho." She falls asleep immediately and dreams of green, dancing bodies forming in the trees, playing catch with her arrows.

Diana practices archery all the next morning, stopping only to eat the acorns and greens Herself gathered the day before. At lunch, despite the stabs in her gut, she begins to worry. Then panic pounces, unleashing a flurry of Furies. *Herself will never come back, because she's not real! You can't survive out here forever. You need to get home immediately! Devin needs you, and YOU CAN'T WALK BACK TO CIVILIZATION WITH NO FREAKING BOOTS!* Diana's gut wrenches fiendishly with every Furious thought.

Eventually, the pain drives her back to what she's learned. Calm the reptile mind. Release thoughts that hurt. Let her meta-self take over. One, two, three. Stillness.

Late that afternoon, as the green begins warming to gold in the slanting sun, Diana goes to retrieve her arrows and realizes she's no longer feeling her way quite so cautiously. She is, however, walking differently. Her balance has shifted onto the balls of her feet, and her body takes each step with a strangely deliberate purpose, feeling for obstacles and sharp objects, moving to miss them.

"Oh, my God!" she says out loud, addressing Cloyd, since no one else is near. "I'm not walking. It's walking me! I'm being walked!"

This realization brings on a giddy laugh, half amazement, half fear, and almost immediately, Diana trips over a large rock hidden in the leaves. She lands on her knee, pain shooting up and down her leg, and curses lavishly until the stabbies remind her to calm herself down again. As soon as she deploys the Tasks, she's up and walking again— smoothly, lithely, more fluidly than she's ever moved before.

"Roy is *not* going to like this," she mutters, remembering his aversion to feet, the story of the native guide with his agile, gripping toes. She feels a slight stab in the gut, but her mental image of those strangely adept feet seems to animate her body even more. She has to confess it—her feet *love* the ground. They want to touch the earth the way her hands want to touch Roy's skin.

At this thought, Diana's feet seem to come fully alive. The pleasure they feel as they touch the soil radiates up her legs, feeding the warm tingle in her solar plexus. The energy rises all the way up to her collarbone, flooding the space around her heart. She feels a cracking sensation inside her ribs, as though a dam is breaking under the pressure of a tsunami.

"What's happening to me, Myself?" Diana whispers. But the boar is nowhere to be seen. And yet . . .

Trust it.

She doesn't hear the boar's advice; she *feels* it. It's blended in with the sweet, warm, buzzing energy rushing up through her legs and surrounding her heart. Really, there's nothing else to do *but* trust it, this surge of pleasure. Diana couldn't stop whatever's happening if she wanted to. Which she doesn't.

All this time her body continues to walk—past the place where her arrows landed, past the edge of the grove onto a field of impossibly green grass glowing against an orange sunset, past any territory she's explored before. Her body is speeding up, her feet finding safe purchase as easily as her fingers would feel for objects in her purse. She is falling in love with the sense of the forest on her skin.

Have you ever felt your heart open, beloved? If so, you know it's not just an expression. The heart, with its own cluster of nerves as big as a cat's brain, can literally feel love's approach, the way a bud might feel the sunlight that has come to unfurl it. As its armor begins to dissolve, the heart both fears and desires what's arising within it; a sensation so sweet it's almost terrible, so terrible it's almost sweet. Then the love breaks through, smashing open your chest, leaving you utterly helpless, vulnerable, and ecstatic. The touch of naked bodies is nothing compared to the touch of naked hearts.

When the love cracks open Diana's heart, the flood hits so hard and strong that there is nothing she can do but surrender. Without protest, she feels herself falling deeper into her meta-self's power, into a body that keeps speeding up and up and up. First, it's her own love of the forest she feels, and that is so immense she must walk much faster to tolerate it. And then Diana feels a different love returning to her, answering her own. It's a love so huge and strange she thinks she might actually explode.

"Feel me," says a whisper in her chest. "Feel how old I am."

Diana gasps, a sob of pure awe.

"Feel all the creatures that are made of me," says the whisper. Diana senses a line of love, absolutely real, connecting the hearts of everything in nature, everything that lives on the soil and in the ocean. Think of the most passionate moment of your life, beloved, the moment of connection when you knew you and your lover were one being. Multiply that by a thousand, by a hundred thousand, and you may be able to imagine what Diana feels as she moves through the forest. There is only one heart, beating fast with ecstasy, forming itself into many hearts, each of them in Love with every other.

Without meaning to, Diana leans forward and begins to run. Her breathing is deep and even. Her feet barely touch the loose sandy soil. They bounce off rocks, spring sideways off tree trunks, throw her body across a small stream as if she were a steeplechaser. So much energy hums through her body that she thinks she might die if she tries to stop, or even slow down. The same three words run through her mind and body, again and again, targeted at so many things Diana can't possibly distinguish one from the other: *Oh, my love! Oh, my love! Oh, my love!*

Each being she feels—Devin, Roy, the boar, every person or animal she's ever known—is meeting her for the first time and has loved her forever. Every tiny mouse and lizard, every elephant and whale, every child of nature is Diana's own being, its huge, intimate life beating like thunder in her single human chest.

She comes to a steep, whitewater stream, just visible in the fading light, and turns sharply uphill. The strain in her leg muscles as they hurl her upward is exquisite, blissful. She can see the moon rising above the mountain she's climbing, and another burst of recognition fills her.

"This, too, is made of me," says the whisper, and Diana can feel how the world dances, every life swaying and throbbing as the moon draws nearer, retreats, draws near again. She feels the clams opening their shells in the tidal surge, the sea turtles following the waves to land at midnight, pulled by the silver lantern in the sky.

She climbs a pile of boulders, and finds that above it, the stream is narrow enough to ford. Her feet love the icy chill of the water, and then the dry land. She feels a bright heart to her left, and realizes that a deer is running alongside her, moving its antlers to dodge branches and thorns the way Diana moves to keep her hair free. She feels another heart above her: an owl, silent as the moonlight, soaring along. Then a fox joins them, a puff of gray fur she glimpses briefly as they run through another meadow. She can feel the animals' hearts, how linked they are to her own. *Oh, my love! Oh, my love! Oh, my love!*

As Diana reaches the crest of a ridge, she smells something wonderful: water, mud, moss, and sedge. The scent of a mountain lake. A few moments later, hurtling downhill and through a patch of scrub oak, she sees it before her: a dark mirror shining its own image of the moon back up into space. She can feel the cooler air around the little lake, the hearts of fish and frogs and herons and blackbirds.

Her body slows to a walk. For the first time, Diana wonders how long she's been running, and where she is. For a moment the old anxiety rises up, and she puts her hand to her side, where a stitch has suddenly grabbed. Step one, step two, step three: calm down, let the thought go, surrender to her meta-self. When she's done that, her heart floods all over again. She feels the boar's love connecting to hers. She remembers how much Herself delights in being asked for help.

"Hello!" Diana shouts into the darkness above the lake. "Myself? Can you hear me? Where are you?"

Not ten feet in front of her, something she thought was a boulder raises its head.

"Well, hello, darling piglet! Fancy meeting you here! *Hoink hoink hoink hoink hoink!*"

"Oh, my God!" Diana shouts. "You're here! I ran right to you! How did I . . . how did this . . ." She thinks for a moment and says, "This is not a coincidence, is it, Myself?"

"Well concluded, sweetheart," says the boar, standing up and yawning. "As I've mentioned before, apparent miracles are the essence of waking up. Do you like this place?"

Diana looks around at the silver-green hills, the dark mass of trees ranged on the other side of the little lake, the silver streak of moonlight on the water. The feeling of nature's heart, and all the hearts that belong to it, still sings in her chest. The running seems to have broken down internal barriers, and now Diana can tolerate the love flowing through her without having to move. The connection she feels to the lake, to this very place, astonishes her.

"Is this heaven?" she asks. "Am I dead?"

The boar gives another long, tickled laugh. "Well, I suppose it would be as close to heaven as any place, if either places or heaven existed. Or death, for that matter. *Hoink!* Death! What a concept!"

"Why am I—why are we here?"

"You've learned the Fourth Task, darling. You've learned to let the world touch your heart. And that means you have to go deeper into the forest, to what the tribes who once lived here would have called your medicine place. So presto, here we are. Well done, piglet! *Hoink hoink!*"

"I need to go back," says Diana. "Just to get my stuff. I'll move here tomorrow." The thought of not bringing her campsite to the lake doesn't even occur to her. This is where everything in her wants to be.

"All right, angel," says Herself. "I'll walk with you. Do you want these?" She nudges something in the grass. Diana's boots.

Diana looks at the boots and shakes her head with a smile.

Herself chortles. "All right, then. They'll still be here when we come back." And without any further ceremony, the boar begins trotting back in the direction Diana came from. Diana falls into step, letting her meta-self guide her feet.

They walk for a long time without speaking, smelling the scents of the night, feeling all the beings around them. Diana tries an experiment: She closes her eyes. She can walk as well as ever.

"*On ne voit bien qu'avec le coeur. L'essentiel est invisible pour les yeux.*"

"What, Myself?"

"I didn't say that, love. He did."

With a sweet jolt of surprise, Diana feels the little silver gray fox who ran beside her on her way here. His bright eyes pierce the dark. His heartbeat is small and fast.

"He doesn't really speak any human language," says Herself. "His thought just came through to you that way because of your ninth-grade French class. Remember? *The Little Prince*?"

It takes a moment, and then Diana *does* remember. "One sees rightly only with the heart," she translates. "What is essential is invisible to the eye."

She feels the fox's absolute delight that she's heard him, that she's given language to the beat of his heart. And then language falls away again, and there is only the love.

STORIES

The sun is straight overhead when Diana finally wakes up. Her legs are sore—though not nearly as much as she would have expected—and her chest is tender, the way her whole body felt after giving birth to Devin. The sensation brings memories of Devin's young life sweeping through her. For a moment Diana misses her boy so intensely that tears spring to her eyes. Then her gut twists, and she wonders if missing Devin is a kind of lie. When she talks to Herself about it, the boar always says, "Separation is only in the dream, dear." Diana doesn't understand this, but the thought relaxes her insides, so she allows herself to believe it.

Tentatively, the way her feet first felt their way over the forest floor, she reaches out with the invisible tendrils of her newly opened heart, looking for her son. She may be imagining it—she may be imagining all of this—but after a moment she can swear she feels him, and that he feels her, too. It's like the moment she first saw Roy on TV, but gentler, almost matter-of-fact.

"I love you, baby boy," she thinks, and the filament of energy connecting them glows warm and bright. "I love you, too," says Devin's heart, and weirdly, Diana is as aware of his presence as if he's standing, large as life, right here beside her.

She climbs out of her sleeping bag carefully, not wanting to jostle her newly fragile heart or the connection to Devin. The air is fresh, overwhelmingly fragrant, as it always has been since Diana learned the Second Task and her senses began to sharpen. She leans against a tree and breathes in a new fragrance. Sometime during the night, little blue flowers have opened all over her grove. It looks as if part of the sky has spilled onto the green, green grass.

Diana hears a loud chirrup, and looks over to see a chipmunk perched just above her on the tree trunk. It runs down almost to her eye level and boldly gazes into Diana's face, its fuzzy five-inch-long tail lashing back and forth like a leopard's. She can feel its heart, a high trill of feisty energy, in her own.

Diana laughs out loud. "Oh, my goodness," she says. "You are so *fierce!*"

The little creature chirps again, flicking its tail. Suddenly Diana finds herself recalling the Great Chipmunk Incident that changed her childhood forever. Maybe you have a similar incident in your own history, beloved. A day when everything you thought was stable and trustworthy shattered, for no reason you could comprehend.

She found the chipmunk on the road outside her first parents' home, in Pacific Palisades. She'd slipped outside while her mama wasn't looking—again—and discovered the animal's motionless body on the road. The chipmunk had been unkindly modified by the car that hit it. Four-year-old Diana, undaunted by the creature's obvious and extreme ill health, carried it home and offered it a glass of water, then a peanut butter sandwich. It refused to partake. After half an hour of fruitless coaxing, Diana saw—and a terrible, guilt-ridden insight it was—that she'd probably made things worse by taking a sick animal away from its home and family. Of course the chipmunk would have a better chance of recovery in its natural setting. Of course! But when she tried to take it back outside, Diana was dismayed to find the door locked.

Now, thirty-two years later, Diana clearly remembers how she tried to solve this problem. She also recalls the precise look of shock, disgust, and plain fear that distorted Nancy Archer's face the moment she entered the kitchen and saw her adopted daughter chopping away at the back door with a meat cleaver, the dead chipmunk dangling by its tail from her free hand.

"*Hoink hoink hoink!* You were such a caution!" Herself trots into the clearing with a backpack full of pinecones with nuts ready to be harvested. "Always trying to fix some little critter. Adorable."

"Or stupid," says Diana, and hisses faintly when her gut cramps. "Oh, all right, not stupid, not stupid!" she corrects herself, rubbing her stomach. "But I could almost never really fix them." She sighs, remembering a childhood full of limping dogs, broken-winged birds, a turtle with a fractured shell. However rarely she could actually help them, she'd always tried.

"It was like some sort of compulsion," Diana mutters. She almost says "insanity," but she feels the stabbies coming on before that thought is even fully formed. But it really is strange: almost from birth, she seemed to detect damaged beasts with some sixth sense that picked up their silent cries: *Help, Diana. Help. You can help.* There was no self-pity in those calls, not even much fear, only insistence. It took Diana years to stop hearing them.

"Roll up your sleeping bag, dear," says Herself. "Let's move to your medicine place. Deeper, deeper, deeper!" She prances a few steps, tusky snout held high.

Diana crouches down to smooth out the turquoise nylon, but she's distracted. She can hear that cry again, flowing through the raw new openness of her heart: a chorus of countless voices, braided into a single compelling message. *Diana, you can help. You're here to help. Please help.* She's starting to feel nervous.

"Myself, what *is* that?"

"What do you mean, love?"

"That sound—well, not a sound, really. That . . . *message*. Who needs my help? And why does it sound so *familiar*? Like I've heard it a million times?"

"Oh, darling! *Hoink hoink hoink!*" The boar twitches her ears. "Much more than a million! A million is *nothing*!"

Diana gapes. "What? Why? Where is it coming from?"

"From living things," says Herself, scratching her chin with one back trotter. "These are perilous times for living things on this planet, Diana."

"Why is it so *loud* all of a sudden?" The cry in Diana's heart has become a persistent tone, so strong it's beginning to physically ache.

"It's no louder than usual, dear," says Herself. "You're just hearing better. You've mastered the first four Tasks, you see, so you're more than half bewildered now. Connected to the heart of everything."

The cry in Diana's chest suddenly swells like a river in a flash flood. More and more voices rush through her, with more and more urgency. *Help. Please help. The babies can't survive this, Diana. Help the babies.*

"I don't like this, Myself." Diana rubs her chest, trying to ease the pressure. "I really, *really* don't like this."

"No," says the boar. "No one said the Tasks are easy. And the Fifth . . ." She shakes her shaggy head, sighing through her teeth.

"The Fifth Task? Already?" Diana hugs her arms to her chest. Her heart feels as if it's stretching to its limit, filled with suffering that keeps growing worse.

"Yes, love. It's happening very quickly, isn't it? I'm so proud of you."

"Well, turn it off." Diana clenches her teeth. She feels as if the strings of her heart have begun to break, one by one. Her gut is cramping, too, but that pain is merely physical. It's the sorrow in her chest, the terrible grief, that feels unbearable. Flashes of story begin appearing in Diana's mind. Animals starving, seeing their infants starve. Finding no food, no clean water, no place to sleep or play or hunt.

"There's only so much I can do, piglet." The boar comes and sits beside her, a comforting warmth that barely touches the cold desolation flooding Diana's body. She feels the pain of mothers, human and animal alike, who have nothing to feed their infants, who love their little ones the way she loves Devin, only to see them suffer and die. The anguish is different from the poisonous gut-stab of a lie. It's as piercingly, unendurably clean as polar ice.

"Please, Myself!" Diana gasps. "Please, *do* something! Help them!"

"Hmm. They seem to think *you're* the one to do that."

"Me?" A sudden flare of anger, heat in the cold. "What can *I* do? I'm, I'm—" Diana gropes for words, and suddenly she hears her Furies, louder than they've been since she mastered the Second Task. "I'm so small!" she says, repeating what the Furies shout. "I'm weak. Powerless. There's nothing I can do!" Her gut spasms.

The only thing as loud as the Furies is the cry of the dying animal mothers, which has now reached hurricane volume. *HELP, DIANA! HELP THE BABIES!*

She covers her ears with her hands. *"There's nothing I can do!"* she screams. "Stop! I can't take this! I can't take this I can't take this I can't take this . . ." Her mind is chaos, filled with the animals' sadness, the Furies' rage, terrible fear that the suffering will never end. She hears Cloyd rattling somewhere nearby.

"Now, angel," says the boar. "You know what to do. Step one . . ."

Diana lets out a garbled scream and clutches her chest as if she's trying to keep the pin in a huge hand grenade. Focusing on the Tasks is like lifting a corpse, but she makes herself do it. *First, breathe. Then ask for help.* She throws a beseeching glance at the boar, who immediately says, "I'm right here, darling." Diana feels a wave of calm. *Now, offer love. Be well, be happy, be safe,* she thinks. Cloyd stops rattling.

"Very good, darling," says the boar. "Now the Second Task."

The Second Task the Second Task what was the Second Task? Oh, yes, don't take poison. Diana realizes that the drone note of her pain, the thought, "I can't take this," is a lie. Whatever this horror is, she *can* take it. She can let her heart be shredded. It's not as if it hasn't happened before. "I can take this," she amends through gritted teeth. "I can, I can." The knife in her abdomen stops twisting. She gasps in a few breaths. The animal mothers, and the Furies, keep screaming.

The Third Task, Diana thinks desperately. *Meta-self. No-thought. Allow.* She feels a rush of energy in her solar plexus, hot and strong. With it comes a stunning realization: Her meta-self is completely comfortable with the vast sorrow and rage flowing through her heart. The meta-self has come here to answer the cries of living things, and to it the thought of answering is not a burden, but a thrill. The thought is so strange that Diana gives a gasp of strained laughter.

The boar is on her feet now, like a sports fan watching a close game. "You're doing so well, my piglet!" she crows. "One more step, now! Just one more!!"

The Fourth Task ... the Fourth Task ... touch nature ... let my heart ... connect with all hearts ... Diana puts both her hands and feet on the bare earth beside her sleeping bag. From her ravaged chest she sends a bolt of energy out in all directions. Almost instantly, the answer comes, from an infinite distance all around her, that vast, incomprehensible love. She's held back the tears so far, but now she begins to sob uncontrollably. The heart of the universe hears every cry of suffering, and loves every sufferer, and is sending help. Sending Diana to help.

"Me?" she sobs. "But why? How? What can I do?"

"You know," says Herself. "Just listen, Diana. Listen to yourself."

Diana tries. All she can hear is the Furies, their volume deafening: *You're weak! You're powerless! There's nothing you can do!*

"So close, my angel!" says the boar. "The Fifth Task is right in front of you!"

"What is it?" Diana screams. "What do you *mean*?"

"Oh, my dear," says Herself, sounding almost distressed. "I can't tell you. You must teach yourself. But you left yourself a clue. Remember, Diana! Remember!"

Suddenly, through the tempest in Diana's mind, a memory rises. She's sitting in her old Hyundai, in the parking lot of the Super Big Mart. It's dark outside. She was fired this morning, and then apparently had one hell of a fugue state. Weak with relief to be in her familiar car, Diana glances over her shoulder to back out of the parking spot. She frowns. Drawn in clear lines on the dusty rear windshield is a line of strange symbols: vòtuɒꞱꝺ ꞁθῶvy."

"What the *hell*?" Now, in the field of fresh blue flowers, Diana clamps her arms even more tightly around her chest and squints at the boar. "What does that have to do with anything?"

"Think!" says the boar. "Think it through, Diana! Remember!"

In her mind's eye, Diana stares at the symbols on her windshield. Something about them feels vaguely familiar. She follows the memory backward, a single bright thread, thin as a spider's web. It's earlier. Morning. She's walking out of Super Big Mart, Buck Guss-man's parting words still ringing in her ears. The cheap fabric of her khakis grates against her legs. She hears the blaring of the car alarm, then feels herself sliding into apathy, giving up . . .

And now the memory turns strange, like an overexposed film, filled with too much light and electricity for Diana to see it clearly. She feels the *other* take over her body, as it does when she holds her bow. The body reaches the Hyundai, opens the door, puts her purse inside, shuts the door, locks it. It walks to the back windshield, pauses for a minute, and writes in the dust: γνῶθι σεαυτόν. Then the *other* Diana turns, pockets the car keys, and runs. She runs like a deer set free from a dungeon.

"What does it mean, Myself?" Now she's in the car again, at night, staring at the writing on the rear windshield. The message might as well be from space aliens.

"Think, piglet, think! When you see it from inside the car . . ."

"Oh! I saw it backward!" says Diana. "I was inside the glass, so it was flipped."

"And to see it correctly . . . ?" Herself can barely contain her excitement.

Diana remembers driving home, exhausted, looking in the rear-view— "Oh! To see it correctly I had to look in the mirror!"

"Yes! Yes! That's it, piglet! Oh, well done!"

"Wait, what? I still don't understand." But Diana feels her mind gaining some sort of traction, as if, somewhere inside her, she's approaching an answer she's known all along. γνῶθι σεαυτόν. She almost, *almost* remembers what it means. What language is it, any-way? Russian? Arabic?

"All suffering is through a glass darkly," Herself says. "The mirror image of suffering is the truth. Try it. Change the story. Change the course of your entire history. Right now."

"You want me to lie about my past?" Diana wipes tears from her face with the back of her hand.

"No, to tell the story a truer way," says Herself. "Any story can be told infinite ways, dear, but listen to me. Listen well. If a story lib-erates your soul, believe it. But if a story imprisons you, believe its mirror image. That is the Fifth Task."

Diana feels a rush of warm prickles in her solar plexus, and knows this was the message her *other* tried to send by writing on the dusty glass.

But she doesn't have time to think about it, because another incredibly vivid, dagger-sharp memory cuts suddenly into her awareness.

It's the week after she tried to save the chipmunk. Her four-year-old eyes are watching her parents, her universe, walk away. She feels her own small hand clench in the sweating palm of a sad social worker.

Diana's eyes open wide. "Oh, no, Myself. Oh, please, no. Please don't make me go there!"

"But you *are* there, my love. This is the story in which you live."

"No, no, no, no, no . . ." Diana begins to keen as the first memory gives way to a cascade of others, in varying shades of unbearable. The Eichenwalds, her first foster parents, teaching her to count blackjack cards, returning her to the agency after she ran away from the casino where they took her to gamble. Her next parents, the Mantons, screaming and throwing things at each other, until Diana became so petrified she lost her ability to speak. They took her back after a week, agreeing aloud that she was retarded, unfixable. Then Mrs. Grover, whose teenage son was the first of Diana's many molesters, and who sent her to bed, dinner unfinished, if she didn't smile all the way through the meal.

"*Stop it! Stop!*" Diana tries to shout, but it comes out as a whisper. Her throat is closing, as if a giant hand is slowly throttling her.

And now there are one, two, three, a dozen teachers talking. Saying, in front of countless other children, that Diana is lazy, undisciplined, not working up to her potential. Now those other kids, the ones with real parents and real homes, are tormenting, taunting, beating her. Here is the man who talked her into quitting school when she was fourteen, pushing her down onto his grimy bed. Here is the numbness she wore ever after that, like a shroud.

"I can't breathe, Myself!" Diana gasps. The stranglehold around her neck closes tighter and tighter. "This is killing me! People are killing me! I hate people! *OOWW—*" Her gut cramps so hard she lets out another scream, which is cut off by the constriction in her throat.

"Well, my sweet love, that's one way to tell your story."

"I only have one story, Myself! AAGH!"

Herself looks at her evenly. "Not true, Diana. Use language to free and wild yourself, not keep yourself tame and in bondage. Tell me what hurts worst, love. The very worst story of all."

Diana can barely see the boar through her tears. She's sobbing so hard it takes a long time to speak, and when she finally does, her voice comes as a thin wail. "I wasn't good enough to have parents!" She pulls in a hoarse sob. "They all just left me, because I'm a stupid, ugly piece of garbage!" She can hardly breathe through the pain in her gut.

"Quite a story, darling," says the boar. "Tell me, does it set you free?"

"Are you crazy?" Diana snuffles. "Of course not!"

"Well, dear, the truth sets you free. That's how you can recognize it. So try the mirror of that story. Its opposite."

"I don't understand."

"Here, darling, I'll walk you through it. First thought: 'I wasn't good enough to have parents.' Does it feel like freedom?"

"No."

"Then tell me the mirror opposite, please."

Diana's tears slow as her brow furrows with concentration. "Umm . . . let me think . . . I was . . . uh . . . *too good* . . . to have parents?"

"*Hoinkhoinkhoinkhoinkhoink!* How do you like that one? How does it feel?"

"It's nonsense," says Diana. "Ridiculous. Stupid. *Ow.*" She grabs her stomach.

"According to your gut, dear, your mind is lying to you. So let's ask your gut this time around: How does it *feel* to think you were too good to have parents?"

A minute's silence. Then, "Huh," says Diana. The constrictions around her gut, her heart, and her throat have all loosened. "I feel sort of . . . lighter."

"Well done, piggly-wiggly! Just notice that. Let's move on. 'They all just left me because I'm a stupid, ugly piece of garbage!' Tell me the mirror-story."

Now that she can breathe more freely, Diana finds it easier to think. Still, the Task is so awkward she finds herself drawing a blank.

"Try switching 'them' for 'you' and 'you' for 'them,'" says the boar. "Remember, mirrors reverse everything."

"Uh, okay." Another minute of silence. "I, um, I left all of *them*? No, that's not right. Ow!"

"As I recall," says the boar casually, "you ran away rather often."

After a moment's silence, Diana's mouth drops open. "Oh, my God, you're right! I did! I left all of them! All the time!"

"Yes, love. And why? What's the opposite of a stupid, ugly piece of garbage?"

"Let's see, I don't know . . . um . . . a smart—"

"Try brilliant."

Diana laughs. "A brilliant, pretty—"

"Beautiful."

"A brilliant, beautiful piece of . . . um . . ."

"Let's say 'treasure.'"

"Treasure?" Diana can't stop laughing, a silly, guilty laugh like the ones that used to bubble up when one of her families made her go to church.

Herself beams. "Wonderful, piglet! I like this story! You left all of them, because you are a brilliant, beautiful piece of treasure. Also, in many cases, because they were stupid, ugly pieces of garbage. I'm only referring to their meat-selves, of course, and only at their worst moments. But still."

Diana giggles harder, and Herself joins in. Then Diana goes suddenly silent. "Myself," she says. "Listen! Something's happening." She bows her head, her gaze turning inward. In her mind the Furies are as loud as ever. But their voices are changing. Clarifying. Not shrieking now, but singing, a chord that slowly, astonishingly resolves into something piercingly sweet. Diana can hear new words, the mirrors of everything the Furies have always said.

"You're weak" has become *"You're strong."*

"You're powerless" is now *"You're powerful."*

And *"There's nothing you can do"* transforms itself into . . .

"Oh, my God." Diana isn't crying any more. All tension has left her body. She's looking at the boar in amazement, as if she's just seen an object fall upward.

"Yes, piglet?"

"There's nothing I can't do," Diana whispers. She is stunned, gob-smacked, amazed by the music in her mind. "I mean it, Myself. There is *nothing* I can't do."

"And there it is." The boar leans over and kisses her very gently on the cheek. "Welcome home to the truth, Diana. Welcome to reality."

For the first time, Diana leans forward and closes her arms around the huge, bristly neck. "I love you, Myself," she says.

"And I love you, too, my baby. My own."

For a long time they stay there, as Diana looks out at the still water and sees every thought in her mind in the clear mirror of the Fifth Task. With each thought, she grows freer and freer, the bond between her and the boar stronger and stronger. Every fear becomes courage, every sorrow, kindness. One by one, Diana begins to lift all her mind's burdens, hold them by a thinning string, release them and watch them fall upward from the field of blue, blue flowers into the blue, blue sky.

REASON

All day, as she integrates the Fifth Task, Diana feels pulled to the little lake, miles away in the deep forest. The sensation reminds her of the way she first felt drawn to Roy, and with some surprise she realizes she hasn't missed him much for several days. Her love for him is still steady; she's just stopped worrying. The reason, clearly, is the Fifth Task. As every story reverses, the thought, "He's in danger," has become, "He's safe." There's no evidence either way, but Diana notices that the frightening story causes physical and emotional pain, so she chooses to believe the second. For now, anyway.

When she and Herself set out for the lake, Diana follows habit by sitting down to don her boots. But when she pulls one on, she feels as if she's gone half blind. She takes off the boot, ties it to its mate by the laces, and loops them around her backpack. In addition to the boots, she carries her sleeping bag, bow, and arrows. The boar volunteers to take the backpack, which contains a few articles of clothing, a considerable amount of foraged food, and (to Diana's faint alarm) Cloyd.

"She'll be fine in there," Herself insists when Diana realizes the snake has been napping inside the backpack. "It would be an awfully long slither to the lake—*hoink hoink!*—and as I told you, we need her. She's an allegorical necessity."

"An allegor— Myself, that is just not *normal!*"

The boar's bright, tiny eyes fix on Diana. "Normal? Really, piglet? That's what you're going for here?"

Diana pauses, sighs, shrugs, and starts hiking.

They've been on the move for an hour before it occurs to Diana that she doesn't know how to get to the lake. She remembers the general direction, but she's been there only in the dark, and in a decidedly altered state. Before asking Herself to navigate, she decides to try using the Tasks. Over the space of a few minutes she goes into a now-familiar state of deep interior silence. There she feels every part of herself functioning like a subtle compass. When she follows a very specific path, she feels healthy and eager. When she gives her mind to her meta-self, trading the thought *"I don't know exactly where I'm going"* for *"I know exactly where I'm going,"* she feels positively dragged forward. Her bare feet sense the ground like fingers reading Braille, seeming to know the way by themselves. It's an odd, almost terrifying, ultimately thrilling sensation.

After several hours, when Diana is beginning to wonder if she only imagined the lake, they emerge from a particularly dense oak thicket and there it is, glowing like an amethyst in the cool evening light. The lake—not much more than a large pond, really—occupies the bottom of a ravine between two steep, thickly forested slopes. The mountains, the sky, and the purple shadows of a few towering cloudbanks are perfectly reflected in its surface. The view is so stunning Diana gasps out loud, but when she tries to speak, no words come. Instead she raises her arms over her head and turns a full circle, a habit she's developed for coping when the splendor of the forest threatens to overwhelm her.

The boar takes the lead, and Diana follows her around the lakeshore, which smells deliciously of green reeds and fresh mud. She notices dozens of footprints at the fringe of the water—mainly deer and small creatures like raccoons and skunks. But one set of tracks makes her stop short. They're a bit like her own bare footprints, but much larger.

"What made those, Myself?"

The boar glances at the track. "What do you think, piglet? Figure it out."

"Considering how my life has been going lately," mutters Diana, "it's probably Sasquatch." Then she notices the marks of long claws digging in an inch ahead of the five huge toes. A moment later she sees a smaller set of matching footprints alongside the large ones. Suddenly, as if a light bulb has winked on, she knows that the tracks belong to a mother bear and her cub. In fact, she sees a vivid flash of them, lumbering down to the lake . . . but no, it's another mirror-lake, on another mountain. The day is hot, the white stones around them peppered with wildflowers. The music of the pipes . . . but then the image fades.

"It's a bear, isn't it, Myself? A bear and her baby?"

"Well tracked, dear heart!"

Diana cocks her head, studying the footprints. As she looks, she can feel the hearts of the two bears. This fills her with a strange surge of affection, so strong she feels herself tear up. The music starts again—a flute, a piccolo? Something high and strange. A surge of inexplicable happiness flows through her. *Arkteia*, she thinks. And then the vision and the word are gone.

She hears the boar squealing in triumph just ahead, and finds Herself standing near a thin, clear stream that trickles from a crack in a tumble of rocks. "Filtered through limestone!" says Herself. "Clean as a baby's conscience! Now we just have to find you someplace to sleep."

Not far from the spring they discover a large oak that has fallen against a cliff face. The tree's trunk leans at an angle, forming a broad ridgepole. The space beneath it is clean and dry.

"It's perfect!" says Diana, peering into the darkness under the log. She laughs. "Almost too perfect. It's like I designed it myself!"

The boar turns to look at her. "But you *did*, darling. Don't you realize that yet? This place—this whole forest—is what you *are*." She studies Diana's blank face and sighs. "Oh, well, you'll get it sooner or later. *Hoink hoink!*"

•

The first several days at the lake are the most peaceful of Diana's life. She and the boar don't talk much, just spend hours foraging and napping in companionable silence. Diana craves silence. She needs it to accommodate the changes inside her. It feels as if all the broken parts of her are realigning in a process as powerful as the shifting of glaciers and continents on a volatile planet. If you are lucky, beloved, something like this may have happened to you. Perhaps a teacher, a book, or an insight once upended your image of the world, opening you to new perceptions. If so, you know it requires your full attention to accomodate such a change, let alone understand it.

Diana is quite swept away by the heart-connection with everything around her—the mountains, the trees, the animals, the sky. The feeling seems to grow stronger by the hour. She sees some animals every day, but she feels many more, not as objects but as pools of emotion. The awareness of them silently watching her isn't frightening; Diana finds no malice in any of these wild hearts. They sometimes feel fear, occasionally a flicker of speculative hunger, but mainly benign curiosity about Diana and Herself. She can feel each creature feeling her feeling it, a loop of shared perception that flows like emotional heart-music, the silent soundtrack of the forest. Devin is there, too, always. His presence feels so real, she's genuinely surprised each time she looks around and doesn't see his meat-self standing beside her.

The drone note under all this heart-music is the continual activity of Diana's mind. She has far fewer thoughts now than before she began the Tasks, but she often hears the Furies singing just below her consciousness, their messages now full of hope and encouragement. Occasionally, the remnants of her old, painful internal monologues rise into awareness. As they do, Diana watches them transform into their mirror opposites: flip, flip, flip.

The thought "I've finally gone insane," a frequent flier through Diana's brain since childhood—and particularly since meeting Herself—turns and lands as "I've finally gone sane." When she thinks, "Roy doesn't love me," the thought flips to "Roy does love me." Just daring to frame this sentence makes Diana feel something close to rapture.

All these changes make the entire world look different to Diana, as if she's taken off a pair of smudged, dirty spectacles. Everything feels fresh and new, continuously changing. Every certainty wobbles and fades until it finally disappears. Into the empty space once occupied by her fears and regrets flows a stream of color, light, warmth, joy. She notices fewer and fewer thoughts, until there are hours when she has none at all.

"Myself," she says one day as they harvest a patch of chanterelle mushrooms. "I think I may be losing my mind."

She notices that there is no answering stab from her gut, and wonders if she should be concerned about that.

"I certainly hope so, dear," says Herself.

Before Diana can reply, something else grabs her attention. Footsteps. Not the scuttle and flick of a squirrel or fox, but a heavier, slower tread, almost like a human's. Diana's heart begins to pound, filling with a sensation very different from the melodious counterpoint of the forest at rest. Whatever is walking behind a nearby screen of scrub oak, its heart is not at peace. Diana feels it as a thick, hot rage. There's no language in it, but if there were, Diana thinks, it would be shouting just one word: *"Me! Me! Me!"*

She creeps into the brush, toward the footsteps. The boar comes up beside her, and Diana is amazed all over again by how silently the big animal can move. Diana goes down onto her hands and knees. A few feet farther into the brush, she sees them: two huge birds pacing slowly around each other, each as big as a beach ball, with thick, heavy legs and claws the size of Diana's hands.

"What the . . . ?" Diana whispers. "Are those turkeys?"

"Mm-hm," the boar replies. "Two fine big toms—gorgeous, aren't they? And there's no need to whisper, darling. They're in full warlust. They wouldn't notice if we started yodeling."

Diana gazes at the birds, understanding for the first time why her teachers always told her to use every crayon in the box to color Thanksgiving turkeys. The feathers are dark brown, but so iridescent that as the toms slowly circle each other, bright colors—fire-engine red, chrysanthemum yellow, leaf green, iris purple—flash from their puffed-up chests. Their naked heads are like candle drippings in blue, white, and scarlet. As Diana watches, both turkeys go into full display, fanning their huge banded tails, pushing their wings out-ward and downward to scrape the earth as they walk. Their beauty is amazing, the rage Diana feels in their hearts as arresting as an elec-tric shock.

One of the turkeys suddenly lunges at the other, shooting his neck out straight, wrapping it around the neck of his opponent, then jerk-ing backward. The other bird, head trapped, begins to kick wildly with the inch-long spurs on his ankles. Then, heads still locked, the toms begin to push at each other like sumo wrestlers, sending out grunting clucks of effort and rage.

"Wow," says Diana nervously. "They're serious, aren't they?"

"As a heart attack, my love," Herself says. "And it's working for them. As a species, I mean. It's kept their kind around for eleven mil-lion years. Such scrappy little dinosaurs! *Hoink hoink.*"

Diana remembers Devin telling her that the dinosaurs that sur-vived the great extinction looked a lot like turkeys. Images begin flickering in her head: the almighty staggering blow of a huge aster-oid, a sky filled with fire, the long dark night that lasted years before the ash cleared away. And death. Everywhere, on a monstrous, incon-ceivable scale, suffering and death. The images feel so real that Diana shudders. Devin must have dragged her to a movie about it.

One of the turkeys seems to be weakening. His rival has pushed him backward and downward until his tail has lodged under a bush. His naked skin pales to a sickly purple, and he writhes free, dipping his head submissively. The other tom comes on like a hurricane, pecking and clawing. The only feeling Diana can find in its heart is a deafening scream of *"ME! ME! ME!"* His beak catches his enemy full in the eye. The fleeing turkey screeches horribly and begins running in a disoriented, half-blind circle. The winner flares huge wings, flies overhead, and lands a spur-kick to the other eye.

Before Diana knows she's moving, her body is on its feet and half-way to the battling turkeys. She swings her bow at the winner, saying, "That's *enough!*" The bow catches the big tom by one wingtip. He tumbles to the ground, where he blinks for a moment as if emerging from a trance, then sprints off into the forest.

Diana turns to the other turkey, which is gabbling like a panicky old man as it stumbles blindly into branches and tree trunks, flapping its wings in a pain-maddened frenzy that fails to lift it into the air. Smoothly, Diana nocks an arrow and shoots the shrieking bird straight through the head. It drops dead without so much as a shiver. Less than five seconds have passed since Diana broke cover.

She stands still with her bow in her hand, great waves of energy pulsing in her solar plexus. A blizzard of images flashes through her mind—a million lethal shots bringing down a million creatures with a million weapons—even though this is the first time in her life that she's deliberately killed anything.

Herself trots up to stand beside Diana. "Oh, heavens," she says. "It's all fun and games until somebody loses an eye, right?"

Diana slowly slings her bow over her left shoulder. "I couldn't think of anything else to do," she says. "He was suffering, and a blind animal can't live long. Why did the other one need to keep going after him like that? He'd already won. This guy was just trying to get away."

"War-lust." Herself twitches her ears. "It's rarely logical, darling, and never fair. Genghis Khan used to say there was nothing he enjoyed more than hearing the screams of a woman he was raping after he'd killed her family in front of her."

Diana recoils. "Sheesh, Myself! Did you have to tell me that?"

"Well, you've got Genghis's blood in your own veins, you know."

"*What?*"

"Oh, yes. Exactly the average amount. *Hoink hoink!* Which is quite a bit, really. One of every two hundred people on Earth is descended from Genghis Khan. Murder and rape are such wonderfully successful strategies."

Diana stares at her. "No, they aren't, Myself! They mean people get murdered and raped!"

"Ah, well." The boar nods. "There is that."

Diana walks over to the dead turkey. "I'm so sorry," she tells it. "I should have done something sooner. Broken things up before you got hurt."

"If you had, this bird might have lived a bit longer—a week, a year." Herself walks up to lean comfortingly against Diana's leg. "Maybe he would have killed a few more rivals, maybe the next one would have killed him. He died as he lived, love. A warrior. And you saved him a good deal of pain at the end."

Diana leans down and pulls her arrow out of the turkey's head, amazed at the difference her heart feels between the living bird and this inanimate carcass. "As long as he's dead, I should probably . . . you know . . . I mean, it would be a pity to waste . . ." She's chagrinned to feel her mouth watering at the thought of a turkey dinner. "Except I'd need to cook him, and I can't make fire without matches. Ouch!" She rubs her gut as the thought flips in her mind. "All right, so I *can* make fire without matches. Theoretically. But I've never done it before."

The boar cocks her head. "Are you or are you not the same piglet who has watched Roy Richards demonstrating primitive fire-making techniques for approximately two hundred hours?"

Diana blushes. "You know about that?"

"You have to ask?"

"Oy," says Diana. Embarrassment surges through in her mind (*"I'm such an idiot!"*), then immediately reverses itself (*"I'm such a genius!"*). This thought makes Diana giggle. "Genius" is stretching it, for sure. Or is it? After all, she did end up becoming Roy's . . . sort of . . . girlfriend. She turns to the boar. "Well, if you were watching with me, *you* must know how to make a fire. Hey, that's an idea! Why don't you do it?"

"Darling." Herself lifts a front trotter. "Once again, the thumb thing becomes an issue."

Diana sighs. "Well, talk me through it, then. That's the least you can do."

"No, it isn't. I can do ever so much less. *Hoink!*"

"Oh, come on, Myself!" Diana laughs. "Please? Pretty please?"

The boar chuckles. "Angel, you know I'd help you if I could. But you see, you've arrived."

"Arrived?" Diana looks around at the endless forest.

"At the Sixth Task."

"Oh!" Diana blinks. "Wow! The Sixth Task is making fire?"

"No, sweetheart. The Sixth Task is learning to let the meta-self use your mind, as you have learned to let it use your body and heart."

Diana's eyes narrow. "That sounds dangerous."

"How so, piglet?"

"You want me to let some . . . some sort of entity control my *mind*?"

"Well, love, what do you think usually controls it?

"*I* do! Of course!"

"*Hoinkhoinkhoinkhoinkhoinkhoinkhoink—*"

"What are you laughing at?"

"Oh, my." Herself blinks away tears of mirth. "It's just so adorable that you humans think you control your own minds."

"What do you mean? If I don't control my mind, who does?"

The boar beams at her. "Diana, darling, until recently *everybody* but you controlled it. That's the whole point of being tame, you see. Civilized. It puts others in control of your mind so that you won't stray outside the lines of group-think."

"In case you haven't noticed, I've never been much of a group-think person, Myself. I'm a nonconformist. Ow!"

The boar laughs again. "Sweetheart, your whole life, you've been worrying nonstop about what others think, how you'll look to them, what will or won't get you into trouble. Authority figures told you how to act. Magazines told you how to dress. Advertising told you what to want. The people you loved—and even more, the people you feared—shaped almost every thought you've ever had."

Diana is silent for some time, taking this in. As much as she'd like to reject them, the boar's words resonate cleanly in her heart and gut. With them comes a deep sadness, a longing she can't quite name.

"You are homesick for your real mind, sweet child," says the boar. "For the mind of your meta-self, which is beyond all fear and shame. Why not give it a chance to operate? See what happens."

The boar's words have that strange seductiveness Diana has felt ever since she first heard of the Tasks. The pull is so strong that Diana reflexively thinks, *"This can't be right."* She flips it immediately to *"This can't be wrong."*

"So, supposing I decide to, um, let my meta-self, like, drive my brain," she says. "How do I do that?"

"Oh, I'm so glad you asked!" Herself gives a little squeal of pleasure. "Think of your brain as a computer, darling. That's what it really is, anyway—or better said, computers are just clumsy imitations of human brains."

"Okay," says Diana. "So, that fascinating advice doesn't help. At all."

"Wait for it, my pigling, wait for it." The boar's ears twitch happily. "You know how you type a command into a computer and then hit 'Enter'?"

"Yeah, so?"

"Just form an intention, Diana. A clear purpose. That's how you type in a command."

"Okay, I get it," says Diana. "An intention. Umm . . . I want to make a fire."

"Excellent. Hold that thought clearly. Picture it happening."

"All right." Diana closes her eyes and sees dozens of images of Roy, on YouTube and television, making fire over and over again. Then she imagines that she and Roy have switched places, that she's the one coaxing flames into life.

"Now, this is the tricky part," says the boar. "Allow the intention to drop away. Let go of your mind."

"Let go of my mind?" Diana opens one eye to peer at Herself.

"You do it every day, love," says the boar. "You just don't notice it. It happens when you're driving in a place you know well, or doing the dishes, or falling asleep. Recently you've been dropping into it naturally, walking around in the forest. Just be here—really be here, with all five senses and no thought of anywhere else—and then let your meta-self move you. It's the same technique as shooting your bow, only for this you must be even calmer. Quieter."

Diana slows her breathing. She focuses on the first five Tasks, in order. The familiar rush of warmth twines up her legs, winds its way through her viscera, fills her heart, relaxes her throat. Her eyes open by themselves. Her head turns. She could stop the movements if she wanted, but before she can, the boar speaks.

"Allow," says Herself. "That's it, Diana. Just allow."

Diana's eyesight seems sharper than usual. Her gaze shifts and scans, finally lighting on a broken branch that hangs by a tendon of bark from a nearby tree. A memory flares: Roy picking a similar branch in a video, saying, "This is good and dry. That's what we need."

She watches her body go to the branch and break it from the tree. She feels languid, detached, very, very still. Just as she's learned to watch her body shoot the bow, she watches her mind calculating, remembering, computing. Her eyes search the ground and find a longer, thinner dead stick. She picks it up. Then she goes back to the dead turkey, hefts it by its legs, and carries it, along with her fire-making sticks, back to her camp. Herself trots joyfully beside her, emitting small grunts of pleasure.

The next several hours are some of the strangest of Diana's life. Each time she decides she knows what to do, her normal mind-state returns and she fails spectacularly to make fire. Each time she goes into the strange, profound calm that is deeper than thought, her brain hums into action, and she—or rather, her meta-self—figures out what to do.

The first time this happens is when she tries to split the dead branch down the center with her Swiss Army knife to make a fireboard. She succeeds only in cutting her fingers. The wounds aren't bad, but they could be, and Diana is chastened. She calms herself, runs through the first five Tasks, returns to the stillness deeper than thought.

This time she feels a strange *sifting* sensation in her head, as if something is riffling through every book in a vast library, looking for just the right page. An image appears: Roy setting a branch on end, positioning his knife on the other end, and hammering the blade into the wood with a rock. Diana watches her body repeat the procedure. It works perfectly giving her a flat, dry wooden surface.

This small victory produces a sense of triumph that encourages Diana so much she resumes controlling her own mind. After all, she knows just what comes next. She sets the point of her long stick against the flat inner surface of the fireboard and begins twirling it between her hands. Her muscles tire quickly and her palms begin to chafe. But she's rewarded by a tiny wisp of smoke rising from the board. "Yes!" she whispers, and twirls harder.

Forty minutes later, Diana's hands are limp and blistered. The fireboard is speckled with small, black indentations. The point of her long stick is a shiny knob. She has succeeded in producing many wisps of smoke. And nothing else.

She glances at the boar, who's lying on her back under a tree, all four legs in the air. "I know, I know," says Diana irritably.

The boar peers at her. "Did I say anything?"

"No, but you were thinking it. Meta-self, allow allow, blah blah blah."

The boar *hoinks* softly as Diana takes another deep breath, lets the first five Tasks run through her, and feels the library in her head open up again. This time she stays quiet for a long time, eyes closed. Not trying. Not thinking. She finds herself imagining her bow, an arrow nocked on the string. As she watches, the arrow twists so that the string is wrapped around it. The bow begins to move back and forth. The arrow twirls.

Diana's eyes pop open. There is no thought in her mind, just the watching. She feels . . . alert. Simply alert.

She observes as her body finds another stick, this one green and springy. Using a cord from the hood of her jacket as a string, she turns the stick into a small bow. Then she plants her foot on the fireboard, twists her firestick into the string of the little bow, and sets the tip of the stick into one of the fireboard's small black divots.

At that point Diana realizes she has nothing to hold the upper tip of the stick in place. She intends to find something, closes her eyes, lets go of the thought. Almost immediately her memory produces an image of Roy making a different fire, this time using a bow drill like the one she's just fashioned. Ah, now she sees: He's using a small stone to hold the upper end of a firestick in place. It takes a few minutes to find a stone she knows will work, one that's just the right size for her hand, with a small dent in one side. Then she watches her body kneel, step on the fireboard, set the firestick in position, and hold it in place with the stone in one hand and the little bow in the other.

It takes another hour of practice before Diana learns how to move the bow. She frequently succumbs to frustration, causing the entire architecture of her fire-making apparatus to collapse. But she can feel success coming. More than that, she can feel the increasingly thrilling sense of the meta-self operating her brain. Other scenes flicker through her mind: making fire with a stick, a mouth-grip, and a strap of walrus leather. With a firestone and dry moss. With animal dung and a stored coal.

Her meta-self, Diana realizes, is far, far more intelligent than her usual thinking. If it's like a computer, it has access to the Cloud, to truths from all times and places. As the afternoon cools to evening, this endless intelligence pops several fully formed ideas into Diana's awareness. She'll need kindling—of course, kindling! The boar cheerfully agrees to collect some dry moss and twigs. Then Diana finds her body carefully pushing together the hot black wood-dust from which the wisps of smoke arise. The word for the clump of smoking dust floats out of some obscure storage compartment in Diana's brain, where it's been waiting, never used: ember.

The sky has dimmed to a deep purple overhead when Diana, not thinking, not doing, watches her arm move the bow quickly and smoothly, twirling the firestick against the board until a smoking ember accumulates. As she tips the ember into a handful of dry moss, another, more familiar word pops into her mind: oxygen. She lifts the bundle of kindling and blows into it. Thick smoke pours from the moss, making her cough. She draws a huge breath and blows into the ember again, once, twice, three times. Suddenly the kindling flashes into orange flame, setting fire to a few stray strands of Diana's hair.

"WOOOOOO-HOOOOO!" she shouts into the purple night. The boar comes running to look, bouncing around like a puppy as Diana sets the ember in a nest of dry twigs, extinguishes her smoldering wisps of hair, and fans the fire with one hand.

"Well done, darling, oh well *done!*" The boar's eyes shine in the firelight.

"No shit, pig!" Diana laughs out loud. Her hands are charred and bleeding, her muscles drained, her face grimy with smoke and sweat. She has never felt so alive.

"I'm like that dude . . . what's his name . . . Promiscuous?" Diana lets go of her mind, and the right word pops in. "Prometheus!" She laughs again, falling backward onto the cool ground, dizzy with joy and exhaustion. "My brain feels like hamburger," she says. And then, "Man, I would love a hamburger! Or a turkey burger." Her mouth waters, but she's so tired she can barely move.

"No worries, piglet," Herself says. "You can cook the turkey tomorrow. It'll keep. I'd say grasping the Sixth Task is enough accomplishment for today."

"Yeah," sighs Diana happily. "But you know what, Myself? I'm starting to feel like I really can do anything. I mean *anything.*"

"The human mind," sighs Myself. "It's such a wonderful servant, Diana. And such a terrible master. Just think: This power, the power of mind, is being used by billions of humans who still think like turkeys—grab, fight, win, breed, repeat."

Diana contemplates this, staring into the purple sky. The turkey battle seems long ago, but she shivers again as she remembers their hell-bent, murderous, silent scream of *"ME! ME! ME!"*

"That's the energy," says Herself, nodding. "The energy that's driven human history as you know it. Whoever dies with the most dead enemies wins. Hurray."

Diana doesn't answer. She stares upward, watching the orange light play against the underside of leaves and branches, observing her mind.

"So if I set my intention and let go, I can solve any problem?" she asks.

"If your intention is true," says the boar. "If it comes from a foundation in the first five Tasks."

"Then I set my intention to help," says Diana. Her heart seems to open even wider at the thought. "To help living things on this planet. To help the babies. To answer the cries."

"Well said, my noble piglet," says the boar. "Now let your mind go."

She does, watching her own thoughts through a veil of drowsiness, feeling her brain search its database for everything it knows, everything it can use. As she falls asleep, she finds her mind remembering the dinosaurs.

The fire they saw in the sky.

The long winter of ash.

The end of everything.

EMPATHY

Exhausted by fire-making, Diana sleeps until the sun is high over-head. When she finally wakes up, brimming with plans, she goes straight into action. First she skins the dead turkey and cuts the meat off the bones. She expects this to be difficult, but her new Sixth-Task skills make it almost automatic. Once she gives the *other* access to her mind, she vividly recalls an instructional video in which Roy, artifi-cially stranded in the far north, skinned and dressed a seagull. She also remembers all the times she and Devin helped cook Thanksgiv-ing and Christmas dinners at homeless shelters—her way of making sure that Devin always had abundant holiday cheer and lots of com-pany, even when they were flat broke.

At the shelters, they always made soup from the turkey giblets, livers, and hearts, so Diana cuts those organs free. Roy, she recalls, always ate the heart of every animal he killed. He said it was a tribute to the creature's life, and also that his old friends in this or that tribe believed eating the heart allowed him to absorb the animal's essence. She remembers him popping the raw rabbit's heart into his mouth on their first day in the Sierras Oscuras, how her stomach lurched just filming the gore. Now, wrist deep in blood, she wonders what she's become. First the deer's raw liver, now this. It's as if the life she recalled before coming here was lived by another person.

"Time for a fire pit!" says Herself as Diana finishes dressing the turkey. "We'll put it right"—she moves back and forth under the huge tree, glancing upward—"right *here*." She begins rooting vigorously with her snout, carving out a depression in the soil. "You go get some rocks to line the pit, piglet. We're going to give you a proper home and hearth!"

The boar digs like a small bulldozer until she's created a good-sized pit, which Diana lines with rocks. Then Herself sets out, empty backpack dangling from one tusk, to gather firewood and greens. Diana gets out her fire-making tools. After a few hours of false starts and a great many repetitions of all six Tasks, she's rewarded with that orange Promethean flare. By the time Herself returns, carrying the backpack stuffed with sticks, herbs, and mushrooms, the sun is setting and slabs of turkey meat are cooking on flat rocks around a hearty campfire.

"Ooh, look what you've done!" squeals the boar. "How wonderful! I found some delectable treats. Let's tuck them into the coals—they'll be delicious roasted."

Diana pokes the bulbs into the coals with a long stick. "It's so true, what Roy always says," she says, flipping a slice of turkey. "Campfires are so *cheerful*."

She and the boar sing for a while, waiting for the food to cook, as dusk turns to dark. Diana never went to camp, so there are no renditions of "Kumbaya." Instead she sings classic rock, mainly the Beatles. The boar harmonizes in her deep contralto and knows absolutely all the words. To Diana, they sound pretty damn good.

After a while, the smells rising with the smoke are so appetizing Diana thinks she may actually swoon. She forces herself to wait until the turkey has browned through and the bulbs feel soft when poked with a stick. Then she wraps a cooked bulb and some mushrooms in a strip of turkey meat, rolls it up, and takes a bite.

"Oh, sweet mother of God," she says reverently. "Myself, taste this."

"No thank you, darling. I prefer my food raw. You go ahead and eat."

So Diana does. She eats like she's never eaten in her life. She eats until she's full, then a bit more. Then another couple of bites. She's almost forgotten what it feels like to be overfed. It makes her extremely sleepy. Her eyes droop shut as she changes into one of Roy's old T-shirts and snuggles into her sleeping bag. A twinge of heart-recognition tells her that Cloyd is down below her feet, already asleep. For some reason, this doesn't bother Diana much. She knows how to keep the snake calm, and she herself is so, so, *so* relaxed.

"Will you watch the fire, Myself?" Diana yawns. It comes out "Wi' oo wash th'furrr?" She rolls onto her back and lets her eyes follow the lazy curls of smoke rising from the fire. Beyond the ridgepole of the dead tree, the Milky Way sprawls like a wash of diamonds.

"Loo, M'sel'! There'z th' Big Dipper."

"You mean Ursa Major?" says the boar. "That's what the old ones called it, you know, dear." She gazes at the constellation. "The Great Bear, Arktos of the north, and her cub, Polaris. Ursa Minor. See him? His tail is the North Star."

Diana feels the same odd affection that accompanied her sighting the bear tracks the day before, and sends up a silent greeting to Arktos and her cub. Then she frowns and cocks her head. "M'sel'?"

"Yes, piglet?"

"Why're the starzz . . . moving?"

"Are they?"

Diana giggles. "Yeah. Movin' in li'l circles. An' they got tails. I like that word." Another giggle. "Tailzzzzzzzz. Oh, wow, M'sel'! You're all pretty!"

In the firelight the boar's eyes are chips of obsidian, sparked with highlights of orange. Everything else about her looks as if she's been wallpapered. Stripes and florets, in tasteful shades of purple and blue, move across her snout. A memory floats up into Diana's mind: a cheap apartment in LA, a boyfriend who had a lot of unmarked bills and a thriving garden inside his bedroom closet.

"M'sel'?"

"Mm-hmm?"

"Wha' kinda mushroo'm di' you gimme?"

"I believe they're called *Psilocybe ovoideocystidiata,* darling."

"Sill-o-sibe . . ." Diana tries to concentrate, distracted by the tiny, pulsating rainbows connecting the stars. Her mouth feels strangely clumsy. "Sill-o-sibe . . . oh, no way, M'sel'! You DRUGGED me? You dru'd me wiv magi' MUFROOMS?"

"Not precisely, sweetheart."

"No' precishely? Whad'zat mean?"

"Precisely speaking, I also gave you a large dose of valerian. It's very calming, dear. They make Valium from it. A nice entrée into the Seventh Task."

Diana's jaw drops. "The Sheventsh Tashk?" she says. "Whadizzit?"

"The Seventh Task, my love, is to release your identification with your meat-self. Completely."

Diana thinks hard about this, and concludes that she should be afraid, very afraid. Her heart attempts to speed up, but can't. It feels like an elephant trying to jump. "Didju poison me, M'sel'?" Diana says sadly. "Am I gonna die now?"

"Oh, my angel, of course not! *Hoink hoink hoink!* It's just that this Task is very difficult for humans. It might take you months of meditation on your own—years. So the plants and fungi like to help speed things up. It's one of their favorite things."

Diana gazes at Herself's bristles, which are laced with twinkling fairy lights that move in delicate patterns, leaving phosphorescent trails. "Bu', bu', but M'sel' . . ." Her brow furrows in concentration. "Drugs're *bad,* aren' they?"

"The way you've used them before, yes," says Herself. "It's so ironic. Tame humans are obsessed with drugging themselves—medically, recreationally, any way you can. Yet you've lost the plant wisdom of your ancestors. I wouldn't recommend you try this on your own, Diana. I'm only engineering a connection with some friends whom you might otherwise . . . well, let's just say it might take you a while to get past your differences."

The boar gets up, trots to the shadows at the edge of the firelight, and comes back with a green bough. She drops it on the fire and pushes it carefully over the hottest coals. Thick smoke billows up to the fallen oak.

"Whacha doin', M'sel'?" Diana's body is vibrating subtly, like a struck bell.

"Just arranging the meeting," says Herself. She peers upward at a cavity in the dead tree, then moves the smoking boughs a few inches to the left.

As Diana closes her eyes and begins to drift away, something lands on her chest—a leaf, perhaps, or an acorn. She's too relaxed to care. Then she feels another tiny impact. And another. She opens her eyes and sees three honeybees on her sleeping bag, over her heart. One is trying clumsily to stand up. The others just lie there. As Diana watches, a fourth bee falls. Then a fifth. Once again Diana considers panicking. She can't.

"Hey, M'sel'," she says cheerfully. "There'z bees fallin' on me. It'sh kinda gross. Ha ha!" She looks up. The hole in the dead tree is almost masked by smoke. Bees are dropping through it like tiny paratroopers.

"Don't worry, piglet," says Herself. "Their hive is up there in the tree. The smoke is making them groggy, but no harm will come to them."

"I'm no' worried 'bout *them*," Diana says. "'R' they gon' shting me?"

"*Hoink hoink!* No, darling. Don't even think about them, for now. Just go through all the Tasks."

This proves surprisingly easy. Diana is fairly sure she couldn't stand up for love or money, but she has no trouble falling into peace and letting her meta-self fill her body and mind. To her surprise, she is suddenly quite fond of the small creatures that continue to land all over her. Her heart welcomes them like long-lost family. She laughs, jostling the bees on her abdomen. "Thiz iz so *weir'*, M'sel'. They're, like, li'l tiny *friends*."

"*Hoink!* If you think it's odd that you feel drawn to them," says Herself, "you should try getting a hive of bees to drop *their* aversion to *you*. Anything without an exoskeleton repels them. They call vertebrates 'guts on sticks.' And humans—well . . ." She clucks her tongue. "No offense, but you don't even have fur."

"Oh," says Diana, suddenly shy. "Bu' you made 'em like me? Th' beeezz?"

"We're getting there," says Herself. "Why don't you sing with them?"

Diana scowls, but after a moment's thought finds this advice oddly compelling. The bees are buzzing loudly, and Diana begins to hum at the same pitch. The bell-like vibration of her body increases, every cell tingling, a delicious full-body massage. After a minute of this, Diana realizes that as well as singing, the bees are also laughing. Their laughter isn't mockery or even amusement; it's surprise, playfulness, and joy. But above all, it is *shared*.

"D' they think 'm funny?" Diana asks Herself.

"They think you're colossally strange," the boar replies. "They're a bit nervous, being so near a vertebrate, but they're relaxing. There's something about you they like."

"That's goo', M'sel'," murmurs Diana. "Cause Ah like 'em, too. Ah rilly do. Ah dunno why, tha's jus' the way i' izzzzzzzzzz."

"Keep singing, dear," says Herself.

So Diana does, for what seems like a long while—she can't tell, because her sense of time is disintegrating. At the moment it disappears entirely, Diana feels a wall of incomprehension collapse within her like a sand castle at high tide—and just like that, she can understand the bees. She feels how they feel, knows how they know, as a group, perception to perception. She understands the way ideas and intentions ripple through the entire colony like wind moving grass in a field, many independent little lives functioning as one.

"*This is so bizarre!*" the bees chorus, still laughing. "*Check this out: It can sing, but it has no wings! How can it sing with no wings?*"

Diana feels the power that shoots her bow pulling her shoulder blades back. They flex down, then forward, then back again.

"*No, there are simply no wings at all,*" say the bees, fascinated by the puzzle. "*And yet it does sing. How is it— Oh, good heavens, it's singing with its mouth parts!*" They laugh uproariously, their humming growing audibly louder. "*And it tastes with its mouth parts, too, instead the normal way, with its feet! How does it walk on things without tasting them? That doesn't seem safe. Good heavens, how does it eat? With its butt?*"

The bees' merriment is infectious, and Diana giggles, jostling laughing insects onto the forest floor. "Wha's happ'ng t'me, M'sel'?"

she says dreamily.

"You're entering a mystery school, dear." The boar gently rights a toppled bee with her snout. "An ancient and sacred one."

"A myshry shool?" Diana blinks. "I dunno wha tha' izzzz."

"Yes, love, hence the word 'mystery.' Just pay attention to our friends."

Strange, vivid images begin drifting upward into Diana's consciousness: Women dancing in skirts striped black and gold, their arms held up high. Children climbing trees, baskets strapped to their shoulders. A dark-skinned man with a blue bee painted on his forehead. They are all, she understands, part of the hive.

"It's all a song," she thinks. *"Everything is a song."* And then it dawns on her, with considerable force, that she's no longer human. She's something larger. Much, much larger. She can't imagine what it is, what it might look like. But she knows it includes the little creatures investigating her body.

"Well, hello, honey!" the bees exclaim, in emotion rather than words. *"Here you are! Welcome to Us. We find you very strange, but beautiful. In your way."*

"Thank you," Diana feels back.

"No offense, honey, but you are very abnormal," the bees feel. *"The way you sing with your mouth parts, instead of your wings. And taste with your mouth, instead of your feet. It is all so strange."*

Diana thinks of her body, a little self-consciously. The feeling of her cells vibrating intensifies. The bees react with great excitement.

"Oh, oh, oh!" they feel. *"Now we understand. You're a hive! You have many little parts, all working together—all for all, always. Just like us!"*

In one golden flash they send Diana a full comprehension of their hive, how they function as a unit, different individuals flowing seamlessly into the roles of nursemaid, guard, scout. Diana sees her body from their perspective: trillions of separate cells, each knowing its role, all of them communicating. She *is* a hive.

The bee-song lowers. *"Oh, honey, there's dissonance here,"* say the bees. *"Keep singing so we can repair it."* The buzz inside Diana intensifies until she feels like an amplifier at a rock concert. Any part of her body that's tense or tired quivers, sometimes violently, and then goes perfectly, slackly relaxed.

"Beautiful! Beautiful!" sing the bees. *"Now you are becoming more normal. You are a lovely hive, really. Very peculiar, but lovely."*

Then Diana senses a small commotion. She can feel mild shock in the bees, and sorrow. *"Oh, honey!"* they hum. *"The hive within you is better now, but we can't find the hive around you. You feel as if you are a hive of just one bee. One thing, without others like you to play and rest and share your being. So alone! So, so, so alone!"*

Tears well up in Diana's eyes.

"Well, I have Myself," she feels to the bees. *"I'm okay."*

"Oh, to have only one self! To call that enough, and never to belong with others of your own kind! No, no, honey. No one can live that way. It would be unbearable."

"You're right." There's no use lying to them. They feel Diana's emotions as strongly as she does herself. And there's no need to hide anything from them, because to these creatures, everything about her belongs. Even her vast differences belong. Even her sense of never belonging, belongs.

"I have people I love," she feels to them, thinking of Devin and Roy. *"And I live in a big city."* She remembers Los Angeles, the millions of cars, the crowded malls. But instead of calming down, the bees become deeply concerned.

"How strange, how terrible!" they feel. *"Almost all of you are out of resonance! You don't feel one another. Even living in such a huge swarm, you still feel alone."* The buzzing intensifies as the bees go to work on this problem. The thought of doing nothing about it never occurs to them. Diana is a part of them now, and so is everyone she loves. To help her is to help themselves.

"There is a way," they finally decide. *"We must make this one a Greatmother."*

Diana blinks drowsily. Her mind has no idea what to expect, but her *other* is as much bee as human, and because of that she knows something unusual is about to happen. Something remarkable.

"Piglet," says Herself, very softly. "Pay attention. Your destiny is unfolding."

The bees' humming intensifies until Diana feels swept into it, as if she's dissolved into nothing but sound waves. Even the thought of "I" vanishes.

A long time later she drifts back into consciousness. Bright daylight dapples the forest beyond her log. The smoky fire is almost out. The boar stands next to her.

"Sit up a little, darling," she says. "Drink." Diana's dented thermos stands beside her. She drinks eagerly. The water tastes gorgeously sweet.

"Is that honey?" she whispers, licking her lips.

"Not quite, love. Royal jelly. The food they give to a baby bee to make her a queen. They call it giving power to empathy. They have never fed a human this way, Diana. It is a great honor."

"Am I still on drugs?" Diana blinks. "Mushrooms and whatever?"

"No, no, my dear. Those left your system hours ago. The bees have entrained your brain into their frequency. The mystery is upon you."

"Myself?" she whispers. "Am I finally going crazy?"

"No, precious piglet," says the boar gently. "You're finally going wild."

"*Lie still, Greatmother,*" said the bees. "*Let us finish. You're not alone now. Never again alone. All for all, always.*"

"All for all, always," whispers Diana, and lets her consciousness disappear again into the song of the hive.

ULTRAVIOLET

For sixteen days and nights, the time it takes all bees to create a queen, the forest watches Diana and her insect friends with considerable interest. The forest has no real objection to human beings, but in general it finds them unpleasantly bizarre. The occasional hikers or hunters who pass through it are like encased geysers, their inner state churning, endlessly unsatisfied, never at peace. (This, beloved, is almost certainly the way you go about the world, and in places filled with other humans, it feels normal. But not good, beloved. It never feels truly good, does it?)

This bee-woman is different, the forest decides. Her energy is less like a boiling acidic geyser, more like a muddy brook after a heavy rain. And as the hive does its work, even that is changing. The remaining memories, traumas, and fears in Diana's mind diminish each day, each hour. Thought-forms that were once boulders become stones, then pebbles, then sand, then nothing. The woman's mind grows deeper, larger, more transparent, a broad river of awareness. One day even the river stops. Now Diana is like an ocean on a windless planet, still and clear.

With nothing to obstruct it, Diana's consciousness begins spreading outward, suffusing everything it encounters. Her usual thoughts are absent—even the memory of identity is gone. There is only love, mind, and awareness, thinly linked to a form made of flesh. The forest shivers with pleasure, realizing that this strange, naked animal, perhaps to compensate for her pathetic lack of instincts, can love it more than any single creature it has ever known. The forest has no defenses; it cannot help but love her in return.

On the seventeenth day, at the moment the bees finish their task, the difference between Diana and the forest disappears completely. Forever after, neither will be able to recall what it once was without the other.

One by one, the weary bees rise from Diana's slack body, flying up from the top of her head in a widening spiral, cheerfully returning to their usual duties as gatherers and guardians. As they leave, Diana's eyes finally flutter open.

•

Light. Light everywhere, coming from everything, shot through with rainbows. A brilliant color Diana has never seen before, like purple but more purple than purple, and dazzlingly bright. Diana's hands come up to cover her eyes.

"Welcome back, darling piglet."

Diana blinks several times. "Myself?" Her voice grates like a rusty hinge. "Myself, are you here?" She stares into the brilliant everywhere, searching.

"Oh, dear, you can't see me, can you?" says the boar. "*Hoink hoink!* Yes, it can be quite shocking to perceive more of the spectrum. I'll just dial it down a notch."

The light dims. Solid forms begin to coalesce out of it, becoming trees and rocks, soil and sky.

Diana laughs out loud. Still blinking a little, she looks around for the boar. "Myself? Where are you?"

"Hang on, I'm adjusting," says Herself's voice. A luminous cloud in the air next to Diana turns milky, then more and more opaque. Finally Diana is looking at the boar's familiar shape . . . almost. Flashes of light flicker out from Herself's bristles when she moves. Her ruff of mane emits beams of gold like a Byzantine icon's halo. Every few seconds, she disappears entirely for an infinitesimal beat.

"You're all flickery," says Diana.

"Still? Hmm. *Hoinkhoinkhoink.*" Herself chuckles. "I think this is the best I can do to appear to you as a meat-self, after what you've just been through." The boar inspects her trotters, which shoot out showers of sparks in response to her attention. "Oh, wait! I have an idea." The golden beams from her mane contract and brighten, gathering at her powerful shoulders. Gradually the light on each side redefines itself until Herself is sporting two small, luminous wings.

"*Hoink hoink HOINK hoink hoink!*" The boar chortles. "Say what you will about clichés, my love, they do get lots of human attention. Makes them manifest easily. Not a bad way to channel the energy, I think. So how d'you like me now, piglet? Which is to say, how do you like yourself?"

"You're amazing, Myself," whispers Diana. "Myself. Amazing."

"How are you feeling? Can you get up?"

Diana gazes blankly at the boar. "What do you mean, get up? I *am* up. And down. I am everywhere."

"*Hoink hoink!* Yes, sweetheart, but I mean your meat-self." Herself puts her snout under Diana's shoulder and boosts it upward.

"What? This thing?" Diana looks down at her body. "But, Myself, I'm not *this*." She raises one hand and turns it back and forth in front of her eyes, examining its structure. "Although—whoa—it's so *interesting*, don't you think?"

"Captivating," agrees Herself. "But piglet, dear," she cocks her head thoughtfully. "Let's see, how shall I put this? You still live in this meat-self. For now. Can you remember how to inhabit it?"

Diana frowns at the boar for a long minute, her eyes scanning back and forth, searching her memory. Then she says, "Oh, yes, I think I can . . . let me try something . . ." She moves her limbs back and forth a few times, then rolls over. This strikes her as hilarious, and she bursts out laughing. "Yes!" she shouts. "Look at this—I can totally move it! I remember this!" Slowly, unsteadily, she gets to her hands and knees, crawls out of the sleeping bag, and sits on the ground.

"I remember this, too," she says, gazing around the grove. The sun of a cool, clear day shines through the pillars of the trees, dappling the lush greenery of moss and shrubs. Then Diana blinks, her eyes lose their focus, and everything disappears back into showers and blossoms of light. "Oops." She giggles. "Now it's gone."

"So form it again," says the boar, who is once more nothing but a cloud of milky golden energy. "You can, darling."

"Really?" Diana is vastly pleased by this thought.

"Yes. Remember, the human body, while of course ultimately unreal, is equipped with considerable imagination. More than any other material thing on this planet."

"That totally makes sense, Myself!" The thought brings on a long belly-laugh, reminds Diana of the way her bee friends laughed as they fed her. When she thinks of them, she feels a huge swell of love in the area around the meat-self's heart.

"That feeling," says Herself. "You can live inside it."

"What?" Diana gives a few more snorts of laughter, then focuses and imagines herself inhabiting the meat-self's love for the bees. She's surprised to find that it feels quite comfortable. Roomy. Around her, the fluid light pulses and flows.

"Good! Excellent!" says Herself. "Now try to remember how your meat-self used to see. Imagine that bees exist as solid objects, rather than waves of energy. Pretend they persist in time. We know that's all illusion, but just *imagine* it."

Diana obediently imagines that bees are physical objects. Suddenly her meat-self can hear them buzzing, not only in the hive above her head but throughout the forest. All at once, she sees a hundred thousand views of honeycomb and sky, water and flowers. The blossoms blaze with patterns Diana has never seen.

"That would be ultraviolet," says Herself. "Not too shabby, eh? You're seeing as bees do. Now imagine that you can see the way your human body once did."

Diana follows the path of the Tasks, becoming very still, open, alert. Then she pretends that the objects around her are solid, rather than clouds of energy. The forest as her meat-self remembers it pops into being around her. Diana gives a cry of pure delight, gazing at the infinite beauty. Everywhere, highlights and shadows glow with the new color. "Dude!" she says, "This is *awesome!*"

Herself sits on her haunches, golden wings folded back, watching. "Do you know," she says, "that when a baby bee is born from its cell, an older bee takes it on a 'play flight,' just to help it learn what the material world is like?"

"The material world? You mean this . . . uh . . . apparent reality?" says Diana, borrowing a phrase she's heard the boar use many times. She still finds it challenging to think of matter as solid, knowing as she does that it's just another frequency of energy.

"Yes, sweetheart. Play is the best way for a soul to learn how the physical realm works. All babies do it. So why don't you just play for a while?"

Diana doesn't answer; she's already playing, studying the interaction of her consciousness and physical matter. She tries to work out how she could possibly have invested this clunky three-dimensional world with reality, making it appear to be an actual *thing*, when of course it isn't. That's obvious, because (just for starters) each moment of this reality keeps disappearing into something Diana's meat-self calls "the past," which doesn't exist except as a thought-form. Nothing that really existed could ever vanish so completely.

After some experimentation, watching how the meat-self's brain works, Diana realizes that it exists only in a moment it calls Now. This Now is like a vast three-dimensional canvas, on which consciousness is painting an apparent physical universe. Her consciousness ripples through the nothingness from which spacetime emerges, creating a series of incredibly brief Nows with a universe in each one, so that from her meat-self's perspective, objects seem permanent and time seems to pass. Diana knows that she could make another reality appear just by imagining it, but she wants to play in this Now-realm, because it is magnificent fun.

"What a wonderful, *wonderful* playground!" Diana grins at Herself.

"I *know!*" The boar stretches like a cat, her golden wings shivering. "Once you know what you really are, this world is a joyride. But remember when you thought you were just a meat-self? That part can be quite dreadful."

"No kidding." Diana grimaces. She can recall her meat-self's tiny little memories now, its persistent illusions of loss and abandonment and pain.

"So!" says Herself. "Now you know you can form matter with consciousness. But here's an even crazier challenge: Can you walk?"

They both laugh. Moving the apparent matter she's created requires Diana to pretend *she* is physical, which stretches her imagination almost to the breaking point. It takes a while, but Diana rises slowly to her feet and sways there, gazing around the grove. "Woohoo!" she says. "Look at my bad self! Driving this meat-machine like I was born to do it!"

"You were, silly," says Herself. *"Hoink hoink hoink!"* She flickers her little wings and rises, like a huge bee, to hover at Diana's eye level. Diana finds this hilarious. Herself zips around the grove, making spirals and figure eights, giggling. Diana laughs until tears run down her meat-face.

"Oh, my stars!" She wipes her eyes. "This is just too—Whoops! Well, hello!"

She's just noticed that a lumpy brown shape at the edge of her grove is not a boulder or a log, as she first assumed. It's a sleeping mountain lion.

"Hey, Myself," she says cheerfully. "What's that doing here?"

"Oh, you mean Warren?" Herself flies to the cougar and hovers above him. "He got here last night, just as the bees finished making you a Greatmother. It's traditional for human bee-acolytes to have a leonine companion, you see."

"What? Why?" Diana briefly wonders what a "Greatmother" is, then has several disorientingly powerful flashes of memory: queen bees, feeling their hives and the human women that share their empathic Greatmother frequency. A golden figure of a winged woman, a lion at her side. A lion guarding honeycomb, looking out over the sea.

"Oh, darling, why not?" Herself gazes fondly down at the huge cat. "He's such a lovely kitty, our Warren. It's actually WrrARR-RNg, of course—emphasis on the ARRRN. Warren is just the English pronunciation."

"You're right. He's magnificent." Diana edges closer to the lion, careful not to wake him. "But isn't he dangerous to the meat-self? Uh, to *me*, that is?"

"Not at the moment." The boar alights gracefully on the ground next to Diana and folds her wings against her sides. "Do you remember, darling, that the night you met the bees, I gave you a plant called valerian?"

"Mm-hmm." Diana can't take her eyes off Warren: his elegant lines, the thick fur, creamy white on his throat that blushes to rich ochre on his back.

"Valerian is quite a bit more intoxicating for cats than it is for humans, you see, and Warren . . . well, he found rather a lot of it. And, all right, maybe a few mushrooms as well. I was a bit preoccupied watching you. By the time I noticed Warren, he was . . . very, um, happy. He spent six hours trying to catch the moon, chewed down a small tree, and groomed his entire body six times. He's exhausted."

"When's he going to wake up?" says Diana. As she forms the thought, imagining Warren awake, the cat abruptly opens his eyes, raises his head, and stares right at her.

Diana feels her meat-self's heart thump a little harder, and then all at once she's not inside it any more. She's in the mountain lion's body, as she was in the bees' bodies a few minutes ago. This doesn't split her from her human body; she is, as she told Herself, everything. But it's delightfully strange, seeing her human meat-self from the lion's perspective. Warren's crystal-orb eyes stare into Diana's amber ones, the same consciousness gazing at two manifestations of Itself.

As the mountain lion, she feels her mouth opening, a single sound escaping. Her human ears hear that sound come from the lion's mouth. "Wow," says Warren. "Wow! Wow! *Woooow!*"

Diana has never seen her body from a distance. All things considered, she has to agree with the cougar. Through his eyes, her human self is gorgeous, its curves and movements richer than anything she recalls seeing in mirrors.

"Hey, Myself! My meat-body ain't all that bad, is it?"

"*Hoink!* It's exquisite, dear. Can you feel how Warren admires it?"

Diana can. The big cat gazes at her, transfixed—and, Diana can feel, still rather heavily drugged. Warren begins to purr like an outboard motor.

"You know what, Myself?" Diana says. "I think . . . I think he kind of . . . loves me."

"All animals love you, Diana," says the boar softly. "All nature loves you. You have come here, taken this form, for its sake."

"So if he loves me, does that means he wouldn't kill me? Kill my meat-self, that is?" Diana feels completely calm; she asks out of pure curiosity.

"Oh, he'd kill you. *Hoink!* He'd kill you in a New York minute if he weren't completely stoned. He's a *mountain lion*, darling! *Hoinkhoinkhoinkhoink!*"

"Okay," says Diana, laughing along with the boar. "Got it."

Then she falls silent again, fascinated by the world through cougar eyes. They can see into the shadows much better than her human ones can, and their peripheral vision is a great deal wider. She sharpens the cat's gaze and watches her human vehicle move. "That thing . . . I mean the meat-self . . . I mean *my body* looks pretty strong considering I was zonked out for . . . how long was it, Myself?"

"Sixteen days, my love."

"Sixteen *days*?" Diana's human form blinks in surprise, and Warren, still mingled with her energy, does the same. "Wow, Myself, why didn't I starve or freeze or, I don't know, at least have to pee?"

"Well, the plants and the mushrooms and the bees got you started, dear. They pulled you into a bit of suspended animation. Arktos did the rest. And Polaris, of course. He was very excited to help."

Arktos. Diana's memory flickers to their conversation under the stars. *Ursa Major. The Great Bear, Arktos of the North, and her cub, Polaris.*

"Wait a second . . . Myself, are you saying there were *bears* here?"

"Yes, of course, dear. They came to put your meat-self into hibernation mode. It lets them lie still for months without losing any muscle mass, you know, and all their wounds heal while they sleep in a way humans find almost magical."

Diana is too surprised to respond. Her consciousness pulls into her human body again, while in her mind a vivid scene appears: Burnished, rocky landscape. The music of flutes. Little girls lined up, wearing fur, dancing slowly. Then the vision is gone, leaving a single word hanging in the air: *Arkteia.*

A few feet away, Warren is struggling loopily to his feet. Herself rises several feet straight up, her wings a golden blur, and flies to him. "Nap time, love." She hovers above him, humming a lullaby. The cougar's eyes close, and his head collapses slowly onto the ground. Then his body drops like a sack of sand. He's still purring.

"Bears!" Diana repeats, amazed. That's when she notices how her consciousness has retracted from Warren's body, and realizes that she can extend it or withdraw it at will, to and from anything. She closes her eyes and sends her energy outward in all directions, scouting for other beasties in the area. She feels them everywhere, dozens of them, watching her from under stones and up in the trees and behind bushes, as fascinated by her as Warren recently was.

"Holy smokes, Myself, this place is *filthy* with animals!"

"Yes, while you slept we had visits from pretty much every species native to this region." The boar kisses Warren's sleeping forehead. "And a few escaped circus animals from entirely different countries. Can't you feel them? You're entangled with all of them now. Your physical form and theirs will always be connected."

"Yes, I can feel a lot of them, Myself." Diana sniffs the air. "No bears nearby, though."

"Arktos and her cub had to leave three days ago. Actual hibernation called, you know. I gave them the last of the turkey to say thank you, and to fatten them up just a little bit more. Have you noticed that your meat-self isn't very hungry?"

"Yeah, now that you mention it." Diana feels peckish, but not ravenous.

"You can go back to eating now, but start very slowly. You're still hibernating just a little. I've been soaking a lot of acorns in spring water. If you feel like snacking, they should be delicious by now."

Diana does, and the acorns are. After slowly munching a few of them, she walks to the lake and sits down under a tree, watching the day and its twin image in the still water, still amazed by the illusory "solidity" of matter. Herself flies up to the crux of two branches high in the oak and perches there, humming.

Diana closes her eyes, the better to sense the animals. Her meat-heart feels almost ready to burst. It's true, what Herself said: All these creatures love her, each in its own way. She feels bobcats and raccoons, squirrels and eagles, fish and dragonflies . . . and then something so powerful and shocking, so utterly surprising, that a small cry escapes her. "Myself!" Diana calls. *"Myself!"*

The boar buzzes down from the tree in a haze of gold.

"Yes, piggly-wiggly?"

"He's here, Myself! He's still in the forest! Roy is still in the forest! *And he's hurt!"* As she speaks, Diana is already running back to her camp, meta-self and meat-self melded more seamlessly than ever before, moving faster than the boar can fly.

REUNION

Diana has been running for at least a couple of hours. Her breath isn't labored, her legs don't feel heavy, her muscles aren't aching. She is, in fact, as fresh as a summer rosebud. It's Roy who's hurting, Roy whose body feels like a war zone, Roy who doesn't know how much longer he can last. Diana feels this—feels *him*—more clearly than she feels the ground beneath her own bare feet.

Since picking up Roy's energy signature, she's been focused on nothing else. She barely paused to roll up her sleeping bag and lash it to her backpack before picking up her bow and arrows and setting out, running the straightest line she can find toward the place where she feels Roy. Where she feels Roy *suffering*.

She's not sure whether the changes she feels are due to what's happened to her, something that happened to Roy, or both. She's far more sensitive now, but all along Diana has always been tuned in to

Roy, able to detect his mood the way a seal follows the scent-trail of its mate through moving water. Never before has she felt such fear in him, like the rapid beating of a huge drum drowning out all other feelings. And the physical pain! Aching, sweating, nausea, chills . . . He must have eaten poison, or caught some illness. Lyme disease? Bird flu? As she runs, Diana's mind goes through the few possibilities she knows. Nothing feels more true than anything else.

She tries to use the Tasks to clarify her perceptions and get more accurate information. But with her mind fixed on Roy while running through uneven terrain, she can't manage it. To connect with him is to sense his fear, and to sense his fear is to share it, which stops even the First Task dead in its tracks. When she begins to worry that Roy may be dying, the wrenching in her gut nearly makes her trip and fall. She's able to find just enough calm to quiet the stabbies and keep running. No, she thinks, he's not dying. Whatever's wrong with Roy, it can be fixed. She'll fix it.

The boar flies high over Diana's head, above the tree canopy. Occasionally she dive-bombs down, swooping through tree limbs like an improbably agile, furry zeppelin, informing Diana about obstacles ahead. There are many. They're moving into the high country, where the oak savannah gives way to pine forest, its floor a thick, soft carpet of dry needles studded with boulders and crenelated by water-cut ravines. The pines block most of the light, and low clouds creep down the mountains like white smoke. The going is very rough.

As she feels Roy's energy signature grow closer, Diana's heart speeds up, not from physical effort but from the thought of seeing him again. She climbs an uneven stair-step of rock and stops on top of a boulder, looking in all directions. Roy is here—or he should be. There's no question that his essence is present. But Diana sees only the jagged teeth of the pines jutting up through the mist.

"Roy?" she calls. The soft pine-needle floor and the fog swallow her voice so fast she feels almost mute. "Roy! Where are you? Are you all right? I'm here! I'm here to save you!" She turns in a circle, listening, searching, feeling him. Just as she opens her mouth to call again, Roy's voice, soft and level, cuts through the mist.

"I don't know who the fuck you are, but you should know that there's an M16 full of hollow-point ammunition pointed at your head. Put down everything you're carrying, stick your hands up, and turn around slowly."

Barely able to repress a wild shout of joy, Diana lays her possessions at her feet, raises her hands above her head, and slowly turns in a full circle.

"Well, you look like her," says Roy, bitterly. "But Diana's dead."

She almost laughs. "No, Roy. No, I'm not. I'm right here." But where's Roy? She still can't see him, though she can hear the exhaustion in his voice.

"What's my nickname for you, then? What do I call you?"

Now she does laugh, in pure happiness. "Brownie. Your brown girl. You started calling me that the first time we slept together, in your trailer."

"Oh, my God!" Roy's voice is softer, with a slight tremor of emotion. "It *is* you!"

Not ten feet away from the spot where Diana stands, a dead pine trunk appears to split in half. Part of it stays where it is, a jagged spike of deadwood. The other half moves toward her, its lines changing and softening. Roy is within arm's reach before Diana can really see him. He's wrapped in a fur cloak the same gray as the pine bark, with gray camo pants and a dirty T-shirt beneath it. His face is streaked with ragged lines of white and black ash that make it nearly unrecognizable, even close up. But the eyes, the storm-gray eyes that search Diana's face, are unmistakable. As he draws nearer, they light up like sunrise.

Diana is the one who closes the gap between them, stepping forward and taking him in her arms. At first he barely responds. She's quietly shocked by his thinness, the jut of his ribs and shoulder blades under her hands. But his muscles are still rock-hard and lithe. Slowly, Roy lets his rifle slip from his hands to the ground. Then he's hugging her back, so fiercely she can barely breathe.

"Brownie! Brownie! My little brown girl, you're alive! You're alive!"

Diana laughs, tears flowing freely down her face. "I am! I am! I am! And you're here! You're here! You're here!"

Beloved, if you have ever spent weeks without company, you know the restorative power that lies in the simple presence of another human being. If you have been reunited with a loved one you thought was lost to you, you know how deep that power can run, how every emotion you have ever felt is beggared by the sheer relief of falling into that familiar embrace. After a long, tight hug, Roy finally releases his grip, and Diana steps back to gaze at his perfect, soot-streaked face. "What happened to you, Roy? Are you all right?"

He takes her face in both his hands. His fingers are calloused and rough. Diana tilts her face up to kiss him, but he doesn't lean in. He just stares at her, his pale eyes burning in their soot-darkened hollows. His cheeks are concave now, his cheekbones more sharply cut. Deep lines furrow his face, the lower half of which is hidden by a ragged salt-and-pepper beard. The inch of hair closest to his scalp isn't sandy blond but almost white, forming a sharp stripe down his part line. He smells overpoweringly of wood smoke and cooked meat. But even with all of that, Roy is still the handsomest man Diana has ever seen.

"I was going for help," he says, still a little dazed. Diana feels his exhaustion, the chills and nausea, the *boom, boom, boom* of his fear. "I was going for help," he repeats, "and then . . ." His eyes leave Diana's face and dart around at the trees. "Things went wrong, Brownie. A *lot* of things went wrong. Too many. This place . . ." He shudders and reaches out almost reflexively to pull her close. "Something about this forest is bad, Brownie. Bad like nothing I've ever seen before. Evil."

Diana blinks. "It is?" The thought is so utterly different from her own experience she almost bursts out laughing. But it would be like laughing *at* Roy, and she would never do that.

"Yeah," says Roy, still looking around warily. "It is." He slowly crouches to retrieve the M16, his head up, his eyes flashing around like anxious silver minnows. "I mean, Mother Nature is a heartless bitch at best, right?" He laughs, a short, hard, bark. "She'll kill you ten thousand ways anywhere you go. But this forest . . ." He swallows. "It's the worst place I've ever been." He tightens one arm around Diana's shoulders, cradling the rifle in the other. "Come with me, babe. I need to get you someplace safe."

"Uh, all right. Okay. I mean, I feel pretty safe—"

"Hush!" he whispers urgently. "They'll hear us!"

"Who will?" she whispers back.

"Shhh!" Roy puts his finger over his lips, and Diana falls silent. She's suddenly conscious of her bare feet, and wishes she'd put on her boots before running to find him. Fortunately, Roy hasn't looked down. His attention flickers in a circle around him, a radar-sweep of fear.

As they walk, she can feel that fear pounding in his mind: *boom, boom, boom*. He's listening for danger, and Diana listens, too—for the buzz of golden wings, a jolly hoinking laugh, a calm alto voice that makes the wilderness soft and inviting. Wait until Roy meets Myself, she thinks. She imagines how his fear will ease. She'll massage his tired, aching limbs. His wired hyper-vigilance will slip into healing sleep. The image makes her smile.

"Brownie," Roy says in a strained voice. "Can you keep up with me if we go a little faster? It's getting dark. Bad things happen in the dark."

Again, Diana almost laughs. "Yes, Roy, I can keep up. In fact, let me—" she's about to say "help you," but just in time, she shuts her piehole, turning her head so Roy won't see her grin. She's gone wild, all right. Forgotten all the nuances of human-to-human interaction. The boar, while a wonderful teacher, hasn't said zip about how to nurture a romantic relationship. Now Diana remembers the advice from that long-ago foster mother: *Always let men take charge*. That's worked so far with Roy. Diana stays silent.

As they quicken their pace, climbing even higher into the pines, she wonders briefly why Herself seems so completely gone. Even the boar's energy seems strangely absent. But Herself has often left Diana to figure out a puzzle—the Fourth Task, when she stole Diana's hiking boots, is a case in point. And the boar obviously knows how much Diana and Roy need time alone together. When this thought occurs to her, Diana sends Herself a silent "Thank you" for giving them space, rather than chaperoning.

"Okay, Brownie Girl, almost there." Roy's voice relaxes as he lets go of her shoulders. They've come to a wall of rock, fronted with thick brush where the low-lying plants have escaped the shade of the conifers. The dead trunk of a small fir tree lies near them on the ground. Roy goes to it, heaves it toward the cliff, and sets its far end right against the stone. Then he holds out his hand.

"Mademoiselle Brownie," he says, finally flashing his real, beautiful smile. "Welcome to my boudoir. It ain't Beverly Hills, but I like to call it home."

Diana takes his hand. As he pulls her up beside him onto the log, she sees that the ground around it is actually a thin layer of sticks with debris artfully scattered across it. The log forms a bridge over a trench some three feet wide.

"*Mais oui, mademoiselle!*" Roy adopts a bad French accent. "I 'ave created ze system de security. To keep *ma chérie* away from ze many monsters of ze forest!"

Diana laughs, carefully following him across the log bridge. When they reach the other side, Roy turns and pulls the log toward them. It knocks away part of the false floor, and Diana can just see that the yard-deep trench is filled with wooden spikes, poking upward. She remembers seeing Roy dig such a trench in one of his videos, when he was "stranded" in a particularly dangerous African jungle.

Roy leads her along the edge of the cliff and moves aside some fir limbs. Diana lets out a little cry of pleasure when she sees the entrance to a cave. The irregular opening is perhaps four feet high at its peak. Roy often extols the virtues of finding a cave in which to avoid weather and predators. "We're all cavemen at heart," he tells the camera with a grin, ducking into a cavern under the burning Tunisian sun or the cold, endless ranks of the Himalayas.

"Let me go first, check for any critters," Roy says. Crouching down, he disappears into the cave. A moment later he calls, "All clear. Come on in!"

Diana leans down and enters the cave, blinking. As her eyes adjust to the dim light, she sees that the cavern is bigger than she would have guessed. After its low entryway, it expands into a space about the size of a motel room. She can feel a cool breeze blowing around her ankles, from inside the cave, not outside. This must be the antechamber of a cavern system that goes deep into the mountain.

Roy is squatting at the cave entrance, near a fire circle made of stones. He uses a steel fire-maker to strike sparks from his knife, igniting a pile of kindling. It takes him less than a minute. As he feeds the fire, Diana shakes her head in admiration. Knowing more about what Roy is doing makes her appreciate his skill more than ever.

When the fire is burning well, Roy looks up with a tired smile, his teeth bright in the firelight. "So, mademoiselle," he says, "how do you like *Chez Roi*?"

"Wow," says Diana. "I mean *wow*, Roy. This is amazing!"

"Make yourself at home." Roy gestures grandly with one arm. Diana sees his sleeping bag laid out near one wall of the cave. She slides her backpack from her shoulders, detaching her own sleeping bag from it and putting all her things, including her bow and arrows, next to Roy's sleeping area. Then she sits down next to him by the fire.

"So, Brownie Girl," he says, his brilliant smile and glowing eyes lighting the whole cave. "I bet you're wondering what the hell ol' Roy Richards is doing here."

Diana laughs. "You read my mind." She can feel that his fear is less in the safety of the cave. He still seems weak, though. She can sense that he's queasy and feverish, and the sooty haggardness of his face speaks of long hardship.

"I was going to get help," he says. "For you. And then—you remember how I was looking for a wolf, Brownie?"

Diana nods.

He grimaces. "Well, I found one. It stepped right out of the bushes and just stood there, looking at me."

"Really?"

"Yeah. I shot it, of course. Then I skinned it and ate the heart, just like the Chuchunk ritual says I should." Roy reaches up and pulls at a leather strip that crosses his throat. The gray fur cloak he's been wearing slips off, and he holds it up for Diana to see. "I used the brain to tan its hide," he says. Diana feels the fur. It's like the coat of a Golden Retriever.

As he looks at the pelt, Diana feels the drumbeat of fear start up in Roy's energy again. "It had to soak, so I carried it along with me in my Mylar emergency bag," he says. "I thought I'd reach a road by the next morning. But then . . . then . . ." He stares into the fire, his eyes strangely blank. "They've been after me ever since, Brownie."

"They?"

"The other wolves. They must have smelled that hide, and they're after some sort of revenge. I almost never see them. I only hear them. But it's like they don't want me to leave this part of the woods. Like"—he shudders (and his fear is pounding very loudly now)—"like they're *herding* me." His eyes come up and lock on Diana's, and she thinks, *So that's what "haunted" looks like.*

"The thing is, Brownie." Roy swallows and licks his lips. "The thing is, they're acting too smart to be animals. Animals *hunt*. They don't keep people trapped, jump out and scare the shit out of them when they try to leave an area, but never close in for the kill. Something's . . . I don't know. Someone is *managing* them. A human, or a group of humans." He catches her eyes and looks away quickly. "Do you think I'm losing it? Think I sound crazy?"

Diana would smile if she weren't busy looking as kind as she can. "No, Roy. I don't think you sound crazy at all."

He doesn't answer, just gazes into the flames with those blank eyes.

"What happened to me is way crazier than that, anyway," says Diana, and now she does smile at him.

"Oh, yeah?" he says, looking up.

"Mm-hmm." Diana nods slowly. She wonders how to begin. Once more, she remembers him saying, *"Brownie Girl, do you believe in magic?"* and *"I've seen things that would turn your brain inside out."*

"Roy," she says cautiously, "you know how you told me the wolf was your spirit animal?"

Roy says nothing.

"And then . . . um . . . remember that wild boar? The one you almost shot?" Diana blushes, hoping he's not still angry that she ruined his aim and stranded them both here. She does feel a flicker of anger in him, but she plunges forward.

"I'm so sorry about that, Roy, but, um . . ." She laughs and shakes her head. "Um, you see, that boar is *my* spirit animal." Another laugh. A happy one.

Roy's brows gather, the new wrinkles between his eyebrows etching themselves deeper into the soot-smeared skin.

"After you left—I mean, when you didn't come back after a few days—I thought . . . well, I thought I was done. Dead. But then the boar came. And, Roy . . . " Diana leans forward, and the story spills out in a joyous rush. "She can talk! She said I should call her Myself, and she taught me how to find water, and plants to eat, and how to shoot my—I mean your—bow, and, and, and . . . a lot of other things, too."

Diana's voice dies away as she feels Roy's mood darken. He regards her with a mixture of pity and horror that chills her own heart. The fear in him has grown overwhelming: *BOOM! BOOM! BOOM!*

"I'm not making this up, Roy," she says, as gently as she can. "Tomorrow Myself will come back, and you'll see for yourself. She can talk, and she can *fly*, Roy, and—" Diana stops. She can feel how insane this sounds to Roy. Small wonder. If he'd told her anything like this when they met, it would have set her back a few solid paces, even as obsessed with him as she'd been.

Roy presses his lips together so tightly they almost disappear. Silently, he stands up and goes to the door of the cave, his back to Diana.

"This place," he says bitterly, looking out into the dimming pines. "This goddamned *place*. It's been almost too much for me—Jesus, of course no one else would stand a *chance* against it. Not a woman, that's for damn sure."

Diana watches Roy's beautiful body tighten like someone bracing to tolerate an excruciating wound. Then an inchoate bellow of rage seems to rise from the soles of his feet, ripping through his clenched teeth. It echoes and disappears into the forest.

"THIS WAS A GOOD WOMAN!" Roy screams into the night. "A WOMAN WHO UNDERSTOOD ME! WHO LOVED ME THE WAY I DESERVE TO BE LOVED! AND NOW YOU GIVE ME BACK HER BODY, AND YOU'VE TAKEN HER *MIND*?"

Another howl of pure pain, pure rage.

"YOU WON'T GET AWAY WITH THIS!" he screams at the forest. "WHEN I'M IN POWER I'LL COME BACK AND BURN EVERY LIVING THING HERE, AND THEN I'LL FIND SOMETHING WORTH STRIP-MINING IN THIS FILTHY SOIL, AND I'LL BRING THOUSANDS—*THOUSANDS*—WITH ME, AND WE'LL GOUGE OUT YOUR GUTS, YOU EVIL SLICE OF HELL!"

Roy goes slack, dropping his hands and bowing his head. When he turns around, the firelight shows pale tear tracks running through the ash and dirt on each side of his nose. Diana wishes desperately that the boar were here to counsel her, to show Roy that the forest is kind—that *everything* is kind. She smiles cautiously at him. He gives her a small, sad smile in return.

"Come on, Brownie," he says, holding out a hand. She takes it and he helps her to her feet. In the dying firelight Roy strips to his boxer shorts. Diana is shocked again to see how thin he is. She feels strangely shy as she undresses, too, donning one of his old T-shirts. She hopes he's watching her. When she glances at him, she sees that he's zipping their two sleeping bags together.

As she climbs into the bag, Diana's own heartbeat quickens until it's beating as fast as his. How long has she waited, how many times has she dreamed of making love to him again? But when he slides into the bag beside her, he only folds her into his arms and lies still. Her heart, pressed against Roy's, can feel an endless abyss of sorrow in him. She aches to fill that emptiness with love.

Tomorrow, she thinks. Tomorrow Roy will meet Myself, and he'll see, and he'll start learning the Tasks. Tomorrow our life together really begins.

As she lies in his arms, loving him more than she ever has before—ever *could* before—Diana hears something far away but very clear. High and strange and wilder than wild, the sound drifts through the dark forest.

The wolves have begun to howl.

DOUBT

"Rise and shine, Brownie. I made you some tea."

Diana rolls over to see Roy crouching by the sleeping bag, holding out a metal mug filled with hot liquid. He's washed the soot off his face, and though it's thinner, lined, and gray-bearded, it's once more the face she fell in love with.

"Fresh mint," Roy offers the mug. "Grows by the stream. I've already gone for water. No wolves today, thank God. Guess you're my good luck charm." He chuckles hollowly, that haunted look still darkening his smile. Diana dimly remembers that during the night she felt him shaking and moaning in his sleep.

She sits up, takes the cup, and sips. "Mmm. Yummy."

Roy stands and adopts his French accent. "And for ze breakfast we have ze 'ouse special, which is ze dried meat, or ze Paleo Plate, which is ze dried meat, or we also 'ave ze Dried Meat à la carte. And

for ze accompaniment, I would recommend a side of ze dried meat."
He grins, his teeth startlingly white in that gaunt, bearded face, and
offers her a strip of jerky. Diana bites off a piece, which takes some
gnawing. The meat is leather-hard and dreadfully gamey.

"How great is this!" she says, chewing. "Breakfast in bed!"

"Anyzing for my *chérie*." Roy kisses her, sliding one calloused hand
down her back and squeezing her butt. "Hey, Brownie, you've tight-
ened up! I could bounce a quarter off that ass. Or maybe some other
. . . hard . . . object. Rowr!"

Diana laughs and blushes, pushing him away playfully. "Are we
going to play caveman now?"

"Yeah, I'm going to knock you over the head and drag you around
a while." Roy gently grabs a handful of her hair, then leans forward to
kiss her again. The kiss feels so good it brings tears to her eyes. She
hopes he'll push her back onto the sleeping bags for what he always
calls "morning glory." Instead he stands up again and goes to his wall
of weapons.

"So while you were getting your beauty sleep, I've been thinking
through a plan for getting out of this hellhole," he says. "We can work
together to get past the wolves. We'll both have guns, and we'll take
turns sleeping so they can't sneak up on us at night. There should be
a road three or four days' walk to the south."

Diana stops chewing. For weeks, she hasn't thought much about
life after the Sierras Oscuras—about anything, really, except mastering the Tasks. The thought of going back to Los Angeles, wearing
shoes, sleeping in her little apartment, driving a car along crowded
freeways, makes her gut clench badly. Then she thinks about seeing Devin again, and the stabbies ease a little. She'll come back here
often, she decides. Camp for weeks on end. And maybe Herself can
live somewhere closer to the city? Diana sends a glance at the cave
entrance in the fleeting hope that a winged boar will zip through it.

"Um, okay, so when do you think we should start?" she asks Roy.

"Maybe three days from now. Two if we're lucky." He picks up
the bow Diana has been carrying for weeks, and again she feels that
small jolt of disappointment as she remembers it's his, not hers. "We
need to store some food. I don't want to have to stop and hunt once
we're en route. I'm going hunting right now. See if I can bag us a

couple of rabbits, maybe a deer." He strings the bow. His muscles are wirier than Diana remembers, but still very impressive. "You know what I love about arrows?" he says, almost to himself. "You can reuse them. Not like bullets."

As Diana watches Roy pull back on the bowstring, experimenting with the tension, it occurs to her that there's a way to convince him she's not insane. When he sees how she can shoot, he'll have to admit that something real and very interesting—maybe even supernatural—has happened to her.

"You know, Roy, I learned to use that while I was with Mys—while I was out on my own."

Roy's eyebrows go up and he gives her a one-sided smile. "Oh, really? So now you're a mighty hunter, eh?"

"Well, I've only shot one animal. A turkey. But I've done a lot of target practice. I got pretty good. Can I show you?"

Roy thinks for a moment, then shrugs. "All right. Let's see what you can do." He waits for Diana to slip on a pair of jeans, then leads her out of the cave.

The sun is just up, the pine trees emerging from the morning mist like great, shaggy, green-shrouded monks. Diana and Roy stand inside the semicircle formed by his makeshift moat. He hands her the bow and an arrow. Diana nocks the arrow and searches for a target. She'll try for something challenging, but not terribly so. No need to threaten his masculinity.

"That stump over there." She points to a broken pine trunk fifty feet away. It's tall but narrow—not a hard shot, but not a gimme, either.

"Right," says Roy. He folds his arms, watching her intently.

Diana aligns her body with the target, nocks an arrow, then closes her eyes and relaxes, waiting for her meta-self to draw. Nothing happens. She's very aware of Roy watching her, and there's a lot riding on this shot. Nervousness stops the First Task in its tracks, and she can't get even as far as the Second.

"Uh, what are you doing?" says Roy after an endless minute.

"I'm trying to calm down," she says. "And waiting."

"Waiting," Roy repeats. "For what? Godot? A bus? The apocalypse?" He laughs, the heartiest laugh she's heard since they reconnected. "A hunter can't *wait* before he shoots, Diana. Animals don't just sit around hoping you'll paint their damn portraits. Watch this." He takes the bow and arrow, turns toward the stump, and fires immediately. The arrow lands six inches from the target.

"Now, that's how it's done," says Roy.

"Okay, right," says Diana. She reaches for the bow again, and he hands it over, along with another arrow. But she's rattled, anxious. She tries to pull off a quick shot like Roy's, and finds she can't bend the bow enough to get any distance. The arrow lands twenty feet away.

"Well, babe," he says kindly, "that's not too bad. You'll get there."

"I can do better than that, Roy!" she says. "It's just that Myself taught me—I mean, I taught *myself* this other method, and it takes a little time to get it right."

Roy shakes his head and turns to go back inside the cave. "I already told you, Brownie Girl. Hunters can't take time." He straightens his back, stretches, and smiles. "All right then! You'll be foraging for plants today—close by, where you'll be safe. What have you been eating since we split up?"

"Acorns, mostly," says Diana. Roy disappears into the cave, and she follows him. "A lot of acorns." She feels weak, crestfallen.

"Really?" says Roy. "Huh!" He goes to his weapon wall and takes a handgun out of its case. "I gathered a few of those, after I started conserving my ammo. But they're so bitter. Did you process them?"

"I like them just the way they are, but sometimes Mys—sometimes I soaked them in water for a while."

"Try grinding them after that," says Roy. "Then soak them and grind them again, a few times. That's what the Indians used to do. Too much bother for me, and not enough protein—I'm a carnivore, all the way." He turns and holds up the handgun by the barrel. "I'm going to let you carry this today, for your own safety. Have you ever shot a Glock nine-mil?"

"Uh, sort of," Diana lies. Her gut twists, but the last thing she wants is to reinforce Roy's image of her as in incompetent burden.

He holds out the gun. "Well, then you know it doesn't have a safety. But I'm reminding you anyway. This thing won't fire unless you pull the trigger, but *keep your fingers out of the trigger guard* unless you want to shoot. Got it?"

"Got it!" Diana manages to sound cheerful and confident, though her gut continues to cramp. She hasn't felt this off balance since she began learning the Tasks—but that was in an ideal environment, with the boar's loving presence. Now Diana is beginning to remember how she melded with Roy to win his love. It comes back easily, like a song from childhood, this ability to leave her own energy, enter his, and intuit what he wants. It happens without her even really knowing it.

"I'll give you a refresher lesson before we start the long hike." Roy hands her the gun, which is cold and very heavy. "Take it with you now just in case of wolves. Don't use it unless you absolutely have to. Now let's get hunting and gathering."

"Roger that!" Diana slings her empty backpack over one shoulder and stands up tall, like a soldier undergoing inspection.

Roy frowns. "Aren't you forgetting something, Brownie Girl?"

Damn! Damn! Damn! She's done something wrong! "Um . . . I don't think so."

He glances down. "Your boots, Diana. Your *boots!*"

Diana stares down at her bare feet, suddenly noticing how grimy they look, how the pink nail polish she put on them before leaving LA has chipped almost completely away, leaving irregular specks of color behind. They look diseased, she thinks, seeing her feet through Roy's eyes, and her heart withers with shame.

"Oh, oh, yes, I'm . . . well, the thing is, I can sort of . . . when I'm barefoot . . . it's like . . . it, um . . . helps me . . . see. Like, find my way?" Her voice fades as Roy's eyes take on the same stricken look they had last night, when she told him about the boar. She can feel the dread rise up in his heart.

"Oh, Brownie, Brownie," he says. "We've got to get you some help." He goes to pick up her boots, which are tied together by their laces. "Put these on, Diana. Right now. Please. The last thing we need is you getting a cut or a puncture wound that'll go septic and kill you. And besides"—he tosses her the boots, and his face goes cold—"I'm sorry, babe, but your feet are disgusting. You need to cover them up."

Diana's face blazes with embarrassment. How could she forget Roy's aversion to feet? No wonder he hasn't made love to her yet. She pulls on socks over her dirty skin as Roy looks away, his upper lip curled back slightly.

"Sorry, Roy. Really. I'm so sorry. My boots are on now."

He turns back toward her, walks closer, and rests both hands heavily on her shoulders. "Babe, just tell me this. You know that pretty much everything you've told me since we met up yesterday is crazy, right? You get that?"

Diana looks into his piercing gray eyes, the eyes that have convinced millions of people that Roy Richards's way of life should be theirs, too. She can't focus, can't think what to say. Yesterday—it feels like a thousand years ago—she felt clearer and more certain than ever in her life. But being with Roy has brought her back to her human senses, and they're swimming.

"It's okay that you went a little nuts when you were lost in the forest by yourself." Roy's eyes hold hers. "I've been there myself, kind of. Once I was lost in the desert with no water for three days, and I saw rivers everywhere. It happens. You just have to stay rational, remember it's all a mirage."

Diana feels tears in her eyes, and fights to blink them back before they spill over. Her stomach hurts. "But I really did . . . there's no other way to explain everything that happened to me, Roy," she says. "Everything I can do."

"Yes, there is, Diana. It's easy to explain." He pulls her head gently to his chest. She can hear his heart thudding. "Here's what happened, babe. You sprained your ankle, and while it was healing the wild boar came back. Maybe you even saw it eating and started imitating it— rooting for ground water, eating raw acorns. That's why you called the boar 'Myself,' can't you see? You knew all the time, at some level, that it was just a projection from your subconscious. It's okay, Diana. In fact, it's *amazing*. It's how you survived. But it's time to come back to reality now."

Diana's gut is a knotted fist, her mind dizzy with growing fear. He's so sure, and it does make sense, and . . . could he be right? Could all the magic of the past few weeks have been one long schizoid fugue state? At the back of her mind, the Furies' music starts up, turning rapidly more sour and discordant.

Roy pulls back and looks into Diana's eyes again, stroking her cheek with his thumb. "I know it's disorienting, babe. It's hard when you realize you can't trust your own perceptions. But you *can* trust *me*. You've got to trust me. Focus on that. I'm your connection to reality."

Diana's eyes fill with tears as she takes in the kindness of those beautiful eyes. "Yes, Roy," she whispers. "I do trust you."

"Good." He smiles. "So—look at me, Diana—so here's the truth. You can't shoot my bow. You can't see with your feet. And there is no wild boar called Myself. That's the name you gave a mental projection, nothing more. Okay?"

Diana's stomach hurts almost unbearably. "But I get these stabbing pains," she says, "when I don't tell the truth. And now I'm feeling them."

"You've been living on raw acorns, baby," says Roy. "It's a wonder stomach cramps haven't killed you."

"But Myself said—"

"That's right. *Your self* said. It was just you all along, Diana. You can understand that, right? I need you to understand that. Because if I'm going to let you handle a gun, and we're going to get out of here alive, you have to be sane—or at least *act* sane. Otherwise I can't be with you. Do you want to be with me?"

"Yes!" Diana nods vehemently. "Of course, Roy!"

"So there is no 'Myself'?"

Diana feels as if her heart is being torn out. "No," she says, focusing everything she is on Roy's steady gaze. "There is no Myself." For a moment there's too much pain to think. Then she finds her way back to the numbness that served her well in all her childhood homes. It fuzzes out the agony, lets her manage an aching, bedraggled smile.

"That's my girl." Roy kisses her lightly on the lips, then grins and tousles her hair. "Don't worry, Brownie. They have amazing medications nowadays, new kinds of therapy. Let's just concentrate on getting you back to civilization, and you'll be fine. We can conquer this!" He holds up one fist. "Right?"

"Right," whispers Diana. Her whole body feels cold, hollow.

"CONQUEST!" Roy roars, his voice echoing in the cave. He smiles, but a thin sheen of sweat is beading on his forehead, and his upraised hand shakes slightly. *He's sick*, whisper the Furies. *You trapped him here, and now he's gotten sick. You've as good as killed him.* Diana shoves the voices behind her wall of numbness.

They leave the cave, Roy pushing the bridge into crossing position, then pulling it after them and covering the space over the moat with sticks and debris. He heads out, following a trail where he says he's seen game, leaving Diana to forage close to the cave. The Glock, tucked into the waistband of her jeans, feels bulky and cold.

Once she's sure Roy is out of earshot, Diana begins calling softly. "Myself?" she whispers. "Myself, where are you?" Tears spring to her eyes again. "It's Diana, Myself! Your piglet! Why did you go away? Why won't you come back?"

She waits for several minutes, listening, looking, hoping, clomping awkwardly through the trees in her bulky boots. There's no response except the rush of soft wind blowing through the pines.

The forest looks strangely dull, and Diana realizes that the extra color she could see yesterday is gone. Don't people with migraine headaches see flashing lights and colors? Maybe her brain has been malfunctioning all along. Maybe she has a tumor that's causing her childhood mental illness to return with a vengeance. *Yes, that's it,* whisper the Furies. *That's rational.* Why didn't she see it this way before?

Forcing herself out of panic and back into numbness, Diana gets to work. She gathers wild parsnips, manzanita berries, miner's lettuce. All the foods Herself taught her to identify—or, wait, wasn't that Roy? Diana remembers him teaching her as they hiked, during her first days in the Oscuras. Maybe she just remembered what he taught her, then projected that subconscious knowledge into the fantasy of a talking boar. That could be. It could all have been a fugue state.

"No!" Diana suddenly blurts, stamping her foot. "It was *real!*" She covers her face with her hands. "The bees fed me, and the mountain lion was there, and I ran back from the lake with my eyes closed."

The memories are so vivid, so real—in fact, they feel more real than this moment. But isn't that how bipolar people describe their manic states? Diana listens desperately for Herself, but hears only the breeze and a few twittering birds.

Fear begins spiraling upward in Diana like a tornado. What's happening inside her unpredictable disaster of a brain? The elation she's felt over the past weeks, the irrational, illogical, magical things she remembers—was it all evidence of some chemical imbalance? Or a weird hallucination and false memory brought on by the psychedelic mushrooms? Didn't every single foster parent who ever tried to raise her conclude she was insane?

Then a thought hits Diana like a cannonball. "Oh, my God," she whispers. "Myself told me, right out loud! All along, she was trying to tell me!"

A rush of memories comes back. *"It's like I designed it myself!"* she'd said to the boar. *"But you did, darling. Don't you realize that yet? This place—this whole forest—is what you are."* Herself was always saying things like that. A thousand times, in a thousand different ways, she told Diana that all the apparent magic was being generated inside her own head.

"No," Diana says out loud, shaking her head angrily. "That's wrong. *She* wasn't trying to tell me. The *boar* wasn't trying to tell me. I was trying to tell *myself. It was just me all along."*

She wants to collapse to the forest floor and sob, but she pulls herself back together, remembering Roy, his kindness, his embrace, his concern for her. Maybe he's right to see the positive, to think that her mind's ability to hallucinate is "amazing." Still, the endless inner torment of Diana's childhood has started up again, Furies Redux: *You're crazy. You were born crazy. You've always been crazy*. Naturally, when stranded in a frightening situation, she went crazier than ever.

You, beloved, almost certainly know some version of what Diana is feeling. You may have had a fantasy punctured or a hope dashed here and there. You remember the shame of it, the embarrassment at having concocted a rose-colored version of your life, and then being found out. It stings, doesn't it, beloved? And it aches, and it burns. And it tells you never to hope again, just pray that others will forgive and forget your foolishness.

Only one thought eases Diana's humiliation: Thank God, thank God, thank God she's found Roy! And thank Roy for forgiving her, after she stranded him here, to get so sick and worn out. He's right; she has to trust him. Who on earth could possibly be more trustworthy in this situation? Roy has faced every kind of trouble in every sort of place, and always used it to increase his mastery of himself and the world. *I may be crazy*, she thinks, *but I'm not alone*. She's going to be okay. Say what you will about her insanity, it's always helped her survive, and now it's led her back to Roy. Good. That's all it needed to do. She can let go of her madness now. Roy will make everything all right.

SALT

When Diana gets back to the cave with her foraged plants, Roy is still gone. The pine-bough bridge is almost too heavy for her to move, but she heaves it into place, then tries to shove it across the spike-filled moat. As it reaches the halfway point, the log's weight pulls it down into the trench. Diana isn't strong or heavy enough to lever it back up and push it to the opposite bank. It takes all her strength just to drag the log back up to its starting position.

Plan B. Diana climbs down into the moat, gingerly placing her feet on the wooden spikes at the bottom. Thank God Roy made her put on her boots. She can see now that anything else would be madness. She wobbles over the spikes like a circus performer, then clambers up the other side of the trench and stops to cover her tracks, replacing the layer of sticks and covering them with dead plants and pine boughs.

Once inside the cave, she sets about making a campfire. It takes several strikes of Roy's firestarter to get sparks, and a few more minutes to get the tinder burning. She remembers seeing him do this, last night and on television, just as she once saw him demonstrate the bow-drill method. Monkey see, monkey do. All along, Roy has been her real teacher. She searches through his supplies and finds a pan with a collapsible handle. She places it on the fire, pours in water from the canteen, and adds some greens. Then she tosses in the remaining shards of jerky. Not the best soup in the world, but maybe not the worst.

Soothed by the simple, ordinary task of cooking, Diana begins to feel almost hopeful. She refuses to think about the magical strangeness of the past few weeks, or her own questionable sanity. She just stays numb, as she did for so many years, and focuses hard on making Roy's dinner taste better than anything he's eaten since her stupidity stranded him in the forest.

After half an hour Diana tastes the broth from the greens and meat, tapping her lips together like a chef. It needs salt—a flavor she's craved often during her time in the mountains. She knows Roy has some, but she can't find it in the dimness. Diana lugs his heavy backpack into the light from the cave entrance and begins going through it more carefully.

Most of the space inside Roy's backpack is occupied by clothes, a plastic water bottle, a trekking towel, insect repellent, toothpaste, a small shovel, a survival blanket, rope, several short bungee cords, and two rolls of duct tape. At the bottom of the pack Diana finds a nylon container, zipped closed, that seems to contain several small containers. Bingo! She opens the packet.

Three amber-colored plastic bottles fall onto the cave floor. Their labels reveal that all of them contain prescription medicine. Looking inside the nylon case, Diana sees several more. The case also contains a few tiny medicine vials—all empty—and a small box holding dozens of disposable hypodermic needles.

Diana's jaw drops, the implications of this find erupting into her mind like boulders from a volcano. Is Roy diabetic? Does he have cancer, multiple sclerosis, HIV? The last thought makes her feel cold all over, and she bats it away like some gruesome flying insect. Still, to be carrying this much medication, Roy must be dealing with some serious, ongoing medical problem.

Heart pounding, terrified by what she might learn, Diana dumps the contents of the zippered case onto the fabric of the empty back-pack to examine everything more closely. At the bottom of the case she finds two empty resealable plastic bags with traces of powder in them. She opens one and touches it to her tongue, which promptly goes numb. It's been a long time since Diana's had cocaine, but the sensation, and the bitter medicinal taste, is familiar. She puts the bag-gie down, picks up the pill bottles, and begins reading labels.

The only prescription she recognizes immediately is a box of blue tablets labeled Viagra—strange, since Roy and she have often joked that when it comes to any kind of sex, he's "Mr. Ever-Ready." Then she finds an empty bottle of Clonazepam, and fishes up a memory: A doctor once prescribed this for her as a teenager, after a fugue state. It reduced anxiety, but the doctor had warned her that she shouldn't go off it abruptly—that it could cause a variety of problems, includ-ing psychosis. She seemed to recall that it killed her sex drive, as well. That might explain the Viagra. At any rate, both containers are now empty.

The next bottle she checks, the largest one, is labeled "Oxycodone HCl, Qty Filled: 200." Diana gasps softly. Roy brought two hundred Oxycodone to the mountains—and he's taken them all? What sort of agony must he be hiding?

A search through the other bottles and vials doesn't do much to solve the mystery. She finds a bottle of "Methyltestosterone," one of "Dextroamphetamine Sulf-Saccharate," another labeled "Deca-Du-rabolin." The tiny bottles that once held injectable liquids are "5-Androstenediol" and "OnabotulinumtoxinA."

At first all these words are gibberish to Diana, but as she rereads them, word fragments begin to pop out: Testosterone. Amphetamine. Botulinum-toxin, which she seems to remember is the technical name for Botox. All the labels list multiple refills, and all are empty.

Diana's head feels as if it might lift off her neck like a balloon. She puts both hands on it, trying to make sense of what she's seeing. Why would Roy be on this cocktail of drugs? Why does he need so much pain medication? So much testosterone? And amphetamines? Those are for energy and focus—and Roy Richards has always had those in spades.

She puts the pieces together several different ways, like someone trying to solve a Rubik's Cube. Maybe Roy has a wasting disease that makes him anxious and depletes his energy so much he needs amphetamines? Maybe the anti-anxiety drugs and painkillers cause sexual side effects, which he treats with male hormones? Maybe the amphetamines ruin his appetite, and he needs hormones to keep up his muscle mass? Whatever's going on, she's quite certain of one thing: Roy is out of all these medications, and when you run out of these medications, you go into withdrawal.

Diana's eyes fill with tears as she recalls all the terrible withdrawal agonies she observed in addicted boyfriends and homeless kids during her misspent teenage years. She never had the money to be a true junkie herself, but she saw plenty of people go through that ghastly passage. Shakes, sweats, nausea, muscle cramps, panic . . . it was always horrible, unendurable. Has Roy been handling all that—plus whatever illness or injury made him need all these medications in the first place? Most people would be curled up in the corner screaming. But Roy is out finding food for her, with a smile on his face. He's always been Diana's hero. Now he's starting to look like her superhero.

She's trying to read the fine print on one of the empty vials when the glow from the cave's entrance darkens. Diana jumps as Roy comes into the space, his face lit from beneath by the fire. The smile dies on his face when he sees her. He looks at her for a long, tense moment. She blinks up at him, tears still flowing.

"What the hell do you think you're doing?" Roy says. His voice is low, soft, uninflected.

"Well, I was looking for salt, and I found— Roy, are you okay?" She wants to cradle him, bring him a cold cloth for his face, rub his aching muscles. "You can tell me, Roy. I can help. I *want* to help."

With one huge step, Roy reaches her, leans forward like a football player pushing off a tackler, and shoves her in the chest, hard. She falls to the floor of the cave with a startled cry. He turns her over roughly, snatching the Glock from her waistband.

"Never!" Roy is shouting, his voice reverberating off the back of the cave. "Never, never, *never* touch *anything* that belongs to me. Is that clear? *Babe?"*

"It's all right, Roy. Honestly, whatever's the matter, I won't judge—"

"Ooh, you won't judge me! You won't *judge* me? AS IF YOU HAD THE RIGHT TO JUDGE ME!" He grabs the zippered case and begins replacing all the bottles, moving very fast. "Goddammit, Diana, I saved your *life!* I risked my *own* life for you, and *this* is how you repay me? By *spying* on me? By *disrespecting* me?"

"I was just looking for salt," Diana whispers. "For the soup."

"SHUT UP!" Roy's hands are shaking so hard, with rage and whatever else is wrong, that he drops some of the bottles and has to lunge forward to grab them. When he looks up at her, his face is red, the veins in his forehead pulsing visibly. Suddenly Diana remembers the male turkey flying at its enemy in battle, claws outstretched, eyes like fire. Then her mind plays a fantastically rapid slideshow of the many times in her past—with foster families, with classmates, and with boyfriends—when she's been slapped, punched, kicked, pinched, or thrown. Her body shrinks away from Roy, seemingly of its own volition.

"I'm sorry, Roy! I'm so sorry!" The bad part isn't his rage, but her knowledge that she deserves it. This is all her fault.

Roy's voice sinks back to normal volume, but he speaks very fast, with suppressed intensity. "There are laws against trespassing on another person's property, Diana. You have broken the law here. You realize that, don't you? You're nothing but a burglar—a batshit crazy little thief. You could do prison time if I decide to turn you in."

"What? No, Roy, I didn't mean to— I love you, Roy! I'm just trying to help!"

He laughs loudly, his voice echoing from all sides of the small space. "Oh, that's a good one," Roy says. "Well, thank golly gosh— Mad Madam Mim is here to help out the billionaire entrepreneur! Wow, Diana, I don't know how I would have managed without you."

Without standing up, Diana pushes herself to the back of the cave, away from the fire, and hugs her knees to her chin, tears running soundlessly down her grimy face. Why, why, *why* does she always screw up? Why has she never been able to make any relationship work, keep anyone happy? After the boar-hunting disaster, after getting Roy lost out here so he's run out of his medications, Diana can't think of anything worse she could do to mess up his life. But, she reflects miserably, she'll probably come up with something.

"I thought you were different, Diana." Roy stuffs the medicine container into his backpack. "Simple, you know? Loyal. I thought, 'Here's a woman who won't betray me.' But what have you done, ever since we came out here to the freaking Sierras Mierdas? You've betrayed me. Over, and over, and over again, *you have betrayed Roy Richards!*"

Diana closes her eyes as tight as she can, trying to block out his anger. It's a tangible substance, like acid in the air. She would rather he just hit her.

"Open your eyes, damn it!" Roy is shouting again. *"Look at me when I'm talking to you!"*

Obediently, Diana opens her eyes—just in time to see him accidentally knock the handle of the pan on the little fire, spilling scalding hot soup on his hand. He gives a yell through his clenched teeth, picks up the pan, and throws it against the cave wall, splashing soup everywhere.

"Jesus *Christ,* you stupid bitch!" he shouts. "Can you do *one single thing* that isn't a pain in my *fucking* neck?"

Diana doesn't move. To her shock and horror, a warm tingling sensation is rising in her body. The *other* is trying to take over. But now Diana knows what it is: Madness. Maybe schizophrenia. A total break with reality, something she must fight to suppress for the rest of her life. She never wants to hope again. Never wants to think she might be safe. Safety is an illusion. Another hallucination.

She shoves the *other* down with every bit as much anger as Roy feels toward her—no, more. Beloved, if you have ever hated yourself for ruining what you value most, you know there's not enough space in the universe to hold the rage Diana feels for her own stupidity, for her rotten, maggot-eaten, treacherous, psychotic brain.

Roy is pacing around the cave, shaking his burned hand, taking huge breaths, and pulling back his shoulders. Self-mastery. She watches him gain more control with each breath, and wonders what hell of illness and withdrawal is racking his beautiful body. No wonder he's so angry. It must tax all his strength, push him to his last nerve and beyond. If only she could *help*, instead of always bumbling along, making things worse.

"I'll keep you with me, Diana," he says in a voice that sounds more or less normal, though Diana can hear a tremor she remembers from the withdrawal agony of a dozen friends. "I'll take you home. I need you to get past the wolves. But if you ever, ever, *ever* disrespect me again—"

"I won't, Roy. I promise I wo—"

"I'm talking, Diana!"

She shuts her mouth tightly. Roy paces in silence for several seconds. Then he goes to the mouth of the cave, reaches down, picks up a dead raccoon, and throws it toward her. It lands with a thud at her feet.

"Anyway, I brought meat," he says. "At least one of us is doing something right. Skin that thing, gut it, and cook it. It'll be enough food for the hike home."

Diana stares at the dead animal. "Okay."

"And clean up this mess." Roy kicks at the cooked greens spilled across the floor. Then he goes to their sleeping bags at the far side of the cave and unzips them. He closes his own bag and moves it as far away from Diana's as it will go. Then he flops down on it, rolls over with his face to the wall, and lies silent. Diana can see from the rigid lines of his body how much pain he's in, and her heart breaks all over again.

It takes her a long time to dress the raccoon's body. The insane part of her wants to grieve the creature like a lost loved one. By the time she goes out of the cave to throw the entrails and skin as far as she can away from the cave, the pine forest is already disappearing into darkness. She makes skewers from the sticks by the doorway, then cuts up the raccoon meat and puts strips of it over the fire to cook. While it does, she cleans up the spilled greens.

She cries the whole time, without making a sound.

When the meat is ready, Roy eats without a word, barely glancing at Diana. She doesn't even try to eat. The greasy smell of the meat, the feeling that the raccoon is a loved one, and Roy's anger all combine to put her guts in such a twist she wonders if she'll ever be able to eat again.

Roy leaves the cave briefly, and Diana hears him pissing into the forest. Then he comes back in, walks past her as if she doesn't exist, and returns to his sleeping bag. After a long time, his breathing deepens, and the tension in his shoulders goes slack. He rolls over with a soft moan, and she can see him grimacing in his sleep—he'd never show his pain if he were awake. His face is bathed in sweat.

Diana sits up a long time, staring at the fire, not feeling anything.

PARAKLETOS

Diana is sinking through quicksand, barely able to move. Her lungs scream for oxygen, her body is spent, her gut aches. Long after she thinks she can't survive another second, she bursts into the air, gasps a huge breath, and shouts the only thing that comes to mind: *"Myself! Help!"*

Then she's standing in the oak forest, no quicksand in sight. The boar, complete with golden wings, stands just in front of her, *hoinking* warmly.

Diana throws her arms around Herself's neck. "Myself!" she sobs. "Myself, you came back!" She holds on tight to the bristly body. "Are you real, or am I dreaming?"

The boar nuzzles Diana's cheek. *"Hoink hoink hoink!* Of course you're dreaming, my darling. I thought we established that the day we met. You're pretty much always dreaming."

Diana's heart plummets. "So this isn't real?"

"Heavens, no!" Herself guffaws.

Diana drops her arms to her sides. "Of course. This isn't real," she says woodenly. "I have to remember that this isn't real. That's what Roy said. If I focus on Roy, I'll remember what's real."

At this the boar laughs so hard she falls over and rolls around on the grass. As Diana watches her, Warren the mountain lion comes from behind her and slides his head against Diana's hip, his fur like warm velvet, his purr making her whole body vibrate.

"Oh, goodness, my dear!" The boar is still laughing. "How you do jump to conclusions! Roy isn't real either, piglet. He's just a different dream frequency."

"Frequency!" says Warren, his voice a low meow. "Freeequency."

"It's like tuning a radio, sweetheart," says Herself. "All sorts of realities flow through your space, just like radio music flows through the air. Tune into Beethoven, and here comes Beethoven, clear as day. Twist the dial a little, and you've got heavy metal."

"So that's why you left?" Diana asks, longing to allow herself the luxury of believing Herself is real. "That's why I can't find you—I mean, that's why I can't imagine you any more?"

"*Hoink hoink!* I never left, my darling, and you weren't just imagining me. Your dream was on my frequency, and you switched it to Roy's. That's all. Now the two of you are creating a consensus dream on his bandwidth. It's the most popular one for humans right now, which makes it a very strong signal."

As Diana ponders this, she feels something pulling her sideways, disassembling her cells and sucking them in like a vacuum cleaner. The next thing she knows she's standing in a huge crowd, wearing heels and a heavy coat. The crowd faces a dais where Roy stands in a biting winter wind, his left hand on a Bible, his right arm raised to the square where thousands throng beneath him. A blond woman stands behind him, watching adoringly.

"Is that—is Roy the President of the United States?" Diana is devastated not to be the blond woman next to Roy. Her longing for his love burns like hot metal in her chest.

"Yes, dear." Diana looks up to see Herself hovering above her head in the cold air, tiny golden wings blurred with speed. "This is the future he imagines, and he may well achieve it. Roy uses the frequency of fear very skillfully. As do all humans like him. Look here, my piglet. I want to show you something."

The scene changes. Now Diana is standing high, high up, on a bare, rocky mountaintop, the boar beside her. Miles below, Roy's presidential inauguration continues.

"Turn around, love," says Herself. Diana turns. The mountain is taller than Everest, incredibly high, but she can see clearly all the way to the far horizon, as if she's looking through a powerful telescope. At first she sees no man-made structures anywhere, just forests, deserts, mountains, oceans. Then she notices a tiny wisp of smoke. Her eyes zoom in on a little gathering of human beings, far, far away.

"This was your planet not so long ago," says Herself. "Now, watch."

Diana sees thousands of square miles of trees go red, gold, and brown, then disappear under a blanket of snow. Within seconds, the snow melts again, and all the trees turn green. This happens again, and again, and again, so quickly Diana can barely follow. And as it does, the number of humans grows. For a few minutes, ice and snow spread to cover much of the landscape even in the green times. The humans move away from the cold, but grow more numerous in the warmer places. As the ice retreats, the humans spread out, creating farms, building cities. Diana sees groups of them beginning to fight. It happens more often as they proliferate, killing one another in larger and larger numbers—but never as fast as more are born.

Then, with incredible suddenness, the humans explode into virtually every space that isn't covered by ocean. Huge swathes of forest disappear as the humans cut and burn them down. Smoke from cities smudges the atmosphere. Sea life begins to die as humans pour strange substances into the oceans. Diana can feel a mighty pulse of energy coming from billions of human beings. At first she can't place that insistent energy, but then she remembers the turkey pumping out that same relentless demand: *ME! ME! ME! ME!*

Beside Diana, the boar sighs. "You see what a nightmare they're having, poor dears," she says. "Can you feel how frightened they are?"

Diana nods silently. The terrible fear under the humans' endless drive is horrible. Fear of loss, insignificance, weakness. Most of all, fear of death.

"Yes, they're so terrified to die, the silly darlings," says Herself. "They believe they *are* those little meat-selves." She clucks her tongue. "No wonder they put people like Roy in charge. No wonder you did, too, piglet. As long as you're tuned to that frequency, you'll cling to the Roys of the world as if they're your only hope for survival. *Hoink hoink hoink!* As if any human meat-self has ever survived for more than a hot second!"

Diana shakes her head, despairing at all the violence she sees, all the poison, all the pain. Then a familiar call arises from the wide, wide world, going straight into Diana's heart: *Help! Please help! The babies can't survive this. Help the babies!* Diana's chest fills with the familiar yearning to find and heal the source of that cry.

"Why do I keep hearing that, Myself?" she asks. "What is it? Why does it . . . how can I say this . . . why does it *move* me so much?"

The boar is in the air, her wings buzzing loudly, turning slow cartwheels at Diana's eye level. "That's for me to know and you to find out, piggly-wiggly."

"Stop that!" Diana scowls. "I mean it, Myself! Tell me what it is!"

The boar stops cartwheeling. "Oh, all right." She opens her mouth to speak. But the voice Diana hears isn't Herself. It's Roy.

.

"Wake up, Brownie. Come on, babe, rise and shine!"

Diana opens her eyes; she wasn't even aware they were closed. Herself is gone. Roy is kneeling beside her, a smile on his face.

"Yep, that's it! Up and at 'em!" he says cheerfully. "Today's the day we're bugging out!"

Diana stares at him. Her head spins, filled with the strange dream and her fear of Roy's blistering anger from last night. She's half elated, half terrified, completely confused.

Roy walks over to his weapon wall, picks up the M16, removes the magazine, checks the action, then rolls the top cover off to inspect the interior. "Don't know why I bother cleaning this thing," he murmurs. "No ammo."

"Roy?" she says cautiously. The dream has given her courage.

"Yeah?" Roy reassembles the gun and straps it across the top of his backpack, securing it with bungee cords.

"About yesterday. I didn't mean to see anything, I wasn't snooping, but I have to know . . . are you sick, Roy? Is there something wrong with you?"

Roy turns, one eyebrow up, the other down. "Sick?" He grins and shakes his head. "What are you talking about, you crazy brown girl?"

Diana feels more confused by the second. "Roy, I—I did something I shouldn't have, remember? I looked in your backpack—just for salt, I wasn't snooping—" She takes a tremulous breath. "Well, I found your medications. A lot of bottles, empty. Are you okay without them?"

"Medications?" Roy repeats blankly. "Brownie, what's gotten into you?" Then his smile fades. "Oh, no. Are you imagining things again?"

"No!" Diana shakes her head. "No, it really happened! Last night! And you were so mad—but I didn't mean to betray you, Roy, I swear."

Roy comes to sit by Diana's sleeping bag. She flinches as his hand moves toward her face, but Roy only strokes her hair. "Of course you didn't betray me, Brownie Girl. You never would. Did you have a bad dream?"

"Yes. No. I mean, I had a really good dream. But yesterday was bad."

"You want me to pinch you?" Roy smiles and lightly presses his knuckles to her cheek. "You're awake now, babe. This is reality. I promise. And nothing happened yesterday. I came back with the meat, and then we cooked it, and ate it, and made love, and went to sleep. Are you telling me you don't remember?"

"I . . . what? No!" Diana shakes her head hard. "No, we had a fight. It was awful! You said I'd betrayed you, and you took our sleeping bags apart, and—"

"A fight?" Roy laughs incredulously. "Babe, if that was a fight, I hope we fight a lot, because you were hot, hot, hot! You seriously don't remember? Think!"

Diana looks around desperately, searching her mind, questioning everything about yesterday. "But look," she says. "Our sleeping bags are separate."

"Yes, of course." Roy nods. "You did that, Brownie. Said you were too warm, wanted to sleep in your own bag. My God, you have to remember! Think!" He looks anxiously into her face. "Diana, tell me something. Do you ever have blackouts? Do you lose chunks of time? Ever wake up and find yourself someplace you didn't expect to be?"

Diana feels nauseated. How did he know? "When I was younger," she murmurs, "it happened. A lot."

Roy presses his lips together, his eyes soft. "We're going to get you through this, Diana. I promise. You'll be okay."

The cave is spinning. Diana has never been so confused in her life. Everything bobs and sinks in a sea of uncertainty, reality slipping away whenever she tries to hold it steady, like a fish swimming out of her grasping hand. Roy's beautiful eyes are the only things that feel stable. His certainty, his strength, are rock-steady.

"This is your frequency," says Diana slowly, remembering her dream. "It's like a radio. This is your station, your channel. *Your* reality."

"Radio?" Roy's brow furrows. "Are you hearing voices, babe? Do you think someone's piping thoughts into your head?" He takes her hand in his. "Diana, those are classic symptoms of schizophrenia. They're all in your brain. Just listen to my voice, Brownie Girl. Feel my hand. You see how real it is?"

Diana nods.

"This is not a dream," says Roy, looking intensely into her eyes. "This is reality. You just hold on to that, and I promise, you'll be all right." He gives her hand one more squeeze, then stands up, breathes in, pulls his shoulders back. "Now get your things together, because we're going back to civilization. Back where we can get you the help you need."

Diana stands up and dresses, trying to move quickly, head whirling, guts knotted up like a tangle of spaghetti. But there's relief, as well. Roy isn't angry at her. He says he never was. The medications, his rage, must all have been part of her dream. As Diana rolls up her sleeping bag and attaches it to her backpack, she half-expects the cave to suddenly vanish. She has absolutely no idea what is real and what isn't.

"You going to eat?" Roy is wrapping the meat from the fire in his trekking towel. He holds up a piece for Diana.

"Uh, no thanks. Maybe later." The sight of the raccoon meat makes her gag.

"Suit yourself." Roy packs the meat away. "Probably smart to save it for later. I'm not sure how far we have to go. Could be two days' hike, could be four."

Diana finishes packing and puts on her boots, turning so Roy won't see her feet. She zips her backpack closed and pulls it onto her shoulders. When she's ready, Roy is just donning his wolf-pelt cloak. The eyeless face goes up and over his white-striped hair.

"I wear this to show the other wolves I mean business," he tells her. "I took out this one, I'll take out all the rest. But I may need your help, Brownie." He stoops to pick up his gun, then hands Diana the Glock she carried yesterday. "Now, listen to me very carefully. If any wolves come at us, climb a tree. If there's no time for that, we stand back to back and fight them as they come. Don't fire the gun until you know you won't miss—I've only got a few bullets left. I'll shoot arrows. If we take down at least one wolf apiece, the others will probably fall back. If not, we fight to the finish. Do you understand?"

Diana hefts the gun in her hand and swallows hard. "Yes, Roy. I understand."

"Good girl." Roy chucks her under the chin. "Cheer up, Brownie. Those fucking mongrels don't stand a chance against two shooters. I've beaten worse odds than that on a bad day." He pulls back his shoulders, "All right! Let's finish this goddam quest!"

They cross the drawbridge one last time and start off through the forest. Shreds of morning mist float between the pine trees, dampening the noise of birds and insects. In the silence, the crunch of their heavy boots on pine needles seems almost painfully loud. Beyond the tops of the pines Diana can see high, bare stone peaks glowing gold in the sun. Then the trees and fog close in again, filling the world with silent shadows.

Roy walks ahead, his bow strung, an arrow nocked and ready. His movements are uncharacteristically tense. He looks around constantly, glancing behind him almost every other step, and often stops in his tracks, holding a finger to his lips, listening.

"I think they're out here today, Diana," he tells her in a low voice as they stop for a sip of water. "I can feel the bastards. This is their territory."

Diana's skin is already prickling with gooseflesh when she hears it: a low, long moan like a foghorn, sustained for what seems like a full minute, echoing through the mist.

Roy drops his water bottle and has his bow drawn and ready almost instantly. He turns in circles, aiming everywhere. "Climb!" he shouts.

Diana jams the Glock in her waistband, runs to a fir tree, and begins climbing. Its branches are like an irregular ladder, and she moves easily upward even with her heavy pack. She can hear Roy run to another tree fifty feet away and begin climbing, cursing as his gear clatters to the ground.

"Damn it!" he yells hoarsely. "I dropped my bow! Here they come! Shoot! Shoot!"

That's when a dry branch gives way beneath Diana's boot. She topples, grabbing at pine needles that break off in her hand, and then she's falling, bumping from branch to branch, the gun flying free, and finally landing with a thud, flat on her back. She can't draw breath or move; she lies stunned, waiting for her lungs to work again.

"Goddammit, Diana! Get up! Get the fuck up!" Roy is screaming from high in his tree. But Diana can't move. She hears footsteps in the pine needles, quick and soft and very close by. She closes her eyes, the one movement she's capable of making.

"*Get away from her, you bastard!*" Roy screams, almost hysterically. She can hear him climbing higher, higher. Then she hears another sound, very close: a whistling whine. A dark wet nose touches her cheek, and she flinches in terror. But the attack never comes. Instead, a warm, soft tongue licks her cheek.

Terrified, she forces herself to open her eyes. She's looking straight into the face of a huge wolf, his breath clouding the frosty air between them. His eyes are golden, his fur a silvery shade of gray. *So this is it,* Diana thinks. *This is how I die. Well, all right.* Her fear disappears, replaced by surrender.

And suddenly her body fills with a prickling warmth. A bolt of heat floods her torso and head. The forest springs into brightness, adding a new shade of purple Diana has seen only briefly before.

The wolf whines again, but this time, Diana understands. He says, "*Greatmother! Diana! Diana, Diana, Diana!*"

She feels her heart connecting to his. His great, warm, loyal, loving heart. *"Do I know you?"* she feels to him, using the silent heart language of the bees.

"Of course!" the wolf replies in the same heart-language. *"It's me! Parakletos!"* He gives her a big, doglike smile.

"Pair of cheetahs . . . ?" she thinks, frowning.

"ParaKLEEtos." The wolf chuckles, whining. *"You remember, Diana! We play together all the time!"* He leaps up and pounces like a puppy. *"Play play play!"*

Strangely, Diana does remember. Her brain downloads the wolf's name and its meaning after a millisecond. Parakletos: Helper. Comforter. Servant. Of course. In her mind a flicker of images rushes past. Running, sitting, sleeping, hunting with this helper by her side, in deserts, mountains, swamps, ice.

"Are you Roy's spirit animal?" she thinks to the wolf. *"Like Myself is mine?"*

"Not exactly, Greatmother." The wolf gives a little yipping laugh. *"Though I have been trying to help him. By making sure he got to you. It's the only way I could think to wake him up. He's past my help. Oh, I'm so glad to see you!"* He licks her face again, wiggling with joy.

Diana's diaphragm has relaxed, and she can breathe again. She rolls onto one elbow. Parakletos drops his head between his front paws, wagging his tail furiously. Then he flops down and rolls over next to her, showing her his belly.

"Parakletos," Diana asks, *"what do you mean, he's past your help? I don't understand. He told me a wolf was his spirit animal."*

"Not so much." Parakletos pants, letting his tongue loll from his mouth, his breath coming in little clouds. *"The only animal that matches his frequency is with him already."*

"What? How? I haven't seen it."

"It's a tick, Greatmother. Bloodblotch the tick. He's a nice guy, and he's really trying, but he doesn't have a lot of power."

Diana frowns. *"Then why are you here, Parakletos?"*

The wolf rolls upright again and fixes his golden eyes on Diana's. *"He called me. He used one of the Old Songs. No wolf in these mountains has heard the Old Songs for thousands of generations. He sang that I should come and wake him up. The Old Songs are beautiful, and very few humans know them, so I was curious."*

Diana's jaw drops as the tumblers fall into place, click, click, click. *"The Chuchunk ritual? So it actually worked?"*

"Well, it got my interest. I even tried to do as he asked. But"—at this point the wolf goes into his yipping laugh—*"I'm afraid it's hopeless. He's so afraid, Diana, and so obsessed with his meat-self's little power. His meta-self is hardly a spark at this point. Whenever I even try to get close to him, he goes nearly berserk."*

"Ah," thinks Diana. *"He doesn't understand, Parakletos."*

"No kidding." The wolf yawns, his pink tongue curling, fangs sharp and white. *"For a while I was stumped. Didn't know what to do. And then I felt you, Greatmother. I could feel that you were nearby, and that you love him. So I thought maybe you'd know how to do for him what I can't. My pack and I have kept him here, waiting for you. We sing to him at night, to let him know we're keeping him safe. It's all we've been able to do."*

Diana's mind is working furiously. *"But, Parakletos—Roy killed a wolf! He's wearing its skin right now! Doesn't that bother you?"*

The wolf nuzzles Diana's face with his cold, wet nose. He's enormous, nine feet from nose to tail, his thick fur a soft gray cloud. For a moment she feels his mood turn somber.

"Yes, the pack misses Aroooo's meat-self very much." He thinks for a moment. Then his great doglike heart rebounds like rubber. *"But his meta-self is always here, and we always knew humans are insane. To be a meat-self that thinks it is ONLY a meat-self, to be a fully tame human . . ."* Parakletos shudders, just the way Diana remembers Herself shivering when she discusses tameness. *"You can't help being monsters. We forgive you."*

Diana reaches out to stroke the soft fur on the wolf's neck, and he licks the tip of her nose. His tongue is very soft, very warm. A bloom of joy fills Diana's vibrating body. The forest is once again full of love, beauty, color. Right now, Roy is seeing undeniable evidence that the world is stranger than his meat-self ever dreamed. Soon she'll ease his fear, introduce him to Parakletos. Then she and the wolf—and Herself, when the boar returns—will teach Roy the Seven Tasks.

He'll wake up. That's what he wanted, the reason for this whole quest. Diana laughs as she realizes she hasn't hurt that quest at all—the truth is in the mirror of the thought: She's *helped* Roy. And she's about to help him even more. The thought makes her feel as light as the morning air.

Which is suddenly shattered by a hoarse, bellowing shriek.

Diana and Parakletos turn to see Roy drop to the ground fifty feet away. He grabs a dead tree limb, raises it like a club, and sprints toward them. The wolf-pelt cloak flaps raggedly behind him as he runs.

"You go, for now," Diana thinks to Parakletos. *"I'll explain everything to him, and call you back when he's calmed down."*

A great bolt of happiness goes from his heart to hers, and Parakletos springs away, zigzagging between trees with that puppyish bounce. Almost instantly, his long gray body disappears into the maze of forest.

Roy reaches Diana seconds later, his face contorted and scarlet. She sits up, smiling at him, heart bubbling over with joy and love.

"WHO ARE YOU?" he screams. "WHO THE FUCK ARE YOU, AND WHO DO YOU WORK FOR?"

Diana laughs softly. "No, Roy, listen. You need to listen to me."

"Oh, I'm gonna listen to you, all right!" he yells, standing over her. "I'm gonna listen to you while you tell me EVERYTHING! I'm going to get the truth out of you, Diana—or whoever you are—if I have to cut off your fucking fingers one by one and make you eat them!"

"Roy, please listen." She shakes her head and begins to stand up.

"DON'T YOU FUCKING HURT ME, BITCH!"

The last thing Diana feels is the rough bark of Roy's pine-limb club smashing into the side of her head.

DESCENT

Pain, pain, pain, pain, pain. Surge after endless surge of it, pulsing in time to her heartbeat. Diana's head aches blindingly. Her whole body feels scratched and torn. Her muscles are cramped from her awkward position on the rocky surface: feet bound together, hands fastened behind her back, on her side. She tries to open her eyes, and finds that only the right one obeys her. The left seems glued shut. When she turns her head to look around, the ache on that side of her head pounds like a jackhammer.

She can see enough to realize that she's back in Roy's cave, on the floor near the back. She can't feel her hands and feet. The ligatures around them are so tight that even the thought of struggling to free herself is impossible. Her back feels bruised and scratched, and where her weight presses into the cave floor, she can feel grit piercing the wounds.

The cave is almost dark, the sunlight from outside fading. She must have been unconscious for hours. A fire crackles near the cave entrance, throwing flickering orange light on the walls. Roy sits next to the fire, poking it with a stick. Behind him on the stone, his shadow is huge, dark, grotesque. Yet even now, when Diana sees his strong profile limned in the light, she's struck by his beauty.

She sees Roy wipe the corner of his eye with the heel of his hand. Devin used to do that as a little boy, to push away tears when he couldn't help crying. Diana squints her one good eye to see better, head pounding. Roy sniffs, then drags the back of his hand across the base of his nose. Diana's first impression was right: He's weeping.

"Roy?" she says, her voice raspy and weak.

He turns toward her and his face goes slack with genuine relief. "You woke up." He closes his eyes for a moment. "I wasn't sure you ever would."

"Roy . . . I don't understand." Diana's mouth is dry; it's hard to form words. "Why am I tied up? Why are we back here?"

Roy stares at her for a moment, then turns and shoves at the fire with his stick, creating a shower of sparks. "Really, Diana?" he says bitterly. "You're really going to keep pretending? You can stop now. I know everything already. I've figured it all out."

"What?" Diana's aching head whirls. "Figured out . . . ?"

He comes to crouch beside her, his body blocking out the firelight. The skin around his eyes is dark and puffy. "You need to tell me who's handling you, Diana. I want names. *Real* names. No playing dumb, no lying."

"Handling me?" Diana stares up at him with her good eye. "What do you mean?"

"Oh, for the love of God." Roy stands up and pushes his hair back from his face. Then his eyes drop, and he looks at the cave floor for a long moment. "You know what hurts most, Diana?" he says, finally. "I came really, really close to buying your whole act. I thought you were so good for me. A simple woman. A soft place to land. Someone to keep me from feeling so . . . alone." His shoulders drop. "So alone."

Even now, Diana can't help it—she sees his pain and wants to help. She knows she can. She knows now that Herself was real, that she really did master the Tasks. She also remembers what the wolf said:

"I have been trying to help him. By making sure he got to you." She tries to relax, to do the Tasks now. But her meat-self hurts terribly, and it's utterly vulnerable, and try as she might, she can't quiet its serpentine, fight-or-flight dread. She can't force herself not to be afraid.

Roy walks back to the fire, head hanging. "All my life, the women I've dated were all so vapid, so self-centered. Sooner or later it was always"—he switches to a high falsetto—"'What about me? What about me? What about me?'" He snorts in disgust. "Incredibly selfish. But I thought you were different, Diana." He turns to look at her. "You know, right from the moment I saw you, I couldn't stop thinking about you. Wanting you. Even though you're nothing special. Just average. And I've been with so many special women." He drops his gaze to the fire, a tear running down his cheek. "The way I felt about you . . . it was like . . . magic."

Diana is crying, too, the glue of dried blood on her left eye dissolving in tears. She's never imagined a scene as strange as this. Her wildest dream—hearing Roy say he loves her—coming true in the very same moment as her worst fear—that he will hate and reject her. Even with her arms and legs bound, wounded, hurting, and terrified, she can see in his face and hear in his voice that Roy's loneliness and suffering are real. Whatever withdrawal, isolation, and exposure have done to him, whatever temporary insanity this is, he needs her.

"I felt the same way about you, Roy," she says soothingly. "From the moment I saw you, I just wanted to be with you, help you. Love you."

Roy turns sharply to look at her. "Stop lying to me, you treacherous bitch. Who sent you? What did you do to me?"

"Do to you?" Diana repeats. Her voice sounds stupid in her own ears.

"Did you hypnotize me? Well, of course you hypnotized me, that's always part of it. But did you also slip me something to soften me up? A fancy synthetic serotonin, maybe? What's Homeland Security dishing out these days?"

"Homeland Security?" Once again, Diana feels adrift in a sea of confusion.

"Oh, yeah. I figured out it's them. Has to be Homeland, because that's how they would justify it. My exploratory committee already knows I'm going to ace a run for the Senate, then the presidency. Did I tell you that, bitch? Did I tell you I'm going to be president? I'm already the most powerful man in the world; I might as well have the title, right? So our dear Commander in Chief is probably telling his henchmen right now that I'm going to kick his party's ass right out of the White House, and that constitutes 'a threat to national security.' Am I right?"

"I don't . . . what are you talking about?" Diana closes her eyes, exhausted.

"Well, whatever you've been using to mess up my head, it's not going to work any more. I'm onto you." He pulls on the short strands of his rough beard with one thin hand. "You know, Diana," he says after a moment, "I fault myself for not seeing through it. Especially when you showed up here, right where I'd set up camp!" He barks a hard laugh. "I mean, really. You just *lived off the land* for over a month, and then somehow managed to find me?" The volume of his voice is rising steadily. "I don't *think* so! No, they swooped in and got you the second I was out of sight, didn't they? And they healed you up at some rich-bitch spa, and then they sent you back to spy on stupid ol' Roy Richards."

The volume of his voice has been rising steadily until he's nearly shouting. His face looks several shades darker, and Diana can see the veins in his temples bulging again.

"Roy, I swear to you," she croaks. "I swear to God I don't know what you're talking about! I was an unemployed retail clerk in Van Nuys. I saw you on TV and fell in love with you, right then. It was just like you said, Roy. Right from the start. Magic."

In three long, strides, Roy walks over to her, pulls back one heavy boot, and kicks Diana in the stomach. She lets out a grunt of agony, then gags and retches, laboring to breathe.

"If you tell me one more lie, so help me, I'll shut your mouth for good!" Roy yells. "Tell me who sent you!"

Diana sobs, her knees pulled up, her torso curling to protect her abdomen.

"Have you forgotten, Diana? *I saw you with that wolf!*" He's screaming now, his voice echoing off the stone walls. "You think I just fell off the fucking turnip truck, Diana? I've seen things most people can't even imagine. I've read the CIA's reports about teaching mind control to their agents. I've read about the dolphins they used as torpedo delivery systems. And a lot more, too. I've watched a *houngan* make zombies out of ordinary people in Haiti. I've seen shamans in the Amazon jungle get jaguars to kill for them. You think I don't know witchcraft when I see it? Think again. Call it hypnosis, call it biochemistry, call it whatever the hell you want—*I've seen it.*"

Roy stands over her, fists and teeth clenched. Diana can't stop crying.

"Don't believe me?" he says. "Feel this." He breathes in and pulls his shoulders back. Diana's whole body tenses, waiting for more blows, but Roy just stands and stares at her with withering hatred, his face going darker than ever, the veins in his forehead throbbing in time with his rapid heartbeat.

"Had enough?" he snarls after a minute.

"Yes." Diana nods desperately. She has no idea what he's talking about, but whatever it is, agreeing seems like the best move.

"You think you're the only one with tricks up your sleeves?" Roy smirks. "I could explode your heart right now if I wanted to, just with my mind. I learned that from an old Special Ops vet. He used to buy a dozen rats a week, kill them with his mind, for fun."

The hope in Diana's heart is dying. She can't follow Roy's logic. She wonders how long he's been taking all those medications, what they've done to his mind.

"Weaponized witchcraft!" Roy says. "A brilliant strategy. Almost sure to go undetected in a world that no longer believes in witches." He reaches down, grabs Diana's hair, and yanks her head up close to his mouth. She screams as a fresh dazzle of pain bursts through her body. "But I believe in witches, Diana," Roy growls softly into her ear. "Oh, I believe." He drops her, and Diana's battered head slams against the cave floor with a fresh explosion of agony.

"So here's an idea, witch." Roy crouches beside her, resting his folded arms on one knee. "Why don't we stop playing this stupid game and have an honest conversation, for the *very first time*? I think you owe me that, don't you? After I've risked my life to save yours—over and over? After I've shown you nothing but kindness and self-sacrifice?" His voice begins to tremble with anger. "After you and your buddies trap me in this hellhole for weeks, set your little wolf-dogs on me, try to break my spirit? Oh, yeah, I'd say you owe me big-time, bitch." He presses his lips together, his eyes filling with tears again.

The hope of reaching Roy, of helping him see reason, is disappearing from Diana's heart. The pain of that loss is worse than any of her physical wounds. She feels herself giving up, going limp. She lies with her throbbing head crushed into the rocks, her eyes fixed straight ahead, looking at nothing.

"I'm going to get the truth out of you, one way or another," Roy says, sniffing back tears and wiping his mustache with the back of his hand. "You're not the only one who's gotten training in mind control. I've broken a lot of men's minds in my time. Tough men. Strong men. Believe me, Diana, breaking a woman is *nothing*." He flashes her a smile that's more like a baring of fangs. "A little rough sex and the job's ninety percent done."

He chuckles, staring at Diana with the empty gray eyes of a fish, then bursts into laughter. "I gotta say, Diana, until today I never thought I'd actually club a woman and drag her through the woods to my cave." His teeth glint as he laughs again. "Check that one off the old bucket list, right? Ha ha! Who says vision boards don't work?" Still laughing, he suddenly lunges forward and grabs Diana's neck with one hand. "Are you going to confess to me now, witch? Say, 'Yes, Roy.'" His thumb is crushing her windpipe, and she gags and coughs uncontrollably. Roy throws her head back to the floor. "Say it!"

Diana gasps for air, then flops like a rag doll, staring blankly at the dancing firelight on the cave walls. She feels the *other* trying to rise in her chest, then dying away.

Roy slaps her across the face so hard it feels as if her head might come off her neck. *"Look at me when I'm talking to you!"* he screams. *"Pay attention! Goddammit, you will show me the respect I deserve!"*

All Diana hears is meaningless sound. The words are incomprehensible. Her body is just a sack of blood and bones and pain. She's disappearing into numbness.

Roy stands up and begins pacing around the cave, his movements wired and springy, a tiger in a cage. "It makes me sick to my stomach!" he hisses. "To think of you and your buddies plotting against me, attacking me, while I rot out here in this shithole. Alone. *Alone,* Diana! One lone man, against all that power, all that treachery, all that *evil.*"

He grabs a burning stick from the fire and throws it at her. "And this whole time, you've been *mocking* me! *Laughing* at me! *Me! Roy Richards!* A man who never did anything to you—to anyone—except give, and give, and give!" The tears are flowing again, trickling into Roy's beard.

The flaming stick lands close to Diana's face. A spark flies off and lands on her cheek. She doesn't move. Doesn't even blink.

"Have you been screwing them, too, your boss-men?" Roy sobs. "Don't pimps usually have sex with their whores? Because that's what you are, Diana. A witch-whore. Selling the love and honor of a good man to feather your own nest. Cheating me in every way there is to cheat." He sobs again. "How could you? How could you do this to me?"

He kicks her again. Then again, and again, so hard that she's propelled backward across the floor. Finally her bound arms and back jam hard into a pile of loose rock.

In Diana's mind a strange video has begun. Dozens of scenes. Hundreds. Thousands. Thousands of women on thousands of floors, thousands of men standing over them, screaming, hitting, kicking. The setting is different in each scene, the faces, the languages. But the women's fear and horror and terrible shame are monotonously similar.

"You were never really mine, were you?" Roy shouts. "You never really loved me. You were unfaithful, Diana." Screaming now. *"I loved you, and you were so, so unfaithful to me!"*

He runs to his backpack and picks up his knife. It glitters orange in the firelight. Diana stares blankly at it. In her memory a hundred thousand men pull a hundred thousand knives on a hundred thousand women. In war, in riots, in gangs, in private. The memories are so numerous she could never count them. Yet Diana's *other* is in every scene, feeling them all, looking out through all those pairs of terrified eyes.

Then Roy is on her, kneeling on the floor, fumbling with her feet. It occurs to her that he might kill her now. They often do. But usually, when it's like this, they rape first. Diana stares at the wall of the cave, not moving, not feeling.

"Well, maybe you weren't mine before, but now I'm going to *make* you mine, witch." Diana hears the ripping sound of the knife cutting through duct tape, and her legs are suddenly unbound. The blood rushes into her numb feet. Roy tears the tape off her jeans.

"So true, what they say," he says with a snarling chuckle. "If it can't be fixed with duct tape, it can't be fixed." He shakes the sticky tape off his hand. Then he reaches up, grabs the waistband of Diana's jeans, and pulls down hard. She feels nothing. Her body is completely insensate now. The memories flow even faster: millions of men ripping and forcing the clothes off millions of women. And in some strange, distant way, Diana realizes her *other* was there with every woman. Every single time.

"I'm going to do you a favor, hoofer, and leave your boots on," says Roy. "Did you wonder why I couldn't get it up when you came back with those disgusting feet? Did you think I wasn't a man? I'll show you what a man is, *babe*. I'm hard as a steel pipe right now."

He yanks her jeans further down, all the way to her ankles. Diana's taped arms rest painfully on the rocky rubble, and her bare hips, pulled briefly upward, land against a large, sharp rock. Diana notes this in a detached, indifferent way. But then something moves against the skin of her back, something cool and rough and soft, and this touch enters her awareness, because it is connected to her *other*.

Roy tries to flip Diana onto her back, but manages only to twist her hips toward him. He climbs up her body until his hands are on her shoulders, pushing her upper torso back across the loose stones. Then he holds her down with his left hand—they often do this, Diana recalls—while using his right hand to unbuckle his belt.

The soft roughness against Diana's back moves again. This is unfamiliar, even to her *other*. It's not something she's felt in all these countless experiences of attack and violation. She gives it more of her attention. As she does, the soft thing swirls against her back. Diana is so surprised she twitches involuntarily.

"Don't you fight me, witch!" Roy slaps her again, on the wounded side of her head. Then his voice drops to an urgent whisper. "You know what every woman really wants? A master. A mate who's man

enough to conquer her. Well, I'm about to conquer you, Diana. You push back, and I'll just—ha ha!—I'll just conquer you harder."

Diana's mind flickers away from the endless scenes of rape to focus on a more recent memory: running back from the little lake to her camp, obsessed with finding Roy. Rolling up her sleeping bag, grabbing her pack, not checking to see what was inside.

Roy has his pants down now. His right hand shoves Diana's shoulder back. He kicks her legs apart with his knees.

From the stones beneath Diana's back comes a loud, stuttering buzz.

Roy pauses, frowning. "What the . . . ?"

As Diana understands, she feels the hum of her *other* meet the buzzing vibration from her back. A bolt of electricity jolts her tailbone, then flashes up her spine and into every nerve in her body. It shocks away all concepts, all thought, all fear. She is suddenly wide awake, *wild* awake, supercharged with an energy that almost throws her into a sitting position, despite Roy's heavy hands on her shoulders. As she sits up, she feels the cool, soft pressure slide up her backbone, into her hair, over her skull.

Roy grabs Diana's face and shoves her head back. She feels cool roughness sliding forward through her tangled hair, then sees a chunky, triangular head. It jabs out, lashing at Roy. Neck strained backward, almost choking, Diana mouths a single word.

"Cloyd."

Roy freezes, eyes and mouth open wide. He stares at the snake as it recoils into Diana's hair and then hurls itself forward again, jaws gaping. A fang grazes Roy's forehead and he screams, lurching backward and scrambling to his feet. Diana feels Cloyd pour rapidly forward, the long, cool body with its buzzing tail flowing over her face, her breasts, her belly. Roy yells hoarsely, backing away, almost stepping into the fire.

Then Diana's body is moving, swiftly and smoothly, as if she had no wounds, no weariness. She works her bound hands under her hips, straining her shoulder ligaments, then pulls her feet through the closed circle of her arms. With her hands in front of her now, she leaps to her feet, pulling her jeans up again so she can run. There are no words in her mind, no ideas, no past, no future. Just wild life, aware of living, wanting to live longer.

As she moves, she sees a flash of Roy grabbing his hatchet, hacking at Cloyd. Then she's at the back of the cave, running into what looks like a narrow dead end, a crevice in the wall of the cave, black with shadow. She's felt air flowing from this place in the past, and even now there's a slight breeze on her face.

She sidles into the crevice, feeling for the source of the airflow. Groping with her taped hands, she finds a small, irregular opening, barely wider than her body, near the floor. She has no fear or hesitation about moving forward. To the snake in her brain, the absolute blackness of the hole, the narrowness of it, feels welcoming, safe. Diana pushes her taped-together hands into the opening, then puts in her head and wriggles forward.

She's wedged into a narrow passage, kicking herself forward with her feet, scraping her shoulders. But after only a foot or so of solid stone, the inside of the wall begins to crumble. Her hands feel the passageway opening up. Diana drags herself forward until her hips clear the narrowest pinch of the opening. Then she half-crawls, half-tumbles downward into utter darkness, finally jarring to a stop against a huge boulder.

Shaking, panting, Diana gets to her hands and knees. Her body is her own again, not the slack, lifeless thing Roy just kicked around his cave. She lifts her hands to her face and begins biting through the duct tape on her wrists. It takes a minute to find the torn edge, but once she does the job is quick. As the feeling flows back into her hands, Diana looks around.

Her first coherent thought is *So this is real darkness.*

Diana has lived through many long nights, has roamed neighborhoods without streetlights, slept in rooms with no windows. She thought that was darkness. Now she realizes that every other darkness she's ever experienced has been floodlit compared to this true, unimaginably total blindness. For a moment her heart speeds up, but Diana begins the First Task, slowing her breath deliberately, refusing to panic.

Her wounds hurt again. Diana gingerly touches her back, wincing at the sting of raw cuts studded with dirt and thorns. Roy must have dragged her by one leg, since all the cuts seem to run vertically up from her hips to her mid-torso, where her jacket bunched up and protected her skin. Her head is still pounding, and she feels dizzy, though that may be as much from dehydration and the lack of any visual references as from blows to her skull.

She's not sure she can stand up—not sure what to do even if she could. Maybe if she waits long enough, Roy will leave his cave and she can somehow climb out the way she came in. Even as she thinks this, she knows it's a pathetic plan: He has food, warmth, light; she has none. If anyone can win the waiting game, it's Roy. Diana is sliding back into despair when she hears a savage cry from above.

"Got you, you bastard!"

Diana feels a tingling sensation at the base of her spine. It slides into her back and up, a pulse of gentle electricity that re-energizes her body yet again. She feels the inward calm of the snake's small mind, without its body now. She feels no sense of loss, no sorrow, in that reptilian consciousness. Just pure existence without judgments or concepts, cool and quiet, at home in the darkness under the earth. It travels in waves along each nerve. Her uncertainty dissolves along with all thought of the future. She is simply here, now.

Diana gets to her knees and feels around her with her hands, assessing the space. She seems to be in a tunnel about five feet wide, four feet high. The cave floor under her feet slopes slightly downward. The rock around her is smooth, water-scoured. This must once have been an underground stream. If there's any way out of the cave system, the water would have found it. She rises carefully to her feet, stooping to avoid hitting her head on the channel's low ceiling, resting in the cool tingling energy moving through her spine. If she can just focus on that and keep moving, in a few minutes, maybe twenty, at the most, she'll be out of the cave and free.

Then, above her, a narrow beam of light cuts the blackness. It roams around, a cylinder of silvery dust motes piercing the dark, then disappears again. Diana hears a clanging sound, then a muffled curse. A pebble skitters against her boots, then another, then several more. Then Roy's voice screams into the dead silence of the tunnel.

"You think you can run away from me, witch? You think I'll give up before I conquer you? You're going to die just like your goddam snake!"

More clanging, more skittering pebbles. In her mind's eye, Diana can see Roy pounding with his hatchet at the crumbly stone around her escape tunnel. Her mouth goes dry again. Her heart beats like a trapped bird. She begins feeling her way slowly forward, downward, into blackness beyond blackness.

Above her, the cold white eye of Roy's flashlight peers into the tunnel, withdraws again. Diana speeds up, her hands in front of her, bumping her aching head against the uneven stone ceiling. Roy's voice echoes down the passage, deafening, seeming to come from everywhere.

"You think Roy Richards is afraid of the dark?" he roars. *"Bitch, I AM the dark!"*

UNDERWORLD

Only if you have spent time in a cave, beloved, can you imagine the darkness gathered around Diana right now. The absence of light is so total that she feels as if she's pushing her way through something solid, a dense black substance her body can absorb the way a sponge absorbs ink. Her lungs gulp darkness. Her heart pumps darkness through her veins and arteries, delivering darkness to every cell in her body, until darkness fills her entirely.

She moves down the tunnel as fast as she can, holding her left hand up in front of her face to feel for obstacles while her right hand traces the cold, smooth stone wall. Her heartbeat is so loud she fears Roy will be able to follow her by its sound alone. Her bruised, aching head pounds in time with her pulse.

After a few interminable minutes, the sound of Roy's hatchet slamming into stone stops, and a series of grunts and curses echoes through the cave as he forces himself through the opening. Then Diana hears a clattering scrape as he skids down the incline to the tunnel floor and hits the bottom with a thump.

Diana is almost paralyzed with fear. Any second she might find herself wedged into a dead end or narrow crevice, waiting like an insect pinned to a specimen board for whatever Roy wants to do to her. She hears his voice behind her, terrifyingly close. He isn't shouting, just speaking loudly, but the sound rushes through the still, barren space as if amplified by a powerful microphone.

"You're making a very, very bad mistake, Diana!" he calls. "You shouldn't have left. No one walks out on Roy Richards."

Diana's left hand, waving in front of her face like an ant's antenna, jams against a column of stone. She explores it with both hands, Braille-reading the rock, and discovers that the narrow tunnel branches in two directions going forward. A flash of hope: If she takes one channel, and Roy chooses the other, she can still get away. What she'll do after that . . . Diana pushes away the thought and heads down the left side of the fork, the darkness pressing in on her aching, stinging, exhausted body.

Roy's shout follows Diana like a boulder rolling down the tunnel. "You may as well come back now and spare yourself some effort, Brownie Girl." He sounds pleasant, diplomatic. "I'll find you anyway."

Diana glances behind her. She can't see Roy's flashlight; he must be standing by the entrance, trying to tempt her back to him before risking his own trip into the cold ink of the cave. Diana creeps along the tunnel wall, placing her feet as softly as she can. When Roy speaks again, his voice sounds farther away. "All right, Diana. Enough children's games. Let's be rational about this. Come back and we'll patch up this whole thing, okay? No hard feelings."

The corridor is narrowing around Diana, the ceiling coming down and the floor rising until she has to crawl to move forward, scraping her shoulder blades. The floor is covered with thick, cold mud. The thought that she might get stuck in it brings on a fresh wave of claustrophobic terror, but then Diana feels the snake-sense pulsing along her spine. It can tolerate the tight dark space; it seems to know instinctively how to wriggle through it. Even so, Diana is hugely relieved when the passageway opens up again. Once on the other side, she feels a surge of gratitude for the narrow space; it may be too small for Roy.

Several minutes pass in silence as she gropes her way to another tributary and turns again. Then, behind her, she hears that clanging sound: metal on stone. Roy must have followed her through the left fork and found the narrow place in the tunnel. She hears him grunting loudly through gritted teeth. The next time he speaks, he's abandoned all pretense of congeniality.

"You think I don't know caves, you stupid whore?" he yells, his voice riding the thick darkness, echoing from everywhere. "I freaking *love* caves. Spent my whole childhood exploring them. That's how Batman got his power, right? Once I read that, I started caving every chance I got. By the time I was twelve, I made Batman look like a pussy."

Diana takes another blind turn. The place is a labyrinth, a Swiss-cheese network of crisscrossing tunnels. She pushes away the sickening thought that even if she escapes Roy, her chances of finding her way out are virtually nil. She'll die here, in this Stygian darkness. Her mind knows that. But the snake energy still moves forward, irrationally bent on a little more life.

A triumphant shout from behind her. "I found your track, Diana," Roy yells exultantly. "Did you forget I'm a tracker? I can track a mouse over solid rock, babe. I can track a bird through the fucking sky. That's how I always find my way back when I go caving. And it's why I always catch what I hunt."

He begins humming loudly, his voice careening through the labyrinth. He must want her to hear him, coming inexorably up behind her. He's scaring her into the open, into a bad decision. It's a classic hunting strategy. And it's working. For a moment, Diana considers turning back and letting Roy have her, just to end this awful, slow-motion pursuit. Only the thought of what he'll do to her before he kills her keeps her stumbling forward.

"Remember, bitch, whoever you're working with, they can't help you here," Roy shouts. Now he's slowly but definitely getting closer. "They won't find you. Ever. I'm the only soul in this world who can get you out of this place."

Diana's head spins, the lack of any visible object spiking her vertigo. She's losing even the memory of light. She tries to picture the woman she was just days ago, a woman who lived under the oaks, who ran for hours toward the man she loved. It's like thinking about someone she barely knows. Confidence, happiness, peace—none of those are reachable from her sick, spinning blindness.

"Hey, Brownie Girl, did I ever tell you about my quest to Central America?"

Diana stops short, shoving her fist against her mouth to muffle a gasp: Roy sounds as if he's in front of her, very close. She turns and begins frantically groping her way backward, feeling for a tributary passage to take her out of his path.

"I went caving down there, in the jungle." Roy's voice follows her everywhere, relentless, endless. She can hear his slow, deliberate footsteps crunching in gravel. "They're magical, those caves," he calls. "I hired a local to guide me. Miguel. We hiked miles into a channel where tourists never go."

The texture of the cave wall is changing under Diana's fingers, becoming smoother, damper, distorted by strange protuberances and hollows. Her fingers find little stone spikes growing from the ceiling. Below them grow rounded stalagmites that catch her boots, momentarily throwing her off balance. Somewhere ahead of her, beneath the constant drone of Roy's voice, she hears water trickling and dripping.

"We had quite the adventure, Miguel and I," Roy says pleasantly. "Hiked almost a mile through this underground river, up to our chests in ice-cold water. No light except for one little headlamp apiece." A pause, then Roy laughs. "Of course, that's more than you have right now, isn't it, Brownie?"

The water ahead of Diana is getting louder, each drip ringing through the cave system like a note struck from a wooden bell. The way sound travels through the tunnels, amplifying and ricocheting off hard surfaces, confuses Diana's ears almost as much as the darkness confounds her eyes. Head aching, body clenched in fear, she pushes forward. Roy's voice echoes on and on, a hound baying after a fox.

"Miguel and I got to this one little grotto—it was *way* deep in the mountain, *way* down that underground river—full of human skeletons. All their skulls bashed in. The old-time priests used this stone axe for the sacrifices, and—ha!—I'll be damned if it wasn't still right there, lying on a little ledge."

The sound of water is louder now, seeming to come from all directions. Diana reaches down and feels a trickle running along the floor—barely enough to wet her fingers, but flowing. Behind her—she can't tell how close—Roy's steady, methodical footsteps crunch and slurp in the wet, grainy mud.

"So you know what I did then?" He begins to laugh. "You know, I've never told anyone this before, but for some reason, I want to share it with you."

Diana notices a strange, slightly sweet smell. It reminds her of a canister of nitrous oxide she once helped a boyfriend steal from a dentist's office. She remembers huffing the gas, getting loose and loopy, blurting out truths they hadn't meant to tell. The boyfriend had told Diana he was sleeping with several other girls, and she'd told him she'd only hooked up with him to get food and shelter. It was their last date.

Roy is still laughing, his voice almost giddy. "So what I did was, I picked up that axe—probably the first person to touch it in centuries—and I bashed in Miguel's head." He laughs for a long time. "Oh, my God, it was such a rush!"

The sweet smell is stronger now. Diana's head feels light. For a moment she thinks it might lift her right off her feet.

"I could've chickened out." Roy is beginning to sound slurred, drunk. "Believe me, it was no picnic, hiking back through that river alone. But that's what's special about me, Brownie—I have the balls to make sacrifices other men won't. That's why I have so much power. Oh, *man,* that ancient power! I can feel it right now. *And you think you can get away from me in a cave?*" The echoes repeat his roar from all around her.

Diana finds a low channel branching off to the right. She crawls into it, then rises to a crouch as the ceiling opens up. Whatever gas they're breathing, it's taking the edge off her pain and fear. Her body feels clumsy, but her mind is growing calmer, sharper. An image flickers in her memory: a woman—no, many women, but only one at a time—entering darkness like this, breathing in sickly sweet air like this, feeling this strange clarity.

The water on the cave floor is an inch deep now, soaking through the air vents in Diana's hiking boots. It's surprisingly warm, almost like bathwater. It must be bubbling up from thermal springs. She hears it growing into a true stream ahead of her, its silvery babble, like every sound, hugely amplified by the cave. Maybe she'll be harder to track through running water. The thought gives her energy, and she begins moving a little faster. But she can't pull away from Roy's voice.

"I'm really enjoying this little talk, Diana!" he shouts. "You have no idea how frustrating it is to have so many wonderful stories I can't tell the world. So many quests I've fulfilled, so much power I've gained."

Diana fights to suppress a cough. She stumbles and falls down, then surprises herself by giggling under her breath. The sweet fumes in the air are definitely affecting her, but not adversely. She feels more aware and alive. She notices her *other* riding along inside her, watching, waiting.

"*Hey!*" Roy suddenly screams into the blackness, his voice slamming into walls, funneling and rebounding through interlaced tunnels. "*Are you paying attention, Brownie? I am right here, and goddammit, I want your attention!*"

Diana feels a gust of damp, sickly-sweet air against her face. That, and a change in the sound of water, tells her the tunnel she's been following has opened up into a large chamber. She feels her way along the wall, then slips and falls, a bolt of pain lancing through her wounded head. Feeling around her, she finds a floor covered with strange raised circles of stone, like children's wading pools. Each one is as slick as melting ice, filled with warm, chemically sweet-smelling water.

"*Aha!*" Roy's voice rumbles through the tunnel, sending Diana's heart into overdrive. "Hahahahaha! Got your track again, bitch! Ready or not, here I come!"

The helium-balloon weightlessness is spreading throughout Diana's body. Her memory watches the sequence of women entering caves, tasting sweet air, sliding from their bodies into another frequency. Head spinning, she tries to get up, slips, and goes down again. Her boots are more a hindrance than a help. She takes them off, clawing at the laces with fingers that feel fat and slow. As she stands up, she glances back—and sees a faint glow of light moving across stone behind her.

Diana scrambles upright, surprised again by the warmth of the water against her feet. Though her body stills feel drugged and clumsy, it balances much more easily without her boots. She sidles along the chamber wall. Roy's flashlight beam grows brighter, swaying and bouncing with his steps. He's grumbling to himself, coughing, laughing, his footsteps splashing, moving much faster than she can.

Diana feels panic rising. She tries to sense the space around her the way she sensed archery targets in the nighttime forest. The memory feels like something she imagined. Nothing seems real but the darkness.

As Roy enters the chamber, he trips. His flashlight skitters out of his hand, spinning two full rotations before coming to rest. In the brief, glancing flash of light, Diana sees that the space is huge, a lopsided cathedral filled with weird, ornate columns and buttresses. Heart slamming, she gropes her way behind a flange of stone that extends out into the cavern. She slips behind it and drops into a crouch.

Roy curses drunkenly as he gets to his feet and retrieves his flashlight. Then he turns in a slow, exploratory circle. Diana's eyes, hungry for light, follow the flashlight beam. The cavern is surreally beautiful. Frills of lacy stone dangle from the ceiling, sprout from the floor, grow from the walls. Some formations look like misshapen bodies, others like patches of flowers, others like strings of stretched gum. Pools and pockets of water glisten everywhere. On the far side of the chamber is a lake so glassy and still that, even from a distance, Diana can tell it's very deep.

She can hear Roy breathing heavily. *"Diana!"* he shouts. Then he freezes in place for a long moment, listening as his echo repeats the word over and over. Diana desperately hopes that the trickle of the little stream is hiding the sound of her own rapid breathing. Then Roy's voice punches through the cavern again.

"Gotcha!" he shouts, and Diana's heart nearly stops. But his flashlight hasn't found her, just her hiking boots, discarded near the series of small, cratered pools.

"Oh, Brownie, you stupid little hoofer," Roy slurs, his words ringing off the strange architecture of the cavern. "You should learn to pick up after yourself!" He bursts into giggles again, staggers carefully over to pick up the boots.

Roy is clearly impaired, moving sloppily. But though Diana's body also feels clumsy, her mind grows clearer with every breath. As Roy crouches down with his light, examining the cave floor near her hiking boots, she realizes that the moment she went barefoot, she became much harder to track.

"Where aaaaare you, Brownie?" Roy sings into the sweet-smelling air. "Should I catch you and eat you, like I did in New Guinea?" He giggles helplessly, snorting in through his nose. "You ever eaten human meat, Brownie? I have! Gotta break every taboo, master every fear, go where other men don't dare!"

The light wobbles in his hand, but he seems to have found her track. He heads slowly toward her, crouching to see her footprints in the mud of the shallow pools.

"Y'know," he slurs, "at first the Karapuna tried to feed me a pig's heart. Said it was human. *As if I wouldn't know.*" Roy screams the last sentence so loudly it hurts her ears. Her position behind the rock buttress is pathetic, exposed. She fumbles along the wall, trying to find some other hiding place before Roy can see her.

"I wanted to kill the guy who gave me that damn pig heart. But in the end, I just made him help me hunt down a man from another tribe. I gave my guide most of the meat—I'm a heart-eater, myself."

He's within twenty feet of her now. There's nowhere left to run. As Diana accepts this, she draws her first deep breath since entering the cave, and lets out a long sigh of defeat. And then, in the space of surrender, she has a very clear thought. It rings through her whole body, just as it did when she first heard Herself say it: *The mirror image of suffering is the truth.*

Everything inside Diana seems to shift, unwind, and click into place. Her gut, which has been twisted in fear, pain, and exhaustion, suddenly relaxes.

"You're trapped now, Diana!" Roy giggles. "You know you're trapped!" In Diana's mind, the sentence flips: *You're free now, Diana. You know you're free.*

"You're food to me now, hoofer," croons Roy. "Food to help me on my quest. I'm going to gain weight on you while I find my way out of this place. You're just meat, Diana. You're nothing."

You're not just meat, Diana. You're everything.

Diana's mind sharpens by the second. Her memory replays everything about her relationship with Roy. Everything she believed along the way is becoming its mirror image. "He's everything I ever needed." *You are everything he ever needed.* "I'm a basket case." *He's a basket case.* The gas in the cave is intoxicating, but not as much as these shocking new thoughts.

She doesn't plan to speak; she just feels the truth rising from her gut all the way to the top of her head, lifting her from that fetal cringe to a tall stance, spine ramrod straight. When she hears her own voice, it's calm, level, relaxed.

"Wow, Roy," says Diana. "You're completely insane."

Roy jumps so hard he drops the flashlight again. He scrabbles for it, then shines it rapidly around the cavern, trying to locate the sound of her voice in the maze of echoes. *"Where are you?"* he shouts. *"Show yourself, witch!"*

"And so afraid!" says Diana, shaking her head. "You're *so* afraid. That's what it's all been about, isn't it? All of it—the money, the cameras, the houses, the 'quests.' Jumping around on stage screaming about mastery. You can't stop talking because you're afraid of what you'll hear if things ever get quiet."

Roy's flashlight finally hits her dead in the eyes. "Well, lookie look," he hisses. "A dead woman walking." He giggles. "You're going to die, Diana."

"Yes, well, so are you," she says, amazed by her own calm.

"There it is!" yells Roy. "There it is! You're trying to kill me! I *knew* you were trying to kill me!"

"No need, Roy. Death will find you without any help from me."

"SHUT UP!" Roy bellows. *"SHUT UP, SHUT UP, SHUT UP!"* He tries to rush at her, slips, and falls with a yelp of rage.

Diana can tell she's much more stable barefoot than Roy is in his hiking boots. Calmly, she calculates that if she can lure him toward her, then sprint past him to the tunnel entrance, she may still escape. She sidesteps along the wall. Roy lunges at her and slips again, the flashlight bobbling. Diana uses the moment to run into the center of the cave, trying to get past him.

"No you don't, bitch!" He rolls across the floor and comes to rest on his elbows, the strobe of his flashlight hitting her eyes again. She freezes, backing away.

Roy rises to a low crouch, holding the flashlight beam steady on her face. She can't see him, only the blinding light, but she hears him scuttling toward her like a huge spider. She backs away, trying to turn left, then right. Roy parries every move. The flashlight comes slowly closer, backing Diana toward the lake. Fifteen feet away. Ten. Five. She can hear the loud *tock!* of a water drop hitting the clear surface just behind her.

"You should look on the bright side, hoofer," says Roy. "At least you're going to fuel the quest of a truly great man. You're going to live on as part of me."

"No, Roy," says Diana. "I'm going to die wild."

And she jumps backward into the lake.

●

Diana expects an icy shock, but the water is weirdly warm, soft. She feels it close above her and looks up just as Roy's flashlight finds her again. His free arm plunges into the water, blocking the light, grabbing for her hair. She hears his voice, loud and angry, the words unintelligible.

Diana turns away from Roy, uninterested, and looks down into the endless dark. All she has left to do, in her entire life, is breathe in. Just open her mouth and draw water into her lungs. After that, in a few seconds—minutes at the most—it will be over. She tries to make herself inhale, to get it over with, but finds that she can't. Beyond all hope or reason, the pulsing energy in her spine wants to live a few seconds more. Diana paddles lightly with her hands to keep herself from floating upward. Despite her body's will to live, she feels no fear. Devin's beloved face flashes into her mind, along with a surge of regret for his pain. But there's nothing to be done about that, so Diana lets it go. She lets everything go.

Absolutely everything.

In the still water she has no sensation of weight, or touch, or direction; nothing to taste, smell, see, or hear. The warm lake doesn't feel like a substance, but an absence of everything. Diana feels bound-aryless, bodiless. She has no inside or outside, no time, no space. As even her snake-sense surrenders its life, Diana notices that though she has only been in this nothingness for a few seconds, it has been in her, filling her, for eternity. This recognition is the opposite of terror, the opposite of horror. The no-thing-ness is so gentle, so tender, so exquisitely soft, and so, so *alive*. Diana's sightless eyes widen as she realizes—or rather, remembers—that the darkness, no less than the light, is made of love.

"Hello, piglet."

The voice comes from below her, as ordinary and comfortable as an old blanket. In dreamy slow motion, Diana stares downward, her hands stroking the water, her body arcing like a dolphin's. Far below she sees a tiny spatter of light moving toward her. It becomes a constellation, then a galaxy, and finally the shining outline of a huge head, four short legs, two glimmering wings. Diana kicks downward and reaches out her arms. The boar swims into them.

"Welcome home, darling," says Herself. "So nice to have you back in my frequency. Hold on tight now."

Diana locks her arms around the great, beloved, shaggy neck. Herself turns a graceful somersault in the dead-dark water, and dives straight down.

ARKTOS

Down through nothing, toward nothing, into nothing. Diana feels the water growing warmer. The pressure on her ears begins to hurt. Then Herself turns and swims sideways, the current pulling Diana's hair across her face. In the light that glimmers from the boar's wings and bristles, Diana sees stone walls flaring and dimming like a subway tunnel as a train goes by. Though everything still seems to be in dreamy slow motion, she can feel by the pull of the water that Herself is swimming very fast.

A breathless while later—fifteen seconds? fifty?—they angle upward again. The pressure on Diana's ears eases, then vanishes. The boar breaks the surface with a splash, and an instant later Diana feels the cool emptiness of her own face emerging into air. She gulps in a huge breath, so shocked to be alive that no other thought or feeling, not even relief, can form in her mind.

Herself swims powerfully along the surface, and by her light Diana sees they're in a tunnel filled almost to the top with water. Stalactites hang from the ceiling like daggers; the boar swerves to miss a few that come close to Diana's head.

Once she's able to form words again, Diana asks, "Where did you come from, Myself? How did you get to me?"

"Oh, darling," says Herself, her voice glubbing a little in the water. "I've been here all along. You just couldn't see me until you completely released all attachment to matter. Then you became the *master* of matter, you see, and what was present in one realm of reality was able to enter another. What humans call a miracle, but it's quite natural. Happens all the time."

As the underground river flows farther from the mountain's thermal center, the water is growing quickly cooler. In a few minutes it's distinctly chilly, and then truly cold, and finally, freezing. As the minutes pass, Diana begins to shiver. Soon her breath is coming in sobbing gasps, her body going numb.

"Hang on, darling," says Herself, swimming hard. "Not much farther now."

The words flow past Diana like the water, not registering. "Wh-wh-why d-d-did you d-d-disap-pear?"

"I didn't disappear, love. You did. You lost sight of me—that is, you lost sight of Yourself—because you changed frequencies. Fell back into an old belief system, one you shared with Roy and most other humans. That's all."

"Oh." Diana feels tears stinging her eyes. "I'm s-s-sorry."

"No, no, no, dear. *Hoink hoink!* There's nothing to be sorry about." Herself's small, shining wings flap through the water like a penguin's, augmenting the power of her legs. "You're just practicing human consciousness. To know yourself as light, dear, is the nature of consciousness. To know yourself as darkness is the nature of humanness. You must all do both, and there's no way to do it wrong. Everything that's happened is just as it should be."

Diana can't answer. Her teeth are chattering so hard she's afraid they might break right off. She closes her eyes and focuses every bit of attention on keeping her numb arms locked around the boar's neck.

"Stay with me, Diana." Herself puts on an extra burst of speed. "Don't you dare die of hypothermia now, after all I've done for you! *Hoinkhoinkhoink!*"

A second later Diana feels sand beneath her feet.

"Come, dear. Quickly, now. Keep moving. You're quite blue."

Diana sees that Herself has brought them ashore on a small sand-bank near one wall of the tunnel the river has cut through the mountain. The boar slips free of her arms, turns, grabs the shoulder of Diana's jacket in her teeth, and backs away from the river, dragging Diana onto the narrow lip of sand near the cave wall. Diana can do nothing to help. In the air, her wet hair and clothes make her feel impossibly colder. Her body quakes uncontrollably. Her mind is torpid, foggy, unsure of anything except a laser-pointed longing for warmth.

"Keep moving, keep moving," Herself repeats. "I'm sorry, dear, but you absolutely must generate some heat."

Diana groans. "I'm so t-t-tired, M-myself. C-c-c-can't you d-do m-m-magic? J-j-just z-z-zap m-me w-w-warm?"

"Not in this apparent world, love. If you want me to work a miracle, I can—that is, you can as me—but there are still limitations in the apparently physical realm. Magic doesn't defy nature, only what you know of nature. Ah! Look here!"

The boar has found a crack in the wall, a strip of deeper darkness in the darkness. As Diana turns toward it, she realizes that she can hear faint night sounds—not the plinking and echoing of the cave, but the trilling of crickets and frogs that fills the forest every evening. She feels a tiny surge of energy.

"Is th-that a w-w-way ow-ow-out?"

"Why don't we check? *Hoink hoink!* Come on, piglet, keep moving!"

With a gargantuan effort, Diana gets to her hands and knees, then her feet. She stands there swaying and shaking like a building under heavy artillery fire. The place where Roy struck her head still throbs, and her torso feels bruised clear through where he dragged and kicked her.

"D-d-d-did w-we l-l-lose him?"

"You tell me," says Herself.

Before the words are out of her mouth, Diana can already feel the answer. Roy's energy is far away, so faint she can barely feel it, and filled with rage at having lost the chance for revenge against her. She turns her attention away from it, focusing on the much more pressing matter of finding warmth.

The crack in the wall proves just wide enough for the boar to scrape through. The top is too narrow for Diana to traverse upright, which is fine, because when she tries to move forward, she falls down. Shivering so hard she can barely coordinate her movements, she crawls after Herself. The forest sounds grow louder, raising her spirits a little. But even if she escapes the cave alive, she won't be able to get warm in time to stop hypothermia. It will kill her long before she can make a fire.

Ahead of her, the boar's glimmering body disappears. A second later Diana hears her jolly laugh. "Oh, piglet! Isn't this wonderful!"

Diana emerges from the passage into another chamber, this one about the size of her bedroom at home. Her heart leaps when she sees shafts of moonlight coming through cracks in the ceiling, dappling the sandy floor with spots of silver.

Herself stands at the chamber's far wall, her glittering bristles lighting an indistinct, enormous dark lump. Then the lump gives a long, contented sigh.

Diana thinks vaguely that she should be alarmed, but she's too cold to care. By the time her brain can name what she sees, her body is already crawling across the chamber, then—this feels completely normal to Diana—wriggling in between the sleeping bodies of a huge black bear and her yearling cub.

The relief is immediate and unspeakable. Diana has never felt anything as soft, lush, deep, and gloriously warm as the bears' fur. It even smells surprisingly clean, like wood and berries. The she-bear is lying on her side, legs outstretched, and without thinking, Diana butts her head between the great forepaws so that she can curl up with her back to the bear's belly. Part of her mind—a frozen, muffled part—protests that this is dangerous and strange. But to the greater part of Diana, the action feels as sweetly familiar as kissing Devin's head.

The mother bear opens one eye as Diana's wet hair touches the underside of her chin. Diana can feel the animal's mild surprise, quickly followed by a burst of pleasure. *"Diana!"* says the bear's heart. *"Welcome!"*

Diana feels her heart respond, *"Arktos, my oldest friend!"* Her mind immediately thinks, "What what what what what?"

The cub stirs a little. *"Hello, Greatmother!"*

"Polaris!" Diana's heart replies. At this, her mind gives up entirely, like a confused substitute teacher, and falls silent. Diana's numb hands move themselves, stroking the little bear's warm ears, his soft cheeks. The cub cuddles into her so that the three of them are nested spoons, Diana in the Goldilocks center.

"Oh, isn't this just *delightful!*" says Herself. She shakes sand off her bristles and sits down near the cuddle puddle of bear and human. "I love this world."

Gradually Diana's mind thaws, suggesting strongly that she do the rational thing and become concerned about her meat-self's well-being. Then she remembers to treat her mind as a servant, not a master. She closes her eyes and begins the Tasks. They come easily this time, like second nature—like *first* nature. She calms herself, releases into the relaxation, lets her hands pet Polaris's muzzle, feels her heart bond tight to these dear, dear friends. Her wounds are healing, her mind is open. As her eyes pick up ultraviolet, more details become visible in the cave. With a huge sigh, Diana finally, totally relaxes.

The mother bear puts her nose against Diana's head and blows a long, hot breath through her hair, then sniffs the lump where Roy clubbed her. Diana feels the bear's huge warm tongue licking the spot, so tenderly she begins to cry.

"There there, my tiny," Arktos says with her heart. *"My tiny tiny. Rest."*

Suddenly Diana comes completely unhinged, an ice sculpture collapsing in warm weather. All the horror of the past terrible hours shudders through her body, shaking her like a rag doll. The agony isn't just from bruises and cuts. The worst pain of all is the memory of watching Roy transform from the person she loved most to something unimaginably horrible.

"M-m-myself?" Diana says. Shaking. Crying.

"Yes, dear?"

"Y-you know the thing with . . . with Roy and me?"

"Mm-hmm?"

"I'm not s-sure it's g-going to work out."

"Hoink hoink hoink hoink hoink!" The boar's guffaw echoes off the walls, and Diana joins in, her body shaking harder than ever with bittersweet laughter. Then the trauma and fatigue pull her into a fresh spasm of weeping.

"That's it, darling. Just let it happen." The boar leans over the sleeping bear cub to kiss Diana's forehead. "It's so different from this perspective, isn't it? The loss, the sorrow, the fear. You've sat through the shakes with so many creatures. But you've never done it this way. Feeling as if you were just one creature yourself."

Another rush of memories passes through Diana's mind. This time the volume is unimaginable, a tidal wave crushing through a keyhole. Infinite memories of being hunted, running, hurt, escaping, not escaping, surviving, dying. Many of the images are bizarre: monstrous animals flitting through the darkness of the deep sea; huge creatures with fur, scales, feathers, chitinous exoskeletons. There are familiar beings as well, animals and people whose names Diana knows. All with the same longing to survive, the same terror of oblivion. So many, even now in this moment, all over the planet, enduring fear, exhaustion, cold, hunger, injury, devastation.

Diana shakes and weeps for all of them.

She has no idea how long it takes for the trembling to abate. Waves of shaking, waves of memories keep flooding through her as silver patches of moonlight drift all the way from one side of the cave floor to the other.

Finally, the torrent of images subsides to a trickle, the shaking becomes sporadic and small. Diana feels hollowed out. Her breathing calms, slows, and then slows some more, then more, then more. Eventually she notices that her breathing is keeping time with the she-bear's, her heart with the bear's heart. It beats at a strong steady pace, but very slowly, one peaceful *thub-dub* resonating through Diana's body every three or four seconds.

When Diana is finally still, Arktos sighs and stretches luxuriously. The huge paw that has been draped over Diana's shoulder reaches outward, its mighty claws spread wide. For a confused moment, it seems to Diana that *she* is the one stretching, that those claws belong to her. The illusion is so strong she has to touch her hand to her chest to make sure she's actually human.

"Myself?" she whispers, not wanting to disturb the bears. "What's happening?"

"The miracle you requested, of course." The boar preens one wing with her snout. "The one you asked for when you were so cold. I always know they're coming, but I'm never sure exactly how they'll manifest. Everything's always a delicious surprise in this apparent world. I mean, really, my piglet, isn't this the *best*? I've said it before and I'll say it again: You do beautiful work."

Diana considers this for a moment, absentmindedly stroking the bear cub's ears. *Polaris, my tiny,* she finds herself thinking. *Sleep the long sleep, my tiny tiny.* She leans forward to lick the little bear's head. Then she pulls her head back, shocked, and clamps her mouth shut.

"But something's really weird, Myself!" she whispers through clenched teeth. "I . . . I feel like a bear! It's like . . . I mean, like, I thought this cub was Devin!"

"No need to be so quiet, love," says Herself. "Arktos and Polaris are hibernating. We could mine for gold in here, and they'd just snooze along in perfect peace. And no, it's not weird at all that you feel like a bear. Don't you recall that you *were* a bear? Or anyway, part of you was. *We* were. To human minds, anyway. For much longer than you've been in your current meat-self."

Diana's mind still feels sluggish, limp with relief, relaxation, and exhaustion. But even if she were fresh and rested, she's not sure this would make sense. "What are you talking about?" she says wearily. "Why don't you ever just talk like a regular . . . um . . . winged . . . wild boar?" She giggles, and Polaris emits a small, happy grunt.

"Hoink hoink hoink!" The boar flicks her shining wings, scattering the last few water drops. "Long ago," she says, "when humans still spoke almost nothing but the heart-language, the She-Bear was their image of a universal force—Hmm, how shall I say it? You might call that force the divine feminine."

An image Diana has seen before pops into her mind, bright and vivid. A line of little girls dressed in fur, swaying rhythmically. Pipes and flutes played on a rocky hillside. The memory intensifies until it almost blots out the present, and Diana realizes that the girls are coming toward her. She's standing at the mouth of her den, blinking, just awakening from the long sleep. Behind her, two newborn cubs grope their way upward, about to see sunlight for the first time.

"We have gifts for you, Greatmother!" the little girls think in the heart-language.

"How marvelous!" Diana feels back, her heart bright with gratitude. *"Thank you, my tinies!"*

The little girls truly are tiny, or Diana is enormous, or both: each child could walk beneath her belly with headroom to spare. They leave their offerings on a large rock near her den and retreat to a respectful distance.

Diana eats the treats in absolute ecstasy. Nothing could be better than the taste of honeycomb after the long sleep. This is Diana's favorite part of the agreement her kind has shared with the humans and the bees, time out of mind. The humans make clay beehives and plant flowers all around them, so that the bees are able to make more honey than they need. The humans share the extra honey with the She-Bear. She protects the human tinies from the saber-tooths and the dire wolves, so they can go on tending the flowers and the bees. It works well for the deer and other grazers, too; they thrive on the greenery. That means the meat-eaters have plenty, and they ensure that the grazers never overwhelm the soil's ability to feed them. All for all, always. In life and in death.

"Ah, those were sweet times on Earth," says Herself with a sigh. "Humans were so much more peaceful before they started communicating in mouth-sounds and lost the heart-language."

The memory shifts, and now the little girls dance in yellow cloth, with choreographed steps and songs to go with the music. Diana sees the scene replayed hundreds of times, every year with a different group of girls. As time goes on, they make a word for the whole ceremony, the ritual in honor of Arktos, the Blessed Mother Bear of the North: the Arkteia.

Diana blinks several times, astonished. Of course all this can't be real, her human mind tells her. But her gut tightens. So she gives in and believes the memory, which is every bit as clear as her images of working at Super Big Mart, or driving on Los Angeles freeways. Her gut relaxes.

"Wait . . . what . . . then . . . Myself, go back, go back. Are you saying I was a *bear*? Like, in a past life or something?"

"Part of you was, yes. Actually a long, long series of bears." Herself lies down next to the cub, who is snoring softly. "All of them chosen to represent the Greatmother of nature itself. That's why the cub in the sky is the constellation of the North Star—because humans once knew that to follow the protection of the divine feminine is to find true north. Later, when their minds were warped by fear and war-lust, humans forgot that wisdom. Which, as you know, is why we're here now."

"As I know?" Diana's chest feels strange, overfull of an emotion she can't identify. It's akin to anxiety, but that usually speeds up her heartbeat, and right now her pulse is still as slow as the mother bear's. She feels the *thub-dub* of Arktos's pulse, a huge velvet gong, sounding its twenty slow times a minute.

"But, Myself, I *don't* know," she says. "Why *are* we here now?"

In her mind another memory pops into focus. This one is more recent, less bizarre. Which frankly, Diana thinks, isn't saying much.

She sees herself—her *other*—leaning over her Hyundai in the Super Big Mart parking lot, writing on the window. There are the symbols again: γνῶθι σεαυτόν. But this time Diana knows, without knowing *how* she knows, what the symbols spell, and what they mean.

"Gnothi seauton," she murmurs under her breath. "Know thyself."

A soft *hoink hoink hoink*. "Very good, piglet!"

A long pause. Diana is afraid to speak the next question. But eventually, it comes out anyway.

"Myself?"

"Yes, love?"

"Who am I?"

25

SPACETIME

Diana breathes shallowly, wanting and not wanting to hear the answer. She stares into Herself's eyes, shadowed by their thick lashes in the silver light.

"My love," says the boar, "you are Diana."

"No, no, I don't mean that," says Diana, with a hint of impatience. "I know I'm me, of course I'm me. But, I mean, who am I *really*?"

The boar twitches her ears. "Let me say this in a different way, darling. And by that I mean in a more important-sounding voice." She drops into her lowest alto register. *"You are Diana. Hoink hoink hoink!"*

"I don't get it." Diana wipes a wisp of bear fur away from her lip.

"You're Diana," the boar repeats. *"Diana* Diana."

"You mean . . . like the princess? She's dead."

"Keep going," says Herself.

"Well, what other Diana could it—"

A long moment of silence. Outside, the crickets chirp, the frogs trill. Diana's face slowly loses all expression.

"And we have liftoff," says Herself.

"No," says Diana.

"Yes, indeed."

"No, no, no." Diana shakes her head. "That's impossible, Myself. That's crazy. I am an ordinary person. I'm nobody." Her gut twists.

"Just notice," says Herself, "that you're making this argument in a cave, to a wild boar, while occupying the center of a bear sandwich. *Hoink hoink hoink hoink hoink!*"

"Nuh-uh." Diana closes her mouth tightly and shakes her head like a toddler. "Nuh-uh, no, no, no! You're wrong you're out of your mind that's absolutely freaking— No no no *no* NO!"

She shouts the last syllable, pushing herself up and away from the mother bear. Arktos reaches out one massive paw and sleepily pulls Diana back into a loving embrace that couldn't be pried open with the Jaws of Life. The goose-egg bruise on Diana's scalp throbs.

"Myself," she says desperately, "listen! I am *not that special*! Ow!" She curls around her stabbing gut. "I'm a trash baby foster child living in a crummy little apartment in Van Nuys. Boring, normal, average Diana Archer."

"I didn't say you weren't average," says Herself. "You're *amazingly* average. And you honestly think that name is a coincidence? Also the surname of every family who ever took you in—the Eichenwalds, the Mantons, the Grovers, the Forrests, the Hunters?"

Diana just shakes her head.

"Look, dear." The boar's voice is calm, reasonable. "Everything you just said about yourself is true. You are Diana Archer. And you're also Diana *the* Archer. The Shining One. Goddess of the Hunt. Mistress of the Oaks. Tender of mountains and forests. Guardian of wild animals. Comforter of mothers giving birth. Protector of those under sexual assault. Also called Artemis, moon goddess, woodland keeper, queen of all bees. And before that, Artio or Arktos, bear-goddess of the wild."

The mother bear responds with a sleepy chuff, and Herself bows slightly in the direction of her head. "You've had thousands of names over hundreds of thousands of years, darling," the boar tells

Diana. "But in your present circumstance—how can I put this in a nutshell—you're as close as the universe can come to incarnating, in one single human meat-suit, a manifestation of the entire divine feminine."

Diana's body is humming with so much electricity that small sparks flash everywhere her body touches the bears' fur. *"Nooo!"* she wails softly. "No, I can't . . . I don't . . . what would that even mean? Even if it were true? Which it *can't* be." The stabbies combine with the electricity to send crackling shocks through her abdomen.

Herself shrugs. "It means we loaded up an entire goddess into a single human body. Well, mostly. There was a little left over, so we distributed that over a few other humans—not that many, just a few million. But every atom of *this* body, Diana, holds the divine feminine in concentrated form. That's why it's always tended to, you know . . . spill out here and there."

Diana's jaw goes slack again. "My fugue states."

"That sounds so negative, dear. They were just moments when your meta-self had to push aside your human mind to save you, or someone else. You've been answering cries for help so long you couldn't quite switch off the reflex."

Diana stares at the wall, feeling the veil of ignorance between her mind and her fugue-state self shimmering, growing thin and translucent.

"It would have been nice to wait until all human meat-selves evolved a bit more—enough to hold the energy of a goddess more easily," says the boar. "But we're in a bit of a predicament, you see. Humans are very, very close to destroying their own ability to survive. They have to wake up, Diana, or they'll disappear quite soon, and not in a fun way. So you volunteered to help. As you always have."

The wall of ignorance shimmers harder, and then begins to rip. It feels like an atomic explosion in Diana's brain. She suddenly remembers all of it—every bit of "lost" time. Time she spent, invariably, going to the aid of a creature in peril. Always the call, *"Help! Help!"* Always the prickling heat. Always the mission to rescue and restore. So many animals saved from trees, drainage pipes, air vents. So many humans in the process of giving up when she'd burst in with a wild energy that struck their aggressors dumb with confused terror.

The memories pop and crackle like firecrackers into her consciousness. The man who ran into his own closet when she'd surprised him beating his son. The pack of drug runners about to rape and kill a prostitute. The bald white supremacist forcing dogs to fight to the death. She'd stopped them all, sailing in with this one, average little meat-self. Her mission is far beyond what's happened so far, but one-on-one rescue is apparently a habit Diana has never quite been able to break.

The sparks of static electricity dancing between her skin and the bears' fur are so bright Diana begins to fear she might set the animals on fire. Her body feels like a lightning bolt in a clay jar. "Myself," she gasps, "I think I'm having a stroke, or a seizure or something."

The boar rolls onto her back, spreading her wings. "Don't worry, piglet, you'll be fine," she says, wriggling back and forth in the sand, trotters in the air. "You can handle this. Remember the Tasks. Use them."

"Right, right. Of course. The Tasks." Diana nods, immeasurably relieved to have a familiar job. She begins. Step one: Calm the reptile brain. It takes a while. She holds the truth in her mind like a strange, large, wrapped package, tantalizing and terrifying. Diana is unsure of its provenance or utility. She can't think how to get a handle on it.

"You're doing fine, dear. Just allow it to sink in," the boar encourages her. "Your presence in a human meat-self has caused a serious ripple already, energetically speaking. Quite a few humans have awakened on their own, just sharing the planet with you—the occasional wacky yogi, monk, nun, and so on. Plus lots of wilderness wanderers and beekeepers no one ever knew about. Of course, so far they've all been completely misunderstood by other humans."

By dint of enormous, slow breaths, Diana physically squeezes the fear out of her meat-self. When she feels completely calm, she moves on to Task number Two. She tastes the boar's strange words, every sense alert for poison. She finds only nourishment. In fact, her gut feels more relaxed and content than it ever has before.

Task number Three: Allow her meta-self to have the meat-suit, to take over, to use her limbs and muscles. As her solar plexus begins to tingle, Diana's fear suddenly spikes, and she loses all alignment. She has no idea what activities the meta-self might have planned for her, but she suspects they will be extremely unusual.

"Myself," she says. "I can't. I can't do this. I don't need to be a hero. I don't want to be. Owwwww . . ." She ends with a whimper.

The boar sits up and shakes sand out of her ears. "Diana, my best piggly-wiggly, there are two kinds of hubris. The kind that makes humans obsessed with being bigger, better, more important than others. We see a classic illustration of such hubris in our friend Roy."

Diana winces.

"You, piglet—most humans, actually—suffer from the other kind of hubris. The kind that makes you see yourself as smaller and less important than you really are. The kind that won't allow you to identify as part of the divine. That, Diana, is the last piece of ego you have left to sacrifice."

"But, Myself," she whispers, "I just *can't* be . . ." The pain in her gut is horrible.

"You are."

Diana's fear spikes into true terror, as if she's skidding toward the edge of a thousand-foot precipice. But the stabbies won't let her run away. She clears her head, calms her fear, lets truth feed her. Then, very slowly, she allows the meta-self to move into her solar plexus, the place where all her motor nerves crisscross. Not much happens; she simply sinks deeper into the comfort of the sleeping bears.

"You see?" says Herself. "This isn't so bad, is it?"

Diana doesn't answer. The warmth is rising from her solar plexus up into her heart, like the tendrils of a vine. The sensation is exquisite. Her heart seems impossibly vast, every slow beat the movement of continents. She feels into it—and into it, and into it. Her heart, she feels, is literally infinitely deep. Each cell, trillions of times smaller than her body, is love. Each atom, billions of times smaller than a cell, is love. Each electron, billions of times smaller than an atom, is love. And each of the infinitesimal particles that make up electrons—each tiny cloud of energy—contains its own universe. And all of those universes are nothing, nothing, nothing but love.

"Oh, my God," Diana slurs a little, drunk on her own heartlight.

"Or my goddess," says Herself. "Or my you. *Hoink hoink hoink!*"

Diana slowly shakes her battered head. "Don't talk like that—it's weird. I'm still not saying I believe it. I mean how could I be . . . ? I mean, I'm . . . It's so arrogant to think of myself as a . . . a . . ." she can barely speak the word, " . . . a goddess."

"Remember the Fifth Task, dear. And remember what I just said about hubris. What's the mirror of that statement?"

Diana has to think for a minute. She's still diving deeper into the sweetness of her heart. "Um . . ."

"It's so arrogant . . . " The boar prompts, and leans forward encouragingly.

"It's so arrogant *not* to think of myself as a goddess?" Now it's Diana's turn to laugh.

"You are consciousness dressed in form, my love. Consciousness is divine. Matter is divine. Creation is divine. Everything is divine. Are you somehow the only exception?"

Diana waves a hand at Herself. "That's not what I meant. I just—"

"Which is truer, Diana: 'I'm *not* divine,' or 'I *am* divine'? Remember the clue: *Everything is divine.*"

"Oh, all right, you silly boar." The love Diana feels for Herself is beyond all reckoning. She gazes at the beautiful shaggy mane, the beautiful little eyes, the beautiful snuffling snout.

"Now you sound logical," says Herself. "Your meta-self is moving into your mind. Can you let go of it, allow it to operate the computer?"

Diana reluctantly moves some attention away from the bliss in her heart and puts it on her head. The pounding of her wound grows fiercer, and she gives a little moan. "My head hurts, Myself."

"So it does, my piglet, so it does." The boar pauses, then delicately asks, "Would you like me to heal it?"

"What? Oh, yes. Yes, please," says Diana. *That's right, I have to remember to ask.* She remembers how the boar sang on the day they met, how her sprained ankle stitched itself up at the sound of that strange song. How long ago was that? Six weeks? Six hundred thousand lifetimes?

Herself leans over the baby bear and touches the swollen cut on Diana's head. "You might want to sing along," she says. "It will go faster that way."

"I don't know how," says Diana. But as the boar begins to sing, her meta-self blooms in her brain, and the melody and words flow into Diana's mind as readily as her own name. She realizes she's using some language other than English, older even than the heart-language, older than this cave. She understands it perfectly.

"*I am the Mother Herself,*" say the words of that familiar, alien tongue. "*I am the force that knits the stardust into flesh.*" At first, the ache in Diana's head intensifies. She can feel cells beginning to shift. Instead of resisting, she surrenders, leaning back into the warmth of Arktos and Polaris.

"*This is the song of mending, of weaving sand into selflets.*" Diana feels the small cuts on her skin begin knitting together. "*I am the Life that makes itself, that flows from one to another, that knows each pattern of Being.*" A bruised kidney pops back into shape, patches its own structure.

"*For this I have come, for this I exist: To hold Life in these limbs and thoughts, to be Love in form, to forget myself and come to know myself again.*"

As Herself and Diana sing, the scar of every wound Diana has ever suffered, physical or emotional, flares up like a moth ignited by a bonfire, then shrivels to nothing and blows away.

"And now the Seventh Task," whispers Herself. "Now the magic."

With no scars to hold it, Diana's mind flows freely out, beyond her body. Like an invisible fluid, it fills the bears and Herself, then rapidly expands into every bat, frog, and cricket in the cave. Then into all the creatures outside in the unseen forest. Then through all the land, for tens of thousands of miles. Then into the sea. All for all, always.

A shaft of cool light drifts across her face, and Diana looks up through a crack in the ceiling to see the bright full moon. She nearly shatters with love—her love for the moon, and the moon's love for her. And then everything in the cave—the boar, the stone walls, the sleeping bear and her cub—is bathing in a cool brilliance whiter than anything Diana has ever seen. It grows whiter, and whiter, and whiter still, until every other sight dissolves into it.

For a moment Diana wonders, *Where is it coming from?* Then, suddenly, she's not in her human meat-self, but in the body of the winged boar. She feels her bulky, bristly shape, her powerful wings, the immense effort of keeping so much non-physical power in physical form. Through Herself's eyes, Diana looks back at her human body, that insignificant scrap of meat wrapped in the she-bear's hug. It's shining like a lighthouse. Like a star.

And with that thought, Diana is no object, but the immensity of spacetime. She is everywhere and everywhen. She glances beside her and sees the moon, her beloved companion. Then, instantly, she's much larger, fitting herself into the shape of Arktos-in-the-stars. She smiles at her cub, the North Star shining at the tip of his tail. Beyond the Milky Way, she sees other galaxies, great storms of jeweled light, beckoning. Diana is still expanding, moving toward every corner of the universe at once, when a different sound cuts through the harmony.

"Help, Diana! Please help! The babies can't survive this," it cries in its countless voices. *"Please, please help the babies."* That braided, infinite choir of fear and suffering and sweetness. The call that has summoned Diana since physical life first appeared. She hears every mother's voice in it, and every grandmother's. The soothing call of the queen bee. The quavering tones of the old woman walking her cats outside a cheap apartment in Los Angeles.

Diana turns toward the sounds of all those voices, and a fresh explosion of love rocks through her like the shock wave of a supernova. There in the infinite blackness soars Earth, wrapped in swirling blue and white silks, embracing its trillions upon trillions of living things. Diana loves everything that ever existed, but oh, oh, oh, how she has loved this one little planet.

Or, perhaps I should say, how she loves me.

And you, my child, as you read these words.

Oh, yes, beloved. Had you forgotten that this is your story, too? That you, too, are an aspect of the divine, sent here to awaken and to heal at the most perilous time in human history? Have you forgotten that you are made of the elements I gathered from the dust and rock of space, the water the dinosaurs drank? That you are flesh of my flesh, bone of my bone, matter of my matter? Every time you have cried for help, and every time another has cried for you, I have heard. And so has Diana.

From outside of time she looks at us—me, a planet; you, a human being born of me. She sees you at this very moment, in all your pain, your fear, your hope. She sees what you can be. What you really are, beloved. She sees the truth of you, and she loves you without measure or judgment, eternally. Just as I love you.

My baby.

My own.

"There there, tiny," Diana feels in the heart-language, wrapping me and you and all my children in her love. *"I'm here, tiny. Rest. Be healed."*

As she offers her help again—she always will—the infinity that is Diana retracts, becomes unimaginably smaller. It gathers itself into a woman of perfectly average physical dimensions, lying between two bears in a cave under a California mountain.

So let us return to her story.

Herself is lying down now, perfectly still. Diana stirs, feeling the sublime comfort of her body, all its cells in order. The moon drifts away from the crack in the ceiling. The bears breathe very slowly. Outside, the night is waning.

"Myself?" says Diana at last.

"Yes, dear?"

"I'm really not from around here, am I?"

"No, piglet, you are not."

"Like, when I sit around the earth, I sit *around the earth*."

"This is what I've been saying."

Another pause.

"So what do I do now?"

Herself gives a dainty yawn. "Use the power of the divine feminine to save the world."

"Okay. Um . . . how?"

"Arktos and Polaris are doing it as we speak."

"But . . . they're sound asleep."

"Exactly. That is their greatest power."

"The divine feminine's greatest power is *sleep*?"

"Often, yes."

Diana blinks in confusion. "Well, how's it—I mean, I—I mean, we—how are we ever going to get anything done?"

The boar raises her head. *"Hoinkhoinkhoink!* How I love those remnants of human delusion that remain in you, darling! They're *adorable!*" She regards the bears, tilting her head one way and then the other. "Do you think the old ones worshipped Arktos just because she was big and fierce? There are plenty of big, fierce animals. But you see, the she-bear is a master of *rest.* She gives birth, forms life, heals its ills, without any effort at all."

Diana reaches up to touch the mother bear's soft muzzle. The long, warm tongue flickers out, kissing her fingers. The bear grumbles comfortably.

"There is too much profane masculine in the human world at the moment, Diana. They think power means killing. Their stories end when the hero kills the enemy, never when he rests and heals himself. *Hoink!*" The boar shakes her shaggy head. "Anything can kill—a virus, a fall, a few years. In school you were taught human history as a series of slaughters. But for every moment a human has killed, there were *years* when that person was held. Every life crushed in a violent second was born, cradled, nourished, tended, hour after hour, month after month. Its hurts were healed, its hungers fed, its needs met. *That,* my piglet, is the power that can save the world."

The mother bear seems to hear Herself in her sleep. With her forepaw, she touches her cub, then Diana, making sure they are both safe and warm.

Herself beams at Diana. "My love, it will take a great deal of lying down and resting, doing nothing at all, for you to save the world."

Diana laughs. "Doing *nothing?*"

"Oh, there will be adventures, too," says the boar. "But at the moment, there's not nearly enough nothing-doing to keep the Earth in balance."

"Myself, that's just ridic— Ow!" Diana grabs her stomach. "Seriously?" she mutters. "I'm a freaking *goddess* and I *still* get the stabbies?"

"Aha!" says Herself softly. "So you've transcended that last bit of hubris. You accept what you are."

Diana strokes Polaris's ears. "Yes," she sighs at last. "All right. I accept."

At once, every muscle in her body goes slack with release. Her head lolls back against Arktos's furry chest. Then, slowly, her *other* raises it again.

"Myself?"

"Yes, love?"

"It's me. All of me. Only me."

The boar sits up and leans forward, ears perked. "Are you sure?"

"Yeah. Yes, I'm sure," the *other* Diana laughs incredulously. "I can just . . . run the body. I don't have to push her aside any more. And—oh, my gosh, Myself, I have her memories! All of them! I remember her phone number—I could never do that before. Myself, I remember the Devin years! I remember how to drive a car!"

"But no suffering?" says Herself. "No sadness? Anger? Fear?"

"No, nothing! I can feel painful thoughts begin, but then they see they have no purpose, so they sort of . . . kill themselves." Diana grins at the boar. "She did it, Myself!" she says. "My mortal did it! She let go!"

Herself is having trouble containing her excitement; her wings, shining like lanterns, beat so fast they lift her a few inches off the floor. "Yes, yes, yes, you have her humanness now," she says. "I can feel it."

"But no pain!" says Diana-the-*other*, awestruck. "Oh, Myself, it's so *quiet* in here now! Feel how quiet!" She reaches out a hand and touches the boar's snout. Herself leans in, hovering, fascinated, exploring.

"Oh, my dear one!" she whispers. "A human mind without human suffering. How glorious you are! How *glorious*!"

After a moment Diana-the-*other* yawns and blinks. "It may be glorious, Myself, but this meat-self is *tired*."

The boar *hoinks* softly. "Well, she's had a sporty time these last few days."

Diana-the-*other* yawns again. "I think I'm going to sleep a while."

"Yes, love, of course," says Herself. "Do the magic! Use your power!"

Diana's eyes are already drooping closed. She gives the boar's snout one last squeeze. "We did it, Myself," she mumbles drowsily.

"We did, my darling, didn't we?"

"At last," Diana mumbles. "At last, at last, at last. I woke up."

And because she knows with every particle of herself that she is wide awake, Diana lets herself fall asleep.

•

WORSHIP

For hours, Diana plays in the sleeping body, watching it refresh itself. For a while, she makes herself smaller than a quark and watches the atoms splay out into what look like random galaxies. Then she increases in size several million-fold and watches biological order emerge out of chaos: tissue connected with tissue in tiny fractal versions of the galaxy clusters she's always loved to visit.

Finally the Diana-body drifts sweetly up from sleep. Before its eyes have even opened, it already detects an unfamiliar sensation: the feeling of being worshipped. Diana the meta-self can't help but worship it, for she *is* worship. Worship is what she receives from the universe, the only thing she can possibly give back. Her gratitude and awe at being fully awake in a form of matter is boundless, ecstatic. The memory of her mortal experience, and the whole of her true, metaphysical being, are wildly in love with this deceptively solid-seeming physical world.

When the eyelids flutter up, Diana gasps and slams them down again. Then she peers through her eyelashes, cautiously. It's still there, what she saw before: a small rock, lit by an arrow of sunlight. Diana manages to keep her eyes open, focused on the rock, though tears form and slide down her cheeks in a steady drizzle. One side of the rock is shadowed by blue darkness, the other lit by the sun. Tiny bits of quartz sparkle where the radiance hits them.

For millennia, people have sung hymns of praise and shouted hallelujahs to this creation, to the Creator, to Diana herself. Now she knows why. Looking at that inexpressibly beautiful rock, she knows there will never be enough hymns to express the beauty of the Earth through human eyes. There will never be enough hallelujahs.

"Oh, Myself," she whispers. "I knew it would be this way, but I didn't know."

"Of course not, love," says the boar's warm voice. "Physical existence can't be expected. Only experienced."

Diana manages to look around the cave, though the sight of the bears and the walls and the light shining through the ceiling cracks is so shatteringly lovely she almost goes into shock. The texture of the bears' fur is inexpressibly marvelous. The way the animals twitch as they dream makes Diana want to hold them in her arms forever. She strokes their muzzles for a while before noticing that the winged boar is nowhere to be seen.

"Where are you, Myself?"

"Within," says the boar's voice, but it comes from Diana's chest. "Inside, where I belong."

"Ah." Diana smiles. "But I love seeing you. Would you mind . . . ?"

"Of course not, dear." The boar flickers into existence across the chamber from Diana, who bursts into tears again.

"Oh, Myself, Myself, you're so beautiful!"

The boar trots over to kiss Diana's forehead. "It's a strange place, this world of illusion, but worth it, don't you think? Even with all the suffering, all the fear and pain."

Diana nods, sobbing. It takes her several minutes to comfortably accommodate her love for the boar. Then she reaches out and touches Herself's snout. "It's weird, having you in that body and me in this one," she says. "Right now, I don't know everything that's going to happen to me."

"No," says Herself. "I'm the part of you that knows the future. Though even I see many possible outcomes from every situation."

Diana tilts her head, focusing on the sensation. "It's fun," she declares at last. She laughs out loud. "Actually, it's *really* fun! I was always certain as a goddess, always afraid as a mortal. Being uncertain without fear is just *delicious*."

"Yes, love, it's the essence of adventure."

Diana laughs again. She remembers her mortal self going on roller coaster rides, giddy at the sense of imminent calamity blended with the underlying knowledge that she was completely safe. The way she feels now is infinitely more intense, but not dissimilar. She examines her hands, fascinated. "I can hardly believe how *real* it all seems."

"I know. You'd swear these objects actually exist, as solid stuff, not just clouds of energy, wouldn't you? *Hoink hoink hoink!*"

"Amazing." Diana touches the floor, which feels firm and unyielding, and giggles. "And the thing about time flowing only forward always sounded so outlandish to me, but from this perspective, it really works!"

"Yes, it took some doing to get the kinks out of that one," says the boar. "It appears pretty steady now, doesn't it? There are still occasions when time speeds up and slows down, but most humans really believe it just marches along, like their clocks."

"Because all the clocks are speeding up and slowing down with the rest of time," says Diana.

"Naturally," says Herself. "But don't bother mentioning it to humans. They're confused enough already."

Diana chuckles and scratches the bear cub's ears. Then she frowns thoughtfully. "Wait, something's happening . . . oh! This body thinks it's hungry!" She grins at Herself, delighted at the way the meat-self works, how its sensations direct her to interact with the rest of the illusion. "Let's find food, Myself! Let's have an adventure!"

Carefully, Diana wriggles backward out of the mother bear's embrace. Standing up feels wonderful. Her clothes are dry now, and the air today is pleasantly cool, not cold. The boar is already headed toward a low tunnel on the far side of the chamber. When she follows, Diana sees that the tunnel is dimly and greenly lit, its entrance thickly overgrown with scrub oak leaves that glow like jade windowpanes. Herself pushes into the brush and Diana follows, moving foliage with her hands, careful not to tangle her hair.

When she finally steps out of the shrub, frees her jacket from one final twig, and looks around, Diana gives a small cry and falls to her knees. It's late afternoon—she's slept through most of the day—and the sun shoots through puffs of purple cloud, cloaking the greenwood of the Sierras Oscuras in golden light.

To anyone, the view would be dazzling. To Diana, it's utterly overwhelming. She leans forward, puts her hands on the ground, and touches her forehead to the soil, letting the surge of energy run through her body and pour itself back into the Earth. She raises her head, looks around again, touches her forehead down again. And repeats. She understands now why the ancient Chinese kowtowed to the ancestors, why Muslims and Buddhists pray this way. It's the only thing she can do to tolerate the amount of worship flowing through the body.

After twenty or thirty kowtows, Diana feels more settled, able to look directly at the landscape without disintegrating. But now there are new beauties arriving from every direction. Animals, hundreds of them, surround her. The grass ripples as the little ones—mice, weasels, chipmunks—scurry through it. Feathers in all shades of blue, white, red, gray, emerald, and ochre flicker in the canopies of the oaks. A colony of ground squirrels gathers in a chittering semicircle a few feet from Diana. Warren the mountain lion glides from a patch of bush, glancing dangerously at the other creatures, but making no move to attack. Bobcats and coyotes, rabbits and deer, otters and opossums join them, all seeming to forget any antipathy in their shared fascination with Diana.

"Hello, my loved ones," she feels in the heart-language. "My family."

Every animal responds with a silent shout of adoration so pure that Diana has to press her forehead to the ground and cry for several minutes. She worships the intricacy of the tiniest knuckle on the smallest toe of the littlest bluebird. She's gobsmacked by her own reflection in each bright pair of eyes. The animals receive her love without resistance, and it flows through their hearts back into hers, which amplifies it and sends it on again. A circle of bees land in a ring on Diana's hair, a weightless crown.

"They've taken good care of your campsite while we were gone," says Herself.

"I dow, Byself," Diana snuffles, weeping. "Dey're all so, so wudderful."

Because, of course, Diana has brought herself home. The bears' hidden cave lies just above the little lake where she made her last camp. Farther down the mountainside, the lake sparkles in the afternoon sun. No wonder humans prayed, built temples, worshipped. To live in a world like this—with clouds, trees, lakes—fuels a gratitude so intense it must act. Not to worship, in the face of so much beauty, would be almost unbearable.

Diana walks downhill, the boar and her retinue of other animals leaping, scurrying, flitting, and pacing along with her. Her body is very hungry, and with delight she notices her brain automatically imagining food. The moment the thought forms, some of the animals race ahead of her. By the time she reaches the cool shadiness of her oak grove, several scarlet-capped acorn woodpeckers are busy piling ripe nuts by the stream, and a raccoon is clambering awkwardly down from the hive in the fallen tree, holding a large chunk of honeycomb in its dexterous little hands, untroubled by the peaceful bees.

Diana accepts an acorn from a scarlet-capped bird, peels it, and eats it. The taste is gloriously bitter, too bitter for most humans to enjoy, but Diana loves it.

"Come, Goddess of the Oaks," says Herself, chewing an unpeeled acorn with her usual loud smacks of delight. "Try them with honey."

Diana does, and the taste so amazes her that she has to spend ten apparent minutes worshipping the oaks and the bees, which worship her right back, as they have done since oaks and bees existed. Finally she's able to keep eating, and does so until her body feels pleasantly satisfied. She sits on a carpet of moss, petting the warm silver-gray fur of her friend the fox as the other animals doze peacefully around her. The sky flares orange as the sun dips below the mountains to the west.

"This is perfect," she says at last.

Herself nods, still chewing. "Everything is perfect," she says. "Always."

"And yet I'm here to bring change."

"Mmm." The boar swallows. "Well, you're actually here to preserve some things as they are."

Diana nods thoughtfully. "So . . . do you have any suggestions about how to save a world?"

"You must start where you are, love. Remember?"

"I do." Diana thinks for a moment. There's nothing in her that still needs saving, but there are others. "I need to deal with Roy," she says. "Don't I?"

Herself settles down on a bed of moss. "Yes, piglet. Our Roy has made himself the very embodiment of the profane masculine—women want him, men want to be him, yada yada. He was drawn to you because his meta-self wanted him to heal. It knows the divine feminine is the balancing force for the masculine. And you were drawn to him because he's your mission on legs—he's everything you came to change and heal. Unfortunately, the profane masculine is rarely interested in changing, and Roy is no exception. He's a raging narcissistic sociopath, dangerous to all forms of life, especially himself. Can you feel him now?"

Diana nods slowly. "Of course," she says. "He's tracked his way back out of the cave. But he's much fainter than before—his energy, I mean. Is he sick? Dying?"

"Oh, no, he's fine physically," says Herself. "That's the profane masculine for you: mad as a hatter and fit as a fiddle, even in withdrawal from all his pharmaceutical enhancements. But now that you're awake, you're feeling things in their true proportions. As a meat-self, you shared Roy's belief in his power. Now you know it's pathetic compared to the other forces in nature. But Roy—and a great many other humans—have managed to do quite a bit of damage with it. And he'll do more if he can."

Diana watches the sky as it darkens to red. "So I must stop him."

"It's not just what he did to your meat-self, dear," says the boar softly. "It's the law of the universe. Justice must be served. He must get what he has coming."

"Yes," says Diana. She sighs and rises to her feet. "Well, let's get it over with."

She strides off along a game trail, animals rippling around her. As the sun sets and the air cools down, the nocturnal animals become more lively, and the diurnal ones begin peeling off, finding safe places to sleep through the night. The moon, one day past full, has just risen when a bee lands on Diana's shoulder and begins to dance—not the happy waggle-dance it might use to describe the location of flowers, but the tremble dance, a call for help and reassurance. Dozens more bees fly down to cluster around the scout.

"The human drone is coming," the scout tells them in the heart-language. *"And he is terribly, terribly heartsick. Greatmother, you were heartsick when we met you, but his heartsickness is worse than anything we have ever felt."*

"I know, love," Diana feels back. The bee's empathy makes the little creature permeable, a sponge for Roy's energy. Diana draws some of it into herself so the bee can survive. Immediately, her awareness of Roy increases. She shudders; he's even more paranoid and angry than he was when she left him in the dark center of the mountain. His fear has sunk its fangs into him as if it were a huge insect, and his rage is a slashing, mindless, continuous attack on everything but himself. Diana feels her meat-self tighten as memories of Roy's violence flare in its memory. The memories don't disturb Diana now. She only shakes her head in wonder, remembering how much her mortal self loved this man.

As the moon rises above the tops of the tallest oaks, Diana and the animals hear Roy thrashing and clomping through the forest. She can also feel, with a little burst of pleasure, that he's carrying the bow and arrows Diana loves to play with. She's so preoccupied with them that when she summits the top of a small hill and sees Roy right in front of her, she's almost surprised to see him.

But not nearly as surprised as Roy is to see her.

JUSTICE

"Gaah!" Roy shouts, his eyes and mouth opening wide. He skids to a halt in the bright moonlight and stands there rigid, his whole body trembling, his lips working soundlessly.

"Ghost!" he shouts, finally. "Witch! You're dead! You don't exist! You can't hurt me!"

Even so, he nocks an arrow and shoots it straight at her. Diana catches it in the air and holds it like a flower.

"Hello, Roy," says Diana. "Nice to see you, too. Have a seat."

To Roy's distress, he finds himself unable to refuse the invitation. His knees give out and his rump lands, hard, on the ground. The bow drops from his limp hands. Diana sits down a few feet away from him.

Roy moans like a terrified dog. "Don't you fucking hurt me, you whore! If you touch a hair on my head, I will bring down a fucking *tornado* of shit on your head! I'll destroy everything you've ever loved!"

Diana sighs. "Roy," she says, "I'm here because you have to get what's coming to you. First and foremost—"

"Don't hurt me!"

"Please, Roy, don't interrupt. First and foremost, I must give you my thanks."

"Wha . . . ?" In the moonlight, Roy's eye sockets are empty pits.

Diana turns the arrow in her hand. "You were a perfect nemesis," she says. "The force of opposition that helped me awaken. I'm not saying it was pretty, Roy, but I think it was necessary. Anyway, it worked. I can't tell you how grateful I am."

A long silence. Then Roy licks his chapped lips, peering at Diana through hanks of dirty hair. "Okay, baby, I see where you're going," he says. "And you know what? You're right. We're good together. We can make this work."

Diana throws back her head and laughs from her belly. "Okay, *that's* not happening." She laughs again, and all around her, the animals join in, chirping and barking. "Roy," says Diana, when she gets her breath back, "your life is never going back to the way it was. Everywhere you go and everything you do is turning this beautiful dream of a world into a nightmare. I won't allow that to continue."

Roy's jaw works, the muscle in his cheek rippling in a way Diana once found irresistible. "Oh, are you talking about all that stuff I said in the cave?" His casual tone clangs like an untuned piano. He gives a horrible imitation of a laugh. "Shit, Diana, can't you take a joke?"

"A joke," Diana replies, "would be letting you continue spinning out your insanity into Earth's reality."

Roy changes his tactics. "Just try and stop me, bitch. There's not a judge on earth who'd convict me of anything I've told you. D'you think they'd care what some little wetback woman has to say? I'm an important man, Diana. I can hire the best fucking lawyers in the world, and if you come after me, so help me, you'll be sorry. Now, we're done here. I've given you enough of my precious time, and I have wolves to kill."

Roy begins to stand up, an effort that ends in a sharp, hysterical shout as Warren the mountain lion glides out of the shadows, rears to put his front paws on Roy's chest, and pushes him backward onto the ground. Then the enormous cat settles heavily, elegantly, on Roy's legs. Roy wrestles to escape, the whites of his eyes flashing and rolling. Warren puts his ears back with a hiss, and Roy freezes, whimpering.

"Why is this happening to me?" he whispers. "All I've ever done is make the world a better place. Jesus, I even volunteered for Special Olympics once."

"Roy, I have a question for you," says Diana. "Has this life ever felt completely right to you? Have you ever felt as happy, as peaceful as you'd like to be?"

"Fuck you," snarls Roy.

"I'll take that as a no." Diana looks up at the moon. "It never felt quite right to me, either, Roy. Oh, parts of it did, sure. Moments. Relationships. My son. The beauty of nature. But human life as we were living it—born astride the grave, hard labor all the way, that stuff—it always felt wrong to both of us. You know why?"

"Do you want money?" says Roy. "Is that what you're after? How much? Just tell me how much, you crazy whore."

"Pay attention, Roy," says Diana. "This is important. You see, life feels wrong to most humans—and death feels *completely* wrong—because it isn't exactly real."

Roy glares at her from beneath the mountain lion.

"It's like a dream," Diana goes on. "It's real—it's a real *dream*—but it's not real the way waking life is." She gestures at Roy and her own body. "These meat-selves are like symbols in the dream. But we have bigger selves, meta-selves. They're the ones who are dreaming, who *know* they're dreaming." Her brow furrows thoughtfully. "Actually they're the One having the dream," she murmurs. "Technically, there's only one Self."

"You are fucking *insane*! Why didn't I kill you when I met you?" moans Roy. "I should've strangled you in the trailer, that first day. Don't think I didn't consider it. But I decided to let you live." He's suddenly furious again. "You *owe* me for that, Diana."

"Oh, Roy, please," says Diana. "You couldn't kill me—in fact, you couldn't resist me. Your meta-self wants you to wake up, and it hopes I can make that happen."

"Oh, is that what you call the desecration of a great man? You say you're going to *wake me up*?" Roy laughs bitterly, glancing from

Diana to Warren. "A little beaner and her trained pussy? Ha!"

"That's the offer," says Diana. "You helped me wake up, so the law of the universe dictates that I help you do the same." She smiles at him. "That's what you've got coming."

Roy chews his mustache for a few seconds, staring at Warren, thinking. Then, quite abruptly, his expression changes. "Wait—okay, you're saying this is a dream? Like, I'm just *dreaming* that you're not dead, and I'm stuck in the middle of nowhere with a fucking puma on my legs and wolves breathing down my neck?" He looks around him with something like his old, handsome face. "Oh, my God, that has to be it! I'm asleep! This is all a dream, and I'm going to wake up in a second and Emilio is going to bring me breakfast and I'm going to go to work—" He exhales hugely. "Oh, *Jesus,* what a relief!" He begins to laugh almost hysterically.

"I know," says Diana, laughing with him. "Isn't it?"

"It's just a dream," Roy repeats, closing his eyes. "Oh, thank God, thank God. None of this is really happening. It's all just a dream."

"So," says Diana. "Do you want to wake up now?"

"You're goddamn right I do."

"Wonderful!" Diana beams at him for a moment before she realizes that she actually has no idea how to awaken Roy. She's about to ask Herself for advice when something crawls from the hair around Roy's left ear. A tiny voice threads up into her ears.

"I'm here," says the voice, a shrill whisper. "I'm ready!"

Diana looks down to see a large, round tick making its way down one sideburn and over Roy's beard, finally stopping on his chest.

"Well, hello, little one!" says Diana.

Roy looks around. "What? Who? Me?"

The tick sighs. "He can't see me or hear me, no matter what I do. He never has. Wait, that's not true. Once, when I was a cockroach, he heard me fair and square. But then he started doing more Oxycontin, and that was the end of that. Oh, but where are my manners?" The tick coughs, stands up on its four hindmost legs, and bows. "Hail, Diana, Greatmother," it pipes in its tiny voice. "I am Bloodblotch, Roy's spirit animal. It's an honor to make your acquaintance."

"The honor is mine," says Diana, bowing her head. "Will you be teaching Roy the Tasks now?"

"Well . . ." says the tiny voice. "It would probably take several years just to calm him down, and now that you're awake, Greatmother, another way is open."

"Oh, really?" Diana arches an eyebrow.

"It's not unlike physical death," says the tick. "His body may remain, but he must go through the life review. Feel everything he has caused in any sentient being, throughout this lifetime."

Diana winces. "Oh, Bloodblotch, is that really necessary?"

"If he's to awaken in this meat-self, Greatmother."

"All right, then." Diana sighs. She looks sadly at the man on the ground. "Roy, this won't feel good. I mean, once you're awake it will feel incredible, but getting there definitely won't be half the fun."

"Stop talking!" Roy shouts. "If you're going to wake me up, then do it! I'm sick of this goddamn dream!"

"If you can hold on through the pain, it will be amazing. Just remember that. This will take courage, Roy."

"Courage?" Roy spits the word at her. "What do you know about courage? You're a woman!" He spits on the ground. "Just *end this motherfucking nightmare!*"

Diana looks at Bloodblotch, and Bloodblotch looks at Diana.

"Well, he's asked me," says the tick.

"So he has."

"I suppose I should begin," says Bloodblotch.

"Must he feel *everything* he's caused other beings to feel?" says Diana. Then she answers her own question. "Okay, I know. Yes, he must."

"It's not a judgment, Diana," says Bloodblotch. "Not something even you can control. Just the law of symmetry."

Diana sighs again, dropping her shoulders and relaxing. "Go ahead, Bloodblotch."

The tick begins to glow, brighter and brighter. When the light illuminates his beard, Roy gapes at his own chest, seeing the insect for the first time.

"I'm in touch with his heart now," says Bloodblotch.

"How do you feel so far?" Diana asks Roy.

"How do you think?" Roy snaps. "There's a killer cat on my legs and a tick on my chest and a crazy witch running my nightmares. I feel fan-fucking-tastic."

"Okay," says Bloodblotch. "I'll start showing him the truth of his life."

Suddenly Roy looks concerned, as if he's just noticed a pebble in his shoe. Then his face blanches. "What's happening? What is this? Oh, no. Oh, no no no!" There follows a volley of curses so vile that Diana, who is no stranger to profanity, gives a low whistle of astonishment.

"Just breathe," she tells Roy.

"Nooooooo!" Roy screams. "No, no, no!"

"Good grief, this doesn't bode well," says Bloodblotch. "I'm just showing him the suffering he created as a boy. The animals he tortured and killed. The people he lied to, the weaklings he bullied. Their pain."

Roy is sobbing, writhing. Warren places a heavy paw on his stomach.

"Can you go faster?" says Diana.

"No," says Bloodblotch. "This is as much as he can stand."

Roy gives a long, groaning howl from somewhere deep in his guts. "No! No! Please don't please don't . . ." Another howl, then a long, hoarse shout. "What did I do? What did I do? Oh, God, I did it all to *myself*!" His voice garbles into slobbering sobs, punctuated by shrieks of pure agony.

The animals, except for Bloodblotch and Warren, edge away. Roy's pain is horrible, his shrieks deafening, his spasms and flailing hideous to behold. And they do not stop.

For hours.

Occasionally Roy falls into exhausted quiet, only to go rigid seconds later and begin screaming again. Warren's ears are folded flat in horror and pity. *"Shall I kill it?"* he asks Diana in the heart-language. *"Usually when something is suffering this much, I kill it fast. I'm really good at it, Greatmother. It's kind of my jam."*

"Thanks, but no," says Bloodblotch. "If he dies now, he stays in the same level of pain he's in until he can finish waking up, which will take a long time without the body. I'm getting to his adolescence now. Things might be a little dicey from here."

"Like they aren't already?" mutters Diana.

A moment later, Roy gives a scream more ghastly than all the ones before it. He begins beating his head against the ground, over and over. "Help!" he shrieks, his eyes rolling frantically at Diana. "Help! *Help! HELP!*" The call pierces her heart. Her whole existence has been spent answering that cry, and of all the creatures who have begged her for rescue, none has suffered more than Roy is suffering now.

"It will pass, Roy," she says. "Nothing in this reality lasts forever."

He looks up at her; the whites of his eyes show all the way around the iris. His pupils are huge and black in the moonlight. "Kill me," he begs.

"No, Roy," she says softly. "That won't work. It will help if you surrender."

"*NEVER!*" Roy breaks into hoarse sobs, and then another wave of pain hits him. With a long, hideous, despairing groan, he resumes his head-beating.

"He's feeling the rapes now," says the tick. "The people whose lives he ruined, even before he actually killed anyone."

Roy's head is bleeding freely, drops of blood and sweat flying as he bashes it against the ground, punctuating his screams and curses and sobs. Warren has closed his eyes and pulled back a bit, too disturbed to watch.

"Please, kill me! *Kill me! KILL ME!*" Roy bites through his lower lip, smashing his bloodied head harder and harder. "I WANT TO DIE! *I WANT TO DIE I WANT TO DIE I WANT TO DIE I WANT TO DIE! KILL ME! KILL ME! KILL ME!*"

Then, with a particularly violent convulsion, Roy forces his hand under the mountain lion's backward-leaning body. When the hand reappears, Diana sees the Glock nine-millimeter Roy carries in his leg holster.

"No, Roy!" shouts Diana. "That won't—"

But it's already done: He's turned the gun, pulled the trigger, sent his last bullet spinning through his own skull. An explosion of blood, brain, and bone spatters the grass and trees behind him.

Stillness.

Even the frogs and crickets pause, listening. Somberly, Diana observes how her mortal mind begins to react with horror, nausea, shock. But even as the pain arises, it sees its own pointlessness and longs for death. Just like Roy, but much faster, with no fanfare, it surrenders itself. No matter where she looks within, Diana has no emotions left but gratitude, love, and acceptance.

"Oh, darn," says Bloodblotch mildly. "He opted out." A tiny sigh. "It would have been so much easier to awaken him here. Now he's taken all that pain with him. Doggone it! He'll keep identifying as a separate being until the whole process is finished. Heaven knows how long that will take, and he'll suffer the whole time." The tick stands up and bows again. "Thanks, everyone, but I'll be getting along now. I have a *lot* to do." It disappears in a pinpoint of red light.

After a while, Diana reaches forward and closes Roy's blank eyes. His face is intact, relaxed at last, though the back of his head is missing. Diana sits there, contemplating the meat-self she loved so much, for an hour or two. As the eastern horizon pales, the boar walks up and puts her snout on Diana's shoulder.

"He was such a beautiful human," says Diana.

"They're all beautiful," says Herself. She's carrying a sprig of flowers, which she sets on Roy's ravaged head. "They're all priceless, piglet. Each of them another face of God."

"What shall we do with his meat-self?"

"Let the forest have it," says Herself. "The natural way."

Diana nods. The carrion eaters, the ravens and vultures and coyotes, will strip Roy's bones and scatter them to the four winds. No one will ever find them.

"Myself?" says Diana.

"Yes, piglet?"

"Do all humans have to go through such pain to awaken?" Tears gather in Diana's eyes. "I don't want to cause this kind of suffering."

"Mmm," the boar murmurs, kissing Diana's forehead. "Roy caused his own suffering, love. You tried to heal it. Your role among the humans is simply to show them what they are. *Gnothi seauton. Know thyself.* That's your only real message. For a few it will be painful, but only because they've created suffering in the dream. It's all just another Earth adventure, dear."

Diana nods, heaves a sigh, and stands up. "It's an intense planet, Myself. Isn't it?"

"Yes, piglet. That's one of the reasons we love it so much."

They walk away as the first rays of sunlight glimmer over the distant mountains. In the red dawn light, vultures ride the warm updrafts of morning air in towering vortices, circling the body that was once Roy Richards.

ADVENTURE

Tonight Diana is sleeping on the bare ground, grateful not to be separated from me even by the polyester of a sleeping bag—though every bed, of every kind, is made from different parts of me. I hold her unfailingly, as I have always held you, beloved, turning the Sierras Oscuras away from my star, the sun, then back into its light. As the dawn warms and brightens, Diana dreams.

In the dream within a dream, she's texting Devin for the first time as her full, complete self. *Hi, sweetie, hope you're not worried about me. I'm fine. Better than you can imagine.* His return text reads, *Oh, but I can imagine better.* For some reason, the message delights Diana so much that she laughs out loud, and this is what wakes her up.

As she opens her eyes, I pour beauty into them. Golden light. Leaf-sparkle above. The bright, curious eyes of rabbits and deer and foxes watching her. Warren the mountain lion sleeps above her, in the limbs of a great blue oak. Goldfinches bathe busily in the lake, shivering ecstatically as the water touches their skin. When Diana sits up, she notices a rattlesnake coiled on the rock not far from her.

"Well, hello there!" she says. The rattlesnake, which is somewhat greener than the late Cloyd, flickers its tongue. "Are you Cloyd's replacement?" she says. "I think I'll call you Cloyd 2.0. You should feel honored. Cloyd 1.0 was a hero." The snake hesitates for a moment, then slithers over to her and twines itself around her feet.

One creature Diana doesn't see is the winged boar. "Myself?" she calls, gently lifting Cloyd 2.0 so she won't step on the snake's long, dappled body. With a hum of wings, the boar zooms up to the patch of smooth sand where Diana slept. Several bees arrive with her.

"Morning, piglet!" says Herself. "I was just visiting our friends. Thanking them for their dedicated service."

"No need to thank us!" the bees say in the heart-language. *"We were just helping ourselves. All for all, always."*

Diana smiles at them. "All for all, always," she repeats out loud, in English. Ultraviolet blazes all around her as she joins the bees' frequency, and now she notices creatures in the forest she never saw before her time in the cave: the bubbles of light that are the spirits of stones, the shifting faces of the tree-sprites in the high oak canopy. Everywhere, there is life. My life.

"You know," Diana says, "even though it's all illusion, and even though it's always dissolving, it really is worth keeping the world this way for a while, isn't it, Myself? For Devin. For his children, if he has any. For all children."

Herself grunts happily. "Well, dear, that's the plan."

"So . . . how do I start?"

"My wiggly little piggly, have you been paying *no* attention?" Herself flies up to nuzzle Diana's cheek. "There aren't any instructions. You became a meat-self to find your way through the mission. Just use its powers."

Diana tilts her head like a curious puppy. "But this meat-self doesn't seem all that powerful. It feels so small and separate."

"Well, you wouldn't be *in* it if it didn't have the power you need," the boar says with a chuckle. "A human meat-self is fancier than you might think. It can reach from this apparent reality—actual solid-seeming matter—into the Absolute beyond all existence and non-existence. It can join with the infinite intelligence that made the universe, that formed spacetime. It can always find out what to do."

"Then why don't I know?" says Diana.

"Well, you can only know what to do *now*. Ten minutes from now—in other words, in another now—the instructions may change entirely."

"Ah, got it!" Diana smiles. "Sorry, I'm still getting used to this. So all right . . ." She closes her eyes and begins the Seven Tasks. As soon as she quiets her meat-self (there's no fear in it now, only slight distraction), she feels a delicious pulse run from her tailbone, up her spine, and out through the top of her head. For a millisecond she considers continuing until the surge of power fills the universe, but then she pulls her consciousness back into the meat-self. Which has had a thought. No, not a thought, a *knowing*.

"All right, then," she says, nodding smartly. "It's time to hunt."

The boar pops twenty feet straight up, like a cork in water. "Yes! Adventure!"

Diana picks up her bow and sets off walking. She doesn't know the quarry, she doesn't know what she'll do when she finds it. She only knows the urge to hunt, ancient and irresistible. Moving with that urge makes her body thrum with rapture.

She breaks into a run. The animals—those that can keep up—run with her for a while, then break away and return to their own lives, feeling the same joy of being they've always felt, but more deeply than before. Diana doesn't say good-bye to them, nor do they feel any loss as she leaves. They're all joined irrevocably, always together. Each creature, rock, plant, and mushroom is content and whole in its immaculate now-ness. They and Diana would feel one another's presence just as strongly even if she moved to another galaxy.

Diana and the boar travel south by southwest through the bright morning, the compass in Diana's meat-self directing her in precisely the right direction, over precisely the easiest terrain. She runs effortlessly, still and still moving, for more than an hour. Then she stops and shades her eyes with her hand.

"Myself, what's that?" Diana points at a cliff a hundred yards away. Something white and shaggy and roughly rectangular is making its way up thirty vertical feet of sheered-off limestone.

Herself gives a joyful squeal. "Well, hello!" she says. "It's Baacchus!"

"Who?" Diana asks, but Herself is already zipping like a rocket-powered zeppelin toward the white rectangle. When it reaches the top, its silhouette reveals it to be a mountain goat. It bears a heavy coat of white wool that tapers down its legs to small, agile feet. Sharp black horns curve elegantly back from its forehead. When it sees Herself, the goat does a double take, then begins bouncing from side to side.

"MAAAAAAAARV!" yells the goat.

The shout sounds so human that Diana stops short in surprise.

Herself lands at the top of the cliff. The mountain goat runs to her, and they begin chasing each other in small circles, like kittens. "MAAARVIN!" the goat shouts again.

Diana runs to the base of the cliff and climbs it rapidly, loving the sense of effort in her back muscles as they help pull her up the rock face. At the summit she finds the boar deep in conversation with the mountain goat, which is speaking in clear, if rather nasal, English.

"Oh, hello, piglet!" says Herself as Diana joins them. "I'd like to introduce my friend Baacchus." She turns to the goat. "Diana doesn't remember you, Baacchus. She thinks like a human while she's in this body."

"Greatmother Diana!" says the goat, extending one foreleg and bowing deeply. "I am so happy to see you. So, so, *so* happy!" He jumps sideways and kicks the air. "Sorry," he says. "This happens when I'm in a good mood."

"Baacchus and I go way back," says Herself.

"*Way* back!" agrees the goat, standing on his hind legs and pawing exuberantly. "I haven't seen Herself in physical form since . . . when was it . . . the middle of the Paleozoic Era?"

"That's right! The Lower Silurian," says Herself. "You were guiding a scorpion, as I recall."

"And you had a horseshoe crab." The goat bleats out a laugh. "Good times, good times."

"And there are even better times to come!" says Herself. "You know, Baacchus, Diana likes surprises." She gives a cheerful *hoink,* and the goat laughs, too.

"Surprises are my favorite thing!" Baacchus bleats. "Well, one of my favorites. Anyway, I think you'll like this one." He inhales and yells again. "MAAAAAARV! MARVIN! OVER HERE!" Diana peers in the direction the goat is facing. Through a stand of scrub oak, she sees two hikers trudging onto the horizon of the next hill. Both men have beards, one white, the other black. Something about the black-bearded man looks familiar to Diana. The way he shifts his shoulders under his backpack; the way he holds his head . . .

"Oh, my God," whispers Diana. "Devin. Devin? *Devin!*"

Then she's pelting downhill, leaping over fallen logs, bursting through thick brush, oblivious to sticks that scratch her arms and catch in her hair. The black-bearded hiker looks up, freezes, then slips out of his pack and runs toward her.

"Mom!" He shouts so loudly that his voice breaks, and for a moment he sounds twelve years old. *"Mom! Mom! Mom!"*

When they're only a few feet apart, Devin trips, but before he can fall, Diana pulls him into her arms as if he were no heavier than a down pillow.

"You're alive, Mom!" Devin is laughing and crying at the same time. "You're alive!"

"What are you doing here?" Diana can't decide whether to hug him close or stand back to look at him, so she holds him at arm's length. He seems older, more manly, but his eyes are still her baby's, dark and deeply intelligent. "How did you find me?" she asks, pulling him back into a tight hug.

"You wouldn't believe me if I told you," laughs Devin.

"Oh, I think I would," says Diana.

"I dunno, Mom, it's all so crazy . . ." He hugs her again. He can't stop laughing.

"Tell you what," says Diana. "Later we'll have a crazy contest, and I'll bet you a trillion bucks I win." She ruffles his curly black hair. "But you go first. What are you doing out here?" "Oh, okay." Devin pushes a few tangled locks back from his eyes. "Wow, where to start . . . God, Mom, I've been looking for you forever. Well, I mean since Thanksgiving, when you didn't come home. At first I called the people from your show, but they were as worried as I was—hadn't been able to contact you—and then I went to the police, but they were about as helpful as bird flu. All they cared about was finding that douchebag Roy Richards. They told me you'd probably taken off with him on purpose."

"Oh, Devin!" says Diana. "No, we got stranded, I hurt my leg, and then . . . well, then it got really strange, but I was trying to get back to you the whole time."

"No one acted like you even mattered!" says Devin, dashing away tears with a grubby hand. "All they talked about was *him*."

Diana nods sadly. "Roy . . . didn't make it."

Devin looks up sharply, his jaw working. Then he takes a deep breath and shrugs. "I'm sorry, Mom. But I gotta say, I never liked what I heard of the guy. And for him, they brought out the National Guard, the California Highway Patrol, everybody but the freaking Galactic Federation. They barely even mentioned your *name*." Devin scowls, then shakes his head and breaks into a huge grin. "But who cares? Mom, *you're alive!*"

"And we're together." Diana stands on tiptoe to kiss him on the forehead.

"The weird thing is, I *knew* you were okay, Mom," Devin says. "And I knew you were still out here in the mountains. Because I could *feel* you. It got stronger and stronger—almost like I could see through your eyes. For a while I thought I was going nuts, but then I told Professor Piper, and he said to trust myself." Devin turns and gestures toward the older man, who's slowly picking his way down the hill toward them. "Professor Piper, this is my mom," he calls. "Mom, Professor Piper."

"Be there in a moment!" calls the older man. Diana can see that his eyes are pink with tears; he's wiping them with a limp white handkerchief.

Devin leans toward Diana and whispers, "Dr. Piper is sort of different, Mom. A lot of people think he's, you know, a few beers short of a six-pack. But he's been great. He's the one who brought me here, even though"—he laughs again—"even though I never, ever, in a million years thought he'd actually *find* you. Coming out here just sounded better than sitting on my ragged ass in my dorm room, losing my mind."

"Oh, sweetheart, I'm so, so sorry you were scared," says Diana. She's about to add, "I'll never forgive myself," when she realizes that, in fact, she has already forgiven herself.

"It was okay, Mom," says Devin. Then his brow furrows, and fresh tears spring to his eyes. "You know what? That's a lie. It absolutely sucked."

Diana hugs him again, more fiercely than ever.

Professor Piper has finally reached them, his face flushed from climbing and weeping. Devin lets go of Diana to throw his arms around the white-haired man. "Thank you," he says, his voice cracking again. Piper pats him awkwardly, sniffling.

Diana meets Piper's eyes. "Sir, I don't even know you, and I have no idea how you found me, but if I thanked you every second for the rest of eternity, it wouldn't be enough."

The professor blinks away tears and speaks in a tremulous voice. "But you do know me, Diana."

"I do?" Diana frowns. "I'm so sorry, I can't—"

"It *is* you!" Piper whispers, staring at her unabashedly. "You *are* Devin's mother! The bees didn't know for sure, but still, I hoped, you know? Sometimes one can't help hoping."

"Bees?" Diana cocks her head.

"I told you this would get weird, Mom," says Devin.

"Yes." The professor nods. "The bees said you were a Greatmother."

"She is." Devin beams. "She totally is."

"But I wasn't sure . . . couldn't be sure until I saw you, that you were the same person . . ."

Diana scrutinizes Piper with new interest. "You can talk to bees, Professor?"

"Well, in a way, sometimes. I have these spells, you see, these attacks . . ." The old man's voice trails off. He walks to a large rock and sits down on it. "So you don't remember me? Well, of course not, why would you?"

Something stirs in Diana's memory as the professor wipes his brow with his handkerchief. The traces of ginger in his white eyebrows, the nervous way he swallows. "You do look a little familiar," Diana tells him. "But I can't . . . quite . . ."

"Why is an octopus like the month of October?" says Piper.

Diana pauses for a second, then smacks her forehead. "Of course!"

"It's not because October is the eighth month," says the professor. "I'll tell you that."

"I know." Diana laughs. "I lied on that one. Sorry."

"You only lied because the test was wrong!" Piper smiles at her. "You acted a little hesitant about that question, so I went back and reread it. The test was wrong, and you knew it. At five years old, you knew it! And you gave me the answer I wanted, which also means you were perspicacious enough to game the test!"

Devin's eyes go from his mother to the professor as if he's watching a tennis match between aliens. "Uh, does anyone feel a hankering to clue me in, here?"

The professor laughs, a long, tickled, infectious laugh. "Certainly, Devin. Your mother and I met once, over thirty years ago. Upon which occasion I had cause to ask her why an octopus is like the month of October."

Devin blinks. "Well, sure you did. If I had a nickel for every time someone's asked me that question . . ."

"I'll explain later," says Piper. "The thing is, Devin, ever since that day, I've been looking for her."

In unison, Diana and Devin say, "You have?"

"Oh, heavens, I sound like a stalker." Piper bites his lip, his white beard bristling. "Who knows, maybe I am. Oh, well." He shrugs. "Anyway, Diana, I've never known why, but you made such an impression on me. *Such* an impression. Not just because your IQ was off the charts. It was something else. Just"—he looks around, then shrugs again helplessly—"just your presence."

"Really," says Diana thoughtfully.

"Yes, really. I don't know why. But whatever the reason, I knew I had to find you again. To help you."

"Help me?" says Diana.

"Or—I don't know, to protect you, perhaps? Or maybe . . . honestly, I think it was to help *myself*. Which makes no sense, I know, but I just couldn't . . ." Piper scratches his forehead. "I was like one of those mystery-novel detectives who can't let go of one particular case," he says. "You disappeared into the system, and I couldn't stand the thought of what might be happening to you." He tears up again, and Diana pats his shoulder.

"I was all right," she says. "Everything that happened to me needed to happen. It was all good."

"I wish I could believe that." The professor looks at her doubtfully. "I took a job with Child Protective Services, hoping I'd run across you again." He closes his eyes and shudders. "That's a terrible job for anyone who loves children. So much sorrow." He breaks down in sobs, hiding his eyes with his hands. Diana puts one arm around him. *"The babies!"* she feels his heart cry out. *"Please help the babies!"*

"I don't know why I'm telling you all this, Diana," he says. "I'm so sorry—"

"No, Professor, I'm exactly the right person to tell."

He looks at her with watery brown eyes. "Really?"

"Absolutely. I'm here to help the babies. Literally. All. The. Babies." Diana holds his gaze, and for an infinitesimal flicker, the Being looking out from the old man's eyes is also Diana: the God-force seeing Itself.

"I *knew* it!" whispers the professor.

"Um, what's going on here?" says Devin. "Why are we talking about babies?"

Professor Piper never takes his eyes off Diana's. It's as if by gazing into them, his parched soul is drinking cool water. "Even when you were a little girl, I *knew*. I saw . . . how can I say it . . . the manifest divine. A walking, talking miracle. But everyone else seemed blind to it. When they looked at you, they actually saw *deficiencies*."

"It's okay, Professor." Diana gives his shoulder a squeeze. "I'm over that. I'm all better now."

"I am, too." Piper sobs quietly, mashing his handkerchief into one eye, then the other. "I stayed on in that job until one night I had to find a home for a child who'd almost burned to death in a fire at his parents' meth lab. I went home and took a whole bottle of antidepressants."

"Dude!" says Devin, softly. He sits down next to Piper.

"I'm sorry, son, but it's true." Piper shrugs. "Anyway, as you see, I didn't die. Instead, I—uh, I ended up connecting with a part of myself I'd never been aware of before." Piper looks at Diana pointedly, gesturing with his head toward the top of the hill, where Herself and the mountain goat stand watching.

The goat waves one cloven fore-hoof and bleats, "At your service, Greatmother!"

"Hello, Marvin, dear!" shouts Herself. "Diana, Devin can't see or hear us."

"I understand completely." Diana nods and smiles at Piper. "Well done."

"After that I went back to academia," says the professor. "I was looking for answers, you see. About what was happening to me, what had happened to you—"

"He's my favorite professor ever, Mom," says Devin.

The old man blushes. "Even though every now and again I have my, uh, pannish attacks?" he says shyly.

"Panic attacks?" Diana queries.

"No," says Devin. "*Pannish* attacks. Like the nature god Pan, you know?"

Diana smiles in surprise. "Actually, I do know," she says.

"When I have an attack I feel . . . I don't know how to say this . . . I feel myself as nature," Dr. Piper says. "All of nature. And I see things, know things . . ." He shakes his head. "I can't describe it, really. But when it happens, I'm always aware of *you*, Diana. Of the little girl I spent an hour with, thirty years ago."

"I had no idea about any of this," says Devin. "I just sort of stumbled into his class! How crazy is that?"

"You know,"—Diana shrugs—"so far it all sounds pretty normal to me. These days I have a new definition of normal."

"So I'd been thinking of you off and on for decades," says Piper, "and you can imagine how I felt when my best student, our young Mr. Archer here, mentioned that his mother's name was Diana. Diana Archer. Could it be the little girl I'd been looking for since I was just a young man myself?"

"I guess it could." Diana squeezes his hand.

"Then, when Devin told me you'd disappeared, I was terrified." Piper's voice breaks. "I thought the whole nightmare was starting all over—the loss, the search, the worry. Thank God for the bees. When the scouts arrived, I knew we'd find you—"

"He understands their dances," Devin cuts in. "Seriously. I didn't believe him either, but it's how we found you."

"I'm not questioning it, Devin," Diana smiles. "Do you see me questioning?"

"I gave the bee scouts some grape jelly to restore their energy, and they danced me your location." Piper stands up. "They did the tremble dance, to say they needed help." He begins to quiver all over.

"And then the waggle dance." He walks in a circle, then cuts across its diameter, waggling his hips from side to side. "The angle from true north tells direction, and the number of waggles tells distance."

Piper reverses his direction and begins moving his arms in time with his hips, approximating the Merengue. "Oh, goodness," he says anxiously as he executes a practiced step-ball-change. "Devin, I do believe one of my episodes is coming on again. I don't mean to be rude, but . . ."

"No worries, Dr. Piper," says Devin. "Mom won't mind. Knock yourself out." He turns to Diana. "Just a pannish attack."

"So I figured," says Diana, laughing.

"I do apologize," says the professor, but his voice is happy. "At this point it's not as if I really have a choice . . ." He moonwalks a few steps backward, then hops into an Irish jig.

In four huge bounds, the mountain goat rushes over and begins to dance with him. Baacchus breaks into song in his honking voice, a song Diana knows, though until that moment she didn't know she knew. It's the music of the Arkteia, sung in the first language human beings ever spoke, but this version is raucous and wild, with a rapid beat. *It is a song I sing to all of you, my beloved. When you awaken— as you awaken—you will remember it, too.*

Professor Piper joins Baacchus, singing at the top of his lungs, throwing in moves from a variety of dances: the samba, the Charleston, the funky chicken.

"Oh, what the hell," says Devin. *"My mom's alive!"* He jumps to his feet and goes into the dance moves he taught himself from online videos when he first realized he was interested in girls.

Diana doesn't intend to move; in fact, she yips with surprise when she finds herself jumping up to dance along. It makes her laugh out loud that the force she knows herself to be, the power that loves creating black holes and supernovas, is equally delighted to shake the booty of a tiny human meat-self on a small blue planet. The boar flies over, singing in unison with Piper and the goat, so loudly it's hard for Diana to believe that Devin can't hear.

And this is how they leave the Sierras Oscuras, my dark mountains. A barefoot woman, an old man, a bearded boy, a mountain goat, and a boar with wings. Singing and laughing, they dance back toward civilization, to hunt for the others who share Diana's soul: who love me and all that is born of me; who feel the longing to awaken; who hear the call of all that is at risk in this perilous time.

To hunt, my beloved, for you.

A GUIDE TO
BEWILDERMENT

"Waking up is the goal, bewilderment is the method."

Be well, my dear one
Be safe, my love
Live in joy and peace, sweet friend

In November 2012, I moved from my longtime home in Phoenix to a patch of land bordering a national forest a few miles inland from the coast of Central California. It isn't the Sierras Oscuras mountain range—that's a place I made up when I wrote *Diana, Herself*—but like the fictional Oscuras, it is a protected stretch of wilderness growing from a primordial seabed that has been lifted by twenty-five million years of tectonic pressure into a rumpled, fertile oak savannah.

I had no rational reason to leave my comfortable life and two grown daughters in Arizona, dragging my partner, Karen, my son, Adam, and assorted dear friends to live in a place frequented by bears and mountain lions. True, I seem to have been born obsessed with nature, but I'd long since outgrown my childhood longing to run away to the woods; traded it in for a modestly successful career as a self-help writer and life coach, living a civilized human existence in civilized human places.

It was something of a surprise, then, when I began to hear a sort of inner call from something—some *place*—wilder than anywhere I'd ever lived. Some mornings I'd wake up feeling that I was already living there. I could see the sloping land, the tall trees. I could feel the texture of the air and the soil. I was on a ranch in California; that was just a simple fact. Then I'd open my eyes, and be dumbfounded to find myself in Arizona.

This happened more and more often, until I knew so much about my hypnagogic ranch I could search for it online, entering data such as the number of acres, the man-made structures, the geographic vicinity of an old-growth forest. There was a place—only one—that fit the description. It was for sale. I called the Realtor, went to see the land, and wandered around it in slack-jawed amazement. Without question, it was the twilight landscape I'd been visiting for years in my half-sleep. One thing I hadn't foreseen: the custom-made gate was carved into precisely the butterfly shape I'd once designed as the logo for my life coaching company.

Here's one thing I've learned: When something that magical happens to you, go with it. Just go.

So as winter began in the Central California mountains, my family and I took up residence in a house much smaller than our previous one, a long way from the nearest grocery store. The only sounds I could hear when I awoke each morning were birds, water, and wind. I expected to be a bit disoriented for a few months, but no. I was only enchanted. I felt so deeply connected to the place—the bobcats and deer, the massive oak trees, the stones filled with the fossils of ancient sea creatures—that it occurred to me I might have some kind of psychological disorder.

Certainly, spending all my money on land, cutting myself off from polite society, and pretty much giving up remunerative work looked like madness. But knowing how crazy I appeared didn't make me act any saner. In moments of anxiety, I'd yank on galoshes, a hat, and a parka (often over my pajamas) and head into the hills around my new home. I followed game trails and animal tracks for hours. I sat in meditation covered with birdseed, so that chipmunks and songbirds came to sit on my knees and hands. I began to lose the ability to think in my usual ways. And all of this felt weirdly involuntary—no, more than that. It felt as if some part of me I didn't understand was pulling me into this strange new life for reasons known only to itself.

Almost as soon as we moved in, a friend offered to help us build a labyrinth on our property. This mazelike circle isn't a puzzle to be solved, but a form that, when followed, is meant to drop the walker into a meditative state. I walked our labyrinth often, and many of our frequent guests did so as well. Over the course of a few months, three people came back from such an adventure to report that they'd seen a brown-skinned, barefoot woman sitting in an oak tree near the labyrinth. She had watched them for a while, they all said, and then disappeared.

I never witnessed this apparition, but as I tramped through the fields I couldn't help imagine her there. At first she seemed to follow me, and then one day I realized our roles had switched: She was in the lead, and I followed. That was the day I came across an unfamiliar animal track in the mud. I snapped a photo with my phone and went home to find (again online) that the creature was a wild boar. I learned that hunters once released Russian wild boars in California to provide interesting prey, and many of these wily, intelligent animals ended up escaping and thriving in the mountains. I also learned, to my amazement, that domestic pigs who escape from farms can revert back to an atavistic, wilder form, becoming dark, bristly, tusk-bearing boars themselves.

The boar stayed on my property for weeks, though I never saw it (I did see others on a nearby property, to which I think "my" boar eventually returned). As I followed its tracks I began to feel a strange sense that the animal was playing with me. On one occasion, after painstakingly trailing the boar for half an hour, I came to a place where it had stood for some time, its front trotters placed primly together, and watched me tracking it.

From then on, I had two imaginary friends with me on all my excursions: the barefoot lady, and the wild boar. Picasso said he worked all his life to learn to paint like a child: I had apparently worked all my life to learn to *think* like the child I'd been before society put a sensible head on my shoulders. I lost all interest in anything my former self would have called "productivity." I just wandered around letting the barefoot lady and the wild boar tell me a story—the story that became the allegory you hold in your hands.

You can see that although *Diana, Herself* is a fantasy, it's not much weirder than my actual life. It's also, to my mind, the most practical self-help book I've ever written. The Guide to Bewilderment you'll find below is my description of a process that began for me when I moved to the forest. This process, as near as I can make out, is preparation for something others have called "awakening," which is impossible to truly convey in words. I can, however, give you the rough outlines.

Throughout human history, certain individuals have experienced a psychological event they sometimes referred to as waking up from a dream. They described this awakening in different words, languages, and cultural images, but despite these differences, all the descriptions seem to point toward the same phenomenon. Awakening includes losing all attachment to most human concerns, shifting one's sense of identity to something infinitely more deep and vast than a human body-mind, and paradoxically knowing that one is nothing (no thing) and everything. The awakened state, by all accounts, is peaceful, joyful, and loving beyond description.

I'm certainly not an awakened being, but I've had tantalizing glimpses of what it might be like to wake up, moments in which it's observably evident to me that reality is nothing like I once assumed. In those moments it simply seems obvious that instead of a collection of nuts and bolts, human existence—all existence—is the play of consciousness creating, becoming, and dissolving form. This sensation is both blissful and mind-blowing. Bewildering.

My hunch is that we humans have reached a point in our history where awakening may be necessary for survival. If we don't change quite dramatically—and fast—we'll soon exhaust our planet's ability to support us. If a sufficient number of people awaken, it might transform humanity quickly enough to keep us on Earth a while longer.

I don't know much about awakening, but I have spent many years becoming more and more deeply bewildered. I can tell you from experience that bewilderment is likely to come from anywhere, at any time, but the Seven Tasks outlined below (versions of Diana's adventures in the book) can galvanize this process. If you give them a reasonably committed try, I suspect you'll end up wilder than you've ever been—by which I mean happier, more peaceful, and more loving. You may begin to feel that you're dreaming, and then—who knows?—you may even wake up. If you're down with that, let's move on.

THE SEVEN TASKS
OF BEWILDERMENT
General Operating Instructions

Awakening doesn't require specific tasks, and no set of tasks can force you to awaken. Enlightened masters seem to share some basic ingredients, including a very strong intention to overcome suffering and a willingness to surrender personal identity to discover deeper and deeper levels of truth. Without these traits, the Seven Tasks won't hurt you, but they won't help much, either. And even if your basic ingredients are present, you'll need three operating instructions to make the Tasks effective.

First, *to master the Tasks, you have to do them, not just read them.* Most of us think of learning as grasping verbal concepts with the cognitive mind. This is like trying to master acrobatics by memorizing a handbook. Actually doing the Tasks means learning throughout your whole body, which is more intelligent than your mind can even imagine. So please, don't just read. Do.

Second, *the Tasks should be undertaken in order.* Starting with Task One lays the foundation for Task Two; both are necessary to support Task Three, and so on. Skipping Tasks is not only ineffective; it can be dangerous (for example, using logic without the ability to calm fear has created most of the atrocities in human history, from your last pointless argument to nuclear war).

Third, *don't take this too seriously.* Some of these Tasks might feel silly. That's a good thing. There's nothing serious about awakening. There is no goal but happiness. Grim determination is part of the dream from which we're all trying to awaken. Bewilder yourself purely for the fun of it, and you're already halfway home.

THE FIRST TASK
Calm All Fear

Awakening can almost be defined as absolute freedom from fear—a state most people never experience. We tend to grip the memory of trauma and imagine terrifying futures—traits that make us the most anxious, neurotic, destructive creatures on Earth. Learning to see the present moment as fundamentally safe and benevolent is bewilderment bedrock, and the purpose of the First Task.

The steps of this Task, which are extremely simple and always available, calm the reptilian aspects of your brain, moving your nervous system out of the fight-flight-freeze state into the rest-restore-rejuvenate setting. I recommend you use them whenever you feel afraid, and at any other moment when you'd like to relax and feel better. If you do this, Task One will gradually become an automatic response, and peace, not anxiety, will become your usual state.

The Task begins with slow, deep, even breathing. Humans are one of the few nonaquatic mammals that can voluntarily change the pace of respiration. Rapid breathing is part of the fight-or-flight reaction; slow breathing is part of the relaxation response. You can fool your brain into thinking you're in danger by breathing shallowly and rapidly, and you probably do this a lot. Happily, breathing deeply and slowly will flip the switch back to your rest-restore system. So start your bewilderment process with a long, sighing exhalation. Then, keep taking slow, deep breaths—not so slow and deep you get lightheaded, but the sort of breathing you do when you're asleep.

At this point, ask for help from whatever benevolent higher power may or may not exist. If you believe in a metaphysical realm, that belief can be useful. Call it faith, or call it the placebo effect; either one will calm you down, which is all we're after. Of course, strongly *disbelieving* in metaphysical reality may create a "nocebo" effect, or the blocking out of any help that might actually be there. Since you can't prove or disprove the existence of a higher power, experiment. Ask for help with an open mind, and see what happens. You may use any method (prayer, spell, ritual, ceremony) you wish. I just say, "Help!"

Next, offer loving-kindness to the frightened part of yourself. You don't have to feel peaceful to do this. At first, it's just noise. But our nervous systems are geared to respond to soothing sounds, especially kind words spoken by a soft human voice. So if you're alone, although you may feel foolish at first, try saying these words out loud: "May you be well, may you be safe, may you live in joy and peace." (These are based on Tibetan "lovingkindness" meditation mantras). If you're not alone when you decide to repeat Task One (and you must repeat it often if you want it to work), just think the kind thoughts, but focus on them as entirely as you can.

I suggest adding terms of endearment, like "sweet friend," "dear child," or anything else that feels soothing. I used to feel ridiculous doing this. If you agree, just notice the stream of worry and misery your inner monologue is used to blathering at you. Is that really preferable? I'm just saying.

THE SECOND TASK
Absorb Nourishment, Not Poison

Only when your fear is calmed can you skillfully choose to keep yourself healthy. When you're scared, you'll absorb anything—cookies, street drugs, the teachings of a suicide cult—without much discernment. So I repeat, before attempting Task Two, make sure you've worked Task One long enough to feel relatively calm and peaceful.

Begin Task Two by eating a meal very attentively, with the stated intention of noticing which foods feel good for you, and which feel bad for you—not what you know in your head, but what you sense in your gut. It works best if you choose your own food, either from your kitchen, the grocery store, or a buffet-style restaurant where many different kinds of food are available.

Instead of just grabbing whatever you're used to eating, slow down. Keep up the calm, deep, even breathing you use in Task One. Before eating anything, simply look at the food. Notice your body's reaction. There may be an initial impulse to lunge at foods that are high in fat and sugar. If this is accompanied by anxiety, redo Task One. Fear drives craving for food that might add precious fat to the body during a famine or natural disaster. Craving these foods indicates you may not be not completely calm. Stick with Task One until you're relaxed. Then select food items that appeal to your whole body.

Once you've chosen your food, sit quietly and take a small bite of whatever you've got. Before you chew, hold the food in your mouth and feel *your entire body's reaction* to it. See if that feeling stays the same as you chew and swallow. Try this with several different foods. Experiment with things you think are bad for you, and things you think are good for you. See if your body reacts the way you expect.

Please note that *this is not a rule-based or regimented diet,* and the goal is not for you to eat more righteously. It's an exploration of your gut-sense, the part of you that tells you how to take in nourishment without swallowing poison. That said, Task Two may lead you to change your diet. For example, it may reveal that eggs make you feel sluggish, or wheat gives you heartburn, and lead you to avoid them.

Practice eating this way until you start to feel your gut-sense fairly easily. Then apply Task Two to other things: events, relationships, your own thoughts. Before you set out to do something, pause. Notice how your whole body reacts. Does it shut down and recoil, or open and rejoice? During any activity, keep "tasting" to see if your gut likes it. Notice that some people and places can give you a kind of junk-food high that later leaves you feeling drained and enervated. Like Diana, you have a "tell," a sick feeling somewhere in your body that lets you know when you're being poisoned. Keep moving away from the people, places, and activities that feel like poison. Go toward whatever feels nourishing.

Mastery of the Second Task occurs when you begin to sense the difference between nourishing and toxic thoughts. With attention and practice, you can learn to "spit out" poisonous thoughts, keeping thoughts that make you feel free, healthy, and nourished. Stop absorbing toxic food, and your body gets healthier. Stop believing toxic thoughts, and *everything* gets healthier.

THE THIRD TASK
Let Your Meta-Self Move You

As you practice the Second Task, you may find that you not only recognize what's nourishing, but feel yourself spontaneously reaching for it. You may be surprised to see yourself picking up a new hobby, or rekindling an old friendship. Certain books or websites may seem to "jump out" at you. This is really your attention being drawn forcibly to them. You're feeling the pull of your meta-self, the intention that comes from beyond conscious thoughts.

Some people experience this in moments of physical danger. Without thinking, they turn the wheel of the car, run for the door, or say the perfect thing to calm down the rampaging ex-postal worker. Oddly, they may feel no fear at all. In an emergency, they drop everything but the here and now. The first three Tasks kick in, and the body-mind calmly, efficiently moves toward safety. If you can master the Third Task, you can live your whole life from this skillful presence. You only have to learn how to stop moving, and let yourself be moved.

Begin by taking at least 15 or 20 minutes alone. Then put on some music you truly enjoy, stand in a neutral position, and wait. If you relax enough, patiently allowing nothing to happen, you may feel an odd sensation of being pulled into movement without any deliberate effort on your part. The sensation may be very subtle at first, a tugging similar to the feeling you get when you hold a refrigerator magnet close to a metal surface. You can easily stiffen and refuse to move. The objective here, however, is to allow movement to occur.

Music can catalyze spontaneous movement even in animals, so it's very helpful when you're first beginning to use Task Three. Once you've begun feeling yourself being moved, turn off the music and simply set the intention to walk—but don't walk on purpose. Just stand and relax. If your body shifts or moves in any way, allow it. Follow that slight pull wherever it takes you. Let yourself be walked.

Continue applying this practice to familiar activities. Let your meta-self wash the dishes, mop the floor, or make the bed. When you have a job to do, sit and contemplate it, using Tasks One and Two. Intend that the job be done with maximum skill. When you feel the pull to move, or have an idea that makes you want to do something, allow your physical body to go along with the sensation.

Awakened masters describe themselves as watching all their own behavior play out this way, without any idea what they may do next (strangely, their careers and relationships work better, not worse). Walt Whitman described it this way:

Apart from the pulling and hauling stands what I am,
Stands amused, complacent, compassionating, idle, unitary,
....
Looking with side-curved head curious what will come next,
Both in and out of the game and watching and wondering at it.[1]

Practice Task Three by inviting your meta-self to do what it wants, and this sensation may begin to arise more and more often, until your whole life is being lived with less effort and more efficiency than seems possible. Your meta-self, you'll find, is better at almost everything than your grim will. As it begins operating in every area of your life, you'll do less and less, while more and more gets done.

THE FOURTH TASK
Connect Your Heart to All Hearts

If you allow safety, nourishment, and movement to flow from your meta-self, it's inevitable that you will fall in Love. This isn't necessarily romantic or sexual desire (though that can be part of it), but the felt experience of your own being as a drop in the sea of Consciousness, the unlimited awareness that brings the universe into being by the power of its attention. You are a small fractal of this Consciousness, and It is a large fractal of you, inextricably intermingled.

Feeling this reality is blissful, ecstatic, and seems to be physically centered in the chest. Your heart has its own cluster of nerves as big as the brain of a cat, which produces much stronger electromagnetic resonance than your brain, and send more information to the brain than the brain sends to it. The Fourth Task, connecting your heart with all other hearts, causes a sensation of your chest melting open. Blocking the connection—for example, by attaching to your fear and believing yourself unloved—can make your physical heart literally ache.

Of the five senses, the most intimately connective is touch. Loving makes us want to touch and be touched, and if touch is guided by the compassion and intelligence of the wild self, it opens us to more love, in a benevolent cycle. A simple way to cultivate this is the method

---

[1] Whitman, Walt. *Song of Myself.* Dover Publications, 2001 p.4.

Diana uses in the book: Go outside, take off your shoes, ground your-self in the first three Tasks, and let yourself be walked.

Our feet are almost as sensitive as our hands, so we wear shoes, just as we armor our emotions, to avoid being hurt. But the sensi-tivity of feet (and hearts) is designed to feel its way through nature, to protect not by disconnecting but by connecting more intimately. You'll find that to walk barefoot without hurting yourself, you have to be very present and attentive. You may notice that this kind of present-moment attention is part of what makes sexual lovemaking so blissful, and that the bliss of physical connection is actually avail-able in many mundane activities.

Your meta-self may walk you toward another being: a person, a tree, an animal. Notice how going barefoot changes your perception of that being. You may feel a circle of energy between you and what-ever you see, as if the earth is completing an electrical circuit that flows through you both.

After you've experimented for a while with walking barefoot, try sitting with a person or animal you love when their focus is on some-thing else. Watch your loved one with the same kind of attention you give to the soles of your bare feet as you walk on the earth. Feel the uniqueness of this being's character, the texture of her or his essence. In all the universe, no other thing is identical to this essence. Your loved one is singular, inimitable, irreplaceable; not a cat, but *this* cat, not a child, but *this* child.

Close your eyes and continue to feel the connection between your loved one and you. Imagine that your heart is emanating an electro-magnetic field that extends around you and interacts with the field emanating from your loved one. It so happens that this is literally true. If you are still enough, you can feel it. As you practice this Task, the bond between you and your loved one will become more tangi-ble, more real. Allow and enjoy.

THE FIFTH TASK
Tell the Truth

We all use language every day, and for the most part, we use it unwisely. Humans are the only animals that can create an imagined future so real and frightening that suicide seems preferable to facing it, and this dubious ability comes directly from language. Without words to describe them, the regrets of the past and the terrors of an unknown future lose virtually all their power.

Task Five is learning to use your verbal mind as the servant of truth, rather than delusion. Once you're in the flow of the first four Tasks, any thought that runs contrary to the felt truth of your experience clangs like a dropped cooking pot, causing your body to contract and your mood to plummet.

Most of us have a few paralyzing or agonizing thoughts we think over and over, lies we believe without question. These are the allegorical Furies. I think they scream so loudly and persistently because they're the lessons we most need to unlearn, the precise mirror images of the truths we're trying to reach.

Start Task Five by simply writing down any thoughts that are making you miserable, and checking to see if their mirror opposites may actually be more true than the original statement. Try it right now. Make a list of any thoughts that are bothering you, such as "I'm not good enough," "I don't have enough money," "Nobody really loves me and nobody ever will." Sitting in front of your list, remember your way through the first four Tasks. Once you're calm, aware, and openhearted, reread your Fury-thoughts and write their exact opposites on a different sheet of paper: "I'm good enough." "I have enough money." "Everybody loves me and everybody always will."

Your knee-jerk reaction to this second list will probably be disbelief, perhaps even Furious disbelief. Return to the first four Tasks. If you allow fear to arise, or stop sensing the difference between nourishment and poison, or force your actions rather than surrendering to your higher self, or close your heart, the positive statements will sound like a barrage of bullshit. If you wish to bewilder, stay the course. Sit still, very still, with each statement. Search honestly for evidence that your self-loathing may be in error, your fondest hopes already a reality.

Are you good enough? Yes, good enough to be here now. Do you have enough money? Well, not enough to calm your mind, but enough to keep breathing right now (the biblical story of manna falling from heaven—but only if the recipients remained confident and refused to hoard—is the story of most people's lives, possibly including yours). Does everybody love you? If you believe in bewildering at all, you have to consider that their true selves do.

You may be feeling outraged and argumentative right now. The Fifth Task violates the ego's strictest rules. If you're stuck, do what I do: Study the methods of Byron Katie, an awakened master who teaches an elegant, powerful way of reversing thoughts. "Like a mirror," Katie writes, "the mind has a way of getting things right but backwards."[2] Use her method, with an honest heart and ruthless logic, and you'll eventually see the truth you need, right there in the looking glass. The Furies, once heard this way, will set you free.

THE SIXTH TASK
Let Your Meta-Self Flow through You

Letting yourself be moved (Task Three) is a strange and delicate art, but not as strange or delicate as Task Six—learning to open your entire being to the flow of inspiration. This means abandoning self-control and allowing your mind, as well as your body, to be run by your meta-self. If this sounds alarming, relax. This won't work unless you're grounded in the first five Tasks, and that means it literally can't cause you to run amok. Quite the opposite. If anything it will make you more yourself, yield huge satisfaction, and reveal your hidden genius.

The simplest way to learn Task Six is by trying to develop a skill or solve a problem that strongly motivates you. Your chosen skill may be running a business, playing the piano, curing feline leukemia, or writing the perfect sonnet. If you feel no motivation for anything, back up and practice Tasks One through Five until your curiosity ignites, or some old interest rekindles. Eventually, you'll find yourself wanting very much to do something beautiful, or change something terrible.

This intense desire is called "talent." Talented people aren't born with skill, but with an almost maddening *desire* for skill. This makes

---

[2] Mitchell, Byron Kathleen, *I Need Your Love—Is That True: How to Stop Seeking Love, Approval, and Appreciation and Start Finding Them*. Three Rivers Press, 2005 (New York, New York), p. 20.

them spend lots of time practicing, which eventually drops them into some version of the first five Tasks, which sooner or later allows all their self-consciousness to fall away, which in turn allows their minds and bodies to act, think, create, and invent something supernal.

Whatever ability intrigues you, start practicing it. Take lessons, go to workshops, join chat groups, but mostly, practice. Here's the method that works best: Focus intently on the precise outcome you want. Do your absolute best to achieve it. Notice where your creation doesn't match your intention. Try again. You'll fail again, but you'll fail better. Repeat. And repeat. And repeat. And repeat.

This is called "deep" or "dedicated" practice, and neuroscience has shown that though it's physically and mentally demanding, it leads to very rapid increases in ability. More importantly, it keeps us at the edge of our capacities, and this is the zone where our brains brew the perfect hormones to create a sensation called "flow." Happiness researchers have found that flow is the single most satisfying experience humans can have. If you do Task Six for the joy of this sensation, not for spectacular results, you'll eventually get both. In fact, things you might now call "superpowers" may become your new normal.

Don't believe me? Consider: Esref Armagan is a Turkish artist who paints realistic landscapes, in fairly accurate perspective and full color, despite being born without eyes. Check him out at www.wimp .com/artisteyes. Isao Machii can stand with his samurai sword in its scabbard as an assistant shoots a BB pellet at him, in random conditions with varying light and wind. He slices the pellet in the air, in less time than it takes for the nerve impulses to go from his brain to his arms. See it yourself at www.youtube.com/watch?v=Qzhs1Z8Rwnk.

Something more than physical neurological processing is happening to—or rather, through—these people. They're allowing their whole nervous systems to be guided by some power that defies what we know of physics and material reality. Realizing that you *are* that power is the gift of Task Six, and the foundation for Task Seven.

THE SEVENTH TASK
Notice That You Are All for All, Always

Task Seven, the full realization of the meta-self, is both a death and a birth. It dissolves the ego, with its illusion of being a separate, isolated physical form. As the ego dies, only the meta-self—the Buddha-nature, the Christ consciousness, what have you—animates the body (though it knows it's not limited *to* the body). In this sense it seems to have been "born." Like death, this kind of awakening can hit like a bolt from the blue. Like birth, it's ultimately beyond our control, but certain activities are necessary for it to occur at all, and the more we engage in those activities, the more likely it is to happen soon.

The lightning-bolt sort of awakening sounds wonderful—bliss without effort!—but it's exceedingly rare, and even people who have it don't always sustain it. Enlightenment isn't a rock, but a river—not an object that lands on us and pins us down, but a current that flows through us when we allow it and stops when we block it. Study enlightened masters and you'll realize that all of them consistently practiced—and taught—some version of all Seven Tasks.

Task Seven happens if you use the first six Tasks consistently, then drop into mental stillness—a practice called meditation (any style can work). You can learn to meditate from a teacher, class, or book, and practice through sheer discipline. Or, if you're using the first six Tasks, your meta-self may begin doing it spontaneously. The magnetic tug you felt when you first let your body be moved in Task Three, the deep fascination of Task Six, might steer you toward stillness. If so, you'll feel an appetite for meditation similar to intense hunger or sexual longing. Give in to it. Arrange your schedule so you have time for it. Be still.

At some point you'll notice that the You meditating isn't a human body, a personality, or even a solid object. Your true identity is the *absence* of absolutely everything, which isn't dead or empty but intensely alive, brimming with the potential for all objects and events to arise within it. This isn't a concept but something you'll simply see, the way you might see a hidden image in an optical illusion. It's been there all the time; you just didn't notice it. Until you did.

This is so intensely bewildering that it's impossible to describe. Nothing looks real in the sense that you once assumed; the entire universe is a product of the Unmanifested—which is both not-you and your real Self—watching and attending. Nothing you can think or say in language is remotely true. You're not here now, you're everywhere and everywhen—except that these words, too, are just labels for illusions.

We've now arrived at the limit of my descriptive ability. I'm not awakened, not even bewildered enough, to say more. I'll let the last words on Task Seven go to Nisargadatta Maharaj, who was a shop owner in a Mumbai tenement when he woke up. Afterward he was still a shop owner, but one prone to saying things like this:

> *Stop imagining yourself to be this or that and the realization that you are the source and heart of all will dawn upon you. With this will come great love which is not choice or predilection, or attachment, but a power which makes all things love-worthy and loveable . . . . When I look inside and see that I am nothing, that is wisdom. When I look outside and see that I am everything, that is love. Between these two, my life turns.*[3]

AND FINALLY . . .

You may have noticed that bewilderment isn't an infomercial process. It won't clean up greasy spills and give you ripped abs in eighteen minutes a day. It won't make you rich or put you on the best-dressed list. It will only make you wild. In T. S. Eliot's words, it is "A condition of complete simplicity / (Costing not less than everything)."[4] Such a purchase is senseless in a world without magic. But sometimes magical things happen. When they do, you can either slam your eyes shut and cling to conventional wisdom, or accept the possibility that convention may not be as wise as you thought.

---

[3] Nisargadatta Maharaj, *I Am That. Acorn Press (Durham, North Carolina, 1973), p. 3 Ibid, p. 236*

[4] Eliot, T. S. "Little Gidding," from "Four Quartets," in *Collected Poems, 1909-1962 (The Centenary Edition)* Harcourt Brace & Company, Orlando, FL., 1963, p. 207.

I don't know how the magic will come to you. For me, most recently, it came as a woman and a boar that seemed almost real, leading me through a place that seemed almost unreal. For you it may come as an illness, a passion, a teacher, a voyage. If you stay wrapped in fear, numb to your gut-sense, stiffened against your spirit, armored in heart, clenched around your beliefs, addicted to familiarity, and sure of your mortal condition, you won't even notice it.

But if you're doing some version of the Tasks, inviting bewilderment, the magic will catch your attention. It will create small miracles, then larger and larger ones, until finally there is no way to deny what is happening. At that point, you'll know what to do.

Go. Just go.

Maelstrom

1

PLEOMORPHIC

At 4:13 A.M., Pacific Time, on a fine autumn day early in the twenty-first century, a strange, pulsating flash briefly outshines the glow of the sprawled stars and the setting moon. It comes from under the earth of the Sierras Oscuras mountain range, through crevices that lead to a cave in which two black bears are hibernating, as is their yearly custom. A pilot looking down from a red-eye passenger jet flying over the Oscuras rubs his eyes, takes a second look, and decides it was nothing.

It takes the light from the cave approximately .016 seconds to reach Manhattan's Seventh Avenue, where Theodore Calvin Victor MacNicol IV is piloting his gunmetal gray Mercedes northward through the near-gridlocked traffic. When the flash of light reaches him—though it's far too dispersed by then for him to notice it—MacNicol is hit by the mother of all migraines.

His first warning is a spot of light that appears in the center of his vision, a ghostly amoeba that seems to hover over the car's dashboard, its rainbow edges undulating. Next come the zigzag patterns, a kaleidoscope of fractured colors that make him dizzy and slightly nauseated. The rectangular lines of the surrounding skyscrapers begin to strobe and flicker. MacNicol ("Theo" to his friends and the public) recalls a random phrase from a medical study he once read, trying to understand his affliction: "The migraine aura is both heterogeneous and pleomorphic." In other words, the electrical storm beginning in Theo's brain can take any form it damn well pleases.

"Oh, no," he whispers. "Come on, not today. Please, not today." He slows down, his vision almost completely obscured, and tries to find a place to pull over. On Seventh Avenue. At 7:15, well into the morning rush hour. "Yeah, right," he mutters. "That'll happen."

From behind comes a deafening honk that makes Theo brace against a shock of noise-related pain. But he finds, to his great relief, that the migraine hasn't progressed that far yet. He checks the rearview mirror, and through all the stripes and spots, sees a large van flashing its lights at him. Flashing lights—just what his brain needs to kick its little lightning storm into Hurricane Theo. The migraine's aura escalates until he's functionally blind, dazzled by the fireworks in his head. Theo closes his eyes and mashes his foot down on the brake.

With a squeal of tires and a Godzilla roar, the van surges past Theo's Mercedes. Theo hears a few screams that sound just about normal for a New York crowd: outraged and aggressive. Then a loud *THUMP*, followed by another scream. This one is *not* normal. It's horrible, hair-raising, the agonized shriek of an animal being clumsily slaughtered.

At this point, things get truly strange for Theodore Calvin Victor MacNicol IV. Despite the headache, that terrible scream makes him reflexively lift his head and open his eyes. He gasps in surprise.

Losing some vision at the onset of a headache is typical for Theo, though it's never been this bad before. But it's not at all typical to suddenly *regain* vision, mid-migraine—and not just normal vision. He blinks several times at a world that is impossibly vivid and detailed. The strobing and zigzags are gone. The whole long, crowded Manhattan avenue, and everything on it, looks surreally clear. Theo glances up at an office window several stories above him. He sees a young woman standing behind it, looking out. He can count the buttons on her blouse. He can see that her nails are shellacked in blue polish, and that one of them is chipped.

Theo is immediately distracted from his miraculous eyesight by the fact that his body is now doing things he doesn't intend. His hands—the right one already going numb from the migraine—put the car in "park," right there in the the middle of the avenue, then remove the blocky electronic key from its slot and open the car door. His legs swing themselves out onto the asphalt. Theo feels as if he's watching all this from a short distance, seeing his own well-groomed blond hair and perfectly tailored suit from the side. His will feels tiny and weak compared to whatever is powering his body. Without any intention or even agreement on his part, the body stands up, closes the car door, and jogs forward.

Initially, Theo's view of the accident is blocked by the van whose flashing lights spiked his migraine. The van stands in the street in front of the Mercedes. It must have been accelerating when it hit a pedestrian, a slender young woman now lying between the crosswalk lines. She's wearing a bright green dress that looks like a waitress's uniform, but it's unlikely she'll ever serve food in it again. All the blood seeping from her torso—punctured by a fractured rib—will never wash out. Also, the waitress may need a new leg. Her left knee is bent at an impossible angle, like something from a Cubist painting. She's still screaming, except for the moments she inhales, when Theo hears an awful, slurping sound issuing from her chest.

With his new, bizarrely precise vision, Theo takes in the van driver—frozen behind his steering wheel, mouth slightly open in horror—and the whirl of other pedestrians on the sidewalk. Some hurry away, faces averted, dialing their cell phones—*I love New York*, Theo thinks—while others, obviously tourists, have stopped to stare. One of them says, "Hey, look, Cindy! Is that Theo MacNicol?" Another voice shouts, "Oh, my gosh, it is!" and Theo hears the click of her cell phone as she uses it to snap photos.

One passerby, a woman in mom jeans and sequined Keds, emerges from the crowd and crouches by the injured waitress. "I'm a doctor," she says in a low, calm voice. "Don't worry, we're going to take good care of you." She takes off her jacket, slides it under the waitress's thigh, and begins tightening it into a tourniquet.

Theo notices all of this at the edges of his awareness, the edges that still feel like himself. Quite apart from him, however, his body is still moving smoothly, quickly. As he reaches the waitress he feels something like an electric shock run up his spine and along all the intricate branches of his nerves, striking his migraining brain with a bolt of pain. The shock wave moves through him and then outward, toward the wounded woman. Theo feels an arc of electricity flowing steadily from his chest to hers, like a current running through an invisible wire. His body drops to its knees by the young woman's head, looking upside-down into her eyes. His hands gently cradle her wild-eyed, anguished face.

The screaming stops.

Later, when memories and dreams of this scene return (over and over and over), Theo will have trouble coping with one thing. Not his migraine, which has hardly begun. Not the waitress's blood, pain, and fear; anyone who's ever seen an action movie knows what those look like. No, what overwhelms Theo is the torrent of love that pours through his body's eyes into the eyes of the young woman. He's never experienced anything remotely comparable. It's as if Niagara Falls has found its way through his pupils, all that force pouring though his eyes into the vast, unguarded openness of the waitress's face.

"It's all right, sweet child," Theo hears someone say. A half-second later, he realizes the voice is his. "Just look at me. You're all right."

The young woman's face is slack now, her eyes wide open to receive the deluge of love. "Am I going to die?" she asks in a soft, ordinary voice.

"Not now, love. Not now," says Theo's voice.

He hears the click of more cameras, and his eyes flick upward for a fraction of a second. Tourists have pooled near the accident scene. In that quick glance, he can read their watches. He can see the unplucked hairs between their brows. Then Theo's eyes, acting on their own, return to those of the waitress. She will never again audition for a Broadway musical, but her injuries will heal completely. Of this Theo is strangely but utterly certain.

He's also certain that, until this very day, he has never in his life uttered the phrase "sweet child."

·

A few blocks away, in a comfortably fashionable brownstone on Eighth Avenue, Dr. Minerva Lao is feeding breakfast to her pet, a Chinese water dragon named Kuan Yin. The lizard is large, about two and a half feet long, and (at least to Dr. Lao) exceptionally attractive. Her jade-green body flushes to orange on her chest, throat, and sides. Dappled lines of turquoise adorn her flanks. She bears a crest of spikes along the center of her head, neck, and back, and her long whip of a tail is striped ivory and chocolate brown.

"Here you go, my beauty," says Minerva Lao, lifting the top of Kuan Yin's chicken-wire terrarium and lowering in a small bowl of dead crickets. "Enjoy."

A voice in her head replies, "Thank you." Dr. Lao smiles. She's been furnishing Kuan Yin's comments in her mind since George gave her the reptile, almost fifteen years ago, for their fortieth wedding anniversary. Even more in the ten months since George passed away.

Dr. Lao doesn't know that, as she replaces the terrarium's trap-door in its slot, a light-burst occurs under the Sierras Oscuras mountains. She has no idea she's about to experience something for which she's been waiting more than sixty years. Through her long and distinguished psychiatric career, she's treated thousands of patients for the recurrent flashbacks of post-traumatic stress disorder. But as of this moment, she's never had one herself.

Many times, in the midst of a counseling session, Dr. Lao has thought wistfully that it would be nice to have at least a few memories of her life before America, of her original home and her father, who raised her alone after her mother died. But she's wrong. When the memory comes, it's not nice at all.

It hits an infinitesimal fraction of a second after Theo MacNicol sees the dancing amoeba above his dashboard. Suddenly Dr. Lao is not in her comfortable living room. She's being shoved between burlap bags of produce in the dark cavern of a covered truck bed. The air is freezing cold, so full of garlic and diesel fumes that she can barely breathe. Outside the truck, she hears a cacophony of shouting, the frightened barks and bellows of animals.

"Back further! Lie down, Min-Min! Lie flat!"

The voice shatters Minerva Lao's heart, because she would know it anywhere, and because she hasn't remembered it, not anything about it, for almost seven decades. "Baba!" Dr. Lao whispers, her eyes filling with tears. In her memory, she's screaming it as he shoves bags of garlic and rice on top of her.

"Hush, Min-Min," he begs her—the flashback is so real it's happening now, not then. "Please, no matter what happens, be quiet. When the truck stops, someone will come get you out. I'll find you later. Just a few days. I'll find you."

The shouts from around them grow louder, and through a tiny crack between the heavy burlap bags, Lao Min-Ba sees her father jump out of the truck, then straighten, turn, and hold up both hands in surrender. His hands are still in the air when the first bullet hits him.

Minerva Lao's seventy-five-year-old body rocks as though she's the one being riddled by rifle fire. "Baba!" she sobs. "Oh, Baba!" A convulsion of grief rips through her. She leans against the terrarium and sobs. She has never felt truly suicidal before, but she suddenly understands all her patients who have. It would be easier to let this pain kill her than to live with it.

"There, there, Min-Min. It's all right."

The psychiatrist, still crying, blinks in confusion. She looks around the room for the source of the voice, which is as dry and creaky as a rusted hinge.

"He loved you, and he kept you safe. You survived. You made a good life for yourself. That's what mattered to him."

Slowly, slowly, Minerva Lao's eyes widen, until they're gaping with a blend of amazement and terror. She stares through the wire of the terrarium, the hair prickling all over her body. Kuan Yin the water dragon licks her own eyes with a long, agile tongue, then says, "Don't worry, Min-Min. I'll always take care of you."

Minerva Lao blinks, carefully latches the door on the top of the terrarium, and faints onto her brownstone's polished hardwood floor.

•

At the same moment, as dawn comes to Austin, Texas, Sophie Andrews—known to her online friends as "Greased Lightning" or simply "GL" for the flash and brilliance of her work—is nearing the end of an all-nighter. She's been coding the biodynamics of a new planet for the game she's helped invent. The challenge is to create an evolutionary process that breeds creatures dangerous and feisty enough for the gamer to fight, but not so powerful they always win hands down.

This particular patch of code has taken far more time than Sophie expected—so much time that when you do the math, she's earning less than minimum wage. But it's never about the money, not to Sophie. It's about the game, the world she's making, and the elegant computer programs for which she is justly famous among the handful of people who understand them. All those people would fit in one gas station convenience shop, but they're her peeps, and their loyalty is true.

At the moment, Sophie is accessing her newly built planet with several browsers. Theoretically, every browser from Safari to Google Chrome should process programs identically, but in practice, numerous tiny differences can create embarrassing messes if they aren't addressed in every line of code. Sophie has just finished patching a troublesome bit of muddled software in a buggy, little-used browser. At twelve minutes past four in the morning, she types in:

```
<!DOCTYPE html>
<html>
<body>

<!-- Do not display this at the moment
<img border="0" src="pic_logo.jpg" alt="evolve">
-->
</body>
</html>
```

She scans the code, nods, and is about to hit "Enter" when disaster strikes.

A strong electrical pulse somehow bypasses the industrial-grade surge protector into which all Sophie's electronic devices are plugged.

With a sickening "pop," Sophie's computer screen flashes all blue, then gray, then black. There's an almost animal sigh from her 64-terabyte hard drive as every machine in the room powers down.

"What the . . . ?" Sophie breathes. Then her voice rises to a painful yelp. "Oh, no, baby! No way! What's happened to you?" She slaps her hand over her mouth, mindful of the neighbors sleeping on either side of her tiny apartment's parchment-thin walls. But she wants to scream, as much from pain as from anger.

"Wait," she says. "Pain?"

It takes Sophie a few seconds to fully register what just happened. The shock of electricity got past her surge protector because it came through Sophie herself. She felt it run up from her feet, through her torso, and out her fingers into the keyboard. It had hurt. A lot.

"But that's impossible!" Sophie pushes back her ergonomic office chair (Staples, $49.99 on sale) and drops to her hands and knees on the floor. She crawls under her desk to examine the cluster of wires bristling from the surge protector's rectangular bulk. The space is tight, but Sophie is a small—if pleasingly curvy—person, and she fits where most men, or even taller women, never could.

She turns off the power switch on the surge protector, then unplugs all her devices and turns the thing back on. The small amber light appears, normal as pie. Slowly, Sophie replaces each plug in its accustomed socket. She expects another shock at any moment, but no. Everything seems hunky-dory.

The last device she connects to the surge protector is the computer itself. No shock. Sophie crawls backward, climbs into her chair, and wheels up to the desk. Slowly, cautiously, she presses the computer's power button. "Please don't be fried!" she whispers. "Please, please, baby, don't be fried."

The computer screen turns gray, which is a good sign, then takes forever to boot up. Sophie doesn't breathe again until the gray screen lightens to blue and a series of icons pops up onto the desktop. Then she lets out a long, relieved sigh and rubs her weary eyes. "Thank you, thank you, thank you!" she says to the computer, then adds, "Thank you baby Jesus, thank you Santa, thank you Ganesh, thank you whoever."

She sighs happily, pulls up her most recent code.

And stares.

The last thing Sophie recalls writing now has several additional lines beneath it. Her eyes scan the new code, which isn't really code at all. She reads it again, and then again, and then one more time, in utter confusion. On the screen it says:

```
<what the/ oh no baby no way/ whats happened to you>
<wait/ pain>
<but thats impossible>
<please dont be fried/ please please baby dont be fried>
<thank you/ thank you/ thank you>
<thank you baby jesus>
<thank you santa>
<thank you ganesh>
<thank you whoever>
```

Beneath the lines of text, the cursor's steady green pulse beats innocently on and off, on and off, on and off.

·

These are not the only unusual events that coincide with the momentary illumination of the cave under the Sierras Oscuras. Later, officials investigating the phenomenon will record many others, none of which seemed connected at the time.

In a dairy factory in Illinois, longtime employee Ernest Olivander looks up from a vat of cheese curds and bursts out laughing. He strips off his hairnet and gloves as he walks out of the curd room, past his fellow cheese makers, and out into the dawn light, still laughing. He keeps walking all the way to the woods, some twelve miles distant.

On the grounds of a Louisiana juvenile detention center, a young drug salesperson named Tawnee Shiverson is preparing to mash another inmate's face into the turf when she suddenly stops, drops her enemy's hair, and stands up. The other girls who are watching the fight fail to respond normally, which is to say they don't kick the crap out of Tawnee Shiverson. When guards rush over, they find all the inmates just standing there, gazing around themselves like a herd of deer, not making a sound.

Most notably, from Oregon to Kansas to Alabama to Winnipeg, people on their way to work, school, or other appointments drive off course, heading with apparent randomness away from their respective destinations toward parts unknown. Even bus drivers do this, to the consternation of most passengers and the incongruous agreement of a few.

From this point onward, all these people and many, many others will begin to deviate from their routine lives. Sometimes this will happen in large and memorable ways. At other times, the changes will be so slight no one will notice them until much later. But even now, without any fanfare or warning, everything has become subtly, slightly different.

It has begun.

Martha Beck is a life coach and bestselling memoir and self-help author. Her books include *Expecting Adam, Finding Your Own North Star, Steering By Starlight,* and *Finding Your Way in a Wild New World.* Readers can also find her unique blend of wit and wisdom every month in *O, The Oprah Magazine.* Martha lives on her ranch in California with her tribe of horses, wild turkeys, bears, mountain lions, bobcats, gophers, and the occasional human.

Visit her at www.marthabeck.com.